Rembrandt's Mirror

Kim Devereux

ATLANTIC BOOKS
LONDON

Published in hardback in Great Britain in 2015 by Atlantic Books,
an imprint of Atlantic Books Ltd.

This paperback edition published in 2016 by Atlantic Books

1 3 5 7 9 10 8 6 4 2

A CIP catalogue record for this book is available
from the British Library.

Paperback ISBN: 978 1 78239 676 5
E-book ISBN: 978 1 78239 675 8

Printed and bound by CPI Group (UK) Ltd, Croydon, CR0 4 YY

Atlantic Books
An Imprint of Atlantic Books Ltd
Ormond House
26–27 Boswell Street
London WC1N 3JZ

www.atlantic-books.co.uk

To Julie Cornwell
In honour of her work

PROLOGUE

Look with the greatest care at the world of things

And at the world where things are not.

The sun has barely crept over the horizon but the gracht is already awash with souls eager to wring a living – or a little more than a living – from the stream of commerce that pulsates through our great city's canals. The water sparkles in the canal below, throwing flecks of light against the walls that rise straight up from its depths. Crates are hoisted up on ropes from barges to the upper storeys of houses, their hungry doors always open for more.

A window glints. That one there, just beneath the stepped gable. And beyond the glass, a woman. Now she is gone again. Or was it merely a reflection? The window blinks again. That glass, that very glass, used to be so clean. It's warm inside. She was here once. Looking out, the glass is full of soot. She would have scrubbed it, with a white linen cloth. Rub, rub, rub, in little circles, her eyes focused on the spatterings of ash.

There, a faint reflection in the handmade glass. A pretty round face. It's her again. She is cleaning the glass. This soot sediment – it's so slow coming off. The reflection, clearer now: a face with eyes translucent as honey. The white cloth is still going round and round, wiping her face in and out of existence. Now her eyes fix on something trapped in the glass. Tiny beads of air. The air from long ago. From when the house was built. Encapsulated.

From the outside, looking in, her face is made fluid by the glass. She opens the window and draws a breath of cool morning air. She takes her cloth, wrings it over the abyss. One more squeeze and a final drop is released. It falls and falls all the way down towards the sparkling wet. A glass bauble suspended in the air. And yet to her it's hurtling towards its destiny, hitting the surface of the canal.

It joins the waters. It now knows all. It created the ripples which are spreading out and out. Back above, Hendrickje's smiling face appears distorted by the surface of the water. How happy she is. She closes the window, just before flotsam would have wiped her from view.

PART I

Amsterdam, 1642

The Night Watch

Rembrandt's house, Sint-Anthonisbreestraat,
June 1642

All is darkness, except for the afterglow of what he saw before he closed his eyes. Two throbbing specks of light. How beautiful they are. And in between the two there's a wisp of luminance, connecting them, like a half-formed thought.

He opens his eyes to let the light in again. For a moment the entire canvas rears up at him, twice his height. He backs away until he's up against the wooden roof support, taking the whole thing in: thirty-odd night watchmen in a restless broil, each jabbing in a different direction; but wait, the lieutenant is about to pull them back into order with his call to march. He squints. The image blurs, letting him see what matters: islands of ivory in a sea of dark. But the dark has teeth, forever gnawing at the light.

He lets his lids part a little more. The brightest of the two islands is Lieutenant van Ruytenburch's coat and there's his visual echo – the girl with the dead chicken hanging from her belt. She's a shade more buttery than him. His ivory calls out, her light form answers, so satisfying to the eye, which loves a repetition. A tension is growing between them, taut as a string, waiting to be plucked. The corners of his mouth rise into a smile.

The sound of a cough. A reminder. He dismisses it from his mind. The canvas is waiting. He opens his eyes fully, struck by the carmine dress of the musketeer. Red is such a pregnant colour, drawing attention by its deep tone alone. He is a choirmaster listening. Right beside the sonorous black of the captain's uniform soars the shining bright lieutenant. Baritone and soprano. Foils to one another. And all around, the choir, singing not with one voice but many: different coloured clothes, textures, characters and vigorous movements in all directions. And yet together they make a perfect harmony. It's just as he intended it.

He is imagining the other group portraits that will hang alongside his. Rows and rows of brightly lit heads, about as life-like as playing cards. Another intrusion. She coughs again. But he needs to take care of the details now. The dark silhouette of the musket butt is similar to the shadow of the captain's hand. He makes them mimic one another – same length, same angle, adds a thumb-like hook to the butt. Now, they chime together – resonant. He scours the picture for more. The carmine of the musketeer and the sash of the captain, both the same red. The lieutenant's partisan, and the captain's outstretched hand. Perfectly parallel. Now the picture hums and whispers like a colony of bees – alive.

More coughing. He listens harder to the bee choir. He won't be distracted. Looks for more enhancements. The coughing stops. He waits, brush in hand, unable to look at the painting anymore, straining to hear. Samuel, his assistant and most promising pupil, seems oblivious to the pause, busy preparing lead white on the grinding stone. The boy is all limbs and yet so full of intent, so serious, at fifteen. Just as he was.

The lean-to is two storeys high and shelters the enormous canvas and several ladders. Supported by a few columns it is open to the yard, making the silence from her open window opposite undeniable.

She coughs again, uncontrollably it seems. The boy looks up at him, his eyes urging him to go to her. So he puts down his palette and brushes, strides across the yard, into the corridor, through the entrance hall, where he notices one of his paintings. He's walked past it a hundred times but now he's caught by it, forgetting where he meant to go. It's her as Flora, wearing a red dress, her left hand resting on her bosom. Saskia. Above her blue eyes is that expanse of luminous forehead that he always wants to kiss, surprised each time that such a simple act can make him happy in an instant. Her right arm is outstretched, offering him a red carnation and some are strewn in the background, too. She smells of them, and other flowers – though not now she is ill. Was it only six months ago that he painted this? Another cough moves him on. He has a thought, steps into the print room on the way, picks up a copper plate and dry-point needle and continues on. It is *her* bedroom now of course. His clothes are still kept there but he has been sleeping in the guest bed in the ante-room so as not to disturb her while she recovers. He has to stop himself from breaking into a run. How could he have stayed away for so many hours?

Her face lights up when he enters. He smiles broadly in response. Her eyes are drawing him to her and her hand lifts from the bed, ready to touch the back of his neck like she always does. He's floating like pigment in too much oil. Then her hand drops, as she remembers not to touch him.

He ignores the chair and sits down on the edge of the bed. Surely that's allowed. Only now does he notice the plump but determined shadow in the corner. Geertje's still there, keeping watch. She gets up, dismissed by an unspoken signal from her mistress.

What to say? Saskia is silent too. Where's her hand? He feels under the warm cloth for her palm. She does not object. There it is, the skin sweaty, the flesh strangely cold. His fingers fold around hers and he's adrift no more. He beds down and rests his head next to hers on that mountain of pillows. Her hair tickles his cheek but he does not move. It's a privilege to be so close to her.

He's tired. How long has it been since they slept in the same bed? Perhaps he could have a little sleep now. Suddenly she jolts up, coughing. He sits up too, wants to help but he can only wait and watch with empty hands. While she's coughing uncontrollably she's searching for something under the covers. Then she pulls out a cloth and presses it hard against her mouth, her fingers blanched.

Then it's over, silence, as if nothing has happened. She takes away the cloth and puts it under the covers. She is still gasping for air. Before he can say anything she asks between breaths, 'How is it progressing? Is it how you wanted it?'

He can't help grinning. 'Yes, yes, it's nearly there. It will burst their little heads when they see it.'

'You've told them, haven't you?'

'I told them they're going to get a group portrait like no other. Maybe I should have charged them twice the going rate as they are getting all the drama and action of a history painting thrown in as well.'

'You *are* charging them nearly twice the going rate,' she says, almost laughing.

'Ah yes, that is true, my dove,' he says.

Her expression changes. 'How is Titus? Is Geertje looking after him well?'

'He's doing splendidly. She won't let him out of her sight. Yesterday, she says, he crawled all the way from the kitchen to the storeroom and then started pulling himself up on boxes. He can't wait to walk. He's a strong lad.'

He wants her to know that Titus will live. Then she'll get better soon, for Titus.

'I'll get him,' he says. 'Shall I? Only this once; I'll stand by the door with him so you can see him.'

She looks uncertain but finally she nods. He's intoxicated by the thought of them all being together for a few moments.

He's only nine months old but Titus is heavy in his arms. He's in a contented mood. Geertje has a way with him or maybe he's just naturally cheerful. The baby tries to finger his moustache but thankfully his hand goes wide of the target. They've reached the door. 'Look,

Titus, there's your Mammie.' He holds him up, hands under his arms. Saskia raises her hand in a wave. 'Hello, Titey. What's your Pappie doing holding you up like a fisherman showing off his catch?'

Then he bounces him up and down in the air and Titus chuckles with glee. Saskia is laughing but she's also close to tears.

'You're beautiful, you know, just like your parents,' he says, nodding and hoping that Titus will nod back. If only Saskia did not look so sad. Her tired smile tells him it's enough. 'All right, Squiglet, time to go.'

He raises Titus's little hand in a wave and Saskia returns the gesture and then they leave. Geertje has been hovering in the corridor all this time as if to prevent any harm to her charge. He hands over the baby.

When he returns to Saskia, even before he can sit down, she says, 'We need to talk about my will.'

'You already have a will.' The words are out before he can make them sound less brusque.

'It is outdated,' she replies.

'We'll go through it when you're better.'

'No, Rembrandt, the notary is coming later today. I will leave my possessions to Titus, as is the way. This might cause a great deal of accounting and expense after my death. I don't want you to have to draw up an inventory and account for every saucer to my family. The notary says this can be avoided if I give you the right to make use of Titus's portion of the inheritance until he comes of age. That way you don't have to worry about a thing.'

He feels the touch of her hand on his. Her face seems luminous; how can this be when he knows that the fine lines that have appeared around her mouth and eyes even in the last few weeks are only the gentlest sign of her suffering?

He tries to forget those little changes. She's here, talking, breathing, looking at him more kindly now. He remembers the copper plate and needle he has brought – he'll draw her. Now. For his pleasure. He sits up to see her better. Just as the figures of the group painting suddenly seemed to organize themselves this morning, so do the features of her face. It's perfectly clear what matters. He'll only need a few lines . . .

He rests the plate on the little table and presses the needle into the metal, incising a line. It's very fine, like laying down a single hair. She settles back into the cushion, looking out of the window. Is she looking at the clouds or at the space in between? He draws her right pupil. Round and round the needle goes. A shining circle of copper burr, reflecting the light. It will be a deep black on the print. He has to stop going round and round, but he's afraid of stopping. With the pressure of his hand on the needle he wants to fix her and him to this moment for ever. Another cough, and another, and another. There might be no end to the coughing. No chance to catch the next breath. Each one drains a little of her strength away. He tries to continue drawing from memory until she can breathe again but his hands won't move. Finally she's released. She sinks back in the pillows, breathing deliberate careful breaths so as not to trigger another bout. He looks at her face again. Picks up where he left off. A line for her jaw, her nose, her eyes. Simple. As simple as her only task: to draw a breath and let it go again.

After a while there are no more lines begging to be drawn. 'You sleep a while. I'll go and do a print of this. I'll show you later.'

Her hand holds him back, then she puts his hand to her chest, presses it to her heart. He can feel the beat of it. Slow, steady. Such a small heart, engaged in restless effort . . .

Then she takes his hand to her lips, kisses the back of it and lets it go. He knows she does not want him to kiss her for fear of infection so he strokes her forehead with his fingers, as softly as if drawing into wax. For a long while after he can still feel the sensation where she kissed his hand.

He's gone over the drawing with a burin, engraving deep lines into the copper. When he's satisfied, he carefully dabs on the ink. Then he wipes the plate shiny again with a cloth. The grooves retain the black. Finally, he polishes off the last remnants with the heel of his hand; there's no better tool to avoid black lines around the edges of the print. Then he beds the plate down onto a thick sheet of the finest quality Chinese paper inside the press, puts the felt matting down and rolls the drum over it. Under the pressure of the drum, the paper rises up into the grooves and licks the ink off the plate.

Now paper and plate are wed and he has to slowly prise the paper away so it does not tear. He looks at the sheet edge-on. Black lines rise like mountain ridges from flats of white. He regards the nonsensical landscape for a moment, then holds it at arm's length to finally contemplate the image.

But there is no familiar face, only thin inky lines that he cannot assemble into anything meaningful. They are floating in front of the paper, suspended in the air, slowly coming towards him. Any moment now they'll drop to the floor in an irretrievable mess, or is it he who is about to fall? They hang in space, separate from all else. Impossible. Then at last he can see her face. There it is, in perfect clarity, but then the lines vanish, as if they never existed. The paper is empty. He lets go and it slowly sails to the floor.

He does not return to her. Neither that day nor the next. He continues working on *The Night Watch*. When she coughs, he wants it to stop, to give her – and himself – a reprieve. But when it's quiet, the silence screams at him.

He pits his brush against it all and paints van Ruytenburch's gold-trimmed buff coat. The more she coughs, the more he works to knit gold embroidery from oil and pigments. When Geertje eventually comes, saying, 'The mistress wants you,' he goes and sits with her. But as soon as she's asleep he hurries back to *The Night Watch*. He must finish it. And as van Ruytenburch's coat begins to warm him, her lazy body is falling away from her. Her face is growing leaner all the time.

He starts finding reasons not to go to her, as if one unguarded look were the beginning of something he cannot finish. He knows that if he looks, he'll have to stay and keep watching. He'll have to walk her right to the gate. She'll pass through to the other side and he'll be left on his own. If he stays away, she simply will have to get better. She would never leave him without saying goodbye.

Even from the lean-to he can hear that her breathing has acquired a rasping sound with a mournful sigh for an exhale. He paints as long as there is light and then beds down on the other side of the house from her. But still he can hear the persistent in-and-out. It's the third morning since he's last seen her. In one of those long silences Geertje comes and says, 'Master, the mistress, I am sorry, it was only a little change, the gaps between her breaths slightly longer. And I soon went in but . . .'

Now he's running – maybe he can still catch her – but it is too late. The body lies collapsed, head and shoulders slumped sideways at an impossible angle. The mouth is open, more of an exit than an entry. A few years ago he thought he'd got Christ's limp body just right when they took him off the cross. He had not. He tries to look but he can't – not at the dead eyes. So he fixes his eyes on her locks. Has the hair just moved from a little breath? Perhaps she is asleep? Everything in his body agrees. She is asleep. Geertje is wrong. He thinks of their dead babies, merely a few weeks old. How he held each of them. How his body insisted that they were alive because they were warm, even as he felt them limp as drowned cats in his arms. Back then, slowly, something in him had come to understand that soon they'd grow cold and then stiff and he would not be able to move their little limbs. Saskia and he had sat with them, their grief bearable while the imitation of life still clung to the babes.

Part of him wants to hold her too, as if to prolong her departure a little. But it is too late. He has no doubt at all that she is gone. He cannot bear to feel her body warm while knowing her to be dead. And most of all he cannot bear his body comprehending, as it had in the end with his babies, that all that is left now is – this absence.

He tries to will himself to step closer, to perform the rites, as she would have wanted: push down the untouchable eyelids with a cloth, use a pillow to keep the head tilted forward so that the lower jaw is brought up to close that dark hollow of a mouth, make her limbs lie less haphazardly – as if she were merely having a little rest that will turn out to last for ever. But death is none of those things. It has torn through her and left him with a pile of bones.

He averts his eyes, backs away and knocks over one of the candles. When he bends down to right it, smoke from the snuffed flame enters his nostrils, sharp like a long needle.

The very next day he finishes *The Night Watch*. He knows it won't be long before his own rigor will set in. After the last brushstroke he starts to pull a thick blanket over things: first over the memories of the girl who was his love, then over the room that holds what remains of her. He never goes back. The blanket is very accommodating; it does not care whether it is stretched over little joys or great sorrows. In the morning he goes around the house and closes all the shutters. He'll live under a shroud – there is no better place to hide from death. Not that he wants to hide; he wants to join her now, as he should have done before.

The house becomes a dim and mute world and even Geertje

appreciates this, hardly producing a sound when she cleans and cooks. And when she gets it into her head to light candles, he simply goes around after her, blowing them out again.

That month they carry two bundles from the house. The rolled-up body of the canvas remains with him for a few more weeks but his wife is gone within a day.

St Jerome in a Dark Chamber

They are getting nowhere. Samuel writes *flowers* on the list of things to arrange for the funeral. His master, slumped in a chair, has all the animation of a sack of swedes. When Geertje askes Rembrandt once again whether to order plenty of flowers, he mutters, 'Why would I want flowers?'

This morning it took their joint efforts to dress him. At first he had protested and tried to push them away but then he merely lay motionless on the bed.

While Geertje wrestled with his arms, Samuel threaded his legs into breeches, reminding him of nothing so much as dressing his father's dead body. Then he tried to push the hopeless lump of flesh into an upright position, thinking a cow's carcass would have been easier to shift. Then, all of a sudden, Rembrandt stood up like a statue, so Samuel took him by the arm and led him downstairs.

Geertje is still stabbing question after question at him. Can she not see that it is no use? Samuel's apprenticeship with the greatest painter that ever lived is most definitely over. The Apelles of Amsterdam could not even get out of bed on his own.

Geertje has positioned herself squarely opposite Rembrandt, still waiting for a reply about the flowers, and the master's eyes are on the door as if he is waiting for the right moment to escape.

Samuel says, 'Let's not trouble him anymore; *we* can decide what to do.'

Geertje huffs, gets up and starts to tackle the array of dirty pots and pans that have piled up on the wooden worktop. Samuel puts his hand on Rembrandt's coarse sleeve, stroking it, as he would a nervous horse.

'You have to eat.'

There is no answer, but at least he has stopped eyeing the door. Geertje plonks a bowl of porridge on the table, way out of Rembrandt's reach, so Samuel has to push it in front of him. Not even a flicker of interest. He takes Rembrandt's hand and places the spoon into his fingers. They close around it, holding it like a brush. No further action follows.

Samuel looks over his shoulder; Geertje is busy at the sink. He prises the spoon out of Rembrandt's fingers. He'll have to try to feed him. To his surprise, the mouth opens and accepts food. Maybe there is hope. Rembrandt's eyes meet his and Samuel tries to find a presence behind the grey-blue irises but his master is not there.

Samuel will have to do his best to hammer out with Geertje the arrangements for Mistress Saskia's funeral. A daunting task considering that the result has to please Saskia's family. He writes *a generous amount of flowers* on his list.

Rembrandt lies in his bed. An ox has gone to sleep on his heart. Breathing is such a chore. Being awake is a chore. At least they've stopped bothering him. Thankfully the boy, not Geertje, brings him food. Samuel ministers to him as if he were a hatchling that has fallen out of its nest.

Geertje has started moving about downstairs and the putrid smell of what she brews tells him it must be morning. Besides, the deep red of the carpet is slowly blossoming out of the dark and strips of light are emerging from the wall where the sunlight filters through the closed shutters. They tremble almost imperceptibly. In another time he would have been compelled to render their tender oscillations in paint.

He follows the pattern all day as it makes its slow journey across the wall, until at dusk it fades and is gone.

Darkness solid as an anvil. So perfectly black that he does not know if perhaps his eyes have stopped working.

He pulls a blanket around himself, clutching its corners. He doesn't mind the darkness. His heart beats with supreme regularity; beat, beat, beat, beat, beat . . . Does it not know? Do all the parts of his body simply continue on without him? The *will to live*, what a useless accessory it is now and yet he cannot rid himself of it; his mouth still opens to each morsel of food that is offered.

*

Mostly he feels nothing, even as her absence tunnels through him. Except there is one particular thought that lances him every time: *You did not do enough for her*. It repeats itself over and over, as if to make sure he's heard it. At other times he hears someone singing. It's a lullaby, sung softly by his ear. And when all is quiet, the same voice whispers: *Have some heart for yourself.* The voice also tells him that it does not matter. Saskia understood and loved him. But he knows it matters; besides, he is oblivious to comfort.

What of the funeral? He should go. They already think him a bad husband. Where is the boy? At last, here he comes.

He's being fed again? Is it to the slaughter soon? His mind wants feeding too. Toothless gums gnawing on fragments of dreams. Incapable of remembering the meaning of certain words like *joy*. The light, despite moving so slowly, is impossible to track. Days both brief and long.

From time to time he crawls to the edge of the bed, puts his hands on the floor and takes to it on all fours, keeping low. The body has to probe the edges of the room. It does this with its eyes closed, fingering at boards and walls as if searching for something. If only it would stop this folly, allow sleep to come.

He wakes on the floor. Something is different. But what? More clattering, shouting and thumping of feet. He burrows back under the covers. It is *the day*. The boy will come to dress him and try to take him there. She'll be in a box, in the aisle of the church, next to the cavity of her numbered grave. They will lower her into nothing and eclipse all light with a slab of stone – until the lease expires on that rented hole.

He tries to stand up but the ground has hands, pulling him down and something's skewering his head. The room's drunk, rotating on a wobbly axis. He waits for it to stop. The sounds come from the kitchen but no one is outside his door. He puts one foot in front of the other, expecting the ground to cant but it stays firm. Out he slips and up the stairs, already half forgetting where he's going. There's a hatch to the loft with a ladder going up. His father used to say, *always hold onto the ladder with one hand, then if you fall you can save yourself.* Mustn't make that mistake again. Don't let go with the left until the right is firmly around the next rung.

There. The top. Close the hatch. Now rest for a moment. Blood's rushing in his ears and veins, bringing with it the dust on the floorboards, weariness and the heart's strange contortions in his chest.

It's a big space, full of crates and boxes. Most of them contain old clothes, costumes or curious things which were irresistible at the time. Some light is squeezing in through the gaps between the roof tiles and the clouds of dust he's trodden loose make visible a fretwork of light beams.

He squeezes himself in where the rafters meet the floor in the eaves, lying on his side, pushing his back into the gap as far as it will go. You're safe. They won't find you. There's a shaft of light right in front of his eyes, and in it dancing specks of dust shining with a light of their own. They are too beautiful. He closes his eyes.

Geertje and Samuel are shouting his name. Then finally quiet. They've given up; the front door falls shut.

His eyes are lured by a single mote of dust, suspended in a smattering of light, in the darkest corner of the eaves. The mote has rough edges. If you look closely, it's an entire world. Something in his heart, an inexplicable light there too. *Saskia*, his mouth forms silently. Then erupts – a scream. A creature pounding the floor. Hands scratched, bruised. Something heaves inside. Terror. Pressing hands to mouth.

'God, where are you?' Voice a rasp.

Mouth moves to scream but no sound comes. Scything grief. Hands clawing at a box, ripping away the lid, digging through clothes. The red dress. Body wraps itself around plush colour, blind for comfort.

Someone's wailing, far away. Sniffs dress, to try to find her.

'No, no, no, no, no.' She's not there.

The box again, hands pull out; garment follows garment, like an endless string. More and more. Enough to get buried in. He lies in his nest of velvet like a baby. Proper tears come. Flow until exhaustion ends them.

Where is that mote of dust now? His world?

Samuel is relieved that the burial was a swift business. The sour looks that Saskia's family gave him and Geertje: as if it was their fault that Rembrandt was absent. He told them that Rembrandt is overwhelmed with grief. They nodded politely but even now they will be saying: *If only Rembrandt had looked less after himself and more after her*. It is not true of course. He loved her dearly; that's why he can't go on now, without her.

Samuel hesitates for a moment before going into Rembrandt's bedroom, afraid to find that he is still gone. But there he is, asleep in his bed or pretending to be.

'It's done. It was fine,' he says, in case Rembrandt is awake. 'She's resting now.' What a stupid thing to say.

Later, he brings him chicken soup. Rembrandt is sitting upright in bed. He looks a little better but smells like a pigsty. The jug and washbasin have not been touched. The stench is beyond cure by perfume. He needs a wash. Samuel starts spooning soup into the mouth and finds his own mouth opening and closing along with Rembrandt's. There is nothing he can do to stop it. Odd that in only a week Rembrandt's skin has turned white as paper. And the eyes: they look as if there is nothing left in the world worth focusing their gaze upon. If only he could see them alert again, intent on a challenge. This will be *my* challenge, he thinks, and then has an idea. He tries to catch Rembrandt's eye. 'Mijnheer Six says it is impossible to produce an etching that depicts impenetrable darkness. I can see his point, for a paper saturated with the blackest black would still only look like ink on paper.'

Rembrandt's eyes slip away from the brief contact. The slurping of spoonfuls of soup goes on uninterrupted.

Samuel says, 'Geertje put some fresh water there this morning so you can wash.'

Rembrandt nods.

'You need to wash,' says Samuel.

Again he nods.

When he comes back with the next meal Rembrandt still stinks. Someone will have to rub him down. Naturally the task will fall to Geertje – it is the kind of thing she does, just as she looked after the mistress.

'No!' she says, arms crossed over her broad chest. 'I am not employed to look after him!'

'What?'

'It's the mistress that employed me to look after her and little Titus and it's just as well she did.'

'But *he* is paying your wages now, always has.'

She huffs. 'He never lifted a finger; she wanted him to care for her but he wouldn't even stay with her for five minutes. Now it's the same with Titus – poor little mite's got no mother and his father is busy doing nothing at all.'

She spits into the spittoon. How can she collect all that saliva when she never stops talking?

'I won't do it, he's filthy, he's mad.' Then, after a pause, she whispers, 'He's probably dangerous.'

'It's women's work,' Samuel replies and regrets it as soon as the words are out of his mouth. Any moment now she'll slap her wet cloth about his face, but instead she bends over, roaring with laughter.

'Ha, ha. You're the one that's done all the women's work so far, so I reckon it's your job. You're his *nurse*.'

'Geertje, please. Yes, it's true. But think about it, I helped you dress him, didn't I? And like you say, I've done everything for him that needed to be done. If I hadn't you would have had to do it. It's only washing him. I can't do it. So will you? Please?'

She pats his head with uncharacteristic gentleness. 'You're a good soul. Of course I will. I've washed a man many times before.' She slings a big pot over the fire. 'And no doubt it won't be the last, as they seem to have trouble with it.' Then she eyes him up and down, steps closer and sniffs his collar. He runs out of the kitchen, buoyed along by her gales of laughter.

Samuel is in the process of answering all the notes that have been left for Rembrandt, asking to see him on business or expressing condolences. He longs to get back to his books, but someone has to deal with the paperwork.

There are sounds of a commotion from below and then a door bangs shut. He goes downstairs and there is Geertje, outside Rembrandt's bedroom, her apron drenched. She wordlessly hands him the half-full jug, cloth and soap, and stomps off.

Bucket in hand, Samuel considers his options: he could forget about it – there is no reason to put himself through so much unpleasantness. But perhaps he can wash away some of the darkness that is suffocating his master? He wants him back drawing something that other people don't even stop to look at until his pen discovers it for them. He has to try.

Rembrandt is in bed, blanket pulled over him with only a narrow opening for nose and blinking eyes. Samuel decides a little lie can't hurt. 'Master, forgive me but the physician says it will be good to rub down the skin. Will you sit on the stool please, it won't take a moment.'

He seems to have special powers, for Rembrandt gets up, albeit shakily, and sits on the footstool wearing his nightshirt. Samuel puts the ceramic bowl on the floor and lifts each foot in turn, placing them in the bowl. He tests the water in the jug for temperature – it is nice and warm – and pours it over the feet. Rembrandt settles into himself and Samuel starts rubbing the shins and calves with warm water and soap. It makes him think of one of Rembrandt's drawings of Christ washing the feet of his disciples at the Last Supper. Jesus hunkered down, scrubbing away at the dirty toes.

When he is done with the feet he tells Rembrandt to lift up his arms and peels away the stinking nightshirt. The skin on his body looks even whiter than on his face. It's no different from cleaning his brushes and palette, he tells himself, and sets about scrubbing the neck with the cloth. There are grey hairs on Rembrandt's head that he has not noticed before. He dips the cloth again into the warm water and wipes it up and down the back, avoiding direct contact with the warm skin. Now the brow, grime-streaked. Samuel dabs at it; the filth does not want to come off but he can hardly scrub it like a muddy boot. Rembrandt leans back, making it easier to see his face, and revealing to Samuel black soot-like flecks on his cheeks. He rubs away at them and to his satisfaction they start coming off. This is better.

He is as docile as a motherless lamb. Samuel does his best to carefully wipe the front of the neck. 'Master,' he says, without really intending to, 'I am so sorry.'

'I know,' says Rembrandt. Then after a while, 'You're a better man than I.'

'It's you who taught me,' says Samuel. 'You taught me everything.'

'I didn't teach you this.'

Samuel sets to work on armpits, chest and arms. That done, he hesitates – down there, what to do about it? He can't possibly, but then again he always finishes what he starts . . . Rembrandt intercepts his hand.

'Come now boy, if I don't put a stop to this, you'll soon be clucking like a brooding hen. Give me the flannel. And tell Jan Six: pitch darkness happens in the vault of the mind, even if the sun shines brightly outside. And *that* can be depicted.'

Samuel hands him the cloth and for a moment he thinks he can smell paint on him again.

Summer

Samuel is at his master's desk. He's just heard the clock chime midnight. He had hoped that things would improve more quickly but it's been almost a month and Rembrandt still refuses to see anyone except him. The pupils are on the verge of moving on to other workshops and since they provide the only remaining source of income he has to keep them occupied, pretending the master has set the tasks. At least Rembrandt now occasionally answers questions, which helps Samuel keep things going. But it is not enough. He needs to show himself soon, or he and his business will be finished. He must speak to him. Chances are he's still awake, as he mostly sleeps during the day.

Rembrandt is lying on the bed, staring at the ceiling, but sits up when he sees him. Samuel pulls up a chair and starts stuffing the pipe he has brought with tobacco. He lights it with the flame from the candle, drawing air until he tastes smoke, then gives it to Rembrandt. They pass it between them until the tobacco is spent. The room is thick with smoke, swirling in the light of the candle.

Samuel says softly, so softly that Rembrandt can pretend he has not heard it, 'What is it like?'

'What is what like?' asks Rembrandt.

'Your condition?'

'You make it sound like a disease.'

Rembrandt's eyes close and he disappears into thought. Finally he utters, 'You know how some fools, greedy for a shiny darkness, add bitumen to their paint without sufficient driers and then a few years later the face of a dear friend, rendered in thousands of careful brushstrokes, develops blisters and then . . .' – he makes a motion with his hands of something flowing apart – '. . . it's ripped apart by ugly crevices.'

His eyes, behind his closed lids, strain as if trying to focus on something. 'When I look where my love used to be . . .'

He shrugs his shoulders and sticks his finger into the spent pipe, scoops out the ash and shows it to Samuel. 'I don't want to talk. Talking is . . .' he sighs, 'I'm just not interested.' He rubs the black ash between his thumb and index finger. 'Funny, to think this used to grow once in a field.'

To Samuel this does not sound like ordinary grief at all but like a canker of the soul. 'So how do we make it better?' he asks.

'Ah, still trying to cure me of my disease?'

'But it's more than grief, isn't it?'

'What makes you think it can be cured?' he says with a defeated smile that isn't one.

Samuel feels the urge to drag him to his feet, thrust a pencil into his hand and make him use it. He can't comprehend this strange apoplexy of feeling. What is the point of loving someone if it results in this incapacity? Samuel touches his arm to get his attention. 'But before, when the babies died, you *did* go on with work?'

With a strange knowing expression in his face, Rembrandt takes

Samuel's hand and studies it. 'You've not been painting either, have you?'

Has he lost his mind? Of course he hasn't painted – he's been running the workshop for him.

Rembrandt turns his hand over and points at the lines in his palm. 'The body changes all the time, new lines appear, sometimes in a matter of weeks. But there are inner changes too, the flux of our natural empathies, the movements of the soul. I've taught you to see and depict them, remember?'

Samuel feels something, yes, he is subject to an inner flow, no apoplexy of feeling for *him*; he is here because of what he feels. How rough the fingers gripping his hand are. He has not noticed this before. Suddenly the window rattles from a draft. The candle splutters and dies. They are in total darkness. Like bitumen, thinks Samuel.

Rembrandt lets go of his hand and Samuel feels a rising panic. He's lost all sense of where he is, or the door, the candle or Rembrandt. It is childish but he's always been afraid of the dark. He can't help reaching out with his hand, feeling for something to orientate himself. He chances upon Rembrandt's arm and holds on to it.

Rembrandt whispers as if telling him a secret, 'We were kin. I was as used to her as to having arms and legs. Of course, it's possible to lose a limb and get on with some kind of life . . . but Samuel, I did not *lose* her.' He pauses. 'I cut her off.'

Samuel wants to shake him – what nonsense. He feels

Rembrandt's hand on his upper arm, like a bridge between them, a conduit. 'I saw that she did not have many days left, so miserable coward that I was I put a gap between us, to make it bearable for myself. Do you hear, Samuel, not for her, but for *me*.' Now Rembrandt's grip loosens to almost nothing. 'I should have waited till after she was gone but I left her, long before she went.'

Samuel understands. He too is frightened. He too has thought of leaving rather than watching his master disintegrate. If only he could put his master's soul at rest about these sins that aren't sins at all.

Samuel listens out into the silent darkness for a long time. He places his other hand also on Rembrandt's sleeve, first softly, then holding on to the arm with both his hands as if to return him to this world and keep him here.

Rembrandt's fingers are gripping Samuel's elbow. 'Why does God teach me to love, then strip me bare, leaving me with nothing?'

Then Rembrandt lets go but Samuel doesn't. He traces the sleeve down to the rough-skinned hand and takes it in both of his. He wants to pour all his own strength into this hand, which is meant to paint. He is glad the dark conceals the moisture in his eyes. Rembrandt sighs and pulls his hand away. He must be trying to lie down, so Samuel helps him and arranges the blanket over him as best he can in the dark. 'I'll go and fetch some light,' he says.

To his surprise, he finds the door easily despite the dark. He hastens up to the studio which has a stove with some embers in it. What a struggle it is to love and yet how easy, thinks Samuel. He puts a candle to them and the wick bursts into flame at the first touch.

He carries the light back to Rembrandt's room and puts it by his bed. His master has already fallen asleep. What a blessing it is to see him look peaceful.

Geertje can't do anything quietly, thinks Rembrandt. If it wasn't for her I'd still be asleep. Can't she lift the chairs instead of dragging them across the stone floor?

It is impossible to produce an etching that depicts impenetrable darkness. Who said that? If he is quick he might not see anyone. How ridiculous to be afraid of encountering another person in his own house.

He reaches the print room unnoticed. Now he's safe. They know better than to disturb him when he is working. He locks the door, turning the key as many times as it will go.

He steps towards the container where the lumps of soft ground are usually kept. Hoping that his assistants have maintained a supply of the right consistency. He picks up and sniffs one of the pieces which are a boiled-down mixture of asphalt, resin and wax. His nose is pleasantly assaulted by the heady smell of asphalt. He inhales the invigorating fumes before wrapping it in gauze and lighting a fire in the chafing dish to heat up the plate.

Once the copper is warm enough he applies the ground which dissolves, passing through the gauze. When the plate has cooled, he opens the shutters to have more light and takes the etching needle and puts it to the plate. The asphalt yields like butter, satisfying – a coppery trail of exposed metal.

The outlines of a small chamber have taken shape but the plate is still mostly black. To the right he sketches a small window, beneath it an old man, St Jerome, who sits at a table with an open book. But Jerome pays no attention to it. His elbow rests wearily on the table, his arm and hand propping up his head. The light is not too bright and yet the old man feels it necessary to shade his eyes.

On the left he draws the outline of a spiral staircase, which continues beyond the edge of the plate. Once he has completed this rough outline of the elements of the picture, the rhythm of his work changes. The plate is still almost entirely black, with only the sketch showing in shiny copper. He imagines it as a print: the red lines of copper transformed into black ink. He'll have to expose much more copper to get the darkness he wants. He thinks of the plate submerged in its bath, the acid eating away at the copper until it has bitten grooves deep enough to retain the ink. He starts a flurry of hatched lines, his fingers and needle a blur. More and more bright copper is exposed. It takes a long time, for it isn't a uniform darkness he wants to achieve but many shades of grey; even the darkest parts still hint at the existence of walls and furnishings, right on the edge of recognition.

He wants the onlooker to see into a special kind of darkness, one that swallows not only ordinary light but the inner light of the eyes, the light of attention. He'll lead the viewer there with his needle, up the dark staircase to the upper room beyond the edge of the plate, where no thought, or light, or glimmer of anything exists, until the onlooker even forgets about himself.

What of Jerome? His head is being disgorged by darkness, but not the rest of him. He remains half-born in a mute world. The shadows are eating him and yet he cannot see them.

Rembrandt turns his attention to the window, the lightest part of the image. It is big enough to allow ample light into the room. But despite his seat by the window, it's as if Jerome exists in darkness, because the light can never penetrate the darkness of his mind.

The boy is terribly pleased when he discovers the etching in the print room. He believes that he brought about a change in Rembrandt but really there is none.

A terrifying noise. It's coming from his chest. A devil's trombone, pummelling him from the inside. And the malevolent thing is vying for control of his breath. It's only with the greatest effort that he gets the bellows of his chest to rise. Air, he needs more air. The drone surges to a deafening roar. His bowels slacken, frightened by his own helplessness. He thrashes the air but there is nothing he can do against the amorphous attacker, except to flee. He gets out of bed, but his knees buckle and he hits the floor.

Another change in pitch – for the better, allowing a breath. But not for long; the pitch changes again. His lungs are paralysed. Breathe, breathe – his lungs don't listen. No heave to suck in air. The door, he has to reach the door. But limbs won't obey. He'll die. He forces out the last bit of air to produce a scream. Pain, but different, on the outside, sharp. Something has hit the side of his face. He opens his eyes: light, white cloth, his bedroom, Geertje. Silence, apart from his own breathing. A dream, he's had a dream. He is on the floor, panting like a dog. Air so fresh and sweet. She's standing over him. His cheek still stings. She must have hit him, to wake him. He's filled with gratitude. She takes a step back. With her long nightshirt and candle in hand she looks like an angel of either deliverance or doom.

He hauls himself up, at last awake enough to feel embarrassed. He must have screamed, but at least he did not soil himself. Why is she staring at him like this? Ah. She probably fears his wrath because she's struck him. He nearly laughs out loud at the idea. A gust of air sweeps through the open door from behind her, cooling his sweaty arms and bringing her smell to his nose. Unlike her wrinkled brow, it is enticing. He wants more but the air is still.

Maybe he *is* still asleep; there are no rules in dreams. He moves towards her, eyes half closed. His hands reach out and touch coarse fabric and a hint of warmth beyond. His nose finds the nook of her neck. He inhales the scent. Divine. He sniffs along her neckline, with each breath more and more awake. Wait. She has not stopped him. And if she has not stopped him, she might let him go further.

He pushes aside the obstructing collar and buries his mouth and nose in the nape of her neck, steals a taste of her skin with a lick of his tongue, disguised as a kiss. Her neck arches. He disbelieves his luck, but goes on. Neck, collarbone, shoulder. Her.

He remembers he has hands. They grab and rumple the linen,

finding flesh through fabric. Hips, clutched and possessed. And there, the fat roundness of her breasts. He seizes them, such malleable softness. No matter how he sculpts and holds them, they resolutely resume their wondrous shape.

How lithe she has become. He never would have thought it. Her thighs pressing against him. A message in that. She wants you, you fool. But he still cannot trust this new world; the nightmare still too real to him. He reaches for her, blindly pulling her towards him. They stumble on to the bed or has she pushed him there? Her skin, so warm. Something else makes itself known: Yes, he's feeling *good*; and his pain . . . ? He can't locate it anywhere. He *is* capable of feeling good. Perhaps he can have a life, some kind of life.

He pushes up the cloth of her nightshirt and lets his fingers dwell on her upper thighs, trying to discern their secret workings, the bones inside and the strands of muscles. Yes, they carry, they bear up and now they tremble softly where he's touching them. He wants to do more – merely to worship is not enough. He runs his hands up from knee to hip, over and over again, to where the shock of thick hair beckons him.

Just as he is thinking of laying his fingertips at her entrance, her hand folds around his cock, and he is lost in her frenzied touch.

At last he knows it. She is his. She has given him back the world and by God he would fill it. And then he enters her with all the languor of certainty, almost laughing when she claws at him for more.

Their encounter becomes dedicated to only one thing. It's a smithy of joy. They forge their pleasure, this way and that, folding it like steel, strengthening it, until it is sharp and bright – so all consuming it at last expunges who they are.

And so the sword comes down and cuts them loose.

PART II

Five years later

Winter

Bredevoort, Gelderland, Dutch Republic, January 1647

'Hendrikje,' my mother shouted through several closed doors, 'the sheets are frozen solid on the line!'

The morning had been so bright and sunny that I'd forgotten it was freezing. I imagined her taking them down and folding them with a crunching sound, angry that I was not rushing out to help.

My hands carried on with the lacework. I felt the bellied bobbins, the wood worn smooth by generations. My fingers crossed two pearly threads in a twirl around one another and then placed them on the side. Twirling, placing, picking up a new pair. The lace on the black cushion on my lap grew like an ice crystal on a window.

My back ached. I'd been resisting the impulse to stop but at last I put the cushion on the chair next to me and let my gaze drift out of the window. I wanted to put my palms on the cool glass. How happy the children sounded outside. They loved the snow. They'd been shouting and laughing all morning. I heard the noise of wagon wheels rattling on bumpy cobbles in the distance and I listened to them until they melted into silence – but still I thought I heard them.

From my seat I could see only a small framed rectangle of sky, the colour of dirty snow.

I picked up the cushion again and returned it to my lap. Why not get up, relieve the strain on my back and readjust the waistband of my skirt? The clock in the corner continued its rhythm – tick, pause, tock, pause – as if it had to inhale before every tick and tock. I glanced at the long pendulum as it swung along its prescribed path. It would never stop; it was wound each day by my mother.

My fingers started again. I watched them. Left, right, left, right, in time with the stupefying ticking of the clock. The timepiece had been my father's pride. It was a rare thing. Everyone else lived by the clock on the church tower. How many more ticks until the collar would be finished? Never; the lace would go on as long as the clock. Tock, inhale, tick, exhale, tock, inhale . . .

My hands continued blind, as my eyes moved away from the sprawling lace. Those pale blue curtains, I'd hidden behind them as a child. They were still there, ready to shut the world out but no longer capable of concealing me. Why could I never get comfortable? It was always there, the pressure of the waistband, the tightness of my bodice and the hardness of the chair. As a child I'd garnered the nickname Mistress Too-Tight for my complaining.

But I'd adapted to my home like a hermit crab to its borrowed shell. I placed my feet on top of the foot stove and arranged my skirt around and soon felt the warmth rise up my legs. Anything could be endured as long as one's feet were warm.

The light suddenly lifted, causing the silver-threaded cloth on the side chair to sparkle. I rested my hands. The sun was blazing through the windows so strongly that it made the glass glow; perhaps it would simply melt, flow away and the room would flood with fresh air. I put the heavy cushion aside and got up, enjoying each step that took me to the window.

I inspected the glass. Many tiny flecks of dirt had accumulated there. And the morning sun caused each of them to light up with their own corona, as if they themselves emitted light. Perhaps they did; perhaps it was the dirt that made the world light up. Still, the windows needed a clean and I wanted to clean them, so I fetched a bucket, climbed on to a footstool and rubbed away at the dirt with a cloth, water and vinegar.

After a while my mother came in. I knew her step. I did not bother to turn or stop; we often talked while we worked. I pushed the cloth right into a grubby corner, determined to remove all the grime.

'Our neighbour, Jacob van Dorsten, has asked for my hand in marriage and I have accepted,' she said.

The clock did not miss a beat, but I was left behind, caught in the moment before the incomprehensible news. My father was barely six months dead; how had she and van Dorsten arranged this? I let my arm drop, and looked beyond the glass as if for the first time: ranks of ice-encrusted cobbles, wild-looking children and a bird's nest that must have fallen out of the tree on to the frozen ground.

'I extend my good wishes to you and Mijnheer van Dorsten.' My mouth formed the words well enough but they were so loud, spoken like this against the glass.

‘Thank you,’ I heard her say behind me. ‘It will be good for everyone.’

One of the little girls outside was bending over with laughter. Had she heard what my mother had said? Then I started to see where the threads crossed over; he was a widower with three children under the age of five and she was a widow. My brothers and sister had all found occupations near Bredevoort; but there was a single thread left, useless on its own: me.

I turned to face her, trying not to lose my balance on the wobbly footstool. She was still speaking to me. ‘I’m sorry, Hendrickje, but it’s time for you to leave home. You’re twenty-one and we will need the space, especially with three little ones to look after. Not right away, but you should make plans to depart for Amsterdam and find work within a few months.’

Then her mouth opened and closed again as if she might say something else. After a few ticks of the clock she turned and left.

I climbed down from the footstool, sat on it and looked at the dirty water in the bucket. Let van Dorsten deal with his windows.

The Supper at Emmaus

Rembrandt's house, Sint-Anthonisbreestraat, July 1647

I arrived at the imposing house with its many windows and red shutters. I ran up the few steps to the front door, lifted the knocker and held it. Once I let it hit the plate there'd be no turning back from my new life. I gave three determined knocks.

The housekeeper, a woman of sturdy frame and resolute airs, opened the door and almost dragged me inside by my elbow. In the entrance hall there were two gentlemen seemingly waiting.

Geertje grumbled, 'Might as well take the lot of you up now. I doubt he'll welcome the interruption.' At the same time she was stripping me of my coat as you would a child. Then she gestured at a tray of mugs and a jug of beer on a side table, but as I made to lift the tray, she told me, 'Wait,' and handed me the jug only. Then she waved her arms, herding us up the stairs like errant sheep.

She followed close behind with the clippety-clop of her clogs and the clanking of mugs on the tray. When we reached the door the gentlemen hesitated and looked at each other. Geertje huffed at the delay and pointed with her chin at the door. One of the gentlemen took a deep breath, lifted his hand and rapped the door so gingerly that he barely produced a sound.

'Enter!' a voice called from inside.

I feared that all eyes would be on me, but instead our arrival was utterly ignored. Everyone in the big room was motionless, as if we'd walked into a religious tableau of wooden figurines. Three young men were seated around a table, which stood on a little platform. The one on the left had a pale complexion and short brown hair, while the one on the right had long trailing locks and a pointy nose. Our preacher at home always said long hair was a sinful pleasure in a man.

Between them sat a boyish-looking youth who appeared modest despite his long brown hair, perhaps because of his air of quiet seriousness. The other two were gazing at him as if transfixed, while the boy was looking straight ahead at a man who I assumed was the master. He sat a few feet away, leaning forward in his chair. He was wearing a broad-rimmed hat, which partially shaded his face but did not conceal his furrowed brow. I'd never seen eyes so still and intent. He held the boy's gaze as if his life depended on it, or was it the boy who held his?

I moved further into the room and around them so I could see better. The table was decked with pewter dishes, tablecloth, wine and some bread and there were also a few scrunched-up napkins. It was not too difficult to surmise that they were posing for a picture but if they were models why were they wearing grubby working garb and why were the boy and master locked in wordless communion?

The boy was holding the broken bread and there was wine on

the table so it had to be a scene from the Bible and I guessed that he was Jesus and this was the Last Supper, where Jesus breaks the bread and says *This is my body, which is given for you*. I'd always thought it very good of Jesus to atone for everyone's sins.

There was something so beautiful about the boy's face that I too could not take my eyes off him; perhaps it was his expression, so understanding and so feeling.

I prised my eyes away and looked again at Rembrandt. I'd imagined him so differently, but his face was entirely ordinary: broad with a biggish nose. The eyes as alive as the boy's, but the rest of his face was slack, lifeless – as if some part of him was absent. And the boy? His face was replete with what his master's lacked – faith and hope.

Then, suddenly, Rembrandt clapped his hands, saying, 'That's it, boys,' and turned to us. He greeted the two gentlemen and I prepared myself to speak, but he just nodded at me with a smile and I curtseyed, something I'd never done before, but a nod did not seem enough. Geertje stood grinning at me, apparently finding my curtsey very funny.

The boy playing Jesus looked strangely moved, almost to the point of tears. I wondered why and warmed to him, because his every emotion was displayed on his face.

'Now take turns and sketch the scene and don't introduce a mountain of objects, like fruit and tableware – they'll only distract from what's important,' Rembrandt told the boys.

Then he instructed the gentlemen to swap places with the boys at the table, calling the one with the locks Johann Ulrich, the one with the short hair Dirck and the Jesus-one Samuel. I made sure to remember their names.

The boys settled themselves with their sketching utensils on footstools either side of Rembrandt.

Geertje was gesturing to me to fill the mugs with beer, which I did on a side table. She watched me as if she feared I'd spill it. I piled the empty mugs on the tray, still observing the goings-on. Rembrandt got up and paced around as he spoke.

'Well, boys, what are we going to do?'

'Choose the most powerful moment of the story,' said Dirck.

'Yes, we want the viewer to hang with his eyes on the painting like a baby on his mother's nipple.'

The boys groaned at the metaphor.

Rembrandt asked them, 'So which moment would you choose?'

'When they finally recognize Jesus at Emmaus,' said Johann Ulrich.

'With their hearts,' added Dirck.

So, it had not been the Last Supper – I should have realized, I thought.

'Why that moment and no other?' asked Rembrandt.

'Because that's when we can show the very strongest emotions on the disciples' faces and by seeing these intense feelings the viewer will be moved the most,' said Dirck.

'Quite right,' said Rembrandt, 'perhaps even be changed by what he sees. That's how you conquer the viewer's attention and keep it.'

They all nodded.

Rembrandt seated himself again and he and the boys started drawing. I could not fit any more empty mugs on the tray, nor were there more to fill, but I remained, hoping no one would notice my idleness. Rembrandt sat in his chair, legs crossed, a wooden tablet with drawing paper on his thigh, wearing a well-worn tabard. There was nothing about his appearance or his demeanour that suggested he was a master, rather his authority was bestowed on him. It showed in the way each pupil worked with perfect single-mindedness and in how they glanced over his shoulder, as if his drawing contained all the answers.

Not quite *every* person shared in this veneration, for when Geertje saw that I now occupied myself distributing the filled-up mugs, she said loudly, 'They'll help themselves if they're thirsty.'

So I made to leave, bending down to pick up the tray of used mugs. I felt the distinct brush of a hand against the side of my leg. When I looked up, Johann Ulrich's eyes were staring at me with a curious expression, as if he'd posed a question to which he half knew the answer. It was that strange look more than the touch which alarmed me. I turned away and left quickly so he would not notice the heat in my face.

When we were in the kitchen Geertje said, 'Never mind Johann.' Did she have eyes in the back of her head? 'If you don't encourage him, he'll soon tire of it, unless you *want* to encourage him?'

This was not said accusingly but with a smile. I shook my head.

'No,' she said, 'these boys are not the pick of the crop, drawing and painting all day. If you'd been here when Carel Fabritius was about, now there was a man worth looking at – despite being a painter. Come, it's time to get cooking.'

I was more than content with scrubbing carrots and leeks – they at least were familiar to me.

Geertje started laying the table with delicate porcelain bowls which had blue dragons snaking around their rims. I'd never eaten out of anything other than pewter, let alone had my soup embroidered with dragons.

'I know,' Geertje said. 'He bought them at a knock-down price. People order china decorated with flowers but the Chinese keep on shipping dragons.' She shrugged her shoulders.

I wondered about a land where dragons were more desirable than flowers. The table was set for three: Rembrandt and the two gentlemen. I'd never served anyone at table before. Geertje lugged the huge *hutspot* we'd made on to the table. Shredded beef and vegetables were floating in the broth.

'Sit down,' she said. 'He's often late – no good letting the food go cold.'

No serving then, I'd have to eat *with* him. I would not be able to swallow a thing. I remembered being in my teacher's study in Bredevoort along with my brothers, looking at prints by Leonardo, Raphael, Rubens and Rembrandt. Our teacher had spoken with the same breathless tone that he normally reserved for the Holy Father: 'Rembrandt – our greatest artist.' Then his voice had dropped to a whisper as he described seeing a portrait by Rembrandt at the Burgomaster's house. 'It was as if there was another person in the room. Only by going right up to it could I convince myself that it was only paint on canvas.'

Rembrandt walked in, tossed his tabard on a chair and let himself fall into his seat. He not so much sat as lay sprawled in his chair, arms and legs everywhere. Geertje ladled soup into his bowl, then placed it wordlessly in front of him. I sat with my hands in my lap. He leaned forward and sniffed the soup. 'Mmm, *hutspot*, just what is needed.'

Then he turned to me. 'So what do you make of our city?'

'It is a well-organized warren, Master,' I said, immediately thinking how rude I was.

'Ah yes, it is certainly expanding at the rate of a warren.' He chuckled and I looked down. 'And there's no need to call me "Master", you're not one of my pupils.'

I nodded, but what was I supposed to call him? At least I had not begun eating yet. It would have been mortifying without the prayers having been spoken. But he immediately started spooning soup into his mouth. How immoral not to thank the Lord for one's food. There was nothing to be done about it except to say a little prayer in my mind. Then he and Geertje discussed what purchases to make as if they were at the market. How could they eat and talk at the same time? At home we'd always eaten in silence. I tried to keep my eyes off the contents of Geertje's mouth.

A little boy with golden locks, about six years of age, burst into the room holding something small and dead in his hand. Rembrandt picked him up and threatened to squeeze him flat as a pancake, much to the boy's delight. 'This is Titus,' Geertje said, soup almost dribbling from her chops. 'And this is Hendrickje,' Rembrandt said, pointing at me with his index finger.

Titus greeted me and said, 'I found a dead bird on the way to school but they wouldn't let me bring it in and show it to the other children.' He shrugged his shoulders in incomprehension, the poor thing still dangling from his hand by its legs.

'Oh.' I was as usual at a loss for anything to say to a child.

Geertje hugged and kissed him too and he seated himself next to her, putting the bird on the table by his bowl, which did not seem to bother Rembrandt or Geertje in the slightest. From then on she talked to Titus incessantly, captain of the voyages of his spoon through the soup. 'Now that big chunk of carrot, no, not the beef again, now for the swede.' Any sign of mutiny was quelled with a reminder that rice pudding awaited the successful captor of the floating vegetables.

I kept my head down but could not help glancing at the master when I thought he would not notice. His hair was a light brown, slightly curly, and he had a moustache which was the only appealing feature he possessed. It was neither too slight nor fluffed out to ridiculous proportions. It was in truth just right.

When he had finished, he declined the rice pudding, saying he'd better get on with things in the studio; the pupils were gone now and he could get down to proper work. On his way out he kissed his son again and turned to me. 'Hendrickje, I hope you'll soon feel at home.'

'Thank you, Master,' I said.

He said to Titus. 'I'm sure Hendrickje would love to see your bird.' Was there a grin behind his innocent expression?

Titus put his spoon down and enthusiastically grabbed the bird by the neck, holding it in front of my face. It was a sorry little thing, a young blackbird. I presented my cupped hands because, dead or not, I could not bear to see it being held by the neck like that. Titus laid the bird on my palms. Rembrandt came closer too.

I said to Titus, 'Look, it's grown a lot of its proper feathers already but I don't think it was ready to fly.'

'What happened to it?'

'It must have fallen out of the nest in a storm.'

'Why did its parents not save it?'

'They couldn't get it back into the nest but they might have tried to feed it on the ground.'

'So why did it die then?'

I looked at Rembrandt for a clue as to whether to divulge the horrible truth. He nodded, so I said, 'They need the warmth of their siblings. It probably died of cold.'

'I have no brothers or sisters either,' said Titus, and poked the nail of his finger into the beak, trying to prise it open. Then he asked hopefully, 'Do you think it's got maggots inside yet?'

'Probably not yet,' said Rembrandt and knelt down on one knee, so his face was level with the bird in my hand. His grey eyes set upon it, his irises moving only ever so slightly as he studied the bird, feather by feather. I hoped my hands wouldn't tremble. His face looked different closer up, coarser. So many lines that I could not make sense of. Too many lines. He had lived too much, making him look more worn than he should. He approached the bird with his index finger. I thought he'd start poking it like Titus had but instead he brushed gently over the bird's neck and shoulders, his eyes still fixed on it, as were mine. The feathers glistened where he'd smoothed them. And then I saw; they were not black or rather the black was made up of many colours. How had I not noticed until this moment? The blackbird might as well have been a bird of paradise for how it struck me now: a parade of amber, brown and black and countless shades in between were visible on each tiny featherlet.

He glanced at me before rising, and I had the strange notion that I'd seen what he had seen and that he knew.

I felt very tired when Geertje finally left the kitchen, which was where I slept. There was a box bed in the corner. From it I could see the embers still glowing in the hearth but the rest was darkness. Where did they keep the candles? I'd never be able to find the chamber pot in the dark. I hugged the pillow to my chest, thinking of my brother Harmen. If only I could talk to him now. When I was little he'd read bedtime stories to me. There was a sick feeling in my stomach. Why was I the one who had to leave? Martijne, being the oldest, had moved out but my mother and my brothers were all snug at home now with the van Dorstens – a merry lot.

Still, I was working in the house of the greatest painter in Holland. That's when it struck me as odd that I had been hired by Geertje so easily and swiftly. First she had stood frowning, clearly having no intention of letting me over the threshold. But then, after a moment's thought, she started babbling as if we were to become the best of friends. She hailed from Gouda. Her name was Geertje. Where was I from? Did I have any experience?

'None,' I confessed.

When could I start?

'Immediately,' I said as nonchalantly as I could, even though an offer of employment from her was the last thing I'd expected.

She'd looked at me with her pale blue eyes, frowning again, and said she'd take me on.

Perhaps she could see that I was young and strong. Perhaps she thought my inexperience meant I was not set in my ways and she could teach me. But why had she not presented me to the master of the house? It was most unusual for a housekeeper to be entrusted with hiring a maid.

I closed my eyes but sleep would not come. The sights of the day pressed themselves upon me: the entrance hall with its towering walls, hung with oil paintings from floor to ceiling. Quite a few of them were portraits he had done of himself. I thought of the one with the fur collar and the fanciful hat. I noticed it each time. It was from 1640 so it depicted him in his mid thirties (Geertje had told me that he was now forty-one years of age). At first the face had seemed remote, haughty even, but when I'd looked at it again, after lunch, a sympathetic humour had appeared that lurked behind the serious expression. I was so close to sleep that impressions jumbled together. The black feathers of the bird that had suddenly revealed their colours. What it must be to see the world as he sees it. The oily ink smell that seeped from the print room. The knuckles of the gentleman, tapping so carefully on the door. The staircase winding on up to his studio and beyond into the dark unknown. And Geertje, the way she'd placed the bowl in front of him as if he were a dog.

In the morning of my second day, Geertje charged me with cleaning the windows of the entrance hall. The glass was very dirty, but as soon as I wiped it, the obscuring veil was lifted from the merchants, carts and children playing on the street. A gentleman was approaching the house. He had light, curly, shoulder-length hair and wore a black doublet and breeches, so well-fitting they seemed to flow with him as he walked.

I'd have to answer the door. I was right next to it. And there was the knock already. He looked surprised, but greeted me cordially and introduced himself as 'Jan Six to see Rembrandt'. I'd never seen such a well-dressed gentleman. Even the collar of his shirt spilled over the doublet in such a smooth fashion that it had to be silk. His movements, too, were trailing, elegant, refined. He headed for the anteroom as though he knew his way around.

Rembrandt burst in and embraced Six with so much vigour that I thought he might break the dainty creature. Both men patted each other's backs as if it was a competition. Then they settled into the seats in the anteroom and I resumed my work in the hall. The intervening door remained open.

'It's been too long, old friend,' said Rembrandt.

'I know, I know. However, given the numbers you sell of these counterfeits of your visage, it's as if I see you everywhere I go.'

Rembrandt laughed and Six continued, 'I must say it was a nice surprise not to be confronted with Geertje's omelette features but a far more pleasant and, if I may add, *appetizing* sight. It's just as well she's not working for me as I might get myself into trouble.'

Did he not realize I could hear every word? How dare he speak in this way? But most unsettling of all, he was of the opinion that I possessed some kind of appeal. Maybe men's tastes in Amsterdam were different from those in Bredevoort?

'Get to it,' Rembrandt said. 'Something is on your mind?'

''Tis true enough, dear friend. I am very concerned for you.'

'What? I've not done anything, have I?'

'You have.'

'What?'

'Windmills.'

'Windmills?'

'Yes, you've been doing a great many windmills. It is said that you've fallen prey to some kind of excessive humour that has you painting them all day, every day.'

At this Rembrandt and Six both burst into uncontrollable laughter, then Six resumed his normal tone of voice. 'Seriously, my friend, certain esteemed and important burghers are getting disgruntled that you've been turning down their generous portrait commissions.'

'Windmills are much prettier than their corm-nosed faces.'

'Yes, but windmills are not in a position to return your affection for them with important and lucrative commissions.'

'That is true but I wouldn't want one or two patrons, no matter how important, to think they had marital rights over my brush.'

Six chuckled. 'I think there's little danger of that as long as you make yourself and your brush widely available.'

'You'll be my teacher,' said Rembrandt.

More giggling. I could not believe the rudeness of their talk or the childishness. Six, while being much younger than Rembrandt, was not a youth anymore. Still, I could see the attraction of having a friend like Six.

Six said, 'I want you to do a portrait etching of me.'

There was a pause, then Rembrandt said, 'What kind?'

'Whatever setting pleases you but I want it to be the epitome of *sprezzatura*.'

'Still trying to be the perfect gentleman courtier, are we?'

Silence from Six, then Rembrandt said, 'All right, remind me of the qualities involved. As you can see, I'm a little out of practice myself.' I thought of Rembrandt sprawling on the chair during lunch.

'The usual, you know, attributes of both a contemplative life—'

'A pamphlet . . .' interjected Rembrandt.

'. . . and an active and courageous one.'

'A sword, scabbard, dagger, cape, maybe a dog.'

'A dog?' Six almost yelped.

'Well, let's say a *hound*, to signify the qualities of loyalty and friendship and that you are a member of the hunting classes.'

'I see. All of this must seem effortless, as if we've put no thought into it at all.'

'We'll have you casually leaning against something, your nose stuck in one of your manuscripts.'

'When can we start?'

'Come by next week.'

'I'm not sure about the dog, though,' said Six.

'Hound!'

'All right, the *hound*,' Six said.

'Just bring it. I'll do a quick sketch first.'

'Do you realize that you're the only painter in town who has his clients cater to him rather than him catering to his clients?'

'What's wrong with that?'

Six laughed and said, 'You ought to draw her. She'd be a better cure for your windmill habit.'

Thankfully, Geertje came in with some beer. As soon as she'd left, Six remarked, 'There goes the true owner of your brush.'

I expected more laughter but there was only silence, then Rembrandt got up and closed the door.

When I'd finished with that great big window, I'd had quite enough of working near the main door and dealing with callers. I wanted to be alone. I grabbed the pile of sheets that Geertje had said needed darning and headed for the linen store. It was perfect – not so much for darning but for hiding. It was up one flight of stairs from the ground floor and was accessed from the mezzanine landing. In the left and right walls of the landing were little viewing windows or peep-holes that looked down into the double-height entrance hall on one side and into Rembrandt's bedroom on the other. And straight ahead was the linen room. I went in, closing the door behind me. The smell of freshly washed linen welcomed me to my sanctuary. It was quite small and lit by only one window at the far end. I shoved the linen on to the table and took off my cap because I could never get used to the pressure of its ear irons against my temples. I settled into the high-backed wooden chair. If I'd had my foot-warmer, I would have felt just as comfortable as back at home. I sat close to the window to get as much light as possible on to the frayed hole. Soon I found a rhythm, bridging the edges with a lattice of thread. I missed the ticking of my father's clock but at least my new surroundings were already beginning to feel familiar. This morning I'd put a candle by my bed in preparation for the second night.

What had Six meant? *There goes the true owner of your brush*. Geertje certainly seemed to be in charge. None of this concerned me. I turned my attention to my own situation. I was twenty-one; it was getting late in the day. I needed to register with the church and involve myself in social activities. They spoke of marriage as a safe harbour after the treacherous straits of maidenhood but I viewed it differently. Maidenhood had been quite lacking in peril and I fervently hoped that marriage would prove to be *my* voyage of discovery. But what if I didn't like anyone, not even in all of Amsterdam? And I always offended people, especially men. Despite what Six had said to Rembrandt, the truth was that I wasn't pretty; I wasn't tall and I wasn't fair. I was as dark as a witch.

The back of the chair had a vertical piece of wood down the middle which was now making itself felt. Stupid chair. I stood up and pushed it away and sat on the floor, stuffing some sheets behind my back. Much better. The door opened and in walked Rembrandt, nearly falling over my stretched-out legs. 'Oh, Hendrickje.'

'Forgive me, Master, I am just mending some linen.' I couldn't decide whether to stay on the floor or stumble to my feet in the small space.

'It's no bother to me, but can you see in this light?'

'Erm yes, thank you, Master. I'm sorry, Master.'

He gestured at the paper he had tucked under his arm. 'I need to get some chalks. They are in the cupboard.'

I mumbled further apologies and tried to get my legs out of his way.

'No, no, don't trouble yourself, I can get there.'

He stepped around me and retrieved a small box. When he reached the door he suddenly stared at the top of my head as if I'd grown horns. He took the paper out from under his arm as if he meant to use it. What was he thinking? This was Six's doing. I pulled the linen up to my shoulders as if it was a blanket. He breathed in and then out with a little sigh. Then he tucked the paper back under his arm and left. 'Forgive the disturbance,' he said.

Maybe he'd not thought of drawing me at all. I got up quickly and sat on the chair. Or he'd seen something behind me? I held the linen where he had looked and a beam of sunlight shone on that very spot; revealing a glowing forest of tiny fibres. My hair, without the cap, must have produced a similar effect. I probably looked as though I had a halo.

Then I remembered the blackbird. The beautiful things I generally missed, how obvious they were to him, while I went about the world with my eyes half shut. I sat down again in the chair trying to find the hole I'd been working on.

But I could not be at peace no matter how good the linen smelled. I gathered up the sheets once more and set off for the kitchen. Geertje was out and it would be warm and quiet there – at least until Titus returned from school.

The next morning Samuel came into the kitchen. Geertje was scrubbing a pan and bubbles were rising up into the air. Samuel was lingering by the door and I thought again of the way he and his master had looked at one another.

'Geertje, we need a model for class,' said Samuel.

A preposterous thought presented itself before it could be stifled. He wanted *me* as a model.

Geertje turned and looked at me. 'You'll have to get one. I must be off to market.'

'Oh,' I replied. I had no idea what was involved.

'Don't stand there gawping, go out and find a body.'

'A body?' I said.

'We'd hardly send you to fetch a proper lady from a mansion on the Herengracht,' said Geertje.

Both of them sniggered. Then she explained, 'It's for the life-drawing class. You go to the harbour – that's where the street walkers are. Make sure you speak to one that you think the master would like the look of and offer her ten *stuivers*. That's more than enough for a morning's work.'

'But how will I know a working woman from an ordinary one?'

'Prostitutes look exceedingly gay and wear fine dresses, almost as gentlewomen do. But they don't seem to know how to move in them with grace and their hands are coarse and marked.'

'And how do I know which one to pick?'

'So many questions from you today. You'll have to guess. I grant you, it is difficult to know what suits his pencil – sometimes the more life's left marks on them, the more he likes to draw them.'

And with that and a chuckle, Geertje left.

I was soon eyeing up the women and tried imagining them doing what they ordinarily got paid for. Being a model must be an infinitely more pleasant way to make money. They were all attractively attired, with low-cut dresses. When I got closer, I noticed that their cheeks and lips were painted with rouge, which gave them a lively appearance. I reminded myself that I was not choosing for a man but for an artist, for him. Were the two entirely separate? Which woman would he like to draw?

I noticed a woman who looked far less pretty than the others. She was at least forty, of squat, voluminous build. While the others made a great show of giggling, waving, smiling and joking with one another, she stood there, looking bored. Every now and then she opened her jaws to indulge in an extended and noisy yawn, which revealed one of her canine teeth to be missing. Even Geertje would have appeared something of a beauty next to her.

I had the power to bestow a favour – a giddying prospect for someone like me. I chose her. Lacking in attractiveness, she was more likely to be in need of money and therefore less likely to turn me down. And with her well-trodden looks she might well suit his purpose.

I began by offering her less than the ten *stuivers*, like Geertje did when she haggled over a joint of lamb. When she answered, I was surprised how well spoken she was, and she had a foreign accent, possibly German. After a brief negotiation we were on our way back to Rembrandt's studio. What a strange pair we must have made, her in a bright green dress and me in my brownish house wear. Like me, she was a fast walker. I thought again about her occupation. It was not only a crime in the eyes of the law, it was a cardinal sin that would be punished by God either in this life or the next and yet she continued in this way. It was unfathomable.

I showed her into the studio, where she was greeted by Rembrandt and the pupils, Dirck, Nicolaes, Johann Ulrich and Samuel. Then I remained, for I was curious. Unfortunately, they were all looking at me – as if the commencement of their work depended on my leaving.

As I descended the stairs, I imagined the street-walker taking off her clothes, revealing what I imagined to be folds of flesh. Would the men be watching while she did this? Then she would pose either lying down, sitting or standing up on the little platform by the stove. Try as I might, I could not picture her stark naked with Rembrandt and the boys all looking at her. And yet it was happening right now, a necessary part of a painter's education.

An hour or so later Dirck shouted down the stairs for refreshments. I took up a jug of beer and mugs and paused before the door, afraid to go in. I put the tray on the floor and knocked.

Rembrandt shouted, 'Enter!'

I waited, still incapable of crossing the threshold and hoped someone would come and fetch the beer. No one came. I shouted through the closed door, 'Will someone fetch the beer, if you please?'

I heard laughter from inside. It enraged me. I picked up the tray and pushed the door open, bracing myself for their stares, but Rembrandt knocked with his knuckles on a nearby table and the boys returned their attention to the street walker. She was sitting on a low chair by the stove, with her legs drawn together and one hand in her lap, whether out of shyness or because the pose demanded it I could not tell, but seeing her bored expression I concluded that the preservation of her modesty was the least of her worries. She was all thighs, arms and two colossal orbs of flesh that hung like cowbells over her belly. I'd never seen a woman like her naked before – I'd never seen anyone naked. Her face was framed by a woollen mass of greyish brown hair which softened her features.

The boys were engrossed in drawing, their heads hardly moving, perhaps to maintain a consistent angle while drawing the woman. What was *he* doing? As I looked at him, I was mortified to discover that he was looking at me. I started to gather up the empty mugs next to the students. He got up and addressed the group. 'You may think that the world is divided into what you can see with your eyes and what is hidden from your eyes: the visible and the invisible. We are here to study the visible. Not what you can see in your head when you imagine something, no, you must study what you see right here.'

He pointed at the model. 'Can you see the indentations on her lower thighs from wearing garters? Don't miss them out, or any other detail; don't call it ugly or beautiful. Study her with the same care as you would search for a painful but tiny splinter of glass in your finger. Let each line of her body draw your attention, just as the nagging pain of the splinter compels you to look for it with the utmost attentiveness. You are a lot of lazy gawkers. Rouse yourselves, for if you miss one mark, one line, one shadow, one curve – you will miss out on knowing this particular woman, right here in front of you, and what have you got then? Nothing. And worse, whoever looks at your drawing will also miss out on knowing her, but not only her – he will miss out on knowing life itself and he will feel cheated. Worst of all, he won't part with a *stuiver* for your work.'

They all laughed, but he continued with great sincerity. 'This poor, battered body is your gateway to the invisible. You can make it manifest in your drawing, but you must use your eyes as if your very life depended on you knowing her body a hundred times better than you know your own.'

They had all stopped drawing and were staring mesmerized at the woman's body. Then Rembrandt added, 'Once you know every single line on her body by heart and can draw her blind, then the invisible part of her will be revealed to you. Her true beauty. Then you will be able to draw her perfectly, using only a handful of strokes with your pencil. But until then you need to lovingly draw each and every wrinkle.'

I left the room quietly as they settled back down to work. What had he meant by *her true beauty*? If even the ugliest of the streetwalkers possessed it, did Geertje possess it? Did I possess it? The *invisible*, a lovely word, so full of promise.

I went down to the kitchen and started peeling apples. The redness of the peel, the wormholes, the frayed edges where my knife had cut – all of it exquisite. Instead of placing all the pieces in the pot to be conserved for the winter, I started devouring them immediately.

After about an hour or so I heard the pupils leave. I couldn't eat any more apples, so some were at last finding their way into the bowl. Samuel came in and sat down at the table, helping himself to a few chunks. He had replaced his tabard with a white shirt with a simple collar and a black jacket which was almost threadbare at the elbows.

'Are you feeling a little more at home yet? I know it's only been a few days.'

'Yes,' I said, 'thank you.' Awkwardness was creeping up on me. What if he liked me? He was probably just passing the time of day.

'How long have you been with the master?' I asked.

'For a few years,' he replied.

'Will you stay on until your training is complete?'

'I'm more of an assistant now.'

'Oh, of course,' I said, mortified by the mere possibility of offence. I sought safety in further questions. 'What were you doing on the day that I arrived?'

He looked confused.

'You know the table, the broken bread, like theatre,' I said.

'Oh, the Supper at Emmaus.'

'Yes,' I said. 'When I walked in, you were all like statues.'

I thought he'd smile but he looked at the wall the way people did when they did not want to talk about something. Then he picked up a long strand of apple peel, leaned back in his chair and started arranging it with his hands as if he wanted to turn it into a whole apple again.

'At times he likes us to take on parts like actors so we come to the Bible in our own way rather than copy the ideas of others.'

I nodded, relieved he was talking.

'Usually,' he added, 'acting is the last thing I want to be doing. I'm hopeless, but something good for my work usually comes from it.'

'I thought you were very convincing,' I lied, without quite knowing why.

'Really?'

'Yes.'

'Maybe I am getting better,' he said, pushing his chair back from the table so he could stretch out his legs. 'You know when he wanted me as Jesus I could not believe it. I mean Johann Ulrich really has the art to do it – and the hair.'

'Yes,' I said, 'but I can't imagine him as Jesus. Far too vain.'

Samuel looked pleased at this, and we both fell silent as I tried to think how to ask what had passed between them as I'd entered the room. 'I heard Rembrandt say that you had to choose a significant moment to depict. I was wondering what happened just *before* I walked in?'

'Oh,' said Samuel, 'well, he told us the story of the Supper at Emmaus. You know, when the risen Christ runs into his disciples on the road to Emmaus, but they don't recognize him. It's only in the tavern that they finally see him for who he is. Rembrandt said that I had to get them to recognize me as the risen Christ. Ha, can you imagine?'

'Why?' I said.

'How do I know what Christ was like, let alone how to be like Christ? Besides, he's been tortured to death, woken up in a tomb, and then somehow come back to life smelling of roses.'

I could not help laughing. 'And what about the *looking*?'

'What *looking*?'

'You and Rembrandt.'

'Oh,' said Samuel, contemplating his apple peel as if he was beginning to realize that it would never rise again, despite his best efforts. 'Don't you want to know how I got them to recognize me as Christ?'

Was he avoiding my question on purpose? I nodded. I could hardly ask him again.

'I said to them, "Oh, how foolish you are. How slow to believe what the prophets have declared!"'

I nodded, trying to keep a straight face.

'And then, I did this . . .' He made the motion of breaking bread and then looked at me as if waiting for applause.

'Uhm, very good,' I said, hoping I was a better actor than he.

He laughed. 'It was a captivating performance. Really.'

'Like this,' I said. I took the apple peel and draped it around his neck like a necklace, blushing at my audacity. Instead of doing the gallant thing and looking away, he stared at me until I had to bury my face in my hands.

'You go so red,' he said.

I groaned, still with my face in my hands.

He laughed. 'Don't worry, I even blushed when I was Jesus. Imagine this: Jesus with a face like he's helped himself to too much wine.'

I giggled through my fingers, but wasn't this blasphemy?

Then he said, 'You understand a whole lot more than you let on, don't you?'

'As do you,' I said, looking at him, not caring if I was red in the face.

'All right,' he said, 'you want to know about the moment when you walked in, the *looking*, as you call it.'

I nodded.

He took the apple peel from around his neck, laid it on the table and scratched his temple. 'Something strange happened when I broke the bread. I felt this ease, as if I did not have to make an effort anymore. There was peace in my heart, perfect peace. And that's when I looked at Johann Ulrich and Dirck. They looked so different than at other times. So touchingly beautiful. When I looked into their eyes, and this is the honest truth, I felt that we were brothers. And when I looked at Rembrandt it was the same and I thought, *this is what he's been trying to teach me all this time*. And then I saw something brimming behind his eyes, something I had not seen there for a long time.' Samuel looked down. 'I have not seen it since before his wife died.'

'What was it?' I asked.

'That which elevates his art above all other art. It was alive in him again. And then it was gone.'

I could not grasp the significance of this thing he'd glimpsed in Rembrandt. 'Maybe it will come again?' I suggested.

'No,' he said, almost angrily, but then he looked as if he was about to cry, just as he had then. 'He's not the man he was. You wouldn't know. I didn't even know myself until that day.'

'Know what?' I said.

'That he had lost something. He can still outdo any other artist without even trying, capture in a few pen strokes the beauty of a leaf or a wrinkle of flesh but . . .' Samuel ran his hands through his hair as if he wanted to pull it out, 'there have been no more miracles like *The Night Watch*.'

After a pause he added, 'A masterpiece does not merely spring from the artist's hands and brains – it is infused with God's breath.'

It was hard to imagine that a group portrait of watchmen could be infused with God's breath; besides, how was God to breathe through someone as impious as Rembrandt?

Samuel sat silent for a few moments, looking as if doomsday was upon us. Then he met my gaze and smiled. 'Then you walked in, with your blue skirt and a jacket the colour of dried cowpats.' I frowned at the insult, and he added softly, 'And eyes the colour of honey.'

Woman on a Gibbet

It was my first day off, a chance to get away. I burst out of the house like the hens when they'd been cooped up for too long. The buildings along the canal stood tall in the morning sun. The air was alive with the trundling of cartwheels on cobbles and shouts from bargemen as they hoisted their wares into open-mouthed gables. But there was another sound, which went unnoticed, like the silence between words; it was the water that incessantly licked at foundations, bridges and the bodies of drowned rats.

It struck me that the whole of Amsterdam was like Rembrandt's workshop, with all the workers dedicated to making it run smoothly. And I too was a mere cog in the giant mechanism, but not today – today I would watch. The thought was delicious.

I entered the narrow passage between the market stalls, enjoying the sight of red chillies, plump foreign fruit and ugly fish. I noticed a stall that sold vanilla pods from Madagascar. It was an expensive luxury and I had never seen more than two pods at once before. Here they were in bundles of several dozen. Pretending to be a serious buyer, I picked up a bundle as if to examine it for freshness. What would a whole bundle of vanilla smell like? I put my nose to it and inhaled deeply. Nothing – except for some almost foul after-smell. A cook once explained to me that vanilla is best used in small quantities and without a fanfare to announce its presence. It likes to enter through some sensory back door, unfolding its beguiling aroma when one least expects it. I put down the bundle. Perhaps I'd been hoping for too much. I noticed something out of the corner of my eye. I looked up and there he was! Rembrandt. Brown leather boots, worn breeches, black cloak and a parcel pinned under his arm. His hat flopping up and down as he marched through the swarming shoppers.

I was pulled along after him like an angler who's hooked a fish too big to land, almost running to keep up. I should not be following him – what if he saw me? The wealthy did not appreciate being spied on by impertinent servants. He might dismiss me on the spot. But I could not stop. What if he was going somewhere interesting? Perhaps I could watch from a distance, to see what he saw.

He walked fast, not looking left or right, possessed by such urgency that I convinced myself I was safe from being detected. But where was he going? This did not seem like a wealthy part of town; surely none of his clients resided here.

Despite our difference in size, my steps fell in with his, following a mere twenty feet or so behind. I wondered why neither he nor I were bothered by beggars. In his case it was understandable, for he had the upright bearing of a man who would not tolerate being accosted. But that was not all. People did not even seem to notice his presence. Nor did he acknowledge the world. When we passed some snarling and fighting dogs he did not so much as glance at them.

Soon the world was lost to me too, his lone figure my only focus, as though we were together in a separate universe. I checked myself: what febrile babble.

We'd reached a vast body of water; it must be the IJ. I'd heard it described as a river wide as a lake with a strong current running at depth. There was a ferry readying to cast off. He boarded it. I followed, paid my fare and sat down not far behind him. He did not notice me. His eyes were fixed on something on the other shore. I followed his gaze and saw it: the Volewijk, an infamous hill that rose up a few hundred feet from the northern shore. It would have looked like an ordinary pasture had it not been for two dozen posts bearing gibbets with bodies strapped to them. They were executed criminals. Despite having often passed by this kind of spectacle before, on the outskirts of my home town, I felt dread. What was his business there?

When we'd reached the other side, I waited until everyone had disembarked, using my shawl to hide my face. Most went to a small shoreside settlement. Rembrandt made straight for the Volewijk. Still I followed but allowed several hundred feet between us. I tried to keep my gaze low, but tracking him at a distance meant seeing the cages that held the bodies. In some nothing but the skeleton remained, the bones picked clean by the crows. Others still had flesh on them, poor wretches, their bodies slumped down, limbs protruding between the metal bars. A change in the direction of the wind brought the smell deep into my nostrils. I breathed through the fabric of my sleeve, but it was no use –the stench was acrid and intent on penetrating deep into my lungs. Not only my lungs, I thought, it wants to infest my very soul.

I tried to banish the thought by getting closer to Rembrandt and fixing my gaze on his heels, not caring if he saw me. He was searching for something, or someone, for he wandered this way and that through the forest of gibbets, until, finally, he stopped. I lifted my head to see what he was looking at. It was the corpse of a young woman strung up on a post. The crows were not pecking at her yet and there were no signs of decay at all. She must have been executed that very morning. He sat down and took his sketchbook out of his satchel, along with pen, ink and brush. I found a spot about twenty feet behind him. He looked up at the woman for a long time, propping his elbows on his bent knees and his head on his knuckles.

Then he took the pen and started drawing. He barely looked down, keeping his eyes almost entirely on her. His hand drew as if by secret communication with the paper, knowing where to make its marks. Finally, he took his brush and ink, probably to apply some shading, and only then did he give sustained attention to the paper, working with fluid, rapid strokes. And then he paused and turned.

He looked at me as if he had known all along that I was there. I stumbled to my feet, unsure what to do. As he approached, I braced myself for his displeasure and tried to think of excuses. He came right up to me and said nothing at all. Not even a greeting. He merely regarded me without quite meeting my gaze. I bit my lip. I could feel the touch of his eyes as they surveyed my temples, forehead and cheeks and then wandered to my mouth, only in the end coming to rest on my eyes.

But he was looking *at* them, not *into* them, taking in colour and shape. Then he blinked and refocused, looking deeper, into a place murky even to myself.

My stomach contracted at the intrusion and he withdrew his gaze. His mouth formed the word, 'Hendrickje.'

Before he had a chance to say more, I asked, 'Master, what brings you here?'

'I heard about her trial and the outcome . . .'

'What was her crime?'

'She killed her landlady, by accident it seems to me.'

'How?'

'Elsje,' he pointed to the body, 'that's her name, could not pay the rent. The landlady started hitting her with a broom. Elsje must have got angry and reached for an axe and in the kerfuffle sent the landlady tumbling down the steps into the cellar. Unfortunately, the landlady died.'

'Oh,' I said.

I looked again at the lone figure of the woman, the fringe of her skirts fluttering in the wind. 'How old?' I said.

'Eighteen. She hailed from Jutland, came here to make a living.'

'How did they . . . ?'

'They strangled her by means of the garrotte and hit her over the head with the axe.'

In what order, I wanted to know. But what did it matter now? I was overcome with a complete incomprehension at the world and its dealings. What laws had conspired to create this cruel, desolate place? Bodies strung up all around me, birds pecking at their remains.

'Come here, Hendrickje,' he said softly, 'take a seat for a moment. Here on this rock.'

He sat down next to me. We were facing the IJ. I gazed at it for a while, that vast volume of water pushing onwards to the North Sea, inexhaustible.

The river was untouched by what happened on its banks. It did not care. I felt a loneliness that reminded me of the day I first arrived in Amsterdam. But it was more than that. The entire world was barren. His face was close before mine. It was filled with a kind of concern. He took the sketchbook out of his satchel and placed it on my lap. It was heavy on my knees. He opened it at the page of the drawing he'd just made.

I did not want to see. I already knew that his art could take the essence of a subject and turn it into a vision so potent that reality itself paled in comparison; still I looked. The drawing showed the woman and the gibbet. Her body was gathered to the vertical post by four or five ropes. One under her arms, the others further down her body, holding her and her skirts tight to the post, to prevent any indecent exposure. There was the axe, dangling in the wind to the side of her head. The murder weapon, like her, put on display to discourage others. I kept looking at the lines of his pen – her arms hung limp, so helpless. Her feet so unsupported by the ground, so far beneath her. Her face at such repose, young and unmarked by life. And my heart cried out, for even in the sleep of death she looked tired. She did not look like a murderess but like someone to be pitied.

His brush had pitied her; her head drawn bare, exposed to the elements, even though I could see, when I looked up, that her head was covered with a cap. Still, there was more truth in his depiction.

There she was as helpless as a babe even now, even in death. I felt tears on my cheeks and looked up at the man who had made the drawing. His eyes were dark and serious. I thought him unmoved but then I saw something else: the same thing that had leapt at me from the drawing. Whether it was compassion for me, for Elsje, or for all men, I did not know.

I looked out again at the landscape. Amsterdam lay stretched out before us on the other side of the river. I thought of all the suffering and toil unfolding at this very moment. Was there a compassion vast enough to hold it all? I was no longer certain it was absent, all because of a drawing.

He touched my arm and said, 'It's time we went home.'

'Yes,' I answered, 'please.'

He took the book gently from my lap and offered me his hand to help me up. It felt soft except for where his skin was calloused from holding the brush. We walked on in silence. I felt unsure about the propriety of walking next to him. But I allowed myself to be borne along by whatever river I had entered.

When we got to the shores of the IJ, he approached one of the smaller ferry boats. He helped me in and I sat on the middle seat. He seated himself behind me. As we set out across the river I noticed strange patterns of ripples. In some places they were like a web of tiny hairs being dragged across the water; in others they were proper little waves. I wondered at the cause. Was it the wind or some deeper current, dragging at the surface from below? His body shielded me from the wind. Every now and then I caught the smell of oil paint, which still clung to him though he was wearing his outside garb. Mixed in with this I smelled something unique of him. I closed my eyes, the boat rocked gently, the wind tousled my hair and the strange aroma gathered me in its embrace.

I wanted to name the feeling that held me like a charm. Ah, it must be what's called happiness. I tried out the word with silent lips: 'I am happy . . . ha-ppy.'

I sucked on it, a comfit of unfamiliar but captivating flavour. The boat rocked and rocked and I settled into the motion. I felt safe. How swiftly happiness had done its work.

It was afternoon by the time we got back to the house. Thankfully no one had seen us arrive together. Rembrandt made for the stairs without a word and I returned to my quarters in the kitchen. Geertje was there and I could see that she had her hands full with washing up, preparing food and keeping Titus occupied shelling peas. A task so brazenly productive would not keep him in good cheer for long. So I helped.

*

It was well past the stroke of ten when I finally crept into my bed. My limbs felt inert and heavy but sleep would not come, despite or perhaps because of my strange happiness. I thought over and over about what had happened; the drawing and how it moved me even now, my recklessness, his unconcern with my having followed him – as if convention meant nothing to him – and his care for Elsje's fate. That fate, I told myself, should teach me to appreciate what I had and not be so careless.

I was plagued by thirst. I got up and walked over the cold flagstones to pour diluted beer from a jug. The fizzing bubbles glistened in the moonlight. I was more awake than ever. The moon was fat in the window, forcing its glare on me. If there had been curtains to pull I might have returned to my nest, but with the moon so bright the idea held no appeal. I had left some knitting in the linen room upstairs. I'd fetch it. Perhaps a few rows would send me to sleep.

The cylinder that held the worn stairs seemed narrow and twisted. The treads and walls absorbed any light that came up from the hall below. I should have brought a candle; I felt as though I was climbing into the gullet of some beast.

Faint moonlight glowed in the small circular window that looked down into Rembrandt's room. I supposed these peep-holes allowed servants to check, without causing a disturbance, if any of the rooms needed attending.

At this time of night there would be nothing to see but no harm in taking a quick look into his room. I stood on tiptoe. My vantage point was high up, just below the ceiling of the tall double-height bedroom. So high that there would be little risk of being noticed even by day.

Moonlight entered through a pair of floor-to-ceiling windows on the left, flooding the room. I could make out the velvet cushions, ornate mantelpiece and the pile of clothing he had discarded on the floor. I could study everything at my leisure. Everything except him, for he was in his bed. As it was a box bed, positioned against the wall with the peep-hole, I could not see in.

A sound. My heart relocated to my throat. The noise was coming from below me. The door to his room was opening. Geertje walked in with a candle, an apparition in her long nightshift. She closed the door, headed straight for the bed and disappeared into it. I don't know how long I stood and stared at nothing. If I'd arrived a minute earlier or later, I would not have seen her, would not have known. After a while my fingers were stiff from gripping the window ledge. There was nothing to do but return to my room. I felt alone again. I descended the stairs as quietly as I could and passed his bedroom door before finally reaching my own bed. My heart was still throbbing all the way to my temples. Was he looking at her now, like he'd looked at the bird? It didn't matter how moving his drawings were. He was a man with no respect for the Lord, who gobbled down his food without saying prayers. They were godless, both of them.

What else was he capable of? I'd been right to worry when he'd looked at me in the linen room. And what a coincidence that I had climbed the stairs just then. Of course it was not coincidence but the goodness of the Lord.

I got out of bed again and fell to my knees. Even if kneeling had been abolished by the Church it was the only way I knew to adequately thank the Lord for preserving me by showing me the truth.

As soon as I woke, I recalled the events of the previous night. I could not help but imagine her and Rembrandt in the act, although this was hampered by the fact that I was not entirely sure of what it involved. Besides, I should not be imagining such a thing at all. But even as I quickly dressed, I could not purge my mind of the vision: them wrapped around one another, cosy in the box bed. So I prayed to the Lord, 'Dear Father, I have sinned, I have noticed ungodly acts and have kept them in my thoughts.'

I tried to submit myself to God's mercy but lacked the faith that I would be forgiven. This reminded me that it was the second day of the two-day holiday – a day for fasting. I would dedicate the entire day to turning my thoughts away from last night and towards God. My stomach growled. I would view any physical discomfort as a reminder to practise governance over my flesh but it would be difficult without any distractions. I'd seen notices announcing a sermon to be delivered in the Oude Kerk by Jodocus van Lodenstein, a famous preacher from Utrecht. I'd go; the sermon would help to keep my mind off Rembrandt and my stomach. But first I drank a good draught of diluted beer to quell the worst of my hunger pangs.

When I arrived at the church, people were queuing at the door, but I managed to squeeze by and find a seat in one of the pews near the front. It was hard to imagine how one man in a pulpit could make himself heard to the hundreds of people in this vast space. Van Lodenstein was small in stature and entirely dressed in black. He was shifting from one leg to the other, and had none of the aura of godly authority that a preacher like him ought to possess. At last he gave a nod to the organist and as the first notes boomed I joined in with the hymn. I didn't know a soul but it was comforting to be here, doing what I'd done at home in Bredevoort every Sunday – although I'd never enjoyed it then. After the last note had rung out, van Lodenstein waited until there was perfect silence. Even the baby in its mother's lap to my right had stopped gurgling.

A thud forced my attention back to the pulpit. Van Lodenstein had brought his fist down on the lectern and spoke. 'Why should we harden our hearts if the Lord wishes us to turn away from our sins? Is the obedience to the flesh and its desires worth losing the Lord's favour and kindling God's terrible wrath?'

I'd never seen someone launch into a sermon like this: the backs in the pew in front had all gone from slumping to straight, as had mine. How could so small a man have such a loud voice? It was as if he was looking at me and only me. Did he know? Had I become soiled simply by living in a house of sin? Had Rembrandt really put his pezel inside her last night? I mustn't think of it. Perhaps van Lodenstein knew I'd stopped listening, for he was glowering at me. Or perhaps he was distracted by the baby, which had started cooing loudly. I'd never been able to remember what we'd been taught at Sunday school despite the inevitable punishments. My stomach was grumbling so noisily that I was glad for the baby's commentary. At the stroke of midnight, the end of the prescribed fast, I'd eat all that remained of yesterday's stew.

Van Lodenstein was leaning so far forward in his pulpit I thought him reckless. 'Humble yourself under the power of God's hand, because He will elevate you in His time. But you must conduct yourselves with the external humility that you display before God's face; above all it appears in your clothing, and your furniture, as well as in your children, yes, in everything.'

Humble. I chewed the word over. Why did it matter to be humble in appearance? Surely the members of the congregation who decked themselves out the most carefully in black were the least humble?

'Humbly we meet him in the heart, in confessing our guilt . . .' Ah, confessing guilt, this was what I'd come for. I certainly felt guilty. If only guilt could be wrapped into a parcel like mouldy pieces of cheese in cabbage, and fed to the cows.

'. . . in the deep feeling for our sins and our sinful nature. With Ezra we can then say: "O my God, I am ashamed and blush to lift my face to thee, my God, for our iniquities have risen higher than our heads, and our guilt has mounted up to the heavens."' A lot of cows would be required for my guilt alone. 'Only then have we made a beginning towards the punishment of unrighteousness.'

What did he mean by punishment? I thought again of Rembrandt and Geertje in that box bed. Were they not afraid of God's punishment? I could not begin to imagine what it must be like to burn in hell for all eternity. Or was *this*, my life as it was, an ongoing series of punishments before redemption? Life did not seem that bad, but perhaps if I'd visited the heavenly Jerusalem then being back here would seem like punishment. Yes, I did want to be with God, so that I would no longer feel separate and incomplete.

The gateway to the invisible – what had Rembrandt meant by that? I could not grasp it with my mind, the *invisible*, and yet I wanted to experience it more than anything, even more than being loved by God. Again I quelled these unbidden thoughts. I was so imperfect, so in need of God's love. I must not become distracted. I put my hand in my mouth and bit down on it until it hurt. I wanted it to hurt. I had sinned, was constantly sinning. Obviously I could not reform myself without God's help. I needed to go to Him and not stand back as I had always done, was doing even now.

Van Lodenstein's face suddenly softened as he invited the congregation to partake of the Holy Supper. How generous he was, even to us sinners.

He looked towards heaven. 'O eternal God and merciful Father, we humble ourselves before thy great majesty, against which we have frequently and grievously sinned.'

I had to hold on to the pew in front for I had a longing again to kneel, even to prostrate myself, to give myself to God at last – such a shame that the reformists had done away with hassocks. I wanted to repent and beg forgiveness and know what it was to be absolved, washed clean of all I had done and was yet to do. I lowered my head in submission to God's will, trying to make each of van Lodenstein's words my own most fervent plea. 'We acknowledge our waywardness, and are truly sorry for all our sins. Wash us in the pure spring of Jesus' blood, so that we may become clean and white as snow. Inscribe thy law upon the granite of our heart. And give us the desire and strength to follow your commandments.'

'Amen,' said many voices as one. Then we all rose and gathered around the table that had been prepared for the Lord's Supper. I pushed my way through the crowds to get to the front, desperate to be absolved.

I was relieved to find my name had already been added to the list, though I had only registered with the Church Council a few days ago. How efficient of them. I took the tiny piece of bread and drank the wine and imagined that it cleansed me of all my sins and my mind of its imaginings.

As I left, I noticed a few people who had been excluded from partaking of the Eucharist. How cruel, I thought, to leave them with their sins.

I emerged into bright sunshine. What to do? I felt too weak to wander about in the heat. I'd head back to the house and find something to do. Put my resolution into practice. Learn to resist the demands of my growling stomach.

When I walked through the front door, I tried to work out who was in the house. It was easy enough to tell if Geertje was there but the master tended to work quietly. Somehow the place felt empty. He must be out. It did not really matter either way.

I went into the kitchen and grabbed the sheets again. They had more holes than a Swiss cheese. No, I had to get something into my stomach first, so I drank some more diluted beer and then sat down on the chair, needle in hand, and set about my tedious task.

As it was growing dark I realized that I'd been helping myself to the beer without checking first that there was plenty left. I gave it a shake – it was near enough empty and it was the last barrel. Tomorrow a normal day's work would resume with a dozen thirsty pupils and assistants.

Geertje was still not back. I'd have to get some beer – but from where? I cradled the barrel as if it was a baby and set off. Samuel was approaching the house. He pointed at the barrel and laughed, 'I suppose that's one way of enjoying the holiday.'

'We've run out of beer and I must get some before tomorrow.'

'Really,' said Samuel, 'I cannot imagine who might have drunk it all.'

I ignored the remark and pushed the barrel into his arms. 'You have to help me or go thirsty. I don't even know where Geertje buys it from.'

'I don't know either and it's late but I think I know of a tavern which also sells beer by the barrel.'

We set off. It was nightfall. I hoped we'd make it back before curfew. I was feeling lightheaded, either from relief or beer.

After a few minutes of walking we saw burning torches ahead, a marriage procession. The bride and groom were in an open carriage drawn by four horses. Members of the marriage party were walking by the side, showering them so enthusiastically with flowers that the couple had to shield their eyes. A few girls who followed the carriage were carrying sticks, with wax cupids and angels dangling on strings.

'A religious holiday is a strange day to choose for getting married,' I said.

'There's not too many holidays to choose from in the year.'

'Why were you going to the house?'

'I wanted to choose some drawings for tomorrow, for the pupils to copy.'

We walked on in silence. I noticed lights being lit in the houses. We passed different windows, almost like pictures; families at table, women preparing dinner, a man playing the lute and children engaged in games.

It seemed like a world so different from out here. How black the silhouettes of trees stood against the fading light. I could still hear the music of the wedding. I looked back. The light of their torches was flickering in the distance.

'What's on your mind?' said Samuel.

'Nothing,' I said quickly.

He huffed, not believing me.

'I'm lonely,' I blurted out. The wretched beer had loosened my tongue.

Samuel stopped and looked at me wide-eyed.

'Never mind,' I said, 'I did not really mean that.'

We walked on and he ventured, 'I know how I felt when I first came here. It takes a while to get used to things.'

'Yes, no doubt I shall get used to them. The things and all.'

The orange light from the windows was reflected in the water of the canal, snaking over the waves.

'I don't think you'll have to get used to being lonely,' said Samuel.

'Why?'

'You're a pretty girl for a start.'

'I don't think so.'

'You must have had lots of admirers at home?'

'Not particularly.'

'There must have been some? Tell me about them.'

I shook my head. What a strange thing to want to talk about.

He smiled and said mock pleadingly, 'Oh, go on, please. We still have a long way to go and I'm curious to hear why you're not married yet.'

Was he making advances? I looked into his face but all I could see was his usual good-natured, honest expression.

'Well, I suppose it is better than talking about vegetables.'

'Huh?'

'The first boy who took a liking to me wrote long letters about the best crops to plant and who'd grown the biggest cabbages. He was obsessed with anything that grew. I suppose it's only natural in a farmer.'

Samuel giggled, 'That does not sound too bad.'

'But the trouble was when he was not talking about how early he'd planted his peas he complained about things.'

'What things?' said Samuel.

'That it had rained too much, or too little, that his shoe hurt his little toe, the dryness of his skin.'

'Ah, poor maid,' said Samuel. 'How did you elude the veg- and complaints-monger?'

'I wrote to him.'

'You did not?'

'Yes, I know, I should have kept quiet, made excuses until he gave up but—' I stopped, suddenly feeling embarrassed.

'I'm sure his beans helped him get over it. Look, there's a seat, let's sit down, my arms are beginning to ache . . .' he grinned, '. . . and my fingers, and my little toe, and—'

I elbowed him in the side, 'Your ribs.'

We seated ourselves on a wooden bench that was facing an empty building plot between two houses, or so I assumed, for it lay in darkness. We sat with our backs to the street, looking into the night. The crickets were chirping frantically.

'What happened next?' said Samuel, looking at me, half of his face in shadow and the other half illuminated by light spilling from the houses behind.

'Oh,' I said, avoiding his eyes, 'there were others.'

'Others you didn't like?'

'Yes.'

'So what's the most downhill thing that ever happened to you with these Bredevoort failures?'

'No,' I said, 'I can't.'

'Why not?'

'It's embarrassing.'

'Even more reason to tell.'

'How's that?'

'First you'll feel embarrassed in the telling but then you'll be less so. Besides, I'd like to hear so I can pronounce judgement on all the men of Bredevoort.'

'No, really, I can't,' I told him.

'At least tell me *when* it happened – that can't hurt.'

'All right, but don't look at me.'

He manoeuvred the barrel into an upright position on his lap so it formed a screen between us. 'There.'

I spoke into the night.

'It was a few years ago on the first of May.'

Without looking at me, he took the cork out of the barrel and spoke into its hollow, producing a spooky voice. 'An innocent enough sounding date, but then Bredevoort has already proved treacherous.'

Then he put the barrel back as a screen and said, 'Perhaps men dress up as tulip bulbs and roll themselves down the high street?'

I laughed, 'No, the custom is for young men to attach a green branch on the ridge-beam of the house of a girl they like.'

'Your ridge-beam must have been strained to breaking point.'

'No,' I said, looking into the black night where perhaps someone might build a house one day. 'No branches.'

Samuel remained quiet. The crickets continued their racket.

I took a breath, 'When I went to look in the morning there was a life-size scarecrow. It had long, black hair, and a decidedly sour look on its face.'

I turned to look at him but there was only the empty barrel. But something touched my hand; his fingers, warm and soft. They folded around mine. I thought he'd squeeze my hand and let go again, but his hand stayed. I closed my fingers around his and disappeared into the black of my closed lids and the sound-swell of chirping crickets. I wondered if they'd ever find one another in the dark.

After a while, Samuel said, 'We'd better go if we want to make it back before curfew.' So we got up, had our barrel filled and arrived back just in time.

I lay in bed aware of the warmth in my belly when I thought of my hand in his. I'd be tired all day if I did not soon bend my mind to sleep-provoking thoughts such as brown leaves floating on the swaying waters of the canal. Or a series of small bubbles rising to the surface from deep inside the murky waters.

When did someone last hold my hand? Not my mother. Perhaps my brother when I'd hurt my knee or my dear father. Perhaps Samuel was courting me or maybe he'd touched me out of sympathy. He always cared for everyone and everything.

Sleep – I must sleep. A gleaming sphere from deep below, getting larger, followed by another and another. A creature blowing them from its nostrils or perhaps they issued from a rotting carcass.

I imagined Rembrandt and Geertje talking in bed about all manner of things, finding great comfort in each other's company. An upright, moving string of pearls. But as soon as the air as much as touched them they burst in quick succession, like musket fire.

The weight of the sketchbook on my legs. His eyes reading my mouth, the rocking of the boat. Him so close behind.

Once more I invoked the bubbles, but they wouldn't come. The dark waters lay sullen. Even the rot had breathed its last.

The French Bed

The next morning I decided it was time to ascend the narrow oak spiral staircase, into mystery – or so I'd come to think of the top floor. It was the only place I had not yet been to in the house, and it would benefit from a good clean. I reached a door, pushed it open and found a large, bright rectangular room. It had the same dimensions as the studio below but contained partitions made of wooden frames strung with sailcloth. From the door I could see into the first cubicle. There was a chair and a desk in front of the window. This had to be where the pupils worked on their own so they did not distract each other when copying Rembrandt's drawings or prints. No doubt their productivity benefited his purse, as he was entitled to sell all of their work. Not a place of mystery at all but of commerce, like all the rest of Amsterdam.

I got down on my hands and knees to scrub the floor by the desk, working backwards. When I'd finished with this cubicle, I continued, still on the floor, around the corner into the next and at last noticed a pair of legs. I rushed to my feet. It was Samuel. I'd not expected to see him again so soon, not now, not here.

'I'm sorry,' I said. 'Geertje thought you'd all be in the studio.'

'Well, I should be, but last night I had to assist in a crisis – far more critical to the smooth running of the workshop than the choosing of a few prints.'

'Oh,' I said, unsure whether to feel guilty or not. But I did notice that he had surreptitiously covered one of the prints on the desk with a blank sheet of paper and now he was nervously scratching his chin. My own awkwardness had one redeeming feature – it disappeared when it was outdone by somebody else's. I felt buoyant, like a bad egg bobbing in a bucket of water.

'What are they?' I asked.

'Uhm, you know, just etchings by the master.'

'Oh, can I see?' I said, pointing at the covered-up one.

'Not this one,' he said.

'Why not?' I said.

He was thinking hard. 'You wouldn't like it.'

I shrugged my shoulders and bent down again as if to resume my cleaning. He turned away, reaching for the packet to put the prints on the desk away. I quickly pulled the paper off the print.

It was a couple copulating in a large bed.

I took a step back, incapable of speech or breath. Samuel spun round, looked at me, then at the print and back at me again.

'Oh dear . . .' I stammered, and tried to look as if the exposure had been entirely accidental.

He was equally anxious to disavow the drawing. 'It's not the one I was going to choose. I've only just come across it.'

The woman was on her back, fully clothed with her legs bent, the man kneeling between them whilst supporting himself on his knuckles. Her left leg was wrapped around his calf and – as if that wasn't enough – she had one hand on his hip and the other on his buttock. How offensive and unlikely, I thought.

Samuel looked like he wished to be anywhere but here. I'd never seen a boy look so embarrassed. 'It was my fault,' I said.

'You didn't know.'

'No,' I said, 'that's true. I had no idea.'

'It's not what you think,' he said, only half looking at me.

Even to my inexperienced eyes there was no doubt as to what was taking place.

'I mean,' said Samuel, 'it is not done the way this kind of picture is usually done.'

This kind of picture? Five minutes ago I had not known that such pictures existed and now it turned out that it belonged to its own category – complete with a set of pictorial conventions for the making of indecent etchings.

'What *would* one expect?' I said.

'I'd better go downstairs,' he said, taking three sheets he'd put to the side. 'they are waiting for me.'

I did not want him to go, with that dreadful thing still on the table.

He added, 'You must not think ill of the master. This kind of print is normally for, uhm, you know, *folk . . .*' he must have meant *men*, 'to enjoy in private, but not this one. It's not for that. He never paints the obvious. It's the work of the painter to lift the veil from what is hidden, to reveal the inner essence of things.'

I nearly laughed. This was hardly a piece of work to start quoting Rembrandt's high ideals over. Then Samuel left. *Kind soul*, I thought, but so gullible. I suppose he could not help always seeing the best in his master. The print was still there. How could an image like this be enjoyed by men? But this one was supposedly different. I had a closer look. At least no flesh was exposed. Except, there, in a shaded area, the man's shirt had ridden up, revealing the curve of his buttock. But it was their faces that claimed my attention; he was gazing down at her and she in turn looked at him with such a sweet smile. Or was she looking past him, lost in some kind of bliss?

I contemplated again the way one of her legs was wrapped around his calf and the other planted so firmly on the bed like a buttress. I tried to imagine his rod inside her and wondered why she was pulling him towards her with both hands. Her legs, her arms, everything added up to her wanting him to come further into her.

The plush bed below, the drapes and canopy above, so sumptuous and warm. I put the print down, but I knew it was as good as etched on my mind. Perhaps there was some truth in what Samuel had said, for there was something unusual about the picture. It moved me in the most surprising way, whether I wanted it to or not. The stillness between the two lovers; the way they were so safe and happy within the canopied bed and within one another. Perhaps it was not only about lust.

*

Later, in bed, I wondered if it depicted what occurred between Rembrandt and Geertje. As if on cue, I heard her leave her room. Titus, who slept in her bed, must be a sound sleeper. I followed her – I had to. I told myself it was because I needed to decide whether to stay or go.

I crept up the stairs, feeling bad because as children we'd always been told not to pry or spy. What was private must be kept private. A matter of respect and good housekeeping. I'd even mastered the art of keeping things private from myself, when necessary.

I hastened past the door to Rembrandt's room, up the further flight of steps to see through the little window. Until now I'd listened in on conversations more or less by accident but this was by design. How I had changed in less than two weeks. What would I become if I stayed?

Rembrandt was standing a few feet away from the bed, wearing his nightshirt. But where was she? Probably inside the box bed. He had his arms crossed and now walked over to an armchair and sat down, arms still crossed like a belligerent child having a stand-off with a parent. Geertje emerged from the bed wearing her nightshirt. She strolled towards him, crouched down and put her hand on his arm. I could not hear what she said. He shook his head, averting his eyes from her. Now he pointed at the door, as though he were asking her to leave. She put her hand on his thigh. He shot up from the chair, again pointing at the door. Her response was to embrace him firmly around his waist; he – despite being taller than her – reminded me of a child who has outgrown his mother's fond embraces. His reluctance was perplexing. I'd come to think of their involvement as one of the established routines of the household. And how dared she be so persistent against his wishes?

Now he was trying to prise her arms away but she held fast – the scene was comic for he looked like a man equal to the task. In the end it required a sudden and almost violent movement from him to extract himself. Then he grabbed her wrist and pulled her towards the door but her feet were braced against the floor. They remained like this, neither of them gaining an inch. All of a sudden, she went towards him, even pushing him, sending him backwards into the sharp corner of the bed. My hand went to my mouth; it looked so painful.

He straightened himself up with an expression like that of my brother Berent when I'd put his playing cards into the fire. He'd pulled my hair so hard that I'd fallen over. But Rembrandt did nothing, except that he shouted, loud enough for me to hear, 'Go, now, please.' But still she did not obey, as if she had some hold over him.

He was staring at her, his mouth slightly open, his chest rising and falling. She played with the long cord on the collar of her nightdress, wrapping it slowly around her index finger and then letting it unravel again. No response from him. I was beginning to feel like a spectator at a boxing match, desperate to learn which opponent would triumph. But in a secret corner of my being I was afraid it would not be the outcome I'd started to hope for.

In the meantime she'd turned her back on him, wandered over

to the mantelpiece and made a show of studying the painting there – a portrait of him – as if she was a visitor touring the house. Rembrandt's fingers curled into fists. And she, bizarrely, started speaking to the portrait. I mean she addressed it with all the looks and smiles with which one would a person. Rembrandt disappeared from view and then I heard the door opening below. For a frightful second I thought I would be discovered, but he returned to the room, and again dragged Geertje by her wrist. But she was unwilling to budge. He gave up and shouted, 'Enough of your games, go now, for heaven's sake!' My hands too had become clenched.

The open door allowed me to hear them easily now. She sneered, 'You are no master, you only play at theatre up there with your so-called assistants who make you all the money because you,' she paused, as if to carefully choose her words, '*you* can't do it anymore. You scratch away at paper with your pencil all day but when did you last produce a proper painting?'

'You wouldn't know a work of art if it turned up between your legs.'

She smiled. 'I think I might.'

What had happened? He seemed less angry now. He went to close the door, took a few steps towards her and pointed at the floor.

She slowly knelt down and got on all fours. Maybe I ought to have quietly gone back to bed, for my own sanity, but I remained, unable to stop watching.

Her head and shoulders were just outside my view no matter how much I pressed my face against the glass. He knelt down behind her, put one hand on her hip and with the other lifted the hem of her nightshirt. I took my face away from the glass. They would do it like animals. I turned my back against the wall and placed my hand on my stomach to keep nausea at bay. I had to pack straight away and leave. But no, I couldn't. It was past curfew. There were only thieves and the night watchmen on the street after ten. I'd have to stay until the morning and leave before daybreak. There were shuffling sounds from the room. I remembered the sight of the farmer's bull on top of the cow, trying to get his long, gangly organ into her, while he tottered precariously on his hind legs. I looked. He'd wedged himself, thighs and all, between her legs. His arms were stretched out, holding on and pulling on her while thrusting his body against her, into her. The bull, compared to this, had displayed finesse. This was brutal, monstrous. *He* was monstrous. Her body was shunted forward each time he pushed into her.

I crept back down the stairs, holding on to the banister, my knees forsaken by bone and sinew. As I passed, the bedroom door rattled; and then something banged against it: *thump*, *thump*, *thump* . . . I could hear it all the way down the stairs.

When I reached my bed I heard strange cries and shrieks. I wondered in earnest whether it was my Christian duty to help her. It did not seem like something anyone would willingly submit to, yet she had knelt down of her own choosing. I was stalled by my uncertainty, my cowardice and the feeling that she was more victor than victim.

The cries and banging from upstairs continued. I grabbed a

bucket and stared at its bottom but nothing came. With shaking hands I set about packing my satchel and then lay in bed waiting for the church tower to strike four, the end of curfew.

I must have fallen asleep because I woke to Geertje's words, 'Up, up, lazy sleeper. You'll need to light the fire in the studio.' It was bright daylight.

How catastrophically stupid to have fallen asleep. Now I'd have to tell him or Geertje to their faces that I was leaving. I transferred the peat that was in the kitchen hearth to a basket. I needed time to think, so it was best to get on with lighting the fire. Strange that he wanted the fire lit. It was summer, after all. Geertje was singing as she scrubbed a pan, looking nothing like the battered figure I'd imagined. If anything she seemed happier than I'd ever seen her.

I was glad to get away from her. I entered the studio and thankfully there was no sign of Rembrandt. The stove was stone cold. I should have brought embers from the kitchen fire. I recalled seeing a tinderbox in the studio's small storeroom. It was little more than a walk-in cupboard and as I entered I could barely see a thing as it was dark apart from the light that fell in through the doorway. There was hardly room to move with all the canvas cloth and other materials that had been crammed in. I waited for my eyes to adjust to the darkness – how pleasant it smelled in here – and then I searched the shelves for the tinderbox.

'What are you looking for?'

I nearly jumped out of my skin. What was he doing here in the dark?

'The tinderbox. I can't find it,' I said, trying to sound unperturbed.

I heard him move about and finally spotted him emerging from a corner. As he came towards me, there was that nice smell again – it was his smell. I took a step back, reminding myself to be afraid and on my guard. His eyes looked sunken and he seemed without vigour. He reached with his arm behind my head to retrieve the tinderbox. Like a fool, I remained standing in his way until his chest was only inches away from my face. My one unhelpful thought: no wonder cats roll around in certain fragrant plants as if bewitched.

He stepped away, tinderbox in hand. 'Here,' he said.

'Thank you,' I muttered, and followed him back into the bright studio. He sat down at his desk.

After layering up the peat, I made a separate pile of straw as tinder. I heard him behind me, sharpening a pencil. I opened the box and took out fire steel, flint and tinder cloth and then knocked the flint against the steel with the tinder cloth next to it. That charred piece of cotton was meant to burn easily but no matter how hard I knocked, no sparks were produced. While I caught my breath, I waited for the sound of his pencil on paper but it did not come. Was he watching me?

'The air is very damp today,' he said. 'My pencil is not catching either.'

I turned around. His elbow was propped on the desk, his hand supporting his head, the outstretched fingers shading his eyes. Geertje excessively happy and him so sombre, melancholy even?

'I'll fetch Geertje,' I said, 'she's got a way with fire.'

'No,' he said sharply. I thought he'd say something else to qualify his response but he only looked down at his paper.

'Should I leave?' I said. 'I'm disturbing your work.'

'There's no work to be disturbed.'

I renewed my efforts with the flint, but there was no spark, no matter how hard I tried. When I turned, he was still looking at me.

'I hope you did not catch cold in the boat,' he said. 'You look a little pale.'

'I'm well enough,' I said, 'but I can't get this to light. I'm sorry, Master.'

He got up from behind his desk and came over. I moved out of the way, partly to avoid inhaling his scent. He looped his left hand through the D-shaped steel, also holding the tinder cloth and then started striking it with his right hand. Again and again. A small spark came a couple of times but the cloth would not light. He brought it closer to the steel and pushed his sleeve up. I could see his paint-splattered fingers and forearm. What Geertje had said was untrue; he was still painting. Then I recognized the shirt – it was the one he'd worn last night when he'd grabbed Geertje and . . . I wobbled on the balls of my feet and had to hold on to the wall. My head was spinning. I waited for it to pass while he continued to try the flint.

In the end he got up too and handed me the bits.

'It's no use today,' he said.

'I could fetch embers from downstairs?'

'Never mind, once the boys get here the room will warm up anyway.'

I returned the tinderbox to the storeroom and re-emerged to find him back at the desk.

'I've been meaning . . .' he said, looking uncomfortable. I nodded encouragement. He pointed at the empty paper, paused, glancing at the ceiling, then sighed and said, 'I'd like to draw you. May I?'

The shock of something hot or cold, or both, rushed through me. I shook my head rather more violently than was necessary.

He nodded and let his pencil drop on to the empty paper.

I was scraping carrots. They were only the first lot of vegetables I had to prepare. Still, my mood had improved: I liked the colour of carrots and I liked eating them as I worked and Geertje didn't mind. Some of them looked like little gnomes.

It was just as well I'd mastered the art of keeping things hidden from myself or I would have had to question why I had not left by now.

A few hours later there was a knock on the kitchen door. I hoped it was Samuel but it was the same street-walker I'd procured for the lesson a few days ago. She must have been hired for another life-drawing session. So it had been for her benefit that he'd wanted a fire.

'Pray, enter,' I said. This time she wore common garb, a well-used brown skirt and a blue jacket. Without the false finery she looked younger. I was on my guard, having heard many tales of whores who took any opportunity to steal.

She asked brazenly, 'Do you have any food to spare?'

My stony face must have told her I needed further convincing, especially as she looked anything but ill-fed to me. 'Ten *stuivers* is good payment for me,' she said, 'but as soon as I return to my lodgings I will have to use it towards my debts because word will have reached the bawd that I've worked. I have not eaten since yesterday and would be grateful even for some bread.'

I was sure that she was lying but it occurred to me that I needed a certain education and she could provide it. And yet how could I question her? I could barely entertain my enquiries in my own brain, let alone utter them. But she was a knowledgeable expert, one who would not be ashamed to speak, so why should I be ashamed to ask? I would boldly beat a path to wisdom. I told her, 'If you answer my questions, when you're done upstairs I'll give you plenty to eat.'

'You're not thinking of questioning me for the benefit of the bailiff?'

I assured her that I was merely seeking to alleviate my ignorance in certain matters between a man and a woman.

She burst out laughing, showing the gap in her teeth. 'Ha, I got a few customers who pay me to talk but so far I've never been hired by a woman.'

The Lord forgive me, I thought. She's right. I've struck a deal with a whore.

I had several hours to regret my boldness and hope she would just leave but she duly walked in and sat down at the table without waiting to be asked. It did not seem right to break my promise so I fetched last night's cold chicken, bread and cheese from the pantry. She set to it without delay and so did I. 'Tell me exactly what happens when you are with a . . .'

'Gentleman,' she supplied with her mouth full. 'I wait on the street and if one looks interested, I look at him and strike up a conversation.'

That was not quite what I wanted to know. Still, I thought, no harm in starting with what comes before. I nodded encouragement and she continued, 'I might say, "Doggy, where are you going?" and if they don't call me a stinking whore but look me in the eye I say, "Come, go with me to my house, we'll share a jug of beer."'

We were getting to the heart of the matter, but now such vast quantities of meat were going into her mouth that, apart from the occasional groan of satisfaction, not a single word passed her lips. I pulled the remains of the chicken out of her reach and said, 'What happens in the room?'

Still chewing, she continued, 'There is a maid who will come when one of us arrives with a man. She brings wine and makes sure the man has plenty, because the money goes to our keeper. But you want to know about what they pay me for, don't you?'

I nodded. She beckoned the chicken carcass with her finger, so I pushed it towards her. With a quick twist she detached a thigh, took a big bite and mumbled, 'There is not much to it. I lie down and they take their plunger and sink it in the place they cannot do without and when they're done . . .'

'Wait,' I said and poured her some milk, 'where does this occur?'

'Well, on the bed of course. I lie there . . .'

'On your back?' I interjected.

'Yes, what else? Goodness, you *are* truly innocent of all aspects pertaining to the procedure.'

I nodded, and wished it were entirely true. The image of Rembrandt and Geertje like beasts came to mind. It seemed that this was an uncommon occurrence even by a whore's standards. She resumed her speech. 'Sometimes I make some noises for their pleasure as they seem to like it. They labour away until their seed jumps out and afterwards they are sluggish like newborn lambs, can barely stand and then they want to cling on to me.' Her face scrunched up as if this was the part least to her liking. 'It takes some craft to get them out on the street again.'

'What about your dress?'

'What about it?'

'Do you take it off, put on a nightshirt maybe?'

She looked shocked and said, 'I'm a whore but I am not indecent. It stays on, of course, skirts and all. The men need to adjust their dress a little but not for long. Where did you get such a notion?'

While I sat, regretting that I'd started this exchange, she did some thinking and then said, 'Once or twice I have been asked to remove my clothes but of course I didn't. I don't oblige unnatural requests.'

I wondered why she had no objection to being painted in the nude but decided to ask a more pressing question. 'What other unnatural requests?'

She hesitated. I reached for a half-full bottle of wine and was beginning to feel like a bawd myself as I filled her glass. This was all the encouragement she needed. 'Some want me to shake their seed out.'

'What?'

'They want a milking-out.'

I shook my head.

'A hand-catechism.'

I had heard enough but now her speech was well oiled and she continued, 'One once asked me for an extremely filthy act,' she paused for effect. 'To suck out his manhood in my mouth.' With that she took another big bite of the chicken.

'What about doing it like animals?' I said.

'What do you mean?'

'You know, like a cat gets on top of another, or a bull or a dog?'

'Ah', she said, digging her fingers into the chest of the chicken and pulling a piece off, 'I've not had that request but a friend of mine has. Very un-u-su-al.'

'Would you?' I asked.

'No,' she replied, 'as I said, nothing unnatural.'

'And your friend?'

'She refused, thought it might hurt.'

'Does it?' I asked.

'What? Oh, you mean when doing it as it's meant to be done?'

'Yes.'

She thought about it. 'Sometimes. It's important to pull up the legs and keep the soles of the feet on the bed, otherwise you can have pains in the stomach afterwards.'

Why would Geertje do something that whores only did because they were paid, especially as it was a sin? Maybe she saw the look on my face, for she added, 'I grant you, they treat us more roughly than when their heart is in it.'

The heart being in it or not. I pondered this, remembering the etching of the lovers, their eyes so soft, as if seeing into another world.

The door opened and Dirck stood there for a moment looking at me sitting with the whore. I stared back at him as if it was him that was at fault. He said almost apologetically, 'The master has asked for more beer, if you please.'

'I will bring it up, Dirck,' I said and turned back to the whore as if this was all part of ordinary business. He left.

The whore got up and said, 'I'd better leave – it is not good for you to be seen talking to me.'

'Wait,' I said. 'How do you know?'

'Know what?'

'What it's like when their heart is in it?'

She did not answer but continued out of the kitchen and up the stairs. When we'd reached the front door she squeezed my wrist. 'May the Lord thank you.'

Her gratitude was genuine and what was more I'd spoken to her more candidly than I had ever to another living soul. How could I treat her like a stranger? 'I will pray that the Lord will look after you when you need Him to. What is your name?'

She made a gesture as if wiping away tears from under her eyes and said, 'Petronella, Petronella Kropts.'

I made to open the door for her but she stayed my hand and said, 'I come from Bonn in Germany, from a good family. I once worked as a maid in Düsseldorf a while before I came here. I was your age. It is hard to believe but I was once a pretty girl. I loved a man. He promised to marry me, so why not share his bed? Soon I was with child and when he found out, he left the province, so I could not use the law to make him live by his promise. No one wanted a pregnant, un-wed woman to work for them. My family would not take me in – or my child. I was hungry. I had nowhere to go. You are in a good place here. Don't be too curious. You have looks. You might even find a burgher who will marry you. Take care of what you have; don't be a fool like I was.' With that she let go of my hand, opened the door and went back out into the street.

I quickly assembled beer and jugs and went to the studio. This time I did not knock but went in quietly. I was greeted with an almost ribaldrous scene. Dirck and Nicolaes were sitting casually on the stage where Petronella had been and the rest were lounging in their chairs, laughing. Rembrandt, too, looked amused. I set about collecting the used mugs which had all been left on a table in the corner. I heard Nicolaes speak as if telling a joke. 'Why do whores never get pregnant?' Dirck replied, 'Grass does not grow upon the highway.' They roared with laughter and then Nicolaes quipped, 'Or in the market place!' Again they all laughed.

Nicolaes was warming to his role as chief jester. 'Why would a burgher shun the street-cruisers and keep himself a chamber cat?'

'I don't know,' came a chorus of replies.

'Because he likes paying for the privilege of having a stinking hole all to himself.'

At this Rembrandt raised his hand and said, 'That's enough, back to work.' I left the room laden with empty jugs and a knot in my stomach. These boys were more wicked than the whore.

That night I lay in my bed feeling glum. How was it that Geertje never seemed the least bit uncertain about anything, least of all her charms, when she possessed none?

She traipsed to his bed of her own volition. I had heard people say that women are driven to things because they are born with lecherous desires. Was that why Geertje went to him? Would these things awaken in me and prove to be my undoing? I doubted it; I felt nothing but revulsion at the vile couplings. My mind turned to the etching. A painter's work was to mirror the visible to perfection so that the invisible was revealed. A better world lived and breathed somewhere beyond the surface of things. I thought of the bed with its posts, the canopy and how it held the couple as if they were in another realm.

It was said by the Church that the soul belonged to the invisible and that it was entirely separate from the body. But what if it wasn't? What if, just as the visible world was the gateway to the invisible, the physical body could be the gateway to the soul?

This was heresy. I dismissed the ramblings of my tired brain. As for Rembrandt, his art was powerful but that did not mean it illuminated some deeper truth – which was what poor Samuel seemed to believe.

It was best to stick with tangible realities and the word of the Lord. Perhaps the most virtuous choice was not to marry at all. I'd live as a spinster, maybe working as a housekeeper eventually. In former times a woman like me, devoted to God, could have become a nun, her body covered in long robes and forgotten. This was such a comforting thought that I fell asleep immediately.

Later, I was woken by the sound of Geertje's feet pattering past the kitchen. She was on her way to his room again. It was like clockwork. The treads groaned as she climbed the stairs and then his door closed above.

I couldn't help but picture what was taking place above. It was as though it was all occurring with the sole purpose of vexing me. She sat with him now, on the bed, naked, their heads moving towards each other in a tender kiss. I was soon disabused of this vision by the creaks of the bed and Geertje's moans and groans. Other people conducted themselves honourably but these two thought they were above the law, God's law. I closed my eyes and tried to shut myself away. Nothing could be heard of him but all the more of Geertje. It sounded more like pain than pleasure.

Before too long I could hear them conversing through the floor boards. 'I wish to stay tonight,' she pleaded. 'Please let me, Master.'

'I am not such a person who can sleep in the same bed with another. Be gone, you shall see me again soon enough.'

There was a long pause; then she said in a pitiful voice, 'My bed is cold.'

'You must light the fire then,' he said with mirth.

'I like to look on you while you sleep.'

'Don't be silly, what would you gain from that? Besides, you staring at me would prevent the very thing that you seek to see: my slumber.' Then firmer, 'Go on, away with you, Queen of Gouda.'

Soon she toddled past my room as she returned to her bed. It was odd that he did not want her to sleep in his bed. Surely there must be comfort in the proximity of another body? Geertje's snoring interrupted that very thought just then. The speed of her fall into sleep needled me. Even her repose lacked decorum.

I remained awake. What about him – had he already drifted off or was he still sharing, with me, the realm of the waking?

The next day was Sunday. Geertje had gone out with Titus, and the pupils would not be coming today. I was free to go on another walk through town. The market was always a spectacle. Except I'd constantly be thinking I might glimpse him there again.

In the end I could not bring myself to leave the house at all, not even briefly. So I dressed and went upstairs to clean the studio. It was a good time to do it. While all the world was taking a breath, Rembrandt too would stay away from work. I started by brushing the grate clean, trying not to inhale the cold ash.

'Are you not going on one of your outings?' he asked from behind me.

I turned around and saw only the high back of his armchair. Then his face appeared as he looked around the side. 'I've heard a big ship from Japan will arrive this morning in the harbour. There will be lots to see.'

'It does not seem like the day for it,' I said.

'I see,' he said.

I returned to scraping away at the remnants of the fire.

'If you must engage with coal and soot I'll show you a better way.'

He walked over and offered me a piece of drawing coal. 'If you won't let me draw you, then you'll have to draw me.'

I could not think how to respond so I remained crouching by the grate. He produced a wad of paper and waved his hand at a chair as if it was a matter of great urgency. I walked to the chair, as if dispossessed of my own will but knew I must be on my guard.

He turned his armchair around and pulled it into the light. Then he settled into it like a bird on a nest of eggs.

I was still standing by the chair. I couldn't possibly sit down with him, much less draw him.

'It's nothing immoral,' he assured me. 'I just want to show you how to draw a face – I'll be the model. Unless you prefer to draw him?'

He pointed to the wizened head of an old goat. It had no apparent use but lingered on a shelf in the studio. The buck's mouth was slightly open, showing his teeth in a demented grin. I took the paper. He assumed a pose, his gaze fixed on some point ahead. I sat down. He was one of those people you could not say *no* to.

'Don't look at the paper, only at this,' he said, pointing at his face, grinning much like the goat. 'Trust your hand,' he said, 'it will do what it does. It's the seeing that matters.'

I looked at him, saw the untidy hair, the collar that was turned up on one side and down on the other, the lines around the corners of his mouth. I leaned in closer. What liberty to look at his face like this.

And then I was a wanderer who had turned a corner into an unknown land. It was spread out before me. I made my first step and followed the line of his left eyelid; it was a smooth curve. The right eyelid, however, revealed itself to have a loose fold of skin that almost drooped over the eye itself. I had not seen any of this before. My hand duly noted these discoveries. The lines in his face all beckoned to be travelled. I wanted to see them even more clearly, so I moved my chair closer – close enough to smell the paint on him, or whatever it was, that reminded me of my feelings in the boat.

I came across a deep line between the brows. It did not plunge straight down the middle of his face but slightly to the left and then took a turn towards the eye socket, where it stopped. I made a map, line after line, noting the texture and terrain. His face was the landscape around the house where I grew up. Soon I knew it so well that I could have found my way home even in pitch darkness.

After a while the lines of his face started whispering to me of something more than their direction and location. They told me why they had been cut.

There, a change in his face. It was more exposed, vulnerable even. He lowered his gaze, almost closing his lids. Had I caused this? No, he had always been vulnerable. I had merely unveiled it, by drawing him. There were yet more veils to lift. I would go on. 'Your eyes, I cannot see your eyes,' I said.

He lifted his chin, but still kept his eyes on the floor. I waited. He took a breath, as if it required an effort to raise his gaze, but then, breathing out, he did. His eyes met mine. Hot pokers into wax. The charcoal slippery between my fingers, all my bearings gone.

I clung to my task and the piece of charcoal. Record the shape of his iris, I told myself. My hand duly made a circle. I kept on looking at his eyes. It was more difficult for him; he was bare before me. There was something like a tremor behind his physical sight. How to record it? My hand moved but I did not care what manifested on paper. Then, something beyond the tremor. I could not name it. The reaction of my own eyes named it for me; they were moist. His eyelids came down and he looked away. We sat in silence for a little while. Then he got up and said, 'I'd meant to teach you something, but I'm the one who's come away with a lesson. It's not so easy to be a model.'

I smiled and looked down at my drawing. It was a wild confusion of lines, criss-crossing all over the paper with only a few features discernible, such as the circles of the irises. He peered over my shoulder and laughed. 'You've drawn the old goat after all.'

Then he added quietly, 'You know how to look at your subject.' He pointed at the billy. 'He'd probably come back to life if you ever looked at him like that.'

I placed the drawing and charcoal on the chair. I excused myself and quickly left the studio.

A Woman Sleeping

I was woken in the middle of the night by a creak of my door. I froze – I knew it was him before he had even crossed the threshold of my room. I kept my eyes closed. Why had he come? Did he think that because of what had happened earlier he could take liberties? I was lying on my side, half curled up, facing into the kitchen.

His footsteps approached my bed and then silence. I slowed my breath to appear asleep. It was my protection; no one could be so wicked as to trespass on a sleeper.

I prayed my blanket-hidden body was of no interest to him. But as he stood – breathing slow breaths like mine – I felt my forgotten hips as his eyes rested on their shrouded apex. Then I knew his attention on the side of my arm, my shoulder, my exposed neck. And then my face. I willed my blood not to rush there and my breath to stay the same.

Finally, his footsteps moved away. I heard him go to Geertje's room, hesitate at the threshold and then she must have woken for both of them tiptoed their way upstairs to resume their inevitable ministrations to one another.

*

When I opened the door in the morning to pour away the slops, the sky looked grey. I was standing with the bucket in my hand. The street was unusually quiet; maybe everyone expected a downpour. I watched the dark green water of the canal undulating in soft-bellied bumps, bringing with them the images of trees and then abandoning them for a window, a door or a piece of sky. The visual world was a disjointed affair. Only the water itself was continuous.

I looked at the house. I did not want to go back inside. The reflections skipped lightly across the waves. If only I could partake in life's joys with such ease or otherwise reach beyond them and be with God as only blessed souls could. I poured the dirty water into the canal.

'Morning, Hendrikje,' said Samuel behind me.

I turned around and greeted him.

'There's a dance next Sunday at The Mennonite Wedding. You know, the music hall. Would you like to go?'

I was without grace in dance but it had to be better than being stuck in the house with Rembrandt and Geertje on a Sunday.

On the night of the dance we made our way to the music hall. So many people were out on the streets: sailors, travellers, servants, country folk and gentlefolk, all clothed in their best garments. I'd concluded Samuel *did* find me appealing – a dizzying thought.

He was dressed so differently from his usual drab attire: white stockings, red puffy trousers and a white shirt with sleeves so voluminous that one had to search for him amongst the swathes of linen.

I had ample time to regard him properly as we walked. His face still retained too much of its boyish softness but his hair was thick and vigorous and his limbs were long.

From the outside the hall was not much more than a door in the side of a house but once we'd passed through it we were assailed by the sound of reckless gaiety. The low-ceilinged space was large enough to hold at least a hundred people. Chairs and tables were lined up along the walls of the long, rectangular hall. There was a fine wooden floor and ornate beams on the ceiling. The dance floor was still empty but couples milled around the sides. I was surprised by the women's dresses; there wasn't a brown or black garment in sight, only blues, reds, greens and whites. I should have worn more colourful attire. You could never tell in Amsterdam whether to be modest or gay. We put our things on chairs and Samuel went off to buy some wine. There were many couples but also plenty of old folk and children. Everyone seemed to be determined to derive as much pleasure from this brief suspension of life's duties as they possibly could.

At the end of the room was a small raised area where the musicians were getting ready: two fiddlers, a bagpiper and a drummer. They started to play just as Samuel returned with the wine. He held out his hand and together we joined the lines of dancers. To my dismay I did not recognize the dance at all, but Samuel with a big grin and his flag of a sleeve motioned where to go next. It was so endearing and enjoyable that I was almost glad to be ignorant of the steps.

There was much spinning and vigorous movement and soon sweat was running down my spine, tickling me. This was what I'd needed: to feel happy, giddy and carefree.

There were quieter moments too, when the couples would lift their arms to form an arched aisle for other couples to process through, reminding me of the sanctity of marriage and the purpose of a woman's life.

After this we sat down and watched the dancers for a while. He sat beside me sipping his wine. I was glad for a chance to catch my breath and tempted to stretch out my legs the way Rembrandt liked to do under the table.

'Why is the place called The Mennonite Wedding?'

'I don't know,' said Samuel, 'maybe Mennonite weddings are particularly gay affairs.' Then he added, 'You're a lovely dancer.'

'But I don't know any of them.'

'That doesn't matter, does it?'

I smiled at him. 'No.'

The fiddler announced that the next dance would be *something quite new* from France and that it was already popular in England and Germany. 'It is called *La Volta*,' he said, raising his eyebrows. He would teach us. Samuel got up, offering me his hand. I took it and got to my feet.

The fiddler had a lady with him on the platform. 'This is how you hold each other,' he said, putting his hand on her hip, pulling her towards him. There were giggles in the room – no one was used to such proximity.

I looked at Samuel, his expression uncertain as he placed his hand above my hip, still maintaining a good gap between us. I was worried where the fiddler would be taking us and it was strange to feel Samuel's hand on my side.

The fiddler said, 'Now it's for the lady to place her hand on her gallant gentleman's back . . .' I wished he'd drop his leering tone; he probably thought himself funny.

'Her other hand – her left hand – in case you're already getting confused, is there to rein in the fabric of her dress in case it flies too high.' The next sentence was punctuated with more excessive eyebrow action: 'Ladies, it is entirely up to your discretion how high is too high.'

More laughs, but not from me. I put my hand on his shoulder. If only we could start dancing quickly. It was awkward standing like this.

'Do not be shy,' said the fiddler, 'go on, move closer. To dance *La Volta* you should be as close together as two babes in a crib.'

No one moved.

'I've never done this dance before,' said Samuel.

'I wonder if everyone will join in.'

'Would you prefer to sit down?' said Samuel.

I wanted out of this but I also wanted to enjoy myself. 'No,' said I. 'Let's try.'

Samuel gave me a warm smile and as I looked into his eyes, my hand settled more easily on to his shoulder.

The fiddler had pulled his partner so close that they were touching all along their legs, with their upper bodies somewhat leaning away from each other. The hall had become very still – from fright, I assumed. No one left the dance floor. But nobody dared emulate the fiddler either, until a couple close to us adopted the wringer pose. Then, like a herd of sheep, everyone followed – except for me and Samuel.

'Well done, boys and girls,' said the fiddler, who ought to be put in the stocks. Now he placed his left hand just below the bosom of his partner. 'Put your hand there on the busk, if the lady is wearing one,' he chuckled. 'Otherwise it may be prudent to place it on your partner's hip, for you will be lifting her in a minute.'

I was not wearing a busk. Samuel probably had no idea if I was or wasn't, for they were stiff plates entirely hidden by clothing. What would it be like to have a hand placed there?

'Ha, ha,' said Samuel, 'trust the French to come up with something like this.' But he did not move and we were still the only couple standing a foot apart – or so it seemed to me.

I took a step towards him, narrowing the gap somewhat. It was only a dance. And in response he put his hand where my ribs joined beneath my breast. His fingers were tentative and light. It was enlivening, a thrill even but then, after a mere breath or two, the thrill grew frightful. My breathing brought my flesh firmly into his palm with nothing but the thinnest fabric between my skin and his.

I wished I could withdraw like a snail into its shell. Curiosity was insufficient preparation for being touched in that soft place. I was just about to push away – faux pas or not – when the music started and Samuel removed his hand and placed it on my hip instead.

The scrawny fiddler demonstrated lifting his lady in big swooping movements and everyone else started emulating him. With the relief of movement came a childish delight at being swung through the air. Samuel lifted me higher and higher until I laughed out loud, only just managing not to scream.

And as we danced to a slower part Samuel returned his palm once more to my upper belly. I resolved to give my weight into his hand, if nothing else than to make our dancing easier but my back stiffened no matter how I tried to relax. I carried on with the required steps but, like a bad puppet master, I was unable to call forth graceful moments from my wooden limbs. All I could do was to try and keep up with his movements but still I lagged behind. He probably hated dancing with me by now. Flushed faces surged in waves around me. I was closer to a man's body than I had ever been – and yet utterly apart from him and from my own soul. Loneliness in company was the worst kind.

No, you're not giving up so easily, I told myself. That hand of mine on his shoulder was an inanimate lump. I moved it to bring some feeling into it. I *will* embrace him like I mean it. This was Samuel, who'd cared and helped me. Rembrandt's main assistant, already a promising artist in his own right. Letting go of my skirts, I placed both my hands on his back. He put both of his on my hips and pulled me closer. It was no use. I wanted out of his embrace but I could not be so rude. I had to endure until the music stopped. Ill-begotten fiddler, why won't you tire? I held my feelings in a tight grip, like the throats of hens before slaughter. How could I have explained my tears to him? I thought of Rembrandt telling Geertje that he could not sleep in the presence of another, how he seemed so reluctant to be with her and yet he carried on. Perhaps he needed something but there always was a price to pay.

I was still being whirled about by Samuel.

Finally the music stopped and we walked to our chairs.

'That was fun,' he said.

'Yes,' I replied.

Samuel accompanied me back to the house. 'Thank you for dancing with me,' he said as a way of leave-taking.

'Thank you,' I answered.

He bent forward as if to kiss me on the mouth but I turned my head away and he kissed my cheek. Then he looked at me for a moment, and bade me goodnight.

As soon as the door was shut, I mopped the remains of the kiss from my cheek. Back in my room I quickly undressed, discarding my smelly clothes in a pile on the floor. It was always the same with me. No suitable man suited me. Samuel would probably be walking home now thinking that he'd had some first-hand experience of what I'd told him about my prickly reputation in Bredevoort. Maybe he had not even noticed. I just hoped things would not be too awkward between us now.

I would let sleep wash away the filthy dregs of the day. I closed my eyes. But the smell of stale smoke and Samuel's sweat still crept into my nostrils.

Saskia Lying in Bed

The next morning was bright and fresh so I decided to clean the dusty *kunstkammer*. I entered it armed with a bucket of water, cloth and feather-headed duster. Every available wall space was covered with shelves carrying sea shells, pieces of armour, costumes, marble busts and books of etchings and drawings. As I wondered where to start, I noticed a book on the floor. Drawings were spilling out from between the blank pages that were supposed to hold and protect them. All the other books of drawings were neatly and systematically arranged on the shelves. Their spines read: *women and children*, *nudes*, *figure studies*, *landscapes*, *animals*, and so on.

I picked the book up from the floor. It had no description on its spine but I set to work re-homing the escaped drawings. I did not pay much attention to them, until I picked up a depiction of a woman sitting up in bed. She looked as if she had given up on the world. Perhaps she had been bed-ridden for a long time. I heard someone enter. It was him. He stood and stared at the drawing in my hand. I got to my feet. We stood facing each other in the narrow, rectangular room. He was by the door, but it was as if the drawing was holding him captive.

'Who is this?' I asked.

Silence.

'Looks like someone who's given up the fight?' I said.

A nod.

I was on the verge of asking if the woman had died when I realized it must be Saskia. How could I have been so blind? I let my arm and the drawing sink. He stared at nothing now and I too was hostage to the paper in my hand.

'I'll file it away again, Master, shall I?'

He did not respond.

'This book is not labelled,' I said. 'Is it all right for the drawing?'

His hand gave a twitch and then a tremor went through him. Whatever moment he inhabited now, I did not share it, and he could not leave it. I studied his face and then I understood more of his plight as his darkness settled upon me too. It was like a weight on the chest that made every breath an effort until one wished one did not have to draw another. I wanted to be back in the kitchen helping Geertje.

I shoved the drawing between two pages and closed the book, then added it to the volumes on the shelf. His eyes had followed the drawing every step of the way.

'I will leave now, Master,' I said, pressing myself against the door frame to avoid brushing against him. His eyes were still on the book.

*

The day wore on. I worked, sweeping and mopping the floors, all the time wishing I had not shown him the drawing and unable to forget the look on his face. I was afraid, not for myself but for him.

When Geertje returned from lighting the evening fires, she said, 'He's in his bedroom, hasn't left it since this morning. I hope we're not going back to how things were.'

'What do you mean?' I said.

'After the mistress died, he wouldn't touch a brush. For weeks he stayed in his room with the shutters closed. Losing the mistress was only the last cruel lick of fate. In the half-dozen years before that, they lost each of their little ones. Rumbartus lived for two months. A few years later, Cornelia lived only three weeks. Then they had a second girl, whom they also named Cornelia. The mistress once told me she was a sweet baby, full of good cheer. But she also died after only a single month of life. And then at last Titus survived. But then the mistress went. Did him in, it did.'

Geertje stood, shaking her head, and then Samuel entered. She must have sent for him. I thought things would get awkward but he acknowledged me with a friendly nod.

'Has he been down?' he asked.

'No,' she replied.

'I saw that the shutters are closed. Have they been like that all day?'

Geertje gave him a look that said he knew the answer.

'I wonder what brought it on?'

'Brought it on?' said Geertje. 'You always make excuses for him. He's probably decided that he would benefit from a little rest while you do his work for him.'

'I don't think it's a matter of his choosing.'

Geertje just huffed, and all I could think was that it was my fault. The drawing had opened some kind of sluice gate in his mind that had held back the melancholy. I ought to tell them.

'Mind,' said Geertje, 'it could be the grief still. Some folk jump right into the grave after their dear ones, or never marry again, and he just can't shake it off even five years on.'

'Will you stop talking like that,' said Samuel.

Geertje looked hurt. 'I was only trying to . . . it's not always easy to make sense of his majesty. What about you? You usually have all the answers.'

Samuel sank into a chair, propped his elbows on the table, cradling his face in his hands. Geertje grabbed her basket with the words, 'I'm going out now to see Trijntje. Not like there's any point in getting dinner cooked.' And to me, 'There's plenty left in the larder.'

After she'd left, I also wanted to go, to avoid being alone with Samuel. But he pulled out a chair for me, so I joined him at the table. I needn't have worried. We were both preoccupied with Rembrandt's fate. I, for one, was consumed with my ill-fated actions and hoped that there might be some other explanation for Rembrandt not leaving his room.

'Maybe he's ill?' I suggested. 'Maybe we ought to knock on his door?'

'He'd let us know about it if he was,' Samuel mumbled into the heels of his hands. 'The shutters are closed, just like when the mistress died. It's a bad sign.'

I could not blame him for being despondent. I'd seen it for myself: Rembrandt succumbing to an excess of black bile from one moment to the next.

'It was me,' I said.

'What was you?' said Samuel.

'I showed him a drawing of Saskia ill in bed.'

'Oh,' said Samuel, 'I don't think so.'

'Yes,' I said. 'He looked stricken and then took to his bedroom.'

'It would have happened sooner or later,' said Samuel.

'What?'

'Like I told you, he's not been himself for years.'

'But why now?' I asked. 'And can he still be missing Saskia after all this time?'

Samuel shrugged his shoulders. We sat in silence for a while.

Then he said, 'He lost his *Beloved*.'

'Saskia.'

'No,' said Samuel, 'not exactly.'

Getting words out of him was like hunting down nits. 'What then?' I said. 'If you've got it worked out, you might as well tell me, so I don't have to feel it's all my fault.'

His eyes focused on me, as if deliberating over something. Then he said, 'I could not understand it myself. Years ago, after Saskia died, he started talking to me about a farmer who'd had his leg cut open when he fell and the plough went over him. The wound turned gangrenous in a matter of days . . . They had to saw the leg off. But miraculously he survived. However, the farmer could not enjoy life anymore. And not only exertions that required two legs, but even having a beer or lying in bed was no longer the same without his leg. He ended up as a beggar outside our house – that's how Rembrandt knew him.'

I had no idea what Samuel was trying to tell me. 'Hendrickje, what prevented the man from enjoying his dinner? Was it the loss of his leg or was it something else?'

I shrugged my shoulders, imagining the beggar sitting all day in the street and Rembrandt wretched in his shuttered room. 'Maybe he's afraid? Maybe he fears he might lose something else? Or he thinks there's an axe hanging over his head too.'

Samuel smiled wistfully. 'There *is* an axe hanging over all our heads. But I'm not sure if it's that. I've watched him. It's as if his hands and arms keep doing what they know how to do so well. But passion, joy, love . . .' He paused for thought. 'They were all amputated when the mistress died. The rest of him carries on, like a cart rolling down the hill without a horse.'

I did not like his fatalistic talk. Samuel's eyes were still on me and now he leaned so close that I could feel his breath on my face. 'A masterpiece is not a thing,' he whispered, 'it has its own life, but you cannot create it without the *Beloved*.' He took my hand. 'You have to dance with her,' he breathed, 'take her in your arms and forget about fear.'

For a moment I feared he would kiss my hand. But he was far away in his mind. He let go and left. I kept thinking about the axe, the end that would come one day. It did not seem like a reason to shut oneself away – quite the opposite.

I could not sleep and lay staring at the dark panelled ceiling of my bed. Geertje was snoring next door, which I took as confirmation that Rembrandt was still unwell. But in truth I would have preferred the sound of them coupling to that deafening silence. Maybe he was lying up there dying. Had they given him food and drink? Had anyone as much as looked through the peep-hole? Geertje's snores seemed particularly grunt-like tonight. I envied her this indestructible sleep. If only I had not questioned him about the drawing. I closed my eyes, praying for better understanding of his grief and his recovery. Thoughts about my own father came to mind. He had lain in bed for months and then died suddenly in his sleep. After the burial, I'd gone back to his room and found his comb on the table. He'd always carried it with him. Then it dawned on me. Where he'd gone, it could not be taken. Not his comb, not his snuff, not a thing, nothing. The comb would remain here, without him, for ever. I reached for it but stopped short of touching it. It was one of his most private possessions. But without him it was just a comb. I wanted to hold it and feel the horn where it had been worn smooth from use. But I still could not bring myself to touch it.

I felt for Rembrandt. He was upstairs now, not dancing with the *Beloved* but in the embrace of an incubus. I tried again to sleep, but to no avail. I fumbled for the candle by my bed and lit it on the smouldering peat. Then I dressed, climbed the stairs and entered his bedroom without knocking or thinking. It smelled musty and acrid. He was sitting in a chair in the dark. I walked towards him. Was he asleep? His eyes opened slowly but remained on the floor. What should I say? I stepped in front of him. His gaze slowly climbed up my body until it reached my face.

'I am sorry about the drawing,' I said.

'Which one?'

'The drawing of your wife. I shouldn't have asked you about it.'

'Oh, that one.' His eyes sank towards the floor again.

It was as if he'd forgotten I was there. And then I knew what to do. I ran up to the studio for some paper and his pen. Back in his bedroom, I approached his chair slowly, put the paper in his lap and offered him the pen. His hand did not move. I put the candle down – I only had to touch his hand briefly, a simple enough thing to do. I picked his hand up; his fingers were cold, lifeless. I lifted his thumb away from the index finger and placed the pen between the two. Then I returned it to his lap and placed the ink within his reach on the table and myself on a stool in front of him, positioning the candle so it would illuminate my face, and waited. After a moment or two he looked up and I saw a quickening of interest in his eyes. The animation spread to his arms and his hands. He picked up paper and inkwell, then studied my face for a long time. I wanted to hide. I did not know where to look so I fixed my eyes on the flame of the candle. Finally, the sound of his pen. Relief. But not for long. When I'd drawn him, the activity had been my cloak; now I was bare before his eyes and there was nothing to hold on to, as if I was tottering on the edge of a precipice.

Scrape, scrape, came the scratchings of his pen. Scrape, scrape. A sound-rope, at the edge of a void. I clung to the rope as any sensible wanderer would. After a while I closed my eyes.

I heard him move closer and smelled the wool of his shirt, a hint of soap and something like pine resin. I let go of the sound-rope and allowed myself to feel his eyes on me. My left cheek warmed, then my chin. I opened my eyes again. I was the sitter now; it would be inappropriate to seek out his eyes while he was drawing me. So I watched the shadow of him on the wall. But then I did look him in the face, causing him to smile a little even though he remained in deep concentration. His attention was like a circle of light. Outside its bounds the world was darkness. Did it even exist?

A moment ago I had been visible and exposed, now I felt as blank as the paper had been. No eyes, no nose, mouth or ears existed until his attention lit upon that part of me. There. I could feel my earlobe brought into being by his pen. Then the rest of my ear took shape, along with the strands of hair that fell across it. Something emerged that had never been before. This was not the girl who had lived in Bredevoort. No, I was being created now. I looked again at him. This time there was no smile of recognition. His gaze was empty, like a mirror. He merely took me in, entirely. I was at last made sense of.

Something fell in me, the wall behind my eyes, it crumbled. His hand noted it. His eyes holding me. Without my deciding it, all was thrown open, his attention penetrated deeper, beyond the remains of the wall, into my most private chamber. I felt him there with the same compassion with which he had drawn Elsje on the gibbet. My anguish was laid bare and he could see it as plainly as a sparrow on the wall. I felt no pain or urge to cry and yet water pooled in my eyes before finding a path down my face. He offered no words. He simply watched. At last the tears stopped.

He put the paper aside and muttered something under his breath that sounded like my name. When I looked at him his skin reddened a little, and he regarded me with his head slightly turned, as if shying away from a bright light.

'I am not afraid anymore,' I told him.

'I know,' he said, 'but perhaps you were right to be.'

Words were so much more clumsy than silences. I was back in the room and in my all-too-familiar skin. Embarrassment crept up on me and I wanted to leave before it showed.

'Wait,' he said.

I paused. He took a step towards me, then slowly raised his hand as if to touch my still-wet face but then he let it drop and said quietly, 'I shall be able to sleep now. Thank you. I hope you will too. Goodnight.'

I nodded and left.

*

That night I dreamed I was walking through a winter landscape. The air was perfectly still and the tiniest branches were covered in thick, precarious caps of snow. I was spellbound by these beautiful creations. But then there were no more trees and the ground felt different too. I stamped with my foot – creak. I was on ice. I'd walked on to a frozen lake. I took a tentative step in another direction – a groan. I shifted my weight back to the other foot – the sound of hissing, then bursting. The ground was gone beneath my foot and icy fingers clasped at my ankle. I woke, heart racing.

In the morning the house was still strangely quiet, although Geertje and I put on plenty of cheer for Titus's sake.

'When is Pappie coming down? I'll go up to him,' the boy asked.

'No, not today, little cherub,' said Geertje, 'your father was working late and he needs to sleep until he wakes up.'

'But why did he not come to bid me goodnight? And I'm not a *little cherub*.' His face grimaced with disgust.

'All right, *Master Titus*. Here's your porridge.'

Soon Titus's attention was diverted by his negotiations with Geertje as to the quantity of the boiled apples to be added. I was trying not to think about last night, so I set about scrubbing the flagstones under the worktop. Samuel came in and looked questioningly at Geertje, who just shrugged her shoulders. Then the door opened and Rembrandt walked in.

'Good morning, Piglet,' he said and tickled Titus's sides, snorting and grunting into his neck. Titus looked tearful and happy all at once. I felt the same, so relieved. Titus was already bashing his father over the head, telling him, 'I'm not a baby!'

'No, you're my little Piglet!' Rembrandt grinned and greeted Geertje and Samuel as if nothing unusual had occurred. Geertje frowned and Samuel stared at him as if he'd risen from the dead.

He finally spotted me and said, 'Morning, Hendrickje.'

I managed a cheerful, 'Good morning, Master.' But for a moment our gazes caught on one another. His eyes still had that soft look that I'd seen yesterday and I was vaguely aware of a third pair of eyes: Geertje's. I forced my eyes away from his face. Samuel excused himself, saying he'd go up to the studio. I continued scrubbing and Rembrandt sat down next to Titus.

'Have you done your Latin?'

'Yes.'

'How is Ferdinand? Is he still ill or is he back at school yet?'

'He's not back,' said Titus.

'Make sure you put your coat on when you run outside to play if it's chilly.'

'Ye-esss,' he said. 'It is summer, you know.'

Rembrandt ruffled Titus's golden locks and Titus tried to push his father's hat off his head and then, as Rembrandt ducked and dived to avoid his hand, they both dissolved in giggles.

'Look, my little shrimp, I'm going to go up now. I need to tidy the place because Jan is coming for a sitting. But see me when you get home if you are not playing with Karsten.' He kissed Titus's ear despite his son's best attempts to prevent it. Then he was gone. Titus returned his attention to his porridge and I to emptying the slops into the canal. I took my time, enjoying the morning air, feeling strangely happy.

Soon Geertje and Titus appeared. She helped him into his coat and he left for school. As soon as he was out of earshot she turned on me. 'What have you done?'

'Me?' I said in a low voice. How could she risk making a scene on Rembrandt's doorstep? Besides, I could not think of anything I'd done wrong.

'I saw how he looked at you,' she said.

I had to calm her down, especially with Pinto, our neighbour, sitting on his bench smoking his morning pipe. She was getting impatient, putting her fists on her hips, elbows wide. 'Like he wanted to make a meal of you.'

Pinto was watching us, happily puffing away. No doubt he could hear every word.

'You know what I mean,' she said. 'You're not that innocent. You're probably not innocent at all.'

'You are mistaken.' I said quietly. 'It was tender thoughts for his son that still showed on his face.'

Geertje breathed out and her shoulders sank slowly to a more sustainable position. She had not been sure. She believed me, but did I believe myself?

The Mill

It was hot, the very height of summer. The occasional bumblebee came buzzing around his legs, searching for the next flower. He'd come here to sketch the windmill by the river. It stood in the sun, the wheel turning with silent purpose. But he'd been sitting idle for at least an hour. He couldn't help smiling when he thought of drawing her.

Nearly another hour passed and still he had not made a single stroke. The sails were utterly absorbing – whoosh, pause, whoosh, pause – flying round their central pivot, never going anywhere, despite the incessant movement. He loved watching them.

Suddenly the entire body of the windmill, tower and sails, spun a little on its axis. The wind had changed direction. It surprised him every time he saw it. How an inanimate construction could be so responsive to a change and yet continue to drive a shaft at ground level at a constant speed.

Geertje would be at home, waiting. He owed her some happiness, didn't he? She'd been there, back then, when it was necessary; had brought him back to life, in a way.

She would come to him like she always did, as if she needed it like air to breathe. How had he lost so much of his freedom without being able to tell when exactly it had happened? No one else was in a position to tell him what to do. He'd not fallen into the same trap as Flinck, who was expected to dine at least once a week at de Graeff's house and to drop whatever he was doing when Prince Maurits as much as farted in his direction. Ha, Flinck was always eager to please, like a boy attending school on charity.

And he did not even rule over his own bed. He'd given her clothes and tokens of affection to keep her in good humour but it seemed to make her think she had *rights*. He shuddered at the thought. Perhaps if he closed the doors to the box bed tonight and bolted them from the inside she'd think he wasn't there? A childish thought. But why could he think of no means to keep her out? She always found a way to get him to do her bidding.

Of course he only had to refuse her, tell her it was not his wish, throw her out of the house if he wanted to. But what would follow? A kind of emptiness, the pull of the past, and he dreaded that even more than doing her. The sport no doubt did him good and she had never conceived a child with her late husband. What more could a man in his position ask for? She kept him going, fucking her kept him going. That's how it was.

The very land he was sitting on would be flooded if it wasn't for the mill. It powered a screwpump which transported the water over a small dyke into the nearby river. In this part of the country, which was lower than sea level, water was always rising up from the ground.

It was just as well that the wind never stopped blowing, powering the mill, keeping the land arable.

Maybe if he made some kind of gesture, it would reassure her? Maybe then she would not demand that he prove his love to her every night. *Love*? Ha, all this flailing about in life . . . so as not to go under. Perhaps that's why he liked those sails, their steady whoosh, whoosh, whoosh; no flailing. A windmill could take even high winds and translate them into the steady turn of the Archimedean screw, in itself a beautiful contraption.

When a serious storm threatened, the wind-wright would simply take down the sails and let the lattice do the work, but the mill would not stop. There was a storm brewing at home right now for which he had no appetite. Was he so reluctant because he cared so little for her? No, he decided, the lack of *amore* was what made their sporting possible.

Later, in bed, he looked at the bundle of prints he'd bought at a sale. He'd put them on the table by his bed with the intention of examining them in the evening when no callers would disturb his pleasure, so he could fall asleep with the images in his mind – the best potion he knew for a good rest. Except, Geertje would turn up any moment now, as predictably as the cows that make their way to the barn for milking. And sure enough the door swung open. She never bothered to knock.

She carried a candle, eyeing him as if unsure of the reception she would get. Perhaps she felt his irritation. The thought pleased him.

As she walked, her thighs and breasts were outlined by the stretched fabric.

He was lying on his back and did not make space for her so she had to bed down close to the edge. He remained motionless.

Eventually she said, 'How did the work go?'

'Good enough.'

Her face was so close that her features appeared grotesque. And now she wanted to be kissed. He fondled her hair instead. Her hand started stroking his neck. He stopped fumbling with the hair. If only he could stretch out, but she was in the way. Once she was gone, he'd lock the door, light some extra candles and look at the new prints. Only him and the quiet of the night . . . But first he had to get her out. She'd probably extract some kind of penance from him.

'Geertje,' he tried, 'it's late. We'd better call it a night.'

She did not answer.

He smelled something on her. Beer and onions. He turned away on to his side, facing the wooden panelling of the bed. Her hand crept around his waist, tentative, unsure – trying to draw a response from him. He would not give it. Her hand brushed upwards on the fabric of his nightshirt from his belly to his chest. Touching his flesh as if she owned it. Then her hand slipped inside the opening of his nightshirt, squeezing his chest. He withdrew inside himself and yet part of him registered her crude touch.

With one arm still around his chest she pressed herself against his back; breasts, thighs and warmth. Despite himself, he was hardening. She pulled on his shoulder and he let her roll him on to his back.

She knelt by his side, bending over him, taking his face between her hands. Then she brought her lips down on his. A sensation like a dog's wet nose in his face. With his lips tightly closed he maintained a line that he would not allow her to cross and yet – the strange notion crept up on him that he might want her after all. His lips opened a little and she was already pushing her tongue into his mouth. He took her head in his hands and thrust his own tongue into hers; she withdrew. Good. But now she was joining into the rhythm of his probing, coming forward again with her tongue, perhaps pleased that she'd brought him into the game despite himself. She strayed further and further into his mouth. He pulled away, clenched his mouth shut and pushed against hers. More of an ambush than a kiss.

She didn't care. Her body yielded. He advanced: mouth, tongue, chest, hips, leg – finally had her on her back beneath him. He stopped to look. She was breathing excitedly, waiting, softer now. He kissed her gently but could not stop thinking of tomcats going to it with their jaws clamped on to the scruff of the female's neck. A nice, quick business.

She sighed, her body becoming lithe. He kissed her prune-skinned cheek. The tips of her fingers brushed up the back of his neck. He liked it and felt something like affection for her.

Her eyes were closed. She was waiting for him to go on kissing her. But now that it had started to mean something he couldn't bring himself to do it.

The pause grew and grew until her eyes flashed open, boring into him. He resented her demand, and himself, for not really liking her and for not being able to go on. She grabbed his cock, rubbing it vigorously, making him lose himself. He would not have to think about her now. She was making him do it. *Fine*, he thought.

He got out of bed, pulled her to the edge, with her legs either side of him, moved her nightshirt out of the way and pushed into her. He had to follow the first thrust with the next and the next as if it was the only thing he could do to keep her away. He was angry and sickened but he could not stop. He pitted his hardness against his shame, willed himself on towards release, but the accumulation would not come. As he laboured away, he watched her excitement with both relish and disgust; she was creaming off for herself whatever she could.

But then he saw her biting her lip. She did *not* fully want it. At first the thought pleased him but then he felt himself shrinking. His body was putting a stop to this. He slowly withdrew from her, as if trying to steal away unnoticed. His nightshirt flopped back down, covering him. He breathed out with relief.

As soon as he stepped away she pulled her legs up and under her nightdress. She lay there with her eyes closed, still breathing rapidly. Then she glanced at him through half-closed lids. Her arm lay stretched out with the palm of her hand open. He ought to go and touch her hand, hold it to restore an understanding that they were still friends. But he could not bring himself to commit another lie. She took her arm back towards her body and laid her hand on her stomach. I've hurt her, he thought and now wished he had at least for a moment touched her hand, to let her know he was sorry, but it was too late. She gathered herself up and left without saying a word or giving him another look.

The next morning he found Geertje in the kitchen. She was alone with Titus. An ideal moment.

'There,' he told her, 'no good them lying about in a drawer – you might as well wear them.' He placed the box of jewels unceremoniously on the table. Titus was excited by the unusual event. She looked incredulous, even a little scared. 'For me?'

'Yes,' he said.

'Open it,' cried Titus, pulling her towards the box.

But instead she put her arms around Rembrandt's neck and kissed him. 'Really, a present for me?'

'Go on,' he told her, 'have a look.'

Titus, in the meantime, had picked up the box, holding it up for her to see the contents, his eyes bright with excitement, and it occurred to Rembrandt that his boy was handing his inheritance to her. Geertje took the box, sat down on a chair, pulling Titus on her lap and asked him to open the lid for her. Titus was only too glad to do so.

Her eyes became even larger when she saw the jewels. She jumped up, placed the box on the table and rifled through it with shrieks of delight, as if she'd personally unearthed a treasure chest.

She had Titus help her put on every single piece until she looked like a mare trussed up for parade. If only they'd hurry up. It would be embarrassing if anyone walked in. Now she was holding a ring aloft.

'Look,' she said, 'what a beautiful gold ring. Is that for me too? Will you slip it on?' Her index finger was poking the air expectantly – so different from Saskia's graceful finger when he'd first placed this ring on it. He willed himself to do as she asked; it caught a little on the knobbly joint but he managed to get it on. At least she was happy now. He kissed her on the forehead and she leaned her head against his chest with a sigh – of happiness, he assumed.

'I'm sorry about last night,' he whispered in her ear so that Titus could not hear.

'Never mind, my lamb,' she said loudly, reaching up to pat his cheek, 'there'll be plenty more times to make up for it.'

Self-Portrait by a Window

Things, it seemed to me, had returned to what was normal for Rembrandt's household. Even their nightly copulations were made un-noteworthy by virtue of their repetition. I was glad I'd helped him that night. It had been my Christian duty of course, but there was also no denying that without him I would soon be out of work and lodgings.

In the morning, when I passed through the entrance hall, I noticed the five faces of him staring down at me. They were so cunningly painted that their eyes followed me wherever I went. I stopped to take a closer look. They were five portraits of him, unmistakable even amongst all the histories, still lifes and tronies, which covered almost every inch of wall space.

I stayed with the one I'd grown to like best. He looked to be in his late twenties, and was dressed in an embroidered velvet cape over a gorget and also wore a gold chain with a medallion. His black beret was adorned with two enormous ostrich feathers, one bright white and upright at the front, and the other ochre at a jaunty angle. This strange and elaborate attire added to the picture's charm, but what I liked the most was his expression. Unlike the eyes in the other portraits, which gazed out directly at the viewer, these eyes were not only obscured by the shadow of the beret, they also refused to meet my gaze. They were raised and unfocused as if indulging in a flight of fancy or pondering something of great importance.

'You like that one, do you?'

I spun around, startled, and there stood Samuel, frowning. 'It looks nothing like him. It's no wonder it hasn't sold in all these years.'

I did not want to hear any more disparaging comments, so I asked, 'Which one do you like best?'

He looked around, studying each of them. 'Pah,' he said, 'I don't like any of these. Wait a minute.'

He ran off and returned with a print.

'There, this one is good.'

The etching showed Rembrandt in his working clothes seated by a window – burin poised over the plate – his face full of concentration. Looking at it, I felt myself to be in the mirror's place, with Rembrandt's eyes looking at me intently. No wonder Samuel liked it: his master at work. And it was clever too, the painter seemingly looking intently at the viewer when he was actually looking at himself in the mirror.

'But why so many?' I said.

'They sell like hot chestnuts.'

'Really?'

'Art lovers just adore them. They like to show them off to their friends. It's largely Rembrandt's doing. He's managed not only to make a *name* for himself but he's made a *face* for himself too.'

'How do you mean?'

'He's distributed many hundreds of portrait prints. So anyone who's got money and inclination to spend it on art knows what he looks like. And when art lovers see a painting *by* him that is also a portrait *of* him they feel they've got their money's worth.'

'Everything always comes down to commerce.'

Samuel smiled cryptically. 'Nothing can persuade him to paint what he has no interest in.'

I regarded the paintings again. Each of them was distinctive, with Rembrandt sporting different clothes, expressions and poses. And I'd seen different clients quickly warm to – nay, become entranced with – a particular portrait and dismiss all the rest, as if they believed they'd chosen the one true likeness.

My eyes chanced across my reflection in the mirror that hung by the entrance door. A demure-looking young woman, in a black dress with a starched white cap that did not sit straight on her head. And suddenly I doubted that the truth about Rembrandt could be found in any of them, or even in a mirror. I regarded myself. Samuel went to stand behind me. Our eyes met in the mirror glass.

'I wonder what he sees when he looks at himself,' I said.

I felt Samuel's hands on my shoulders as he put his head next to mine, scrutinizing my face in the mirror.

'Just look,' he said. 'Focus on what's in the mirror. There's the cap, with that bit of stitching coming loose. The eyebrows, the colour of the skin and lips and your eyes. Where do you see those things?'

I had an urge to elbow him, for such a silly question. 'Well, in the mirror of course!'

He squeezed my shoulders and I could feel his breath on my cheek. 'But what is right *here*?'

I knew my face was here, but it did not feel like that, more like a window without glass. As if I did not possess a face at all, but that I was made of looking. It frightened me. I turned around to face him. His face was very close. So close, I could even see the bristles of his beard, the hairs of his dark eyelashes. I nearly touched his face, for in its solid physicality it was a marvel compared to the transparent peep-holes of my eyes.

His eyes were bright as he looked at me and said, 'Freedom resides in the looking, not in what you're looking at.'

I don't know what came over me but I stood on tiptoe, put my hands on his shoulders and kissed his cheek. And then immediately regretted it because I didn't want him to think I meant anything amorous by it.

He stroked his hand down my arm, giving me yet further cause for worry. Then he held my hand between both of his, studying my face. I looked away.

He said, 'You don't want to come out with me again, do you?'

I stared at him surprised, relieved and, of course, embarrassed. 'Um, how did you know?'

He let go of my hand. 'I had a feeling.' Then he shrugged his shoulders and pointed at his cheek. 'Maybe it was that kiss just now. Urgh, so friendly.' He gave a shiver of disgust, making me laugh. Then he added, 'An improvement, though, on getting a letter like those chaps in Bredevoort.'

I embraced him with both arms.

'And now this!' he protested. 'You're a nightmare!'

Jan Six with a Dog, Standing by an Open Window

In the afternoon Geertje and I delivered beer to the studio; Six and Samuel were there. Six was resting with one elbow against the windowsill, dressed in dove-grey breeches and a matching jacket, finished off by white stockings and golden garter bands. At his feet was a well-behaved greyhound sitting on its haunches. Six always was better dressed than even the richest burghers. The dog was of a similar grey to Six's clothes – he had probably chosen the dog to match.

I offered mugs of beer to everyone; Six declined as he was posing. Rembrandt did not look at me when he took his mug off the tray, but Samuel gave me a warm smile and then settled back into a chair in the corner of the studio. I'd never known him sit idle like this, watching his master work.

Rembrandt was in his chair, legs casually crossed, paper and wooden tablet on his thigh. 'Get the hound to put its front paws on your leg.'

'But that's the very thing I've had him trained not to do,' said Six.

'Indulge me.'

Six called to the dog, which pressed its ears to its head and eyed its master nervously.

'It's all right, Rupert, come on, here boy, here!'

Rupert placed his front paws on Six's thigh, wagging his tail in delight. A moment later he was down on all fours again. I looked over Rembrandt's shoulder. He was still sketching what had just happened. It took him only a dozen or so strokes of the pen to capture the hound rearing up. Then he gave the drawing to me to pass to Six.

Six looked at it. 'No, you're overdoing it; there is too much going on. The dog, the leg, the ornate stuff beneath the window. Above all, the leaping dog destroys the very poise and stillness we're trying to create.'

He handed it to me to take back to Rembrandt. Geertje was standing in a corner with her hands on her hips.

'You are right,' said Rembrandt, and then to me, 'Take that chair and put it where the dog was.'

Then he addressed Six. 'There's another change we need to make; turn a little more, so that your back is to the window.'

Six smiled, clearly pleased to be rid of the dog. He turned as if he was a dancer, on tiptoes and all, and cooed, 'We've not done it like *this* before.'

Geertje glanced at me, rolling her eyes. Six was such a peacock.

Rembrandt ignored him. 'I want the light to come at you from behind.'

'Oh, that *is* different.'

Geertje sniggered and Six looked at her with a raised eyebrow.

'Turn your head sideways a little so the light grazes your cheek and put one foot in front of the other. Yes, that's it, lovely as a windmill.'

Six laughed. 'High praise, but my face is entirely in shadow. We cannot have that, can we?'

'Do not be fearful; we'll make you sparkle yet. Here. Hold this pamphlet in your hands. It's a stand-in for your manuscript. The paper will reflect the light on to your face. You'll feel it.'

'Ah, it pays to be *done* by a master,' said Six, looking at Geertje as she placed the beer mug within his reach. His eyes fastened on the expensive bracelet and ring she was wearing. I too had noticed these. She must have put them on only this morning. How could she have come by such riches?

'Look at you, Geertje,' Six said. 'Have you got yourself a well-heeled admirer?' Then he patted her behind and quickly resumed his stance. She turned red – from anger, not embarrassment. She looked at Rembrandt, but he was intently studying his drawing, the corners of his mouth twitching despite his best efforts not to smile.

She held up the mug of beer in front of his face. Oh no, I thought, she'll slosh it in his face. Why did Rembrandt not do something?

Six spoke while managing to keep his head perfectly still. 'Be a good girl and put it on the table for me. I'm not allowed to move just now.'

She plonked it on the table, spilling some of it.

'Thank you. That will be all.'

Geertje replied with a dismissive grunt and swept out of the studio as if she had a train and entourage. I lingered, not wanting to follow her just yet.

Six said, 'She needs reminding who is master and who servant. And you can't have her flouncing around in Saskia's gems.'

'I know,' said Rembrandt. 'I've taken care of it.'

Six laughed. 'By my arse, you have.' Then he paused and added, 'But why this deference, my man? Show her the door if she's a nuisance.'

Rembrandt glanced at me, loitering at the open door. I took the hint and left.

As soon as I walked into the kitchen, Geertje handed me a plucked chicken.

'Needs skinning,' she said, prodding the fire back into life under the roast. 'Who does that prancer think he is? And the master himself sits in his chair smirking like a six-year-old.' Then she said loudly, 'Do I look like someone who will put up with insults?'

I shook my head dutifully.

'He's given me these,' she said, pointing at the necklace and ring, 'for my good service and because we are . . .'

I kept quiet.

'Living like man and wife.'

I did not want to hear any more, but once Geertje had started she could not stop. 'First he gives them to me and then, a few days later, he says they are a loan. They really belong to Titus. I have to change my will so Titus gets them after I die. *Yes Master*, I say. Not like I have a choice. *You can still think of them as yours while you are alive*, he says. *While I am alive* – what is that supposed to mean?' She looked at me. I shrugged my shoulders and continued to tug at the skin of the chicken. She held up the bracelet and looked at it with alternating expressions of triumph and doubt.

'Six had no right, and Rembrandt should have put an end to it. What sort of man lets his woman be mocked like that?' She took the chicken carcass out of my hands and with one swift movement stripped it of its skin. Then she handed it back to me.

After Six had left, I went up to the studio to collect empty mugs and to tidy up. Samuel was still there, cleaning brushes. I noticed the open satchel by the door, bulging with his work clothes. He got to his feet and said, 'I've decided to leave.'

'Leave?'

'Yes. Leave Amsterdam.'

'Why?'

'Don't look so dismayed. It's nothing bad and anyway, it's time I set up my own workshop in Dordrecht.'

'I see,' I said, wondering if it was because I'd rebuffed him. 'I wish you much success with your travels and your workshop.'

He thanked me formally.

Then he picked up a rolled-up piece of paper from the table. 'I made this for you.'

He handed it to me. I unrolled it, shaken by the gift and the news.

It was a very fine drawing. A beautiful woman was holding up a balance scale with two pans suspended from the central beam. One pan contained a sphere with a map drawn on it and the other pan was completely empty. Samuel pointed at the sphere and said, 'That's the world that we can see.'

'And the other side?'

He smiled, leaned forward and whispered conspiratorially, 'That's where what truly matters dwells.'

It was intriguing but I was too troubled to converse about what dwelled where. So I asked, 'So why leave now?'

'Ah, still not too fond of mysteries?'

'No.'

He smiled. 'They are coming back.'

'Who?'

'His powers.'

'Oh.' I still did not share his view that Rembrandt had somehow been lacking in ability since Saskia's death. My pancake batter did not turn out perfect every time either, especially when I tried out a new recipe.

'I found a drawing,' he said, pointing at a piece of paper on the desk. 'I don't know where he made it or whom it depicts and it only consists of a few lines but it's perfect – a masterpiece.'

I went to look and as I approached I could see broad sweeps of ink.

'The freedom in the strokes . . .' said Samuel. 'It's as close to something alive as a work of art can get.'

I saw that the drawing was of me. The face could not be recognized, it was too broadly drawn, but I knew it by the pose. I was on my side, my body loosely curled up, as I had been on the night he'd stood by my bed. And there was my black hair in broad swathes of ink. He must have made the drawing from memory after seeing me and yet it was so faithful to how I'd lain.

Samuel and I both stood contemplating the drawing and then he looked at me and then back again at the drawing. 'It's you!'

Long seconds passed. As he continued to look at the drawing I watched his face; first it expressed vulnerability, then regret, then love, then joy and then sadness.

It was as if the drawing exposed far more than the fact that he had drawn me. I had an impulse to deny it was me.

He looked at me and said, 'He's not conventional you know, not in any way. Look after yourself.'

A warning? 'What do you mean?' I asked.

'I mean, I would not trust him as a man.'

And this from Samuel, who'd never said a bad word about his master. But before I could question him further, he kissed my forehead and was out of the door.

I knew things would not be the same without him. He'd kept us all in balance.

You would think that having been made a gift of a drawing I would have sat contemplating it, but instead that evening I lay in my bed still thinking about the other drawing. I wanted to see it again so I lit the candle and made my way up to the studio, as quietly as the creaking stairs allowed and past his room where all was quiet for once.

I entered the studio, which was cast in starlight, and placed my candle by the drawing. It was composed of only a few flowing lines, each capturing perfectly a fold in the blanket. The folds themselves combined to give a sense of the body beneath; its profound repose suggested a serenity I did not know I possessed. Each line had been drawn with a dizzying combination of delicacy and speed. I could not help feeling that the brush had cherished the subject, had enfolded it like the blanket did the sleeper. I stood cradling the paper in my hands for a long while.

I did not consider it a flaw that the artist had failed to register that not only had I been wide awake but terrified. Instead I revelled in the picture's beauty and chose to believe that his eyes had perceived some *greater* truth about me.

I gently returned it to the desk and descended the stairs. My candle was almost burned down, illuminating only the next one or two uneven steps.

When I reached the peep-hole into his room I could not resist having a look. His room was also steeped in starlight. It was peaceful. I continued down and reached his door. How easy Geertje found it to lift that latch. The candle spluttered. I did not want to be stranded without light so I hurried back to my room.

As sleep claimed me, I imbued the soft weight of the blanket with the touch of his gaze; lines applied by his hand brushed on to my leg, my hip, my arm and neck. Had I given birth to them or they to me?

The lull of sleep was not to last for long. The loud creaks told me that Geertje was on her way to his room. Oh, not tonight, I thought, something would die in me to hear them at their game. But I got up, driven by the need to know how they would be with one another. I took a glass with me, so that I could press it against the wall to listen.

Geertje had placed her candle on a small console table. She stood in front of Rembrandt's bed and was in the process of taking off her nightshift. I assumed from her artless movements that he was asleep. Why did she have to disturb him every night? She removed every last item of clothing. Everything except for the ring that sparkled on her finger.

For a moment she stood, pondering what to do. Then she walked to the window, looking at her own reflection and smiled. She is more happy naked than dressed, I thought. And how she moves, as if she was royalty. I'd always thought of her as ugly, but not anymore.

She finally disappeared into the box bed. I put my glass to the wall and heard him groan and say, 'Get off, leave me to slumber.'

Geertje was back in sight in front of the bed, now trying to look coquettish, running her fingers through her hair like a young girl at a fair. All this while she was naked as an eel. I was alternating between looking and listening with the glass.

His voice complained, 'Go to your bed – the bull cannot tend to his cow tonight. He can only think of the pasture of his dreams.' And then, 'Let a man have his rest!'

She put her hands on her hips for a moment, pondering her next move. Then she disappeared into his bed and immediately there were shuffling sounds and then something emerged from the bed: his feet with their soles pointing at the ceiling, followed by his legs. It was a strange sight, as if his legs and feet were levitating. Next came his behind, clearly visible as his nightshirt had ridden up. I wanted to look away but it was too late. His white buttocks gleamed much like the ring had done.

Now his feet were grappling for a foothold against the floorboards but an invisible force was still holding on to his right arm and shirt from inside the bed. So he employed his left arm to advance ownership over his nightshirt, but to no avail; the tug of war over the shirt continued with neither party gaining more than an inch or two until he finally found a foothold and dragged not only his shirt but also Geertje out of the bed.

She landed with a thump and a vexed screech on the floor and let go of him. The shirt was almost entirely over his head, depriving him of sight and the mobility of his arms, but his modesty was preserved by the shadows. He took the opportunity to arrange the garment somewhat more traditionally about his body. Geertje had no such concerns. She stood stark naked, howling like a fury, 'It is her. You want *her*!'

He mouthed something like, 'What?'

She screamed, 'That sly, half-faced innocent!'

I was so desperate to hear his response that I made sure the glass was well against the wall. His wits must have undergone restoration at the same time as his dignity for his response was calm, almost forgetful. 'Oh, you mean the maid. God, no.'

I could imagine the bored expression on his face. But then to my complete shock he added, as if by the by, 'Geertje, you know we cannot go on living like this. People are . . .'

'It's never bothered you before.'

'Yes, *I* don't care but Six says it's affecting our business – to the point where it's untenable.'

'*Our* business?'

'It sustains you too,' he said.

'There is one way to stop them talking. Marry me. You promised.'

At this, I quickly peeked through the peep-hole again. Geertje stood like a battlement, holding up the ring in front of his face. It was impressive that she could hold her own in an argument without so much as a thread on her.

He raised his voice. 'I did not.'

'You did!'

'No.'

'You liar!'

'You knew that I was not in a position to . . .'

She interrupted, 'You cannot dispose of me like this, now that you've had what you wanted.'

'You also wanted it,' he pointed out.

She opened her mouth but no further words came.

He too remained silent. I shifted my position again in anticipation of lowered voices. I needn't have, for she spoke with force. 'But that's not right. It's just not right. Where would I go, how can I live? Think of everything I have done for you. Think of Titus. I am the only mother the boy has ever known.'

No response from him.

They both stood unmoving. Then he went to Geertje's nightdress which still lay in a crumpled heap on the floor. He picked it up and gently straightened it as if he cared for the garment. Geertje sank into the armchair; for once she was stock-still. He knelt and gathered the sides of the shift as you would for a child and presented it to her. All she had to do was put her arms through. She did not move, and so he threaded it over each arm in turn and then slid the garment over her head.

She leaned against his chest, closing her eyes and resting her head on his shoulder. I'd never seen them so close. He put one arm around her and then the other and then whispered something into her ear.

I no longer felt like an innocent bystander. I'd caused this. The only moral action was to leave – I had to think of poor Titus.

Rembrandt detached himself from Geertje and looked at her. He was still kneeling and took her hands into his. I pressed my ear to the glass as if my life depended on it. 'You won't be without means,' he said. 'I'll see to that. We will come to an arrangement that you are happy with.'

She looked at him and slowly stood. 'All you want is to get rid of me so you can move on to her. The only person you truly care about is Rembrandt van Rijn. Everyone knows it but no one wants to believe it.'

She paced across the room a few steps and he got to his feet. She turned to him again. 'I know something of the law and I will see to it that you pay what you owe me.'

With that she walked from his room closing the door with deliberate quiet. I would have been less worried for him if she had slammed it shut.

Autumn

The next day I thankfully had time off, so I could stay out of Geertje's way while her wrath was still fresh. I doubted she'd believe Rembrandt's insistence that I had nothing to do with his decision. In the grey dawn I dressed quickly, packed some bread and cheese and slipped from the house. The greengrocers were already setting up their stalls and deliveries were in progress on both sides of the canal. The place was swarming. It was uncommonly warm and sunny for October so I headed towards the south-east, where on a previous outing I had come across a woodland strewn with streams and pools. In less than half an hour I arrived, sweating and panting. When I saw an opening in the fringe of thick undergrowth I delved into the forest. I soon came across a clump of majestic oaks. They towered above me, their thick trunks sprouting into many arms, which fingered into branchlets. Some still held red or yellow autumn leaves, trembling softly in the breeze. Dappled light played on the leaf-littered ground as if the entire forest was decked with the finest lace.

Striding further into the wood, I heard rustling in the leaves and saw shiny black beetles crawling amongst them. Then I spotted a brown spider waiting in its web for prey – or perhaps a spider did not wait as man does. How dull waiting makes all things, how it narrows our view, obliterating most of the world while we drum our fingers in despair for the one thing we've set our heart on. Today I was not waiting.

I sat down on a mossy rock next to the spider's web. His long legs and body were in the centre of the web, where all the silken threads converged. If anything as much as brushed a far corner of his universe, he'd feel it instantly. My feet were on the soggy ground, my hands felt the springy moss on the stone.

My eyes closed – the odd bird singing far and near, wind spreading through the leaves. And in between the sounds – an eternal quiet. A long breath out. Then silence.

A flicker, a thought – of him. I smiled, brushing it aside, trying to regain my timeless bounty, but I could not. So I started walking again, drawn by the burbling water. I held my skirts up as I stepped over fallen branches, picking my way towards the sound. I found a glittering stream which meandered ever deeper into the forest. I followed it, balancing from rock to rock along its bank. After a good hour I came to a small grassy clearing beside the stream. The grass was not the familiar, thick-bladed kind but long and delicate; shocks of maidenhair sprouting from little mounds. My early rise caught up with me, and I wrapped myself into my coat and bedded down on the soft grass. Earthy perfumes soon carried me off.

*

When I woke again, I felt as if I'd slept in God's own lap. And then I saw the figure of a man, sitting in the grass a few feet away. Him!

I sat up; his entire demeanour was as if this place was his home and I should not be surprised to find him here.

After a few moments he asked, 'Did I wake you?'

'I don't know . . .'

'You have slept for a long time, very peacefully I think.'

I could not believe he was here.

'What an enchanting place this is,' he said.

He must have followed me, perhaps running even, for I'd been fast. I nearly laughed out loud at the thought. His eyebrows arched up and I attended to my dress, making sure all was where it should be.

When I looked up again his eyes were still on me. I could not meet them so I got up and walked towards the stream and leant against a sturdy oak, to steady my trembling limbs.

Our silence was filled by the gurgles and murmurings of the stream. It approached in a broad sway and then narrowed into a channel studded with rock. There it quickened, zipping and spilling across big boulders. He remained on the ground, resting his hands in his lap. I still could not look him in the face and yet I knew his eyes were on me by virtue of a kind of warmth; first on my legs, then my hips and arms and finally where my heart was beating. And with that my heart slowed and grew more restful.

He rose and came to stand in front of me with a few feet between us. Still I kept looking at the water where it tumbled from a rock into a whirlpool. And then it was as if we met right there, within that gyre, for he was looking at it too. Our separate gazes – one.

With two steps he brought himself closer, his body an inch or so from mine. I felt the warmth of him, his chest, his arms so close. My fingers on the furrowed bark behind.

The bottom edge of his coat brushed against my stockinged leg. His breath quickened, as had mine. My fingers further tightened on the oak, to stop myself from touching him. My eyelids closed and in that dark I wished that he would close the gap between us, so I could feel his chest on mine. But he did not. He waited and waited until at last he moved, his arms reaching either side of me. Now he would cradle me – but no. He kept himself away, still braced against the oak.

I wanted to un-buttress him. But I remained inert, afraid to reveal my wanting.

Then soft and sudden, his hand on mine; pressing. And mine, turning, finding his fingers, wringing them for more. Our breaths one rhythm now. In, out, him, me, unfastening. My lips pressed tight from wanting more.

And then he pulled his hand slowly from my grasp and brushed my face, with fingertips so feeling and minute in touching. I looked at him, saw eyes of grey, first smiling, then thinking. He stepped away from me but took my hand and helped me to the grass where we both lay down with a few feet between us. He did not touch me again.

After a while he said, 'What are we going to do?'

I could not see the need to do anything ever again.

The only other words that passed between us were those of leave-taking. He was due to meet a client back at the studio and off he went.

I remained, my eyes aimless, except that they kept returning to the spot where he had been. The waters were sparkling just as bright and yet the forest now was wanting. You are love's fool, I told myself. My thoughts crept back to him and to the house. I had acted without thinking. I needed to know what had caused his tender actions. Love or lust? He had told Geertje to leave and then followed me into the forest. It seemed simple enough. He wanted rid of her so he could have me. Most likely he wanted to have me in the way he'd had Geertje, and what good had that done her . . . No, it was not the same as Geertje. It was different. But then I thought of Petronella's warning, to preserve what I had and not be a fool.

I could think of nothing better than to hurry back to the house. I slowed only at the threshold to the kitchen, remembering that Geertje might not be well pleased to see me. I heard Titus laughing in the yard and as I approached the kitchen window I saw him with Geertje, throwing a rolled-up piece of linen back and forth over the half-empty washing line. She was a child's delight, always eager for a game. Her back was to me so I thought I would remain unnoticed. She launched the little parcel in the air with vigour but as it winged its way to Titus she suddenly turned and looked at me. Did the hairs on her neck announce my presence? I sat down at the table listening to their cheerful voices and waiting for the inevitable storm.

I'd rather have had a tooth ripped from my jaw than endure Geertje's wrath. I thought again about Titus. He was about to lose a mother – of sorts. I too had lost a mother when she made me leave our house. I had been twenty-one then and he was only six. I would have to be a mother to him. I remembered a farmer's cow that had at first rejected her newborn calf but after a few minutes had started licking it and allowed it to suckle. There was no hope of me suddenly knowing what to do with a child. And the streets were littered with chicks, babes, puppies and infants crying out to be coddled, fed and soothed. The thought made me shudder.

Titus came running past me on his way upstairs to his father. Geertje followed, poured herself some beer and fell into a chair. I would tell her how sorry I was, how truly sorry. I would offer to leave. What could be simpler than that? I opened my mouth and then closed it again – the words did not come.

Geertje stared at the table and said, 'It's no surprise. To be noticed by him is no small matter. Especially for women like you and me.'

There, she had not been fooled by his denials. Whether through observation or deduction, she knew his eye was on me. But surely the sting in her words was yet to come.

'We strive for a secure position, a good marriage – for the means to keep ourselves in comfort.' She looked up, her eyes straining to make out some fact in her distant past. 'I had a husband, mostly a good man, but then he died.'

Perhaps she counted this amongst his failings. Her finger was tracing a knot in the wood grain; round and round it went.

'I felt so very sorry for Rembrandt,' she said. 'After Mistress Saskia died he was in a pit of despair. Could not find his way out, poor soul. I don't know why I cared,' she added. 'It was bad, you know. He needed me more than Titus.' She looked at me for the first time. 'What I did not know then is that he has a way with folk. Look at his patrons. They're always ready to forgive what by rights ought to have ruined him: his whoring with me, his tricks to squeeze more money out of them, his shuffling of debts instead of paying them. He has paid hardly any of what he owes on this house. He's been in contempt of the purchase agreement and it's not for lack of funds, but he prefers to buy useless things instead. Any other man would be called a fraudster, certainly not be given work. But our Rembrandt, he can do as he likes.' She paused. 'It's because the master's other great gift is to make people love him.'

This had the ring of truth. Even from what I'd seen he'd not conducted himself well.

'It's strange they don't realize they are not even getting a foul egg in return. No, it's stranger still. They *do* know it. I knew it too and still I had to help him.'

Her speech had been delivered in a measured voice up to this point but now she spoke with vehemence. 'He made me promises, you know.' She was holding up her ring. 'He gave me a marriage medal too, un-engraved, only a matter of time, he had me think.'

I got up. I wanted to keep her unbidden words away from my ears.

She leaned back in the chair. 'You think it will all be different for you; I would think the same. Well, not knowing what I know now.

I'm telling you he's seeing a dealer this afternoon. He won't think twice about paying a hundred guilders for a bunch of prints to gather dust in the storeroom but he wants me to survive on sixty guilders a year, a pauper's wage.'

She continued calmly, 'You think he'll love you and respect you but it's as inevitable as the lambing in the spring. If you stay, you'll be his new whore, no more and no less.' She grabbed a pot and started scrubbing the burned bottom. 'Yes, I would fair see you gone but not to get him back. No, he's done with old Geertje. I just don't want him to play the same old trick again and – God knows this is true – I don't want to see a young girl throw her life into Rembrandt's cesspit.'

No doubt she'd get the pot clean and shiny again in the end. Life would go on here, now. This was no magical forest. Dirty pots had to be scrubbed clean, slowly and laboriously. The only way of avoiding too much unpleasantness was to not let the milk get burned in the first place. She was right – I had to get out of the stupefying circle of his attention.

A few days later Rembrandt called Geertje up to the studio – I assumed to discuss terms with her. When she came down she said through gritted teeth, 'He wants to see you. Go up now.'

He was behind his desk and gestured to the chair on the other side. I sat down uneasily, but he could not seem to make a start.

'Master,' I said, 'what can I do for you?' How pathetically eager I sounded.

'I would like to make a request,' he said, 'which you must flatly deny if you feel uncomfortable in any way.'

He studied my face for a reaction and continued, 'Geertje will be leaving us and we have come to an agreement. I want her to be financially secure, and there are some other matters that need tidying up. The notary will come tomorrow for the agreement to be signed and I require a witness, a discreet witness. In short, some of the content of the agreement might tarnish my good name if it were to become public knowledge.' He coughed.

'I see no reason not to oblige,' I said. 'I will witness the statement if you wish.'

He jumped to his feet and stretched out his hand to shake mine. This was usually the means by which men sealed an agreement. I took his offered hand and shook it firmly.

'Thank you,' he said, and looked relieved.

It was true, he had a way – one wanted nothing better than to say *yes* to him.

The next night and morning passed just like any other. Titus still had not been told that his world was about to lose its strongest pillar. In the late afternoon, the notary arrived with a stout, red-faced woman. Geertje's witness, I assumed. No introductions were made. Geertje ushered them in and once Rembrandt had joined us we all traipsed in single file down to the kitchen. The notary was a little, wiry man dressed in black. He shook hands with Rembrandt, who was ensconced behind his desk. The notary turned to us. 'This won't take very long; I will read out what Mistress Dircx and Rembrandt have agreed and then you will sign as witnesses. Please be seated.'

I sat down on a chair which was close to the wall and so did the fat, red-faced woman. Rembrandt seated himself at the table. The notary took out his papers and then eyed Geertje, waiting for her to be seated, but she remained standing with her arms crossed. He gave a shrug and started to read:

'Present, Geertje Dircx, widow of the late Abraham Claesz, and the honourable painter Rembrandt van Rijn. As witnesses, Hendrickje Stoffels and Trijntje Harmans . . .'

'Wait!' Rembrandt interjected. 'Make that the honourable, *famed* painter.'

Geertje scoffed but made no further protest when the notary amended the draft. He continued to read, 'The aforementioned Geertje Dircx has resided for a considerable length of time with the aforementioned Rembrandt and she now wishes to leave and depart.'

Geertje's fist slammed on the closest available surface. 'When did you put that in?'

Rembrandt said, with the exasperated calm normally reserved for addressing three-year-olds and idiots, 'Geertje, it will look better for you, when you seek future employment, that you have chosen to leave, rather than having been dismissed.'

Geertje scowled but nodded. The notary continued, 'The same has acquired her possessions, though few and insufficient to sustain her, for the most part at his house. All this induced her to come before me, the notary, on 24th August 1647, to bequeath her possessions, which she might leave behind, to Rembrandt's son Titus van Rijn.

'The aforementioned Geertje Dircx and the aforementioned Rembrandt van Rijn hereby declare to those present that they have come to an irrevocable agreement as to her maintenance. Rembrandt van Rijn will pay her a single payment of one hundred and sixty guilders. In addition, for decent sustenance . . .' another huff from Geertje, '. . . the sum of sixty guilders annually, for the rest of her life but no longer. However, with the explicit condition that the last will, drawn up by Geertje Dircx before me, the notary, in favour of the young son of the aforementioned will remain inviolate. Both parties promise to abide by the terms of this contract.'

Geertje made her mark on it and the rest of us signed and that was that, or so I thought.

A few days later I had just finished eating my porridge when Geertje burst into the kitchen, holding aloft a piece of paper, shouting at the top of her voice, 'You're a she-devil, a street sow!' Then she breathed, 'No, you're a silent whore.'

I'd heard of silent whores; outwardly they appeared respectable but plied their trade at home unbeknown to their neighbours. Why was I a silent whore and why was she so angry? I had to pacify her somehow but I might as well have tried to stop a stampede of bulls. She snatched my cap, not minding in the least that she'd pulled out some of my hair with it. I felt it, of course, and yet I was like an onlooker at the theatre.

The piece of paper she held was the drawing he had made of me when I had sat for him that night. Apparently, it was proof of some despicable crime.

She now turned her back on me and fumbled with her skirts. I only understood the purpose when she lifted them and slapped her naked backside: a grave insult. However, I somehow found it funny. I'd seen more than my fair share of buttocks lately.

I still could not fathom what had upset her. It was not like he'd drawn me in the nude or in any other way that was unusual. It was just another face study, like the hundreds that filled the books in the storeroom.

Perhaps my failure to react made her even angrier, for now a pan was hurtling towards me. To my own surprise I managed to duck, and it clattered behind me against the wall. The next missile, a ladle filled with steaming porridge, was on target, soaking my sleeve with scalding sludge. This brought me to my senses. I shouted, 'What is the matter with you?'

'Oh, *the matter*?' She aped my country accent. 'The matter is that you spend all day with me, behaving like a child and letting me look after you, and then you go to him and *display* yourself.'

'But he sketches folk all the time.'

For a brief moment she looked away, hiding her face, and I finally grasped what was eating her. He'd sketched the beggar, the whore, the noble, the dead, the young and the old but he had never sketched her. He'd thought her fit for his bed but not for his pencil. As I wondered if this was a deliberate oversight, she launched herself at me. We tumbled over backwards and I hit my head hard on the stone floor. My vision blurred but I could see her hand stretching for the kitchen knife. 'I'll put a red ribbon across your face,' she cried. 'There'll be no more drawings of your smirk.'

She rolled on top of me, pinning me down with her body, her right hand still reaching for the knife. I slipped off my clog and as she lifted herself off me to get to the knife, I quickly got my knee and then one foot between her body and mine. I catapulted her off, got on my side and stretched my leg to ram my heel into her nose, feeling the odd sensation of cartilage and then bone being compressed under my foot. She groaned, holding her face. By then I was on my knees and sank my elbow into the pit of her stomach for good measure.

She lay there doubled over, struggling for breath. I was glad that I'd wrestled so often with my brothers, even feeling pride that I had brought things to such a swift and satisfying conclusion. But now her right hand was searching for another weapon. She needed finishing off.

I got up and grabbed the handle of a wrought iron pan, the obvious answer to every single thing that pained me. I had only to bring it down on that brittle skull of hers.

I raised my arm for maximum impact and then in my mind's eye I saw the image of Elsje strung up on the gibbet. My arm sank and I placed the pan back on the table and turned to walk away.

Titus was standing in the doorway, his face white, his eyes on the whimpering Geertje. He stared in terror at me. I turned on my heels, grabbed a wet cloth, went to Geertje and started wiping the blood off her face. Her nose was bleeding in streams. I did not know how much he had seen. I whispered to her, 'Titus is watching us.'

She instantly stopped groaning, sat up and said with an admirably normal-sounding voice, 'I'm not hurt, don't worry, little lamb.'

He ran towards her, hugged her and dissolved in sobs and cries. I carried on cleaning up her face, feeling quite the villain. Then I offered her some beer, which she took and sipped, still sitting on the floor with the sobbing Titus in her arms.

Then she told him, 'Listen, little one, Hendrickje and I had a fight. You know how you sometimes fight with your friends. She did not really mean to hurt me. It was an accident. See how she is helping me now.'

He looked suspiciously at me. I tried to summon the innocent demeanour of the girl I used to be. I asked him if he wanted some milk but he shook his head.

'No point putting it off,' she said to herself more than him, 'there won't be much time now.'

'What?' said Titus.

'I'm going away, little lamb.'

'No,' he cried in despair and clung to her.

'I'm sorry I have to go, but your father will always be with you.'

'No, you can't, you can't,' he sobbed.

'There is another little boy that has no mother *and* no father and he needs me.'

I knew this was a lie but it was a good lie. He gave a little nod.

Geertje continued, 'Hendrickje cares about you and she will help your father to look after you.'

He shook his head.

'It's best when everybody gets on, isn't it?'

Nodding.

'So now we'll all have a sip of milk from the glass to show that we are all friends again.'

I fetched a mug of milk, hoping her blood would not drip into it. She took a quick sip. I drank too and offered it to Titus. He took it and drank without looking at me.

'You did well, Tity-Mighty. Everything will be all right,' Geertje said, stroking his hair.

I walked away.

Using the handrail, I pulled myself up the stairs. In the storeroom, I sat on the floor against the far wall. If only my hands would stop shaking. I'd never have thought I'd have the lust to kill in me. Heaven was forever barred to the likes of me.

I heard the front door close. It must be him. I hoped he would attend to Geertje but his footsteps were coming closer. I prayed that he'd pass by the storeroom. I needed time to gather myself.

The door swung open and he walked in, carrying an old helmet. He stared at me. I wanted to get up and pretend all was well but I was as good as part of the floor.

'What's wrong?' he said.

I shook my head, unable to produce a sound.

He knelt down on one knee trying to read my face but I hid

it. He said, 'Come into the studio. There's a chair there and a fire, come.'

I tried to get up but apart from leaning forward nothing happened. He hooked his arms under mine and pulled me to my feet. Then, with his arm around my waist, he helped me to the studio. He was worried, worried for *me*.

I must tell him what happened, I thought. Geertje might need help. But I could not get the words out. He helped me into a chair and I listened to the shouts of cabbage vendors from the street below.

'Come, you Amsterdammers, take a look. The firmest, cheekiest and plumpest cabbages you've ever seen.'

I envied them. They had a cart of cabbages to sell and by about four in the afternoon the cart was empty and they could go home.

'And don't forget – a cabbage a day keeps the neighbours away.'

My chest contracted in the motion of laughter but then I realized it was tears that were trying to get out. But my lower jaw was locked in place as if secured with an iron bar. Tears would not be shed; words could not be spoken.

He tried again. 'Will you please tell me what happened?'

It was the strangest feeling. Another part of me wanted to tell him, wanted to be comforted like a child and told that everything would be all right, but I knew it wouldn't be, it would never be all right again. I'd come so close that it was as if I had actually murdered her and she was lying dead on the kitchen floor, a horrible secret yet to be discovered by the rest of the world. I closed my eyes, trying to summon composure, but now my throat was tightening and I started coughing.

'Water, I'll get you some water,' said he.

I shook my head. I did not want him to leave me. I wanted him to stay. I shook my head, the coughing subsiding at least.

There was something I was supposed to be telling him but it was hard to remember.

'It's Geertje,' I said, my voice hoarse.

'What about her?'

'She's bleeding. And Titus saw it all.'

'Where is he?'

'I left him with her.'

He nodded. 'I'll go downstairs and see to them. I might be a while – wait for me here. You are not hurt?'

I shook my head.

As soon as he was gone, I grew afraid. The devil knew my evil now. I pressed my hands to my face. Was there a shadow on the wall? I stared at it and then at the easel and the chair. The shadow was not theirs – it was a cause unto itself. And it was oscillating too, as if it had its own breath. And wasn't that the shape of a wing? No, it was just a fiend conjured up by my strained temper. It had no substance. But what if it was Beelzebub, the prince of demons, come to take me for my sins?

I'd murdered her in spirit. Nothing was left of the girl who'd lifted the door knocker to a new beginning. I laughed. *A new beginning* indeed. I tried to stop these thoughts, to see the window and the warm stove right next to me. But the shadow grew and grew upon me. I was easy prey, sinful as I was. 'Dear God, protect me, please.' I prayed, convinced I could feel Beelzebub's breath and that my soul was his. 'Mama,' I said, 'mama.' She would not come of course, she never came. And then I remembered, waiting and waiting as a child, eyeing a shadow on the wall. Maybe the devil had already taken her. I don't know why my past and present had converged in this way – but they did and I was lost.

I heard the sound of raindrops against the studio window, rousing me. I looked. A layer of tiny water droplets had also formed on the inside of the glass and as I ran my finger down they merged together, running away like teardrops.

Beyond the glass a woman was hurrying along the canal, a bag over her head. She probably had a husband, children, relatives, friends. A life full of obligations, but also full of connections, like a web of arms and hands that would instantly hold her should she ever lose her footing. What if I fell? I had no friends or family in Amsterdam. Samuel had gone and the pupils were nothing more than casual acquaintances. The only other person who'd cared for me was a whore. And he? He was the cause of my fall, if not now, then later.

The canal was so far below, a chasm between tall and narrow houses. Its emptiness an invitation. I turned away. I would only have to go down the steps and out of the house. Rembrandt and Geertje were in the basement; no one would see me. I could easily rent a room before curfew and later send for my wages and belongings. I'd never have to see him again. I walked to the door, put my hand on the latch and stood for a minute or more, incapable of lifting it.

The sound of footsteps. He was back.

He said almost cheerfully, 'They are both fine. Geertje is a tough old nut.'

'I saw you with her.' My words took me as much by surprise as they did him.

'What?' he said.

'You were using her body as if you were animals.'

His mouth formed the word *how*, but no sound came.

'I watched through the little window in the wall.'

His hands went up to his face and he started rubbing it as if he wanted to wash something away.

'You wanted me next, so you got rid of her.'

How different my voice sounded.

'No,' he said, looking like a man who has just seen all his possessions swept away by a flood.

A plan took shape in my mind that would see me delivered from his house even if my volition failed me again. He gently put his hand on my arm. I snatched it away. He made a step towards me and that's when I lunged forward, pushing him hard, with both hands. But he stepped aside so quickly that I fell into thin air. I would have fallen if his arm had not caught me.

But I was set on my course. I'd break all our tomorrows. My fist flew towards his head, striking flesh and bone. The skin of his cheekbone was burning red, but he stood there, calm as an angler by his favourite pond. Then I realized: he'd *chosen* not to duck the blow. My body was too heavy for me. At least he'll throw me out now, I thought, as I swooned.

'Ye gods!' he said, as he helped me to a seated position on the floor. 'Have you considered becoming a prize fighter?'

I shook my head. Why did he have to joke now?

'Don't dismiss it,' he said, looking down at me, 'you could make good money.'

'Please,' I said, 'be quiet and tell me to leave.'

'I can't do both at the same time, you know,' he said, crouching down next to me.

I grunted, in despair.

Shielding his face with his hands, he said, 'Please don't hit me again.'

He sat down on the floor opposite me, still behaving as if we'd had nothing but polite conversation. And then, like a feeble idiot, I burst into tears. He put his hand on my back.

'Why are you not angry with me?' I sobbed.

'What? You mean because you felt like hitting me?'

'I did hit you!'

'Only because I was too slow.'

'No, you let me!' I cried.

'I think you needed to,' he said. 'After all, you didn't get a chance to finish off Geertje.'

He was almost grinning. It was not funny.

Then he said, 'You know, you are not the first person to get angry when someone hurts you.'

'Nobody hurt me,' I protested.

He pointed at the bruises on my arms and came to sit next to me, inviting my body towards him with his arms. I gave in, letting him take my weight. I felt the warmth, the shape of him. And yet how alone I was and soon would be again. People like him did not bother with people like me. I pushed his arms away but he held on. I drew a breath and then another, but the air imparted nothing to my lungs. I wished for solitude. To be alone was to be safe.

'Rika,' he said, 'it's not so bad.'

No one had ever called me this. 'Please,' I said, 'let me go.'

He finally opened the girdle of his arms.

'I . . . I can manage,' I said, pushing out the words.

'I know,' he said.

I moved to sit away from him but he reached out again and stroked my arm in sympathy. And so, despite myself, I was made flesh again. He shuffled closer until I felt his knee against my thigh and his care. My head grew heavy and rested on his shoulder. I pulled his arms around me like a cloak.

He brushed loose strands of hair from my face and then I felt him bending down and then his lips kissing my cheek. I touched my face against his beard, wishing for his lips.

They found me, as if he knew, first soft and unsure, then without hesitation, plunging me into a jewelled darkness – a sensation so vivid I almost withdrew from our communion. But I stayed and let it reign – and in the precious dark, I sensed like the chime of a distant bell the approach of bliss.

But how could I, so undeserving of grace, how could I abide in bliss? To find such joy in flesh was wrong. And with that thought my lips had turned to clay. He let go of me and I of him. I told myself that it was good I'd called a halt to lust (if it had indeed been lust).

He leaned back a little so he could look at me but I glanced down, unable to face him.

'You are right, you are the reason I am sending Geertje away. I have no design as to how things will be from now on, but they could not have stayed as they were. Change is the way, no point opposing it.'

After that he went downstairs and bid me stay in the studio.

After a while the pupils started to arrive. It was now late morning and Dirck had brought in a bust from the *kunstkammer* as a drawing exercise. He told me, 'You are to stay here with us.'

'Where is he?'

'Making arrangements.'

I watched them gather around the bust and start to draw. Rembrandt finally returned a few hours later and told me to go downstairs and prepare lunch. That was all he said.

I wondered if Geertje was really gone so I checked her room. The few personal things she had possessed were no longer there. The shelves were empty, the bed was tidy and made up. I wondered about Titus. Rembrandt must have sent him to school. I hoped he at least got to say goodbye to her.

I set about preparing lunch the way Geertje would have done.

I did not stop to have a day off until two months after Geertje's departure. The Christkindl had come and gone, or rather had not bothered to stop by our house. I had no way of knowing if servants would customarily receive a gift from their employer, but was glad anyway to be spared the embarrassment.

It was the first week of January 1648 and I went for a walk. It was freezing cold but soon the tulips would be poking out of the earth in the countless private gardens that dotted the city. The owners would have to keep a watchful eye on their pricey flowers, for they were a thief's favourite. I had no particular destination in mind but after a while I became aware that I was heading for the watery woodland.

The last months had passed quickly. There had been a great deal to learn. Looking after Titus had been both easier and harder than I'd anticipated. Easier, because he seemed to like me, and harder, because he required so much of a warm sort of attention that I was not used to supplying.

As for Rembrandt, at first I'd been in a continuous state of apprehension as to what would happen with Geertje gone. But absolutely nothing did.

We spent a great deal of time together going over matters of a practical nature and Rembrandt treated me with a constant but distant kindness. No mention was ever made of Geertje, not once, as if her name alone could summon demons.

He taught me how to order supplies and keep the books, and said I should approach him whenever I needed to. However, if a client came while he was working I was to send them away. When I went to him, he answered my questions still holding his brush and palette. At lunchtimes we went through bills and accounts. I noticed that large sums were spent at auction houses, just as Geertje had said.

So here I was happily ensconced in my new role, feeling safer with him than during all the months she'd been in the house and in his bedroom.

I'd reached the boundary of shrubs and undergrowth. Now I had to find the way into the forest. Last time I was here something unthinkable had occurred; something so different from anything I'd ever known that I doubted my own memories.

I looked back at the road by which I'd come. How silly to imagine that he'd follow me a second time. I continued along the edge of the forest. How naked those trunks looked, like corpses. I was quite convinced that they would never sprout again. I could not see a way into the forest. It was fringed by thorny, bone-white bushes, twigs tightly interlaced. I took a deep breath and pushed my way through. A lone bird sounded a warning at my intrusion. I continued further, hoping to find the stream. The frost-hard earth did not yield under my foot and the forest was wreathed in eerie silence, without so much as a rustle of a leaf. But then something – gurgles. The stream! It was frozen over entirely in places but in others it was rimmed by brittle ice shelves. Spring would come. Soft grass and flowers would grow again. I wondered who I would be by then. Change was inevitable, Rembrandt had said. Already I was but a distant relation of the girl who'd kissed him in the studio, who'd learned that rapture resides in the smallest of things. The man I saw every day, had he changed too, like the seasons, to and fro? The moment Geertje had left the house we'd all become like fish in a dark, murky sea – bored and sullen.

I smothered these pointless thoughts. I'd have to try to go back to being that unknowing girl again. I could still make friends through church as I'd intended when I first arrived. I gave several of the ice shelves a good kick, enjoying the sight of the little pieces floating downstream, and then made my way back to town.

As I passed by the harbour area I recognized Petronella. She wore exactly the same clothes as last time.

I quickened my steps and walked towards her, shouting, 'Petronella, it's me.'

She said nothing until I was closer and then admonished me. 'What are you doing, announcing to half the town that you know me?'

'I need to talk to you,' I said, forgetting all my manners.

She rolled her eyes and drew her thick eyebrows together but then her mien softened. 'Come to the third house in the Huitersgracht at one hour after midnight. The door will be open. Make sure nobody sees you enter.'

'But it's after curfew,' I said.

'It can't be helped. If you are careful and don't take a light no one will see you.'

I nodded, not feeling reassured in the slightest.

*

In order to merge with the night I'd wrapped a thick dark shawl around my head and face, feeling a bit like a tulip thief. Out of the shadows, a drunken man staggered towards me. I stepped to the side but he mirrored my move, barring my progress. My heart was beating a tattoo in my chest while I stared at him. He said, 'Please wait, I just wanted to . . .'

'Do not block my way!' I said.

He stepped aside and I quickly walked on, mightily satisfied that I'd seen off the drunkard. I peered around each street corner to avoid stumbling across one of the night watchmen who would throw me into a cell.

I found the house and entered. A door was ajar at the top of a set of stairs. I pushed it open. The ample figure of Petronella filled the only armchair in the room. She got up with surprising ease, closed the door and motioned for me to sit down in the chair she had vacated. She sat on the bed, which creaked under her weight, and said, 'You look like you've been through the wringer; what's the trouble?'

'There is no trouble.' I glanced at the innocuous-looking bed.

'Have you become his bedfellow?' she asked.

'What? No!'

'Good, so he's got some other woman?'

'No.'

'I'll hold my tongue and let you speak,' she said, grinning.

'He's thrown out Geertje, the housekeeper. He used her in his bed but sometimes I wondered if it was the other way round.'

'A lusty one, was she? A born whore. So why did he throw her out?'

I said nothing.

She looked at me and said, 'I can see why.'

'No, no, he's not interested in me.'

She raised her eyebrow. 'Is that why we are talking? You want him to be interested?'

'No,' I protested loudly. 'It is the opposite. I feel revulsion. I have had unchaste feelings.'

'That's not the opposite.'

I ignored her and continued, hoping that sooner or later the purpose of my visit would become clear both to her and to me. 'I don't understand how you can do what you do and not be afraid of God's punishment. The devil fuels our lust. We must be chaste or burn in hell for our sins.'

'How do you know that's the truth?' she said.

'Your question is blasphemous.'

She was calm as a catkin. 'Have you ever wondered how it is possible that there are Anabaptists, Remonstrants, Counter-Remonstrants, Catholics, Calvinists, Quakers, Jews, Mennonites and they all say that different things are true? They cannot all be right, so how do you know any of it is true?'

I could not think of a suitable reply. It was odd to see her sitting on the bed, looking so coarse and yet she spoke with such eloquence and education. How far she must have fallen.

She continued, 'Who is God more likely to forgive, the whore who is starving and has to make a living, or the man of means who pays her and commits the sin for his pleasure?'

I considered this; she hardly looked like starvation was a problem.

She studied my face. 'Have you felt desire?'

I could feel my colour rise and this seemed answer enough for her.

'So have I,' she said, 'a long time ago.' She was still looking at me intently. 'What did you do when you felt it? Did you feed the fire?'

I thought of the kiss in the studio many weeks ago. 'No, I put it out.'

'I see,' she said. 'But some fire is necessary – remember we keep one going in the hearth.'

I was growing irritated. 'What are you telling me?'

'You've resolved to keep putting out the flame in you, but it's God's flame too. You're stifling the very life in you.'

I looked at her and glimpsed how she must have been, when she herself still loved. But what of her warnings that I must not make the mistake she made and fall pregnant? Where was the sense in her contradictory counsel?

She spoke again. 'You'd better decide if you want to be a whore or a virgin.'

'I want to be neither,' I said.

'Then you'll have to be something of your own making, but most people won't see you for who you are; they can only think in terms of what they know. To them you will be either virtue or vice.'

'What do you see when you look at me?' I asked.

She studied me again. 'I'll show you what I see. Go and lie on the bed.' I was frightened of her now. She had something to prove and I might merely be the means to prove it. But I was far too curious. So I lay down on the quilted bed.

She spoke quietly. 'Loosen your limbs until you sink into the bed.'

Tiredness crept up on me with a softness.

'Now imagine a man coming through the door. A man you like.'

There he was, standing in the doorway wearing his painting coat. I could even smell him.

She continued. 'He's walking towards you, sits down next to you. Can you feel his warmth? He lies down beside you and kisses you. He goes to lie on top of you.'

'No,' I said.

'What?'

'I don't want to play your game.'

'Oh,' she said, genuinely puzzled. 'Don't you want to study the flame? We're only making a little fire. It's quite safe.'

'It's not that,' I said.

'What is it then?'

Something was bursting out of me – I did not know what I was saying but the words came anyway. 'I want something more, something brighter, a shining light that pierces the heavens.'

She laughed, walked over to the bed and put her arms around me. I thought this strange but I returned her embrace, my bosom against hers. Then she put her hand on my heart. I felt a growing warmth inside. I had not been held for a long time. I hugged her closer. Her hand was still there on my heart, on my breast. Her touch changed. Her hand enveloped my breast. I stayed against better wisdom, a sensation between my legs keeping me there, a flame, first soft then violently alight. She pressed my flesh the more, causing a throbbing that spilled into an ache, reaching up deep inside me.

She let go of me and went back to her chair. 'There,' she said. 'There's more colour in your cheeks now. That was lust, my dove, perhaps not so bright as to pierce the heavens but still it's what keeps you and the world breathing. The church, remember, is full of withered old men. Now, time to go. I'm expecting a man who wants some of that.'

'But what about you?' I wanted to say, for I remembered that she felt nothing, but she quickly ushered me out.

I staggered back home, in a state not much different from the other drunks and no closer to knowing what I'd wanted to ask her, let alone what the answer was.

In the Depth of Winter

He'd been looking at me for quite a while before I realized I'd pulled a strand of hair out from under my cap and was winding it around my finger. I let go of it. He smiled with a kind of curiosity. Titus was not back yet from school so Rembrandt and I were at lunch on our own. I noticed that his beard was made up of many different colours, including red. The morning sunlight brought them out.

'Rika.' It was the first time in a while he'd used the familiar form of my name. 'I've been wondering whether Six is right and I should emulate Gouvert for at least an evening?'

'What?' I said.

'Not his tedious, tight-arsed brushwork but his panache for entertaining guests.'

'Oh,' I said, thinking with terror what this would mean for me.

'I've got an appetite for painting their faces again. So perhaps it's time to get them to part with some guilders. Six thinks a dinner is a good idea.'

I supposed it was – given that he was barely breaking even.

'I thought we could come up with a list of fancy ingredients for a lavish banquet – curly cabbage looks nice, doesn't it?'

'Yes,' I said, 'but I'm not sure if it's what you would serve to impress.'

'True,' he said. 'Rose water – I heard you flavour cakes with it; that'll have them guessing.'

'Yes, that's good,' I said, and made a note.

He took the pen and paper from me, brushing my skin accidentally. But could a hand capable of painting light reflections the size of pin pricks do anything unintentionally? He started making scribbles on the paper, then something recognizable, a mouse. This was also the hand that had touched Geertje and now it was innocently holding a pencil. There was no outward sign of its encounter with her flesh. Was the hand guilty of the sin? Now it transformed a white sheet of paper into a beautiful drawing and had it not painted many pictures of our saviour, inspiring devotion in anyone who laid eyes on them? Did virtue reside in his hand, his heart, his brain or any other part of his body? Surely the sin was attached to him – no more and no less – than the blessing of his ability to render God's word in paint.

'Don't buy any parsnips – they taste like a dung beetle's ball at this time of year.'

No, I thought, the hand was just a hand. Dung beetles rolled dung, that's what they did. I was a woman in possession of a body. Bodies responded to bodies, just as mine had when Petronella knew how to minister to it. If God had not wanted the dung beetle to roll dung, why did he give it a love for such dirty work?

'You must get saffron, Rika, it sweetens rice and colours it the most golden of yellows.'

There was a knock on the door; not a plain knock but a fist rapping with insolence. I ran upstairs to open it. Rembrandt followed; like me he must have thought something was wrong. A man dressed in black burst in past me with the words, 'I must deliver this to the master in person.'

'I am Rembrandt.'

The man handed him the letter and walked straight out again. Rembrandt read the missive there and then, his face transfiguring itself into a fortress. 'That greedy, never-satisfied sultana. She wants to milk me for more.'

'Who?' I said.

'The old carp, it says here, is suing me for breach of promise to marry her and this is the summons to the hearing. And,' he took a deep breath, 'she pawned the jewels – Saskia's jewels. Remember she agreed to leave them unencumbered so they could pass to Titus, when at long last she relieves this good world of her presence. Of course a contract means nothing to her.'

He tore up the paper. 'As long as there's an opportunity she'll put a spoke in the wheel. She thinks she can get the better of me. But not this time.'

I didn't like to hear him speak like this. 'But what can you do?' I said.

'How dare she . . .' he muttered, as if he had not heard me.

'She's probably struggled to make ends meet and therefore had to pawn the jewellery. Sixty guilders a year is hardly a sum to survive on.' He glowered at me but I continued. 'If you offer her a decent amount of money she won't have to trouble you anymore.'

He turned his back on me, wandering off next door, making me regret my words, but then returned.

'Perhaps you're right.' He picked up one of the torn pieces. 'There's an address on here. Send word that she should come with a witness in order to re-negotiate terms.'

It took a few moments for the sound of his words to assemble into intelligible meaning. I could not believe he'd taken my counsel. He put his hand on my shoulder, squeezed it and left. I felt that I'd moved up in the ranks.

Geertje arrived a few days later with a witness, whom I later learned was the cobbler Octaef Octaeffsz. Rembrandt did not wish me to be present, and neither did I. After they had left, he told me that he'd reached an agreement with her but that it had been like having hairs slowly pulled from his temples.

Exactly one week later we all piled into the notary's tiny, dingy room. Everything – floor, walls and ceiling – was fashioned from the darkest wood and for some reason the place reeked of fish oil. It was like being in the belly of Jonah's whale. There was exactly a chair each, lined up against the walls. Thus we sat, with hardly enough air to breathe.

Geertje and her witness were on one side, me and Rembrandt on the other. For someone who liked to stretch out his legs he had them pulled very close to his body and his hands folded in his lap. The notary's chair stood against the third wall, separating the parties. He had lit a single candle on a side table to augment the light from the tiny window and began by assuring everyone that he had drafted the document according to the new agreement between Rembrandt and Geertje. Only the signing remained to be done.

I would have signed anything just to get out of that stuffy little room. The notary was about to read out the text when Geertje started shifting in her chair and exclaimed, 'I won't listen to this thing read out.'

'Come, come,' said the cobbler, patting her arm, 'no harm in hearing it read, is there?'

At this she seemed to quieten down and the notary read out his draft. It was similar to the previous version except that Geertje was promised an additional one-off payment of 200 guilders with which she was to redeem the jewels, and an annual sum of 160 guilders, a generous improvement on sixty. During the reading her face grew red and her hands curled into fists.

The notary had barely said the last word when Geertje stood up and proclaimed with her index finger stabbing the air, 'This is a piece of piss out of a cow's arse. I won't sign such a thing!'

The notary looked with raised eyebrows at Rembrandt, who looked at the cobbler, who looked at Geertje. She was gesticulating wildly to embroider a torrent of language that would have made a sailor blush. Rembrandt gripped the arms of his chair but said nothing. And then the cobbler – blessed be his honest soul – said, 'But Geertje, these are all things you agreed yourself in the last meeting.'

'What if I get ill and need to get a nurse?' she said.

Rembrandt said with effort and through gritted teeth, 'I'm sure we can accommodate your concerns in this draft, as long as we can get this dealt with today.' He turned to the notary. 'Can you propose a wording?'

The notary scratched his head with the end of his quill and said, 'The applicant is willing to adjust the amount, at his discretion, should this be required due to a change in Mevrouw Dircx's circumstances, such as illness. With some luck the court might be moved to uphold the last agreement.'

Everyone was nodding, as if we could pull Geertje into agreement by our tide of nods.

'At *his* discretion,' she laughed, pointing at Rembrandt. 'If it was down to *his discretion* he'd see me shipped to the Far Indies. No – ill or well – he owes me more than a hundred and sixty guilders.'

She stepped close to Rembrandt, so close that he couldn't have got up even if he'd wanted to. For a moment I thought she might spit on him but she merely looked down at him. Then she turned around and left and the cobbler scurried after her.

We all leaned back into our chairs and drew a collective breath. Then the notary said, 'A shrewd woman, with a penchant for theatre. She probably knows she might get more in court than a hundred and sixty guilders and that you would do anything to avoid public embarrassment. She'll be hoping for a better offer from you and if it is not forthcoming, then her attendance here today will still work in her favour.'

'How's that?' said Rembrandt.

'The court favours reasonable plaintiffs. Now she can demonstrate that she has at least made an attempt to resolve matters amicably.'

Rembrandt groaned and put one hand over his eyes as if trying to shield them from some horror.

The notary said, 'Not all is lost. I'll redraft the agreement, taking care of the concern she voiced regarding her getting ill. This will show you to be reasonable. Either she accepts it or she won't and we'll go to court.'

The two men shook hands. And we were finally free to leave the stinking belly of the whale.

Geertje, of course, turned down the new draft, so a few weeks later we found ourselves at court. I'd imagined something more grand but it was a sober, medium-sized room, completely unadorned. There was a small area to the side, fenced off with wooden rails, where family and friends were seated. I was there on my own. On the other side were public benches filled almost to capacity and at the front was a raised area with a desk, occupied by the three commissioners of marital affairs. I recognized the grey-haired men as wealthy burghers who could easily have counted amongst Rembrandt's clients. Now they never would.

Geertje was called upon to present her case. She took to the floor like a commander to the decks of a man-of-war. Her voice was clear and calm and as she spoke she looked at each of the commissioners in turn. 'Rembrandt made verbal promises of marriage and gave me this ring. Further I declare that he has slept with me on several occasions and I request that I may be allowed to marry Rembrandt or alternatively that he support me.'

The chief commissioner turned to Rembrandt and asked him to comment. Rembrandt waited for Geertje to be seated again, rose to his feet and said, 'I deny having made promises of marriage and, with respect, I do not have to admit that I have slept with Mistress Dircx. It is for her to prove it.'

The honourable gentlemen had their work cut out in stifling

a laugh. But the spectators on the public benches showed no such restraint and chuckled to their hearts' content. After a brief deliberation, one of the commissioners got up.

'We have studied the paperwork and much of the case depends on whose word we can trust. Does either party have anything else to add about the conduct of the other?'

Geertje immediately raised her hand and took the floor. Rembrandt was stone-faced.

'I was first employed by Rembrandt's late wife, born Saskia van Uylenburgh. I nursed her to her final hour and then cared for their son Titus for almost six years. The master never found fault with my work or with us living as common-law man and wife until,' she paused for effect, 'there was another change in the circumstances.'

She looked at me and kept on looking until every head in the room had turned in my direction, including Rembrandt's.

'Not long after enlisting the services of a new maid, Rembrandt and two of his assistants threw me out of the house, leaving me entirely without means and poor Titus without a mother.' She walked back to her seat like a broken woman.

I supposed in a way it was true. I wondered if he had actually physically thrown her out. The room was awash with whispers and chatter. Finally the head commissioner told the crowd that if they wanted entertainment they should go to the theatre and threatened to have the room cleared.

It was Rembrandt's turn to respond.

'As I have demonstrated to the court, I have made numerous

attempts to settle the matter to Mevrouw Dircx's satisfaction, but there is no pleasing her.'

The commissioners withdrew for a brief deliberation while we all remained where we were. Geertje had branded me publicly as Rembrandt's whore, which was ironic considering that she had been and I had not. She'd not said so, but, as Rembrandt taught his students, what you don't paint has more power to move than what you depict in great detail.

When the commissioners returned they announced that Rembrandt must pay Geertje 200 guilders and act in accordance with the draft of the most recent contract.

Rembrandt grew red in the face and Geertje spat into her hands in delight. True to her word, she had more than tripled Rembrandt's initial offer of sixty guilders. I felt Rembrandt's humiliation as if it was my own but I also marvelled at a legal system that made it possible for a woman like Geertje to get justice. Still, not everyone did. Petronella had not been so lucky.

As soon as we'd left the court building, he hailed a carriage. The cobbles were black, wet and shiny. The sky was covered in dense clouds, bathing the world in a muted twilight that barely reached inside the carriage. He was opposite me, his hat in his lap, his mood as heavy as the sky. I said into the gloom, 'Are we going home?'

'Yes,' came the toneless reply.

Only more shadows would be waiting for us at the house.

'Can we go somewhere else?'

He looked at me, his eyes two dark hollows. 'For what purpose?'

'To forget about what happened. It's finished now.'

The sockets turned away from me and looked blindly out of the window.

'We might have a walk in the forest. You know the one,' I said. I could not believe I'd been bold enough to ask.

He replied, with strained forbearance, 'Hendrikje, it's not a day for outings, not the weather for it.'

'We don't need sun to get air.'

He continued to stare at his nothing world outside. He would not be moved.

The carriage continued its journey, bumping me along with it, the rhythmic clanking of the wheels as inevitable as the drab days that lay ahead. I had to do something to get his attention. I leaned across, and touched the thickest part of his sleeve. I felt that his eyes, though hidden, were on me now.

I told him, 'You know, the forest will look quite different in this weather. It will be dark but cast in this eerie light.'

He laughed. 'Dark but light?' I took my hand away. 'I am not three years old; next you'll be telling me if I come with you to the forest, I'll get a sweet.'

He told the driver to take us to the forest.

To the left of the track, fields stretched all the way to the horizon; on the right was the bristly woodland that I was so keen to enter again, today of all days.

'Come,' I said, 'let's hide the satchel in a bush. We'll pick it up later.'

He threw it behind a shrub. I picked a path for us through the low-growing willow and hazel shrubs. Once we'd passed through this curtain, we stopped. This was an entirely different scene.

Trees stood like sentinels, dark, slick and unapproachable. If I touched them my hand would not find hold. There was a lifeless quality about the trunks, affirmed by the absence of birdsong. The ground was in its perpetual state of rot; the odour of decomposition climbed into my nostrils. What had possessed me to bring us here, as if a dark mood required an even darker setting?

He started walking, stomping his feet as he went, kicking at leaves and earth. I followed behind. As we penetrated deeper, less and less light reached us. I did not know where we were. There was no sight or sound of the stream. He picked up a rotten branch, thick as an arm, and smashed it against a tree; with a loud crack it splintered into fragments.

'How dare she use me like this,' he muttered, more to himself than to me. 'Could they not see that she was out to bleed me dry?'

He pushed against an oak as if he wanted to shift it. Then he walked on, still treading the ground heavily. 'You can't get justice in Holland anymore.'

'I suppose she'd see it differently,' I said. He turned and glared at me but I had to say it. 'Does she not deserve a decent living after everything that she's done, after what both of you did?'

'You're still carping about that?'

First her, now I was the carp. His steps quickened away from me. I ran after him, barely able to keep up in my dress. Grabbing his sleeve I said, 'Wait!'

He tore it away from me but stopped. As he stood in front of me I realized how tall he was. I avoided looking at his face and instead my eyes settled on his black hat and then on the black doublet. A fine satin thread ran through its fabric, glistening like a lure. I looked at his face. His stormy features were cast in the reflected light from his collar. That's when it struck me. He was handsome. I'd never thought him so before. His arms hung loose, the sleeves unmoving for the air did not stir and neither did we. His breath came in short shallow bursts and his hand was at the top of his shirt, loosening a button and another on his doublet. He said, 'We should not have come here, I need to get back to work.'

'If you wish, Master,' I said.

'Don't now call me Master after having been quite the mistress about how I should handle my business.'

'I was not,' I protested.

'By God's teeth, you told me what I should do.' Then, aping me, '*Give her what she wants and she'll go away*. I thought that you understood her, having worked with her and being a woman and all that. Turns out you did have a special understanding but it was all about what was good for her, not me.' And then in a whining voice, '*Sixty guilders is hardly a sum to survive on.*'

He'd never mocked me before. Something in me felt loose, like it had slipped out of place. He walked off again, this time in the direction we'd come from. I staggered after him, feeling as I did as a child when Mother was angry with me. I reached for the bottom edge of his doublet and held on with both hands.

He stopped and turned to face me. I let go. His eyes focused on mine. There was nothing soft about them now. My father told me never to corner a bull in the edge of the pasture. He continued to glower at me. I swallowed.

'By the heavens,' he swore, then clenched his jaws tightly. His eyes darted about between me and the trees but I caught and held them – grey and archaic. His arms shot forward, grabbing me and pushing me backwards. He'd loosed off his bridle. I stumbled but felt no fear. He stopped, his fingers still pressing into my arms.

Then he pulled me towards him, his face only inches from mine. He forced out the words, 'What do you want?'

In answer, I closed my eyes. Instantly his lips were on mine – salvation. My hand between our bodies, feeling his shirt and warm flesh beneath. Then I withdrew my hand, his chest now fully against mine. My body drawing him further in.

For a moment, the forest seemed to pause and he paused too, resting his cheek against mine and then, with his warm breath against my ear, he whispered, 'Rika.'

His pausing did not still me. Leaves were falling all around. I kept my face by the nook of his neck, trying to calm my breath. I wanted more of him, but he continued to hold me in his quiet.

Breath after breath, I felt a surge of life within. My fingers pressed into his back. Oh to fall, and be borne away by the wind. I'm a natural whore, I thought, taking to lust like this.

He took my head between his hands and lifted it so I would look at him. And there was something in his gaze which I trusted beyond belief, beyond experience and even beyond my shame.

'More,' I said. 'More,' and closed my eyes again. His lips became like butterflies' wings, brushing my mouth, my cheeks and forehead. My body gave itself away and then I felt the touch of his leg edging between mine. I tried to pull him closer but he responded by touching the skin inside my collar like a reverent pilgrim – his breath quickening as he did. And then he leaned away to look at me again. And upon that touch of our eyes, I slipped my moorings. His mouth found mine. His leg now pressing full between my skirts and thighs. The earth had dropped away. I fell so fast no thought could follow.

When our mouths finally parted, my head dropped down against his chest and his chin touched my hair. I breathed out – still from the deep. And slowly, slowly the world returned, lighter on this, the dullest day, than I had ever known it.

The Return of the Prodigal Son

I was still fearless, the day after and even the next. I was not used to bliss. I neglected my duties and coaxed Titus into going to his friends after school. All so I could wander the fields, marvelling that there was not a blade of grass, a cow, a tree, a man or a drop of water that was separate from anything else.

When back inside the house, I was like an actor who had lost interest in the part she plays. I was in one of the storage vaults using a shovel to transfer uncooperative lumps of coal into a bucket. It was not the coal, of course, that was at fault but my indifference to the task. I wanted to think incessantly about what had happened, to make it last as long as I could. But after a day or two the memory of his touch had lost its potency and the dusty coals became real once again.

We were back to kindness and respect, back to ordinary life. But not quite, because he flinched every time there was a knock at the door. He was so distracted that I had to repeat things when I spoke to him.

Then one afternoon Jan Six came for a sitting and I remembered the lavish dinner we were meant to be having. Maybe he'd been too busy to pursue it.

Six strode straight into the studio and boomed, 'How are things with you, old hog?'

'Quite satisfactory,' came the answer, as Rembrandt pulled Six into a rough embrace, thumping his back.

'Not so fast, sailor,' said Six in a pleading voice, and then the two broke into raucous laughter as I reluctantly closed the door behind me. I envied their boyish high jinks. Between him and me things were always weighted whereas he could talk to Six, perhaps even about what was on his mind. I pressed my ear carefully against the wood of the door. If one of them emerged I would pretend I had come to ask if they wanted beer. I heard Rembrandt's voice clearly.

'Why don't you drape your fetching frame over there against the window and I can get on with the drawing while you tell me what you've been up to and who you've been up to.'

Six chuckled, 'Now van Rijn, I should think you're the one with saucy tales to tell. Rumour has it that you're keeping a pretty chick right here in your back yard.'

One look from Geertje at court was all it had taken to mark me out to the gossip-mongers.

'Don't believe the rumours,' said Rembrandt. 'Geertje's caused enough trouble.'

'Yes,' said Six, 'funny that women just don't understand that it sometimes is necessary to move on.'

'Be quiet, Jan.'

'No, *Mijn Rembtje*, I'm not poking fun at you, I'm speaking from experience.'

'I'm sure you are. Let's get you into a suitable position . . .' And after a pause, 'Yes, that's it, keep it like that. I'll make a start. How about you, have you had much leisure to roam?'

'I have been confined to the stables most of the time. But I have been making approaches to a lady of premier connections. And have been well received, but there are plenty of others who'd like to stick their oar in. So I'm afraid I'm having to be well behaved so as not give those blabberers anything to blab about.'

'What does this lady have to offer that you are willing to wear a gob-string of your own making?'

'Well, she makes a pretty picture but more importantly she will marry up the chairs of power with my handsome arse.'

'No doubt your buttocks will derive great joy from sitting on them.'

'Ah, you don't approve? No beautiful princess could tempt you into a life of luxury?'

'I like to do as I please. That's my luxury.'

'Yes, I know, my friend, but even your freedom has limits. It is one thing doing what you do in private but it pays not to be too public about one's taste for the lower orders. They don't tell it to your face, but it has not done your reputation much good to have Geertje drag you into court.'

'Are you telling me my clients will flock to commission some piddling paint-pissers because they don't approve of who warms my bed?'

'No, not exactly, but now no one will risk sending their daughter to you for a sitting. You've painted the last young lady for money.'

'A bad smell does not last for ever.'

'That's true, but you keep on adding to the dung heap.'

'Well, she had me.'

'She certainly did.'

'Yes, but . . .' I could hear the smirk in Rembrandt's voice.

'But . . . ?' asked Six.

Then there was another pause. 'Come on,' said Six, 'out with it.'

I too was dying to learn the cause of Rembrandt's cheer.

'As you probably know,' said Rembrandt, 'I was ordered to pay her two hundred a year . . .' he made a rude retching noise '. . . so along comes her brother to collect my hard-earned money. Amiable host as I am, I bid him sit down, cut off a chunk of Maasdam, open a bottle of wine and we get talking.'

'As you would, with the brother of your enemy,' added Six.

'Investments, cheese-making in Germany not rivalling ours because they cannot keep their cow sheds clean and then suddenly he starts twittering about Geertje and how she's like a bad case of gout and how even her neighbours in Edam think so. How he always has to sort out her problems and that he is, well, sick to death of it. The poor fellow had to take her in after her husband's death. So naturally we have plenty to compare and agree upon as regards the rigors of living with her.'

'Naturally?' Six sounded incredulous. 'You're not seriously

telling me that her own brother agreed with you? And this is the brother she trusts to conduct her business?'

'You got it lightning fast.'

'Maybe he was merely relieving his ire?' said Six.

'No, my friend, he had a purpose in mind.'

'All right then. What more?'

'She gave him power of attorney.'

'Of course,' said Six, 'so he can collect the funds but . . . You did not? Is it possible?'

'Yes.'

'No.'

'Yes.'

'Stop it,' said Six, 'what are you saying?'

'Well, I started throwing looks at the bag of guilders that's sitting on the table and he took this as his cue to say, that there are places for keeping difficult women – you know, places that take proper care of them.'

'Unbelievable. You mean a Spin House?'

'Precisely.'

I was sickened. The treachery of the brother was as appalling as Rembrandt's. He continued in the same gloating tone in which he'd told the entire tale.

'Funny thing was, I was slow to catch on. It was him leading me by the nose. But who minds being led where they want to go?'

'Yes, quite.'

'So then it dawns on me that if she's in the Spin House I don't have to pay her maintenance; that's how the law sees it. So I say to him that I'd much rather the money, or what's left over after paying the Spin House, went to someone responsible like a caring family member.'

'No doubt he wholeheartedly agreed with you.'

'After that we worked together like two boys planning to relieve a neighbour's tree of its cherries. He'd get her acquaintances to sign depositions that she is unhinged and then the court would have her sent off for safe-keeping.'

I felt as outraged as if it were me he'd cheated out of tenure and possessions.

'So what's the latest?' said Six.

'That's it. It's all been done. She's in Gouda now, learning how to spin a good yarn, which should play to her strengths. And as she's signed her rights away to her brother, she's trapped as trapped can be.'

'If anyone other than you'd told me this story I wouldn't have believed it,' said Six.

'Best thing is I no longer have to worry about tripping over her every time I step outside my house. It's perfect.'

'Sounds like it.'

I'd been worried for him all these weeks and all he'd been doing was plotting his revenge. How convenient that he could bury his public embarrassment along with her. A tidy business, except she'd have to pay the price. This was the same man who had looked on the limp body of Elsje with so much compassion. Now he had become judge and executioner, locking Geertje away in a pitiless institution full of thieves, criminals, lunatics and whores, condemned to spinning all day and being gawked at by passing visitors. She would have little food but a limitless supply of infectious diseases. I doubted she would last five years. What an open-mouthed fool I'd been to have admired him for his compassion. I wanted to spit the word out; by association with him it had become dirty. Geertje had always seen him for what he was and tried to warn me.

Days passed. I hardly said a word. He was a stranger to me now. I wondered when he'd mark the change in me. He did not seem to care or notice. At mealtimes Titus's little face glanced from him to me as we all ate silently.

After about a week, I felt worn down to the knuckles and went to bed early. Despite my tiredness I could not sleep. I thought again of Samuel's drawing. It was comforting to think that Samuel had cared enough for me to make it. If only he was here now. I took the drawing from behind my woollens and carefully unrolled it. It was far more detailed than Rembrandt's work. Even the heads of the tiny screws that held parts of the balance scale together were rendered complete with slots and light reflections. On the left, as I'd remembered, rested the globe of the entire world. The continents, though, were drawn less confidently than the screws. The pan on the right was, of course, empty. But it was lower than the left! Whatever *nothing* it contained weighed heavier than the entire physical world. I smiled, thinking how Samuel liked to be clever. I wondered what invisible thing it held; one's eternal soul or perhaps the heavenly Jerusalem? While I studied the drawing I noticed the odd popping and hissing sounds from the fire, the breath of the wind squeezing through the gaps in the windows and the clomp-clomp of distant footsteps on the street. Samuel had said that the 'empty' pan contained what was most important. No doubt he'd learned these ideas from Rembrandt.

If a man like Rembrandt – who could see the deeper truth of things – behaved so unfeelingly, then what hope did the world have? As soon as I let go of the drawing, it curled back into a roll.

There was a knock on the door to my room. My chest contracted. I quickly rolled up the drawing and pushed it into the gap between my bed and the wall. Rembrandt might decide it was his property if he found out Samuel had drawn it while still employed by him. And I had no intention of parting with it.

'Yes?' I said, and the door opened. I sat with the covers pulled up under my arms, for I was only wearing a shift. He stood at the door for a long time, still in his paint-spattered tabard.

At last he said, 'You've not been talking much all week.'

I did not answer. He came closer and placed his candle on the table beside my bed so he could see my face.

'I don't want the candle there,' I said.

He looked taken aback but picked the candle up and put it on the kitchen table instead. Then he came to the bed again and kneeled on the floor, putting his hand softly on the cover where my shin was. I'd been hoping for such a gesture for I don't know how long. I slid my leg away from his touch. His hand collapsed into the void. I pulled my legs against my body. He walked to the sink and clasped its edge with both his hands. I swaddled the blanket around me and stood up. His body was black against the dimly illuminated window.

He turned around. 'Why are you looking at me as if I've infested your flour?'

'Because of what you've done.'

'What have I done?'

'I was so wrong about you. You're nothing but a vindictive scoundrel.'

He ignored the insult and asked quite calmly, 'How did you find out?'

This incensed me further. He was more concerned with the means by which I'd come to know than the wrong he'd committed.

'By accident,' I said.

He moved towards me, hands outstretched in a placating gesture. I moved away, keeping the table between us. He moved, I moved. He stopped, I stopped, like children playing a game, but we were not children.

'I had to. You know what she is like, breaking every single agreement. She'll never change.'

'She could not have broken what the courts decided. That was the end of it.'

'It makes no difference to her whether she's signed a hundred agreements with a notary or a judge. Not if she gets something into her head. Hendrickje, she attacked you. I had to do it for our protection.'

Why did he have to bring me into it? And what *our* was he talking about? As far as I could see, there never had been an *our*, except when it suited him.

'How very thoughtful of you,' I said. I wished he'd call his hatred by its proper name instead of trying to pass off his revenge as a good deed. 'I've been such an idiot. She warned me about you.' Tears amassed behind my eyes. I refused them.

He was tugging nervously at his tabard. 'No, it's not as you think. You probably listened to me speaking to Six, which you shouldn't have done.'

'Seems we're conveniently back to master and maid,' I said.

He tried to wipe this aside with a wave of his hand. 'I was just bragging to Jan. Besides, it was the right thing to do. She causes problems everywhere. All her old neighbours say it too.'

'Problems?' I said. 'A few pawned jewels, that you gave to her yourself; perhaps she should be garrotted for such a crime. Wouldn't that wrap things up nicely?'

He replied, 'You keep forgetting she was trying to hurt us.'

'She was out of the house. It was over.'

'It was not. It never is with her.'

'So, what if I become a little difficult, will you lock me up too?'

'She was more than a little difficult.'

'No. You're the one that's difficult.'

'That's enough, Hendrickje.'

'It's not!' I took a breath. 'You loved her. How can you not feel for her?'

'Love?' He made a dismissive grunt. 'It takes a heart more tarnished than yours to understand these things.'

I stared at him. 'Explain it then.'

He stared back at me and said, 'You want the truth?'

I nodded.

He turned away and said, 'I don't care whether she lives or dies. All I care about is that she's under lock and key and can't interfere anymore.' And then so quietly I could barely hear, 'I never cared for her.'

At first I received it like a confession, but then my anger rose at his inhumanity. I grabbed the shiny lid of a pan. He stepped back a few paces but I had no intention of hitting him.

'How many times have you produced "noble" pictures of yourself for your clamouring customers . . .' My voice was turning shrill. 'They are all failures.' I held the lid up to his face and stepped towards him. 'Why don't you take a good look at yourself?'

He could not help glancing at his distorted reflection.

'No wonder you don't depict yourself as you really are. Who'd want such a hideous portrait.' And then I shouted, 'Least of all me!'

With that I dropped the lid. It fell clattering on the stone floor.

He looked like he needed a chair. The feeling of power temporarily glazed over my pain.

I noticed my own grotesque reflection staring back at me from the lid and for a moment I feared that things were not as clear as they seemed. I stepped aside to let him leave. He looked like a beaten dog.

‘I’m sorry,’ he mumbled as he went.

Sorry – what a meaningless word when spoken without insight or regret.

By the next morning my anger had left and with it my courage. I felt almost as if *I’d* done something wrong. Titus followed me from room to room, trying to sit on my lap, whether I was peeling shrivelled carrots or sewing. In the early evening he went to the studio to be with his father and I could hear him laughing and screaming for Rembrandt to stop tickling him. Only a month ago he had declared he was too old for such things.

A few days later we were in the kitchen. Titus hugged his father around the legs and then ran over and hugged me the same way. Then he stood, waiting expectantly, as if relayed hugs might bring grown-up people to their senses. For a moment the palms of Rembrandt’s hands seemed to open towards me and I thought his arms might follow. But they did not. If they had, I would have refused him of course. I looked down into Titus’s hopeful little face. If only by magic all could be forgotten.

An entire week had passed. Night had fallen and I could not think of anything else I could possibly clean without rubbing it into oblivion, so I sat down at the table. I had not felt the true extent of my sadness until now. I allowed my upper body to rest on the table just for a moment. But then my throat tightened until a sob prised it open.

The crying that followed was so violent that I felt I was a stranger to myself. Spasm after spasm shook me. The world was flawed in some fundamental way. I didn't want it. Any of it.

This was exactly how Titus had cried when he'd lost Clarence, the wooden horse. He'd taken the toy everywhere. He'd been Clarence's voice and animation. Then suddenly there was no Clarence. We'd searched the whole house but found no trace of him. Titus had dissolved in a great fit of wailing and tears that lasted for well over an hour. I was mystified how the loss of a wooden horse could provoke so much grief. But now I understood perfectly.

I wanted the old Rembrandt back but he was gone. You might say that Titus was not upset by the loss of a sculpted piece of wood, but by the loss of the living, breathing Clarence that dwelled in his fancy. And yet I thought I'd lost something more than an imaginary Rembrandt.

The next day he came down in the late morning and said, 'Rika, I have to buy materials and I need your help carrying them back to the house. When can you be ready to leave?'

He usually had one of his assistants help him, but I was in no mood to argue. 'I can go any time now.'

He grabbed some baskets and off we went, bypassing the food markets and heading straight for the harbour and the warehouses of the East India Company. The closer we got to the IJ, the narrower, darker and smellier the alleyways became. Whenever we came across a begging leper he would toss him a coin and make sure to put himself between the leper and me. I inwardly scoffed at this show of protectiveness.

Finally we emerged from one of Amsterdam's gloomy passages into the open space at the IJ. There were two dozen large ships, most of them anchored, and a handful making their way in or out of the harbour with billowing sails. One massive ship nearby was disgorging goods on to a host of small man-powered barges. They'd ferry its cargo to canal-based warehouses all over the city.

We stopped to watch. The ship was majestic with its three large masts. Her wooden hull was smooth and elegantly curved, lying quite low in the water. I wondered what was in the crates; spices I'd never tasted, silk from China made by little worms, tea, sugar and all manner of curiosities. A large part of these marvels was only channelled through our city before being sold on to those abroad who could pay for such extraordinary pleasures.

He said with a smile, 'If you could buy anything you wanted, what would it be?'

'Chocolate,' I said without hesitation.

He laughed. 'Yes, I've heard of it, both good and bad.'

We'd reached the warehouses. He bought reams of the cheapest cartridge paper. With pigments he was more choosy, taking a long time examining various chunks of lapis lazuli until settling on a particularly vibrant blue. Then he purchased some small quantities of Chinese paper. By that stage we had so many parcels that he asked me to wait in one of the offices while he went off to buy some brushes.

*

When we got home I carried everything up into the studio. He remained in the kitchen, which was odd as he normally liked to put materials away himself. I piled the items at the entrance to the small storeroom. When I returned to the kitchen he held up a steaming cup and said, 'Chocolate.'

Before him was the pestle and mortar he had used to grind the cocoa and the room was filled with the unfamiliar aroma. He pulled out a chair and placed the cup on the table. I hesitated but the cup steamed so invitingly. I sat down and took a sip. What an awful bitter taste! I must have grimaced as he quickly took the cup and tried it himself and gave a shiver. Then he got the jar of sugar that was reserved for special guests and lopped several spoonfuls into the mug.

'Try now,' he said.

I could not believe the difference. The bitterness had been transformed into something utterly delicious. I pushed the cup towards him so he could have a taste but he pushed it back.

'No, you have it. I'll enjoy seeing you drink it.'

It was almost midnight. I lay awake, listening for his footsteps from the studio to his bedroom. For some reason I still could not sleep until he was resting too. But lately he had taken to working late into the night. At last I heard the creak of his body sinking into the bed above. But still I could not sleep.

*

Day followed day, much as before. I occupied whichever rooms he did not and gulped food down at mealtimes. One morning, after a week or so of avoiding him, I heard him go out. So I rushed up to the studio with a bucket and cloth, out of guilt that I had not cleaned there for so long. Not that he had complained. I ran my finger over the surface of the table, raking up a clump of ash. It had settled on everything like a veil. I smoothed it between my index finger and thumb. It was impossibly soft, softer than anything I'd ever felt. Without thinking I put my ash-covered finger on my tongue, perhaps wanting to know what annihilation tastes like. It was harsh and metallic. I spat it out repeatedly but the acrid sensation remained. I rinsed my mouth with clean water from the bucket, but it would not wash away.

The table top needed wiping. I moistened my cloth. The wood was covered in a film of grey, on top of which lay a new drawing. I sat down to have a closer look. It depicted an older man embracing a younger man. The younger man seemed to have no strength left to hold himself up so he had his arms around the neck and shoulders of the older man, whom I took to be his father.

The father was leaning on a cane, so he could embrace his son with only one arm and yet he held him unreservedly. His head was tilted as if listening to his son's very breath, his shoulders curved to meet him, his chest soft to receive the young man's weary body. It had to be *The Return of the Prodigal Son.*

I knew this Bible story well. The youngest son had asked for his inheritance, left home, gambled and whored. Having lost everything he'd returned home to ask for charity. He did not even have to seek forgiveness, for as soon as his father spotted him coming over the hill, he ran towards him and ordered the best calf to be slaughtered in celebration of his homecoming. The father must already have forgiven him, I thought, but when was the moment of forgiveness? When he was in his arms? When he saw him coming over the hill? Or even long before that? Did he think to himself, *I won't hold a grudge anymore* or was the meaning of true forgiveness that there was simply nothing to forgive? I looked at the embrace again. There was no space between them. None.

My heart fluttered open just for a moment, and then closed again when I heard the sound of Rembrandt's feet strumming the stairs. And there he was, walking in. I felt myself a dead weight. He sat down on a footstool on the other side of the desk. Neither of us said a word. I had lost the sentences I had composed night after night with which to hold up his wickedness to him. We remained sitting, me chair-locked, him elbows on knees, head in the heels of his hands. Seconds turning to minutes. I stopped searching for words. I looked at him, the shape of his sunken shoulders. He scratched his beard briefly. The damp cloth still in my hand, the water slowly draining out of it, making a puddle on the floor.

How small he looked, hunched like that. My hand opened, dropping the cloth. His eyes glanced up at me. I looked at the drawing, avoiding his eyes. It was nothing more really than a piece of paper. I touched it, letting my fingertips rest on it, as if it could take me back to him across the sea of ashes.

I withdrew my hand, noticing too late that his was, just then, reaching out to touch mine. He placed his fingertips where mine had been, the paper still warm from my touch.

After this, meals became embroidered with words once more, mostly for Titus's sake. But I continued to be haunted by the drawing of the prodigal son. The father's embrace was a riddle I could not solve. It hovered at the bottom of the dirty dishwater, it appeared at night as a reflection in the window. I walked through the house with my right arm gathering empty space in imitation of the father's gesture.

How inevitable suffering seemed, like a great sea tide, which could even reverse the direction of the IJ. No compassion was vast enough to make the smallest difference. Certainly not mine. I could not forgive, least of all the unrepentant.

And anyone who dared love in this flawed world would surely suffer.

Then one afternoon, a few days later, I passed by the studio. The door was ajar. He was at the easel in deep concentration. His brush hopped from palette to canvas, like a songbird after a worm, applying paint to a golden sleeve. Then he did something I'd never seen him do before – he turned the brush on its end and stabbed the wooden handle deftly into a bowl of discarded, dried-up paint, scooping some up and mixing the paint crumbs with some yellow and ochre. Then he took the palette knife and applied the thick mixture to the canvas, sculpting the sleeve more than painting it. Even from the doorway I could see it rise into being. A miracle; not that he had rendered gold brocade from oil paint, but that he'd invented something new with the same casualness with which I drank from a glass of water.

It was the essence of how he worked. The hundreds of thousands of strokes he'd made before had no bearing on this stroke, other than his manual skill. He was guided only by what was to be achieved in painting the sleeve – for this crest of paint to catch the light. He was perfectly free in this. If only I could be too.

I continued to watch him paint. It was like a tonic.

The sleeve was all there now. He'd turned waste into gold.

That night I woke from dreams of burning effigies and urns bursting with ashes. I tried to get back to sleep but rolled around until my bedding slipped off the bed. How to forgive? I could and would not forget nor could I un-love him. Round and round I went like a mouse trapped in a glass bowl. And there was something else; my not forgiving kept me safe from him – an iron breastplate, weighing me down day and night.

In my despair I clung to the hope that one day he'd change into a man I could safely love. I kept on going round and round. Until I saw; my hope was my prison now. Better to let hope die, than to die hoping.

I lay defeated. The black waters of the IJ slowly moving through me. Ripples dancing prettily on the surface but below – in those crypts of our soul we reach only in dreams – I felt its deepest current, a great sorrow, making and unmaking me. The sorrow of all men.

And then I was the father. I was the son. And I was God. A tiny bird soared high up into the sky, singing as it went. I watched the little creature in the boundless blue. Yes, I would love. Love did not require knowing. It thrived brilliantly beyond the edge of the known.

I got out of bed, feeling perfectly awake. He was upstairs. I must see his face.

I opened the kitchen door, placed my hand on the banister and slowly pulled myself up, step by step, on the winding staircase. The latch of the door into the studio lifted easily. He was behind his desk, wearing his golden reading glasses.

His face was there – a landscape of lines, stigmata of a lifetime. I remained on the threshold, seeing his body, his tenderness and his cruelty.

He looked at me over the rims of his glasses then he took them off and put them down. I closed the door. His eyes were steady. I took a few steps into the room. He rose from his chair, arms by his side. My body mirrored his, learning about him that way. The palms of his hands were slightly turned towards me. I knew the meaning: *This is me.*

Something in me came undone; nothing was more extraordinary than the ordinary. I put my hand on my mouth to try to hold myself together. I really saw him now – just him. And not just him, for I saw every man in him. His eyes were bright, their colour both green and grey like ancient rocks. His chest, his face, his arms and legs, becoming full and fuller of what it was to be him. I'd never seen the very life in him before.

His arms opened and we embraced. We stood like this for a lifetime. I held him in his maturity, as a baby and as a dying man. I sank deeper into his chest as if into Mother Earth herself. I felt his care for me as I grew younger, and younger still, until I was a newborn and then nothing at all.

This *nothing-me* felt the touch of his lips. Felt them but not the way I'd felt them before, more like the ocean holds the fish that swim in it. I was each wavelet and the stillness at the bottom where no current stirs. His hands worked slowly to free my body from its clothes. I felt sleeves slide down my arms and skirts fall from my waist – the warmth from the stove enveloping my skin.

My hands tugged at his shirt as if I'd never carried out a manual task before. He rid himself of it and of the woollens he was wearing underneath. His chest was white and new and warm. I closed my eyes, touching his chin, his cheeks and the soft skin beneath his eyes, as a blind person sees the immortal face of a dear friend.

I opened my eyes again and he led me by the hand to a place in front of the stove. He spread out his tabard for us to lie on and opened the door to the fire. I lay down on my side, naked but not feeling naked, my head propped up on my arm. He knelt down, his upper body a dark silhouette against the flames. The red glow licking his shoulders and haloing his head.

Then, to my perfect dismay – a knock on the front door. I willed whoever it was away. He frowned, still looking at me, and said,

'Let them knock – they have no business knocking on a Saturday night.'

'No,' I said, 'they don't.'

'Such bad manners,' said Rembrandt without taking his eyes off me.

Knock, *knock*, *knock*. He bent forward and whispered into my ear, 'Maybe if I answer, they'll go quickly?'

Before I could reply, a male voice shouted, 'Remmmm . . . brandt! Are . . . you . . . home? I want to see the *Miracle of our Age*!'

'Sounds like a drunk,' said Rembrandt, getting up. He opened the window and shouted down, 'I'm not home. Any further disturbance and the *Miracle* will summon the night watch.'

The man muttered something and Rembrandt closed the window and resumed his place on the tabard. I'd grown aware of my nudity, especially as he was still half-clothed. He smiled at me. Then he reached behind me and pulled the tabard up and around my body, 'So you don't get cold.'

All was quiet again. His eyes roamed my body beneath the cloth, making a study of me. Then he laid his hand on my stomach as if to assure himself of my existence. I thought of innocence and that I'd be dispossessed of mine, but never by him. He'd not judged a single thing I'd done.

He moved his hand and laid it on my breast, listening with his palm. I watched his hand. So other-looking, on my never-touched skin. Petronella had said I must decide to be a virgin or a whore. I would be neither; I'd live the way he painted and the way he was looking at me now. I met his eyes and touched his hair, feeling the strands glide between my fingers, gripping them.

'Ow,' he said.

I laughed and tugged again a little. He swept his hands up behind my neck, causing me to abandon my business with his hair and recline fully and as I did, he went to lean on me with his chest, causing a dizzying, urgent wanting. I pulled at him to lie on me the more.

He shuffled off his breeches, under-breeches and under-drawers too. I had no idea men liked to keep so warm. Then he returned to my side and held me close. I felt something against me, fleshy, solid, searching: his rod. I had to touch this secret part of him. My fingers closed around the soft-skinned thing. He made a noise, a groan, but did not move, as if transfixed by my touch. There was a gathering stillness in him, a readying. I gripped more tightly – an intake of his breath and a twitch of recognition in my belly. How could it be so soft and solid-seeming? A riddle in my hand. I loosened my fingers, weighing its portentous heaviness and noticing the pulse, his heart-beat right there in my grasp.

I looked into his eyes, once more moving my fingers. A shiver ran through him but he kept them open. And then he put his mouth on mine, with all the greed of necessity, quickening an urging in my womb, that he be inside me now. I rolled on to my back, my legs wrapped around him, pulling him with me. He lay on me. Oh, to be new. To die.

His firmness pushed against the place I most wanted him to push against. I could finally have him all but – my body did not open, as if an obstacle had interposed itself.

My eyelids pressed together in vexation. He whispered, 'It takes time,' then kissed me again, softly like lapping waves against the shore. And then I felt him pressing again between my legs, small motions, which rolled through me like forgetfulness. The boundary was gone. Wave after wave of more than pleasure – joy. The kind of joy I thought had been reserved for the next life. Far away I registered a stab of pain, but it meant nothing to the ocean.

After a short while he stopped his moving, but remained inside me. We stayed like this for a while, with him on his elbows until he finally removed himself. I grew aware again of my body and my nakedness. We lay on our backs and I thought how I'd never looked at the ceiling in the studio before and then felt an ache.

'Is there blood?' I said. How harsh my voice sounded.

'I don't know, there might be,' he said, 'do you want me to check?'

I shook my head. I wanted to be dressed again. I reached for my shift and put it on. He too sat up, still naked but for his stockings. The part of him that had filled me was almost nothing now. I continued getting dressed. It seemed to be infectious for he did too and now I wished that we'd stayed naked or him at least. As if each piece of clothing charted a step away from where we'd been. He picked me up and carried me all the way downstairs into his bed and said, 'Lie here and rest. I'll get you something to drink.'

By the time he returned I must have fallen asleep for when I woke there was beer on the table and I could see the stars through the big window in his room. But where was he?

She was sleeping now, unknowing of his absence, the ice-encrusted ground crunching under his feet. He'd quickly reached the marshes outside the city gates but his thoughts returned to the house. He'd carried her to his bed with the intention of them falling asleep together. When he returned she was already inhaling the gentle breath of sleep so he carefully slipped into bed next to her. Then, he lay there watching her face in the moonlight. Such repose. Was this his doing? Had he made her happy, despite the brevity of their joining? He'd not been able to fully unfetter himself even while inside her. He continued to watch her sleeping face, and at last felt pulled towards the heaviness of slumber. But he could not surrender himself to sleep either. So he lay listening to her breath. It was the softest purr, deep and easy. His breath followed hers. She was teaching him to sleep – what a blessing that would be. He turned on to his other side, bedding down the way he usually slept, facing the window. How bright the stars were, so far away, unaffected by the precious moments of joy they'd just experienced. How many more such moments were in store for them?

He turned once more. Her breath brushed his face, sweet and warm. He sipped it like honeyed milk but he was still wakeful – like overripe fruit, refusing to drop from the tree.

So he got up and went downstairs, not bothering with a candle; he liked the dark. When he'd felt his way into the kitchen he saw the glow of embers in the grate and found the chair. He mused that he and Rika had changed places. She was in his bed and he was by hers. He considered lying in it but that would be the most effective sleep deterrent yet.

He continued to sit by the burned-down fire. Another soul had reached into his heart. With Saskia he'd not felt the need to even think of consequences. That's probably what they meant by innocence, to be ignorant of the fact that joy and love brought pain and sorrow in their wake. He touched his lips to his fingertips and blew a kiss to the dying embers.

The grate was still so very hot. Perhaps the wintry air would cool him down and strip him of whatever humour was riding him. He went to lace up his boots.

It was good to be out. The houses had dwindled away and the marshes held sway. Still the evidence of man was everywhere. The land had been drained, the water corralled into tight canals. They dissected the land, with the occasional bridge allowing passage. He saw an old boat frozen into place alongside a rickety pier and a hut. The mere sliver of a moon made the stars inordinately bright. He liked this kind of night. Starlight was not like ordinary light – it made it possible to see without taking the darkness away. He remembered something else about darkness. It had once meant something to him. Shelter. He wanted to get further away from the city. The road was straight, the land flat, as if stretched out by a giant's hand in all directions, right to the sea. The flats curved away under him, keeping him perpetually at their apex.

Then there were no more huts, or barges. He was separated from his fellow men. The frozen ground unyielding under foot. He relished it. An unambiguous world. Straight, clear lines.

Marshes and ditches, no sign of any creature. He sighed, his chest relaxed. Alone now, he looked at the firmament. The vastness stripped away the very air around him, his skin and even his heart. Making him empty.

He was glad to be empty. It was better that way. Better than joy. He could stay like this. Never go back.

He sat down by a tree. Ice crystals were glittering on the grasses. He slung his arms around his knees and let himself grow cold. He'd stay and let the frost rise up from the ground and embrace him, until he too became part of its hardened shell.

He leaned back against the tree. It too was in the rigor of winter but its roots were stubbornly dug into the ground, penetrating the earth, intent on staying alive. Something between his stomach and his heart contracted as if from a distant terror.

The tree felt warm against his back. He touched the bark. His fingers noticed something frayed. A hole and in it, soft, rotting wood, a kind of wound. He turned to look. The hole was not frozen but soggy. As a boy he'd picked away at rotten wood like this until no more loose bits came away. He pulled on the bark and innards until a large piece of dead wood came loose. Something was moving in the hollow. A bed for grubs. They nestled there, deep within the tree. Even now they were trying to burrow deeper with their heads pushing down into the soft wood. He carefully pushed the piece back into place.

His fingers were bestrewn with bits of wood and dark, rich compost, dead wood transformed into soil. It smelled of the possibility of life.

The constriction in his chest returned. He leaned his head against the rotten piece of wood that covered the sleeping bugs, his ear against it, like a pillow. A spasm rose from below his heart and he felt tears filling his eyes. His body shook as his hand went to lie on the piece of wood that sheltered the life beneath. He did not realize he was crying. He could not comprehend the courage of the bugs to stay alive through such a winter. He wanted to stay out here by himself, never to return to the warm hearth.

End of Winter

In the morning I woke in his bed. Why had he not come back? It did not matter; I would see him now. I would go downstairs and he'd be in the kitchen and I could look at his face. Most people had to travel further for a blessing.

I was still in my shift – the rest of my clothes were in the studio. I decided not to fetch them as nobody was in the house yet except him and Titus.

There he was, eating porridge with his elbow propped on the

table, as if he did not have the strength to lift his arm. He must have made it for himself. He looked up at me, dark shadows under his eyes, as if he had not slept at all. I had a wish to kiss his head. I approached the table very slowly, as if he was a bird that might take flight, and seated myself next to him. It seemed difficult to touch him, but I commanded my hand to lie on his. His fingers welcomed it with a soft squeeze. Then he let go of my hand and brushed across his face as if trying to wipe something away, before rubbing his eyes with both hands.

'Looks like I've taken all the life out of you,' I said.

He laughed and said, 'I've been out, walking.'

'It was a night for it,' I said. 'The stars were very bright.'

'You were awake?'

'Only for a little while. Where is Titus?'

'He wanted to see Ferdinand, so I took him over there. They're happy to have him till early evening.'

He looked so very tired. I suggested, 'Why don't you go up and sleep? Hopefully all will be quiet on a Sunday.'

He nodded, ran his fingers briefly over my shoulder and left. Later I found his cloak thrown over a chair in the entrance hall. It was soaking wet. I was glad he was asleep now, in his bed.

He came down at midday, a changed man, and informed me that we would go ice-skating. What a delight. We walked down to where the Ververs Gracht joins the Amstel and it seemed as if the whole town had taken to the ice. There were brightly coloured sleighs drawn by horses, scores of children of all ages and even old folk being pushed along in wooden chairs. We climbed down and put on our skates. After only a few strides my old confidence returned. He too took to the ice with ease. Soon we were skating side by side towards the Blue Bridge, beyond which the Amstel would take us past the city walls.

There were fewer skaters now, allowing us to go faster. And soon our feet moved in a steady rhythm interrupted only by the occasional swerve to avoid children who liked to court collisions. We slowed down when we reached the bridge for fear that the river might not be frozen solid beneath it, but the ice looked firm enough and we skated on and out of the city. Out here there was even more of a festival atmosphere, with colourful stands selling hot drinks, wafers and a hog roast. On the other side, young men were skating very fast.

'They look very serious in their efforts,' I said.

'They are probably practising for the race. You know the one, from Zaandam via Amsterdam and back. It's over a hundred and thirty miles.'

A little later I noticed people from our neighbourhood. There was Pinto, our neighbour. He'd draw his conclusions about me and Rembrandt. We continued along the banks of the Amstel at a more leisurely pace. The fields were under a blanket of snow with only the occasional windmill sticking out. He put his arm around my waist and I put mine around his, as other couples were doing. He did not seem to care about being seen like this. I took heart from that and we glided along, further and further away. I closed my eyes, trusting his guidance. The wind was cold on my cheeks but I could feel his warmth against my side. Then I opened my eyes again, looking straight up at the sky. My vision filled with blue, I could almost believe that we were flying.

Eventually we stopped at a little hut on the bank which sold hot drinks. He purchased a large goblet of spiced wine for us to share. We sat down on some logs by a fire in the shelter of a large elm tree. I could smell the cinnamon in the wine. He cradled the goblet with his hands. Whirls of steam rose from the blood-red contents, fast and pretty, until they dissolved into nothing. I looked at him, thinking he too would be watching the eerie display but his eyes were focused on me through the curtain of steam. We leaned towards each other and kissed. Afterwards I put my hand on his knee and he offered me the wine, holding the goblet while I drank. His eyes looked bright under the open sky. The whirls were still thick and furious and I sliced through them with my finger creating a multitude of eddies. I cupped my hand over the mists to collect them, but they soon spilled out, rising a little further and then vanishing. I kissed him again, this time holding his face between my hands, drinking in his scent, wishing that the wine would never grow cold. This kiss was different – steam-like it swirled this way and that, finding every corner in me and when I thought it was fading, there came a new beginning.

A couple with two children walked by. They looked at us from a distance as if we were a picture, and the woman said something to the man. Did we remind her of how she once had felt, maybe still felt?

After they'd passed, I started to feel restless. 'Let's go on,' I said.

'Not yet. Let's finish the wine.'

'All right,' I said grudgingly. Dusk was approaching fast.

He held the goblet under his chin, still gazing through the vapours at the empty expanse of frozen river. Finally he put the goblet down, took off his glove and formed a tight little ball of snow. Then he turned to me and touched it to my forehead. It felt pleasantly cool on my hot skin and water droplets trickled down my face. He wiped my forehead dry with his woollen glove, and said, 'Every year I cannot imagine that so much snow and ice can ever melt again.'

'It always does.'

'So it does,' he said.

He was looking at the ball of snow, holding it between his index finger and thumb as if evaluating a precious stone. Then he looked at me, with an expression I did not know how to read, took both my hands and pulled off my gloves. He placed the iceball between my palms, with his on the outside, pressing my hands together.

I could feel the ice melting and his gaze was fixed on me, the way I'd seen him look at an object he was drawing. My hands, despite the warmth from his, were growing icy. I wanted to let go but he was playing some kind of game. Not quite a game, for it was serious to him. As if he wanted to see if I could melt the ice. So I kept the ice between my palms, ignoring the ache. 'Kiss me,' I said.

He let go of my hands and kissed me, pulling me tightly into his chest. He'd forgotten all about making me melt the ice and so I dropped it down his collar, on his skin. He cried out and let me go. I collapsed laughing but quickly got to my feet when I saw him scooping up snow. I skated away like the fast skater I was, while he threw snowballs from the bank, but none of them reached me.

At the start of the week the house filled once again with pupils invading our special world. Evening would come, they'd finally leave and our life together would be restored. In the meantime there was plenty to do.

I moved the table and chairs away from the wall so I could scrub the floorboards. I was on my hands and knees and noticed a crack in the wall. I'd seen it before and thought nothing of it but it had grown both in length and width. Some of the plaster had come off; maybe some kind of shift had taken place in the wall. It was impossible to tell if it had been sudden or over many months.

Daniel in the Lions' Den

After the evening meal, once Titus was in bed, we at last sat by the fire. He drew while I mended holes in some woollens, a task made more bearable by the scratching of his pen and my stolen glances at him.

He was sitting in the broad wooden armchair, one leg over the other, a tablet with paper resting on his upper thigh. The hand that held the pen was broad with fleshy fingers and yet the lines that flew onto the page reminded me of the speed and accuracy with which swallows scooped flies out of the evening sky.

I'd tell him about the crack in the wall later, after he'd finished the drawing. The girl I used to be would have been horrified to learn that while he drew I almost prayed that we would share a bed. I was possessed by a strange fear that the joy and love I'd felt would never be repeated. If he'd experienced the same as I why was he not compelled to embrace me as soon as Titus was asleep?

His pen had stopped moving. He was contemplating his drawing.

'What are you thinking?' I ventured.

'What it would be like to be thrown into a den of lions.'

I leaned over to have a look. There was Daniel kneeling upright amidst four large lions with thick manes. I'd seen etchings on the table in the studio by other artists that he must have studied. And they'd all shown Daniel with his hands tightly clasped together in a prayer of despair. But this Daniel's palms met most lightly in a gesture of communion with his Maker. His face was remarkably peaceful considering the predicament he was in. To his right was a triangular grouping of three of the four beasts, sniffing Daniel and baring their teeth. And yet on his lips was the kind of happy smile that reminded me of the Virgin Mary when she was holding the baby Jesus. The fourth lion, which stood taller than the kneeling Daniel, had come up from behind Daniel and was rubbing its enormous head against his arm, much as our neighbour's cat greeted me in the morning.

Daniel's head and the lion's were inclined towards one another as if they were the best of friends. Despite the teeth gnashing on the right, I felt that Daniel was perfectly safe.

'How can he be there without being ripped apart and how can he be so unafraid?'

Rembrandt scratched his head. 'I don't know.'

'But you have answered it in the drawing,' I said. 'Daniel is as trusting as a babe in his mother's arms.'

'You think that's all it takes to avoid the blows of fate?'

His response made me feel foolish, and yet the drawing was so convincing. How could he have drawn something that contained truth, without being able to see it himself?

'I cheated,' said Rembrandt, as if I'd asked the question out loud. 'When I drew Daniel I imagined him in the presence of the Lord rather than with the lions.'

'Maybe if faith is strong enough it does protect one from harm? God looks after the faithful.'

Rembrandt laughed.

'Unshakeable faith can make life seem like the Garden of Eden, even if you're in the jaws of a lion? But the end result is still the same – death.'

I thought of the Virgin Mary again; she'd been in the presence of the Lord but she had suffered gravely, losing her son. Could she still trust and love?

'Look,' I said, 'his face suggests he is not in the grip of fear, and that's why the lions behave differently. So it *has* made a difference to him; he's not been eaten.'

'It's just a drawing, Rika.' He put his pen away and I knew he would now leave. I wanted to reach for his hand, but didn't.

He did not get up immediately, his eyes focused on something in the distance, maybe a shadow cast on the wall by the fire or something in his fancy. I tried to think what I could say to keep him with me.

'I must go to bed,' he said, stood up and walked out of the door.

I wanted to go after him, wring an embrace from him, but Geertje's example kept me rooted to the spot.

I remained by the fire, watching the shadows flicker on the wall, imagining them as prowling lions or flying bats and me being as brave as Daniel. I remembered when I'd first come into the house and looked at his face and thought, perhaps I have faith and hope, and he has not. It was difficult to love without faith, let alone go into a den of lions.

In the morning there was a knock on the door. It was our neighbour, Pinto. He looked agitated and asked to see Rembrandt. I showed him into the anteroom. Rembrandt was already coming down the stairs so I left them to it. When Pinto left he slammed the door, or perhaps it was just caught by the wind.

After dinner we sat by the fire again. He said, 'Rika, when did you last visit your family in Bredevoort?'

'I haven't yet,' I said.

'Not since you left?'

I shook my head.

'I was thinking you might miss your parents,' he said, 'if you haven't seen them for so many months, and no doubt they miss you.'

'Parent,' I said.

'Oh, I'm so sorry.' He looked at me. I wanted him to stop pursuing this fruitless topic so I poked the fire and put on more peat, making as much noise as I could rummaging with the iron.

'Was it your mother or father who died?'

I sat back down, pulling my chair away from him and closer to the fire so I could carry on with breaking up the lumps of peat. 'What does it matter?' I said.

‘It matters,’ he replied.

‘To whom?’ I said.

‘To you,’ he said, ‘otherwise you would have told me by now.’

I was murdering the fire with my poking.

‘My father,’ I said.

‘I’m so sorry, Rika,’ he said again.

‘It happens,’ I replied. ‘One ought not to be surprised at death. I’ve seen many a bride in Bredevoort getting married in black so she could use the dress again at the funerals to come. So why should I feel hard done by?’

Then I remembered that he’d not only buried both his parents but three babies and a wife.

He said softly, ‘Because when you love someone you don’t expect to lose them, even if you keep a black dress in the cupboard.’

I put down the poker and sat back in my chair again, smoothing out my skirt. His face was turned towards me but I didn’t dare look at him for fear he might notice my mood.

‘Rika, will you write to your family? It would be nice to visit them with you.’

His words shot hot through my insides, but I nodded calmly. There was but one reason for a man to ask about a girl’s family and want to visit them. It all made sense, the skating together, the proposed visit. He would never have done anything like this with Geertje. Maybe I’d been wrong about him being hesitant. Maybe he wanted to observe propriety, but wasn’t it a bit late for that? And then there were the things he had done for Geertje and not for me: the jewels, the ring. I agreed to write to my mother nonetheless.

A few days later, Christoffel Thijs burst into the kitchen with Rembrandt following close behind. Thijs was so tall that he had to duck his head under the doorway. His trousers and doublet were of the deepest black, with not so much as a grain of dust on them. His pink face floated above an old-fashioned millstone ruff – like a hog's head on a platter. His features were contorted into an angry grimace, possibly because Rembrandt had grabbed hold of the sleeve of his jacket to prevent him from walking further into the kitchen. But Thijs easily managed to pull Rembrandt along behind him.

'If you expect me to pay for it, I have to see the damage to the wall.'

At this Rembrandt let go and Thijs straightened out his jacket, which had come halfway down his shoulder, and saw the marks of lead white Rembrandt had left on his fine black sleeve. His face was a picture of perfect dismay. Rembrandt did little to conceal his glee and declared, 'This is my house, now leave!'

Thijs made a few strides towards him, towering over him, a good head and a half taller. 'Why don't you pay for its maintenance, then, and while we're at it, why don't you pay for the house in the first place. It's been fourteen years since you "bought" it. I've been more than patient, but to have old Pinto come knocking on my door for the cost of underpinning your house, that, van Rijn, is you mistaking me for one of your sycophantic customers. And you know what, Pinto is even within his rights to hold me responsible as the owner of the house because you've paid for less than half of it in all these years.'

Rembrandt did not back away. What if they came to blows? I stood as far out of the way as possible but I would not leave them alone. Rembrandt barked, 'The purchase agreement allowed for instalments.'

'Who would have thought the great Rembrandt would make instalments befitting a flea?'

'You've had a fair lot from me!'

'About a third of the purchase price, after a decade and a half. I suppose I should be grateful. At this rate, I'll have been in the ground a trifling twenty years by the time I get the rest. Mind you, even the trickle has all but dried up lately.'

Then all of a sudden he looked like a little boy about to cry – I felt for him. And his voice was almost a whisper as he said, 'I even paid your taxes for you all this time. I regarded you as a friend and you played me for a fool.'

Rembrandt stepped back, giving Thijs some breathing space. 'Christoffel, I'm sorry, it's with the recent losses at sea . . . shipments of commissioned works to Italy.' He touched Thijs's arm. 'You are right, you have been a good friend and I've been at fault. The payments will resume promptly, you have my word.'

It was as if Thijs had not heard any of it, or maybe he had as his face hardened. 'I've come here to see what Pinto is on about.'

'Go on then, have a look. It's nothing. Pinto prefers someone else to pay for his decorative urges. He must have thought who better to foot the bill than my famous neighbour who – he thinks – is shitting guilders.'

Rembrandt pulled away the table and pointed at the crack in the wall. I could see even from ten feet away that it had grown much bigger in the short time since I'd noticed it. It was shaped like a wedge, widening towards the rear of the house. Thijs went down on his knees to inspect it. Rembrandt stood, hands on hips, and said, 'It hasn't changed in a decade.'

'It looks fresh,' Thijs said and turned to me. 'You must have noticed it before?'

They were both looking at me. I felt for Thijs. It was obvious that he was more affronted by Rembrandt's treatment of him than the money. I did not want to tell an outright lie, so I finally said, 'There are so many cracks in the walls. I never pay them any attention.'

Thijs looked at me like a lost cause and then turned to Rembrandt and inhaled as if in preparation for a big speech. 'You'll be hearing from me. I cannot afford to go on being charitable. I too have financial commitments that I need to honour and you need to honour yours both to myself and Pinto.'

'You tell me what you need and it will be dealt with,' said Rembrandt.

'It's not what I need. It's what you owe me. You are not doing *me* a favour. I have been doing *you* a favour for the past fourteen years and it is about time you learned the difference. I'm not the only one who feels this way. You will pay the full amount of what you owe me forthwith. You will receive a summons.' Then he walked out.

In answer to my questioning look, Rembrandt said, 'I'll pay him and that will be that.'

'How much?' I asked.

'Eight thousand or thereabouts.'

An incomprehensible amount. I knew from doing the accounts that he did not have the money. Could he possibly earn enough in time to pay it? I knew that he sometimes charged as much as five hundred guilders for a commission but if he could earn that why had he not paid it back in all those years? I knew the answer. He'd spent the money on other things. I glanced at the crack. I doubted that as things stood the house was still worth the unthinkable amount he'd paid for it. Our quarter was no longer popular and the house itself was probably in the process of slowly sinking back into the boggy soil.

In the evening we were sitting by the fire in the kitchen. I wanted to question him about what he was planning to do about Thijs but wasn't sure if it was my place. I unwound a length of thread and cut it with my teeth. The doublet and the loose button were in my lap. He was still idle as if preoccupied with something in his mind. I held the needle up to the window in order to guide the thread through the eye. How the wind howled and whispered around the house. My thread missed the eye every time. I looked around. We might not only lose the house but also the furniture, the beautiful copper pots and everything . . . I'd seen it happen in our neighbourhood, especially with trade currently being at a low ebb. It was ironic that just when I'd felt myself in reach of a secure life and marriage it was more likely than ever that I might be without means.

I was about to ask about his finances when the wind pushed a plume of smoke into the kitchen. He put more peat on the fire in the hope that it would increase the draw. I knew it wouldn't work. When the wind came from the north-east, the air sat about the house and no joy was to be had with fires. In fact, he was making it worse by smothering the flames. Why had he not told me about the loan? You'd think it was the kind of information you'd volunteer to your accountant. Smoke was now hanging in the air like banks of fog. Another gust delivered a cloud of ashes into the room, making it difficult to breathe. I'd been thinking everything was balanced, even if only precariously. Geertje had told me that he'd only paid off a third of the house. How could I have been so stupid as to forget? The smoke made me cough so hard I went into the hallway. Back in the kitchen the air was thick with it and yet he was still trying to relight the fire.

I went into the adjacent storage room and opened the delivery door, watching as the smoke was whisked away by the wind.

He came up behind me. 'Why have you opened the door? We'll turn into icicles.'

'Better than being smoked like eels, look!' I pointed at the plumes.

He shrugged his shoulders. 'All right, what shall we do?'

'Put out the fire and go to the anteroom,' I said brusquely.

He nodded.

We settled ourselves in the anteroom. Me cocooned in several shawls and him with a blanket on his legs. He'd fetched his drawing things and was working now. I stared at the empty fireplace and felt even colder for watching it. My teeth started chattering. He looked across at me. 'You're really cold. Come and get into the guest bed – you'll catch your death otherwise.'

He lifted the blanket up for me. I crept in and he tugged it tightly around my body. 'There,' he said smiling at me, 'you'll warm up soon.'

In an instant my annoyance was gone and I found myself holding on to his sleeve. He looked at me, an expression on his face almost of fear. I did not let go. He remained where he was, neither pulling away nor coming closer.

'Just help me get warm,' I said.

His elbow softened and he came under the covers with me, lying on his back. He smelled of smoke. I looked at his pale face. It seemed to me that by entering this guest box bed we had entered a different world. He opened his right arm, an invitation. I lay within it and moved closer against him, putting my head on his shoulder. I felt almost at peace now. We lay like this for a long time. Then I grew restless; why did he have to lie there like a dropped acorn? I gave up waiting and closed my eyes. Then I felt his head incline towards mine and come to rest against my forehead. I put my hand on his heart. I felt it beating – so fast as if he was fretful. I propped myself up on my elbow and kissed his temple. I thought of my older brother Harmen and how he'd sung a song to help me go to sleep when I was a child. So I started humming the tune and then the words came and I sang as softly as I could:

When our ship sails the sea to a faraway land
We lie there sleeping, love holding our hand,
The waves come so softly, rocking to, rocking fro,
Now sleep little baby, for there's marvels to come.

I've watched the horizon all day for your sails
I know it is coming for the wind blows so sweet.

His eyes remained open, blank, staring at the black ceiling of the box bed, but then his lids sank lower and closed. I wanted my voice to carry what calm I had so he could rest.

I pray you may sleep until you are home.
I pray you not suffer the tiniest storm.
When we're together we'll sail once again
The waves gently rocking, our two hearts to one,
As vast as the ocean, till all else is gone.

When I reached the end of the song, I started again but singing ever more softly, as if the air itself could be lulled to sleep. He turned on his side, his back to me, his body relaxing and then his breathing changed to the slow, deep breaths of sleep. I lay down beside him and soon fell asleep too.

Spring

The carriage took us ever closer to Bredevoort. I had written to my mother, unsure what to say about Rembrandt. In the end I'd told her that we'd got to know one another and it was his heartfelt wish to visit my home and meet my family. It was the truth as far as I knew.

He had hired a coach and man for the journey. We were sitting side by side on the leather seat being jolted against one another. If he intended to ask for my hand in marriage surely he would have said something to me by now. Or perhaps out of decorum he wanted to meet my mother first. Given the debt he was in, it was hard to see how he could provide for a family, but then again he'd lived with the same debt for over a decade and was paying me wages nonetheless. At least I'd be seeing Harmen.

I kept looking out of the window. The entire land was dissected by small dykes which bordered the newly drained polders. Without the dykes the land would be flooded again. So much audacious effort for so little earth. Most of the Low Countries were below sea level and yet we thought we could wrest every ounce of it from the waters.

I'd grown up amongst the waterlogged plains and was sad to see them changed. Water always found the lowest point – it would win back the land one day. I wondered about seeing my mother. My memory of her was like a faded drawing.

There were the fortifications of Bredevoort already, clawing the air. We thundered over the wooden bridge across the moat and through the city gate and we were amongst the tall, narrow houses which huddled together within the confines of the city walls. We passed the soot-blackened church tower which stared down on everything with its clock-face. The wheels rattled over the cobbles. Not far now. I clasped my hands together.

He continued to look out of the window, his usual unbothered self. I tried to do the same. My stomach started to gurgle. The wheels continued on.

After some final directions from me, we arrived outside the small timber-framed house of my birth. It looked old and weathered and the trees in the garden had grown huge. The thatched roof needed renewing. He offered me his arm as I climbed out of the carriage. The fur-trimmed collar made him look rich as a merchant. I'd never seen him wear this particular garment before. I wanted to feel pride in him, as I would be entitled to if we were married. For my own dress I had vacillated between wearing modest black from head to toe or a loose-fitting burgundy jacket with a white shift underneath and black skirt. In the end I'd chosen the more colourful attire. It was a special day after all – at least I hoped it would be.

We walked towards the door, which had been repainted the colour of green bile. An ill-judged choice, unless van Dorsten meant to induce nausea in his visitors. Rembrandt knocked. The bilious door receded and there was my mother, smiling. I'd been prepared to see some grey in her hair but not the stoop that bent her back.

Her eyes wandered from me to Rembrandt and he bowed saying, 'Mevrouw van Dorsten?'

'Yes, and you must be Mijnheer van Rijn. Please come in, be heartily welcomed.'

We stepped inside. She kissed me briefly and then Harmen's arms were around me. Before I knew it, he'd lifted me up but stopped short of swinging me around in a circle as he had done when I was a little girl. When he put me down I noticed how low the ceiling seemed and how small the windows were compared to Rembrandt's.

Then I was formally introduced to the children even though I of course knew them all, having lived next door to them less than a year ago. There were the two boys of four and six and a girl of seven. While saying their names my mother touched their heads, stroking their hair. They all had an unfortunate likeness with their father. Even the girl had his bony chin and pokey blue eyes.

Van Dorsten signalled to the children by a wave of his hand that they were to return to their play. They ran to a corner of the room which was full of playthings: a horse without a head and some wooden farm animals.

We seated ourselves on chairs, except van Dorsten and my mother who took to the settle in a way that made me think it was their accustomed seat. How frail he looked, like a starving pigeon, well into old age. My mother appeared less old now that she was sitting next to him.

A maid entered the room and started furnishing everyone with cakes and boiled apple water. Rembrandt turned to van Dorsten.

'Thank you for your kind welcome. If I may ask, now that the war has ended, has there been an impact on the garrisons of Bredevoort?'

Van Dorsten launched into a long description of the decline of the local garrisons. My father's clock was still there, ticking, and there was the chair I'd sat in for so many hours doing lacework. I could not understand why my mother was sitting so close to van Dorsten – there was plenty of space on the settle. At one point their hands were even resting against one another. I was getting impatient with Rembrandt, who was holding forth about his investments, the art trade and how prices failed to take into account the true value of art.

My mother's eyes met mine, a question in them.

Then Harmen asked, 'So how have you been? How is life for the two of you in Amsterdam?'

'Good,' I said, feeling awkward. 'There's much to do. The workshop is busy.'

They'd start asking further questions now. We should never have come. If there was a time to announce his intentions, surely this was it.

'I must see the garden,' I said, already on my way out.

Everyone looked surprised, but Harmen got up and offered to accompany me.

The yew tree had been my refuge as a child. I climbed it and Harmen followed wordlessly. Despite my cumbersome skirts I managed. Soon we were many feet up, sitting comfortably on thick branches in the dark green cave, sunlight sparkling through the gaps between leaves.

'I missed you,' I said.

'I missed you too. Why did you not visit sooner?'

'I did not want to see our mother with that man.'

Harmen nodded. 'It was all too soon after Father's death but you must not be too hard on Mother. It's better she's with someone than on her own.'

'Hm,' I said, 'I suppose it is.'

'She needed something to do,' said Harmen.

'Marriage is an excellent remedy for idleness,' I said.

He looked at me and shrugged his shoulders. And then he said, 'I've seen how he looks at you, he cares.'

'Who?'

'Rembrandt.'

'Oh,' I said, 'do you think so?'

'Yes, it's obvious,' said Harmen. 'And do you care for him?'

'Yes,' I said, 'yes.'

'I thought he was about to announce your engagement when you got up.'

'Did you?'

'Well, yes.' He studied me. 'That's why you're here, isn't it?'

I hesitated. 'I don't know.'

Harmen looked first puzzled and then worried.

'Be careful, won't you?' he said.

I nodded. Thinking that *careful* was probably not the best way to describe my conduct.

We sat in silence for a while, the wind fanning the branches. I remembered seeing caterpillars once in another tree in the garden and having a little reverie about a metamorphosis so complete that one remembered nothing at all of one's former life. Perhaps complete and utter change was best. I should have stayed in Amsterdam.

Harmen was the brother I was closest to and even to him I could not be truthful. We sat in silence for a little longer and then returned.

On a whim I went upstairs and slipped into the room where my father and my mother used to sleep. There was the old box bed and the large cupboard. I could hear laughter from downstairs. I opened the cupboard. It was filled with van Dorsten's clothing but at the bottom stood my father's leather boots. When I was a child, upon coming home, he would pretend he could not get them off until I helped him pull at them. The leather was dry and brittle now – it was surprising that my mother had bothered to keep them.

I heard footsteps so I quickly closed the cupboard. It was my mother.

'What are you doing here?' she said.

'Nothing.'

'I've been looking for you. Amsterdam has done nothing for your manners, just running off like that.'

'Let us go back downstairs then,' I said.

'What's he come here for?'

I shrugged my shoulders, trying hard not to say, *Why don't you ask him?*

'I thought you'd come to announce your engagement?'

I wondered whether I was the most angry with her, with Rembrandt or with myself.

'Hendrickje, have you become his whore?'

'No!'

'Of course you have. Look at you. Those colours.'

'I choose my own wardrobe these days.' I had not come to fight with her but it was inevitable.

'How hard I tried to instil God's tenets in you . . .' She raised her hands as if to heaven.

I had the strange urge to run to my father as I'd often done in moments like this. But there was no one to redeem me now. If only I could take the boots with me, I thought. But if I asked for them she'd know something of how I felt.

When we returned to the drawing room van Dorsten and Harmen were smiling at an impromptu sketch Rembrandt had made of the big-bellied widow who lived opposite. He rose, offering me once again his arm and we stood there framed by the window with all eyes on us. My hope rekindled that this might be the time. But Rembrandt just stood smiling, patting my arm. Then we took our leave. As my mother came closer to bid me goodbye, it was as if the lines in her face prefigured the ones that were to come in mine.

She was tired, yes. She'd lost a husband. At least she'd cared enough about him to keep his boots. Harmen was right; it was good she had van Dorsten.

I reached out and held her hand in mine – but when I sensed her discomfort I let it go again.

We rattled back over the cobbles, past the church tower in silence. My metamorphosis was incomplete and perhaps that's how I'd remain. I sat as close to the window and as far away from him as I could.

Portrait of Jan Six

He put down his brush; the loud hammering had ruined his every moment since the early morning. He still could not believe that Pinto had had the audacity to go ahead with the work on the foundations without his consent. Six would be here any second now. Perhaps he should have gone to his friend's house instead. But there was always a chance Six might see something he liked and buy it. On the other hand, with that racket going on, he doubted even the generous Six would be in the mood to make a purchase, let alone do him a favour.

Six surprised him, walking into the studio, his knock on the door must have been drowned out by the noise.

'Thanks for coming, Jan,' said Rembrandt.

'I'm regretting it already,' said his friend. 'What's going on and how can you work like this?'

Rembrandt showed him the balls of beeswax he kept in his ears. 'Not that it makes much difference. Pinto's decided to embark on another one of his little projects.'

'Pardon me?' shouted Six, putting his hand behind his ear.

Rembrandt gestured at Six to follow him, and once they were outside the front door, he said, 'I think we'd better go for a stroll.'

'Or a ride,' said Six and waved at a small canal boat. They climbed in, taking seats opposite one another, with Six facing in the direction of travel.

'Take us around the Herengracht,' his friend told the boatsman. It was a relief to be away from the noise and he saw his chances of a favourable response from Six increasing with each pull of the boatman's oars. Rembrandt sat back and watched the houses go by. Neither of them felt the need for conversation as the boat glided through the balmy – if rancid – air.

Soon they turned into the Herengracht. Completed mansions stood next to empty plots or building sites. Everything was designed for grandeur. Two lanes for traffic and still plenty of space for moored boats on each side. He could not help but admire the ambition of the burghers and merchants who could afford to build here. The houses were sky-high, with enormous windows and a wealth of sculpted stonework.

No wonder other perfectly fine quarters had fallen out of favour, including his.

Six finally said, 'So why did you want to see me?'

There was no way of putting it diplomatically, so Rembrandt answered, 'I'm in a bit of a squeeze.'

'But not in a good way, I take it?' said his friend with the boyish grin Rembrandt felt sure Six would still be sporting in his sixties.

Six laughed, making it easy for him. Then a massive boom shook the air, like a canon going off in the distance, but it was probably just a pile driver. He could not afford to get distracted. 'I'll come straight out with it,' he said. 'I need a loan of one thousand florins.'

'Whatever for?' said Six, looking only a little taken aback, and *boom* came the noise again. He tried to get his reply in before the next one. 'Thijs demands I immediately pay off the house. It's in violation of the contract, but I *do* want to pay him back.'

'You've been there for some time,' said Six.

'Yes, indeed,' said Rembrandt, 'and he says he's under pressure himself. It's the right thing to do. Cornelis Witsen will give me four thousand.'

Six raised an eyebrow and Rembrandt was not sure whether at the sum or the creditor. *Boom*. It sounded like a shot and an explosion all at once, so loud he could feel it in his body, and even the surface of the water rippled slightly.

'Our new burgomaster himself will lend you money? You know Cornelis Witsen did not become chief administrator of the Dutch East India Company by being careless and now that he's burgomaster you won't be able to wriggle out of anything.'

'It will be fine,' said Rembrandt. 'I know I can pay it back, and Isaac van Heertsbeeck will also give me four thousand, but I'm still a thousand short, taking into account bits and pieces here and there.'

Boom. Six swallowed and pointed in the direction they were going. 'We are coming up to the Golden Bend. Look at that new house over there; splendour's the name of the game. I've heard that Witsen has bought a plot here too. It will have cost him.'

Rembrandt could not help thinking that it had been a long time since he last had a commission – *boom* – from this part of town. Six craned his head to see where the noise was coming from. There was a scaffold about forty foot high, consisting of four poles that met at the top. A giant lump of metal was being slowly winched to the top via a system of pulleys and ropes drawn by twenty or so men. Once it reached the apex they would let go and it would crash down on the wooden pile and drive it into the ground. They had skimped on piles when building his own house, and now he had to pay for it. The men let go, the hammer hurtled down in free fall, landing on the wooden pile with an ear-splitting bang.

'Of course I'll give you the money, but I'm worried about you. Knowing you, you'll not put it all where it ought to go.'

He thought it best to say nothing in reply.

'I want something for it,' said Six.

'Name it,' said Rembrandt, uncomfortably aware that he was in no position to refuse.

'Keep the loan quiet and accept a commission for which I will pay your usual rate on top of the loan.'

What generosity! He could not help but slap Six's thigh. He saw the boatman's eyes widen. At least the hammer blows were getting quieter now as they moved away.

'You're a true friend,' he said, feeling a little guilty for having underestimated Six's devotion to him.

'I try to be,' said Six, 'but once I'm married to Margaretha I might not be able to be so open about it, depending on how you conduct yourself, and I will also be more constrained in terms of what I can do financially.'

Rembrandt could see his future was assured, if even his friend felt the need to use a loan as leverage to get a portrait out of him, but he'd gladly do it. 'What do you have in mind for the picture?'

'Well, something astounding, dazzling and original, of course,' said Six.

Rembrandt stood up, causing the boat to wobble, and held one hand a foot over his head and the other just below his crotch. 'From here to here?'

'Yes,' said Six, 'that covers all the important aspects. Oil not ink.'

'Rough manner?' said Rembrandt.

'Of course.'

He sat back down again and gave the boatman a big grin. Six leaned across, patting Rembrandt's knee, and said in a low voice, 'It's bad enough that your wretched neighbour has decided to have the house propped up but that will be nothing compared to the disruption if you get into serious financial trouble. It would be a waste of your talent. Do you hear?'

'You lend me money and yet you don't seem to have much faith in my finances?'

'I don't have any faith whatsoever in your financial acumen but I have faith in your art.'

'My art can always save me from pecuniary wobbles,' said Rembrandt.

'No, it can't. It's a miracle that this has not happened sooner.'

There was a rat swimming by, fat, healthy and agile. It seemed there was more than enough in this town for everyone.

'Besides,' said Six, 'you have more than money to worry about.'

Rembrandt had a feeling of dread before Six even began to elaborate.

'I have a friend in the town council in Gouda,' Six said. 'He tells me that a Trijn Jacobs, a close friend of a certain plucky housekeeper of yours, is trying to convince them that poor Geertje really deserves to be released, being now ill and having been incarcerated for some time. He also told me that you've been trying to prevail on them not to grant the request with such "well-reasoned and persuasive" arguments as that if she got out she would live to regret it. Have you lost all sense?'

Rembrandt asked through gritted teeth, 'Did your friend say what they'll decide?'

'They will release her,' said Six. 'I thought you should know so you can stop wasting your time. She's in a bad way and they've taken pity on her. Perhaps she'll die before she can cause any trouble.'

Rembrandt stared at the water.

'Mind you,' said Six, 'if she recovers she'll probably sue you for wrongful imprisonment so she can claim the maintenance you owe her. And she'll be joining quite a queue of creditors. I'm sorry to have to say this, Rembrandt, but you must tell me when the time comes to sell on the credit note before it becomes a worthless scrap of paper.'

Rembrandt could only nod his agreement. Why did Six not

believe in him? As for Geertje, if she tried anything he'd simply counter-sue her, with her brother as witness of her being deranged.

Six told the boatman to take them back by a different route to avoid the noise.

They sat in silence for a while. It was such a shame, that rank stench. There had been many attempts to circulate the water in the canals, using the tides or windmills, but none of them had worked. Amsterdam remained a beauty with bad breath.

'How is it with your amour?' said Six out of the blue.

'What?' said Rembrandt.

'The girl I prophesied would get you into trouble. You can't marry her of course, can you?'

'I don't see how,' said Rembrandt, surprised to find himself willing to discuss the matter. 'I'd have to find the money to pay Titus his portion of the inheritance, as stipulated by Saskia's will.'

'So, if it wasn't for that, you'd actually consider it?'

He shrugged his shoulders. 'It might make things easier for her.'

'There's a keen groom.'

'You're one to talk.'

Six smiled cryptically and said, 'I *am* one to talk.'

Rembrandt was about to ask what he meant when Six said, 'That business with Saskia's will gives you the perfect excuse.'

What was his friend insinuating? Why wouldn't he want to marry Rika?

'Don't be so sure,' he told Six.

'Ah, Cupid's arrow has struck then?'

How pretty the ripples looked, reflecting the buildings. He liked the scum too and the fallen leaves.

'Well, has it?' said Six.

'Has what?' said Rembrandt.

'Are you in love?' His friend's eyes were sincere.

Rembrandt fished out one of the leaves and looked at it. It was mostly of a uniform brown but a few tiny yellow dots remained.

He tossed the leaf back. 'The world is moving too fast for me,' he said.

'What is that supposed to mean? Perhaps you have not quite woken up to the truth yourself. So here's a piece of advice by Horace. *While we speak, envious time will have already fled: Pluck the day as it is ripe, trusting as little as possible in the next.*'

Rembrandt recognized the verse; he'd studied it at university. '*Carpe diem, carpe diem, quam minimum credula postero,*' he added. 'Unfortunately knowing and doing are not the same.'

'Don't be such an ass,' said Six. 'Go pluck! *Carpe domina!* No doubt she's ripe.'

'It's always the same with you – salaciousness before salvation.'

'One must maintain perspective on what's important in life.'

The reflected light from the waves was flickering on Six's face and there was a change in his features; it was obvious now that he saw it.

'You and Margaretha,' said Rembrandt, 'you had me think that it was all about politics but—'

'Shush,' Six interrupted, 'it's nothing.'

Seeing Six squirm, Rembrandt could not help laughing. 'Ah, Cupid has been busy.'

'Women,' said Six, 'they make us soft and a little frightened.'

'Indeed,' said Rembrandt, feeling inordinately pleased that his friend was finally smitten.

Six pointed at a gap between buildings. 'Look, I'd like to buy this plot, not in the Golden Bend but still, 610 Herengracht has a ring to it. When I have a son, I want him to have a decent address.'

'It's a fine site, Jan, and I'll do you a portrait so you'll never be forgotten, by all the Sixes to come.'

'Thank you, my man; that would make me very happy.'

After we'd returned from Bredevoort I was not sure how to be with him. Not that I saw much of him. I was confused or maybe I was angry but what right did I have? He had not made me any promises. But why take me to Bredevoort if not to ask for my hand in marriage? I tried not to come to any conclusions but they wanted to come to me. I told myself I was not biding my time. But I was. And a mere handful of nights after our return my wait was finally over.

I heard Rembrandt call my name in the middle of the night, so I ran up to his bedroom. He was sitting amongst a tumble of pillows. I put my candle on the little table. 'I heard you call out.'

'Oh,' he said, looking at me through half-closed eyes, 'I think it was a dream.'

I climbed into his bed but sat at a distance. 'What about?'

He reclined on the pillows. 'Our house. I came to it but it was deserted because we no longer owned it. Still, for some reason I tried the door and it was open so I went inside.'

Had he said *we* owned it?

'We'd moved out long ago and yet all our things were still there, even things that we'd sold.'

'Sold?' I said. But he did not answer, apparently caught up in memories of his dream.

'Then, the floor started to tilt, a vase fell off the mantelpiece because the entire house was at an angle. I had to crawl on all fours to get back outside.' He paused, looking at me. 'I did get out.'

It sounded like a nightmare and yet he'd spoken about it as if it had not distressed him at all. But then why had he called out?

'Anything else?' I said, hoping there wasn't so I could go back to bed.

He remained silent for a long time, as if weighing something and finally said, 'Saskia was there.'

My hand reached out to the woodwork of the bed and held on to it.

He closed his eyes as if to focus on something in his mind's eye. 'She was on the bed. And even in the dream I knew that she had died.' He smiled. 'It was such a blessing, to be with her for a little while.'

He reclined into the pillows and looked so happy, presumably reliving these moments with Saskia. Perhaps I should leave him, let him fall asleep again. Several minutes passed as he lay there with his eyes closed. I thought of all the portraits of Saskia, decked in flowers. She must have been such a sweet, kind woman.

His breathing was now deep and regular. Was he in a kind of waking dream? Was he still with her? His face looked so different, as if a burden had been lifted. I wanted him to remain this way, even if he never woke again to be with me. Such a strange thought, but that's how I felt just then. *Dear Lord*, I prayed, *please let him remain in peace and joy for ever.*

But as the minutes went by, I noticed the night's penumbra on the walls. He and I were mere shadows compared to how he and Saskia had been. The fact that a dream could bring him such happiness showed how he had felt about the real Saskia. He was living in a lost world – or perhaps not lost, for it would remain alive in his heart until he died.

I was surprised to feel the touch of his hand on mine and mechanically closed my fingers around his. He embraced me.

'The house,' I said, 'the crack in the wall, is there any chance of it really sinking? And Thijs and the debt – will he force you into bankruptcy?'

He looked me in the face. 'No, of course, he won't, and the house is not going anywhere thanks to Pinto doing the underpinning.' He grinned. 'It will be fine, Rika. I'll pay Thijs but I won't bother with

Pinto. He'll give up on the money sooner or later. I should let you get back to sleep.'

So I kissed him goodnight and made my way back to the kitchen.

The next morning, as I stood stirring the porridge, I thought about everything. He could have asked me to stay with him last night. Ha, that bed would remain his and Saskia's for ever. No wonder he'd never married again. He was still wedded to her. He could not even bear to visit her grave. There was more devotion in that than if he'd decked it in flowers year after year.

The porridge had become a thick sludge. I slopped it into a couple of bowls. Titus was already at school. Only me and Rembrandt in the house.

Outside there was a fog so dense it looked as if someone had obliterated the world. I walked right up to the window until I could see nothing but the rolling vapours. I felt the ground shift under my feet but it was only the fog moving – a harbinger of my future, awash with intangibles.

I went to the wardrobe and regarded my few belongings: some skirts and dresses, a few ornaments and my skates. I reached for a canvas bag; in went a dress, then the old clogs. Last night, by the fire, he'd angled his chair with his back to me. In went my comb and hair pins. On the other hand, he did draw me a few times, and he never drew Geertje. In went my woollen under-things. He'd never marry me. I packed my favourite mug, not caring that it was his property. The gateway to the invisible; another fancy for which I'd fallen.

Better to live some kind of life than starve on dreams. Yes, he'd flickered into life a few times but mostly he was dead – keeping dear Saskia company. I redoubled my efforts, assembling things on my bed to speed up the packing process.

He walked in, staring open-mouthed at my bag and the pile of things.

'What are you doing?'

'It's no use.'

'What's no use?'

'You.'

'What?'

I carried on.

'What are you doing?'

'Going.'

He tried to take the bag out of my hand but I pulled it back and continued filling it with my endless socks and stockings.

'But Rika,' he said, 'is it something I did?'

'No.'

'But you must have a reason?'

'Must I? Find me another bag. I am out of space.'

He went off to find one. I was both pleased and put out by his compliance.

'Is it because I can't marry you?'

'Oh,' I said straightening my back, 'I did not realize that such a notion existed, even if only as a rejected notion.'

'What?'

'Marriage,' I said.

'Well,' he said as if we were talking about buying runner beans, 'I did consider it but I'd have to pay Titus's share of Saskia's inheritance to her family. It says so in her will. And I don't have the money.'

I shrugged my shoulders. Nothing had ever prevented him from doing what he wanted. I thought of the stacks of prints he'd chosen to collect instead of dealing with this 'small' impediment to his personal freedom. There was only one explanation: not-being-married was exactly how he liked to be.

I went upstairs to the linen room where I kept some sheets that were mine. He followed me.

'It *is* about marriage then? A piece of paper is meaningless.'

'Not to Geertje, it wasn't,' I said, 'and not to most men and women either. Only to you.'

I regretted having given away how I felt, for now he'd answer back and I wanted to get out as quickly as possible.

'It made no difference to Geertje's rights,' he said. 'As you were privileged to witness, she got what she wanted, married to me or not.'

'It was a privilege I could have done without, and I don't think being locked up in a Spin House was what she had in mind.'

'Why are you dragging that up again?'

'So inconvenient, I know.'

He swished his hand through the air as if to cleanse it of what I'd said. 'Anyway, Rika, Geertje's got nothing to do with any of this . . . and I love you.'

The words had slipped out, which made them harder to ignore. I stared at the pile of folded sheets in the cupboard, trying to remember what I was doing. My sheets were hard to tell apart from his. Had he really said he loved me? I pulled out the whole stack of linen and looked through the packets of white.

'When you arrived in the house; it was only the second day and you were sitting right there on the floor. I nearly fell over you coming in and there you were with glowing hair.' He gestured with his hand as if this was the self-evident explanation for everything that had occurred between us.

I'd finally found the two worn sheets that were mine. Perhaps love and truth did dwell in those junctures, but there'd been precious few of them. I bagged the linen and descended the narrow stairs again, with him still following. When we reached the kitchen I put the linen bag next to the other bag and rummaged for some candles in the cupboard. I'd never wake in a new place in the dark again.

When I got my head out of the cupboard, he was standing there holding my two bags and then he made off with them. I followed him down the corridor into his bedroom.

When I caught up with him, the bags were on the floor and he stood next to them, chest puffed out like a town crier.

'I want you to stay with me,' he said, taking my hand. 'Will you always share this room, my bed and my life as my wife, not in the eyes of the Church but in my eyes and the eyes of the world? I know I've been . . . obtuse, obstructive, obstreperous. Whatever you want to call it. Not very helpful and forthcoming, anyway.'

I stared at him, feeling like the participant in a piece of theatre, but I was moved. In fact I had to take my eyes off him to gather myself. The swirling fog was blanketing the high windows of his bedroom. He wanted me to stay as his wife, but not his wife. Was there a difference between the non-wife I had been and the non-wife he proposed I could become? I thought of Daniel amongst the lions, of his hands that met so tenderly as he communed with his Maker. Could I trust and have faith, that very way that he himself could not? I'd have to live without the certainty that resided in the habits, morals and beliefs I'd relied on all my life. And he did not seem to understand the vulnerability of unmarried women.

'I'm not the fool you think I am,' he said, as if he'd been privy to my thoughts. 'I will look after you and any children we might have.' He raised his right hand. 'I vow to that. Please.'

Before I could say anything, he opened the big wardrobe. 'Will you help me choose some old things to throw away to make space for yours?'

He stood back, pointing at the five or six doublets he possessed.

I knew at once; the badly cut doublet I'd detested ever since I'd known him. It was the colour of pus and completely threadbare under the arms, because he wore it virtually every day. I pulled it from its shelf and held it up. His face was a picture of injury before he made an effort to conceal it.

'All right,' I said. 'I can see you love the thing.'

We both stood there for a moment then I held it to my nose.

'Hmmm, it smells better than it looks. Perhaps we ought to keep it.'

He grinned.

'There is no need for you to part with anything. I can continue to keep my things in the kitchen. I'll only want to put my nightdress somewhere.'

He nodded and opened one of the packed bags, knowing exactly where the nightdress was. He took it out and then, carefully refolding it, placed it in the cupboard on top of one of his night-shirts.

Then we carried my things back to the kitchen and I unpacked again.

When they retired for the night, he let Rika go up the stairs ahead of him. She hesitated at the door and looked at him over her shoulder. He smiled encouragement and she lifted the latch. It did not escape him that she glanced up at the peep-hole as she walked in. An unwelcome reminder of the past. Then she opened the wardrobe and took out her nightdress.

'I'll let you change,' he said and went into the studio to put on his nightshirt. He'd have to live by his promise now. When he returned, she was in bed, lifting the cover for him to get in. He felt happier now that he could feel her. She was lying on her back. He put his arm under her neck and she turned towards him and they embraced. Her face lifted to him and soon they kissed and he was lost. It was so instant. No doors between them now. But his mind took him away again: the canting floor, the dream. The box bed sliding towards the wall. And Saskia in it. Trapped.

'She was in the bed.'

'Who?' Rika looked at him, confused.

'Saskia. I should have saved her.'

'You couldn't have, she was too ill.'

'No, in the dream, I mean she could not get out. She called for me to help her, but I just ran away, trying to save myself.'

Rika was nodding, but how could anyone comprehend his sin.

Her hands were on his back, brushing in little circles, like his mother used to do. But he hardly felt them – as if he was clad in thickest leather. And then, suddenly, he was bare. Her fingers vivid on his skin. And not just on his skin, but reaching deep inside, infusing blessings into his secret sorrow.

He did not deserve this. And now she whispered, 'Have some heart for yourself. I love you so.'

Then, to his embarrassment, he sobbed. He tried to stop but couldn't. Wretched sounds, unabating, from his throat, while her hands held his heart in perfect grace. As if he'd been forgiven.

And then he cried like a madman. She stroked his hair, and he felt perfectly safe – as if death was just another tomorrow.

He let his head fall in her lap, abandoning himself. His arms around her hips, his mooring. He looked up at her – she was so pristine, so new. He brushed his palms up and down her back to welcome breath into her lungs. She sighed and then she smiled at him.

I'd never seen anyone weep like this. I held him until it stopped and then I lay with him, our heads touching. We'd entered the heart of stillness, the currents of life diverting around us. We were beyond time's reach.

And yet it flowed close by, licking at our sides, coaxing us into the stream once more.

His lips roused me. And then our breath kindled the fire that breathes God into all things. I unbuttoned his shirt and emerged from mine. I sat in his lap, folding my legs around his waist. I felt his hardness. I could have him now, in his fullness. I lifted myself up and brought him inside me. He made a sound – a groan – but let me rule him until I found my pleasure.

After a while I slowed our doing, breathing quietude, always with him alive in me. Then a cusping from the stillness, rousing us again. A spreading of sensation, of him, far beyond his cock, into my breath, my blood, my heart. He rocked us vigorously, back and forth, back and forth.

The sun burning behind white wings, setting them on fire. Gone in an instant, leaving me – the sky.

PART III

Fifteen years later

Self-Portrait

Rozengracht, Jordaan,
July 1663

I sat in the plush chair, staring at the back of the half-finished canvas on the easel. An incongruous thing without him. When would he be back?

Cornelia was still playing in the kitchen, judging by the clattering sounds. She could not understand why I wouldn't allow her to be with her friends, no matter how carefully I explained the danger. She was eight years old, but in the absence of playmates had resorted once more to stacking pots into precarious towers or making a 'soup' from onion peelings, bits of peat and scrapings of dried oil paint that her father had given her. There were more hours in the day than any of us knew how to fill, except for Rembrandt who always had his work. I got up and looked out of the window. A few moored boats were bobbing on the canal. The trees were beginning to look a little tatty even though it was still the midst of summer. The world looked as if it was obscured by layers of darkened varnish and yet I'd only cleaned the windows two weeks ago.

I heard the rattling of wheels and the tolling of the bell, by now a daily occurrence, warning people not to come near. On the other side of the canal was the death cart piled with bodies, some of them naked. Lately the heap was so high that I feared the bodies would fall off. One of the men walked in front of the cart, swinging his arm, clanging the bell; the other led the horse.

They came to a halt at the house opposite. The letter 'P' gleamed white on the door. It did not stop them. They entered the house and emerged only moments later with a body, one man holding the wrists, the other the ankles. The corpse looked very thin; they all did. It looked to be a young man. He was clad in nothing but a nightshirt. They swung him back and forth and then, with a big heave, threw him on the cart, on top of the other bodies. He landed haphazardly, one arm under his torso, the other to the side, like a doll cast aside by a child. My eyes returned to the house. There was the ghost of a woman's face behind a first-floor window. Had it been her son, her husband? She pressed her palm flat against the glass as the cart carried on, jostling its cargo of loved ones towards the pits.

The weather had been very hot, causing the distemper to thrive, sending the weekly death count into the hundreds. Cornelia and I had stayed in the house at all times, but Rembrandt and Titus, now twenty-one, had to go out for supplies. The black market flourished as food was scarce; farmers did not like to come into town for fear of infection and they could easily sell their wares to those of means who had fled to the country. We had not. In order to eat we had to carry on with our business of buying and selling art. After Rembrandt's bankruptcy, Titus and I had set up an art dealership which employed

Rembrandt in order to prevent income from his work being claimed by creditors. Thankfully, demand for his art had never dried up entirely.

Despite the risks, a few brave and wealthy souls had remained in the city. They'd either chosen to stay because their livelihood, like ours, depended on the city or because they trusted the Almighty to preserve them. Or perhaps they simply did not object to joining the Lord sooner rather than later. I was surprised we still managed to sell art. Why would anyone, in times like this, be interested in luxuries? Perhaps there was no better way for the wealthy to reassure themselves of their longevity than to purchase an expensive painting to be enjoyed in the years to come.

Most of those who'd stayed had taken the precaution of barricading themselves in with months' worth of supplies, believing that the illness could be kept out by closed doors. I touched the glass with my hand and looked down at the street and the canal below. Different realms. Life inside, death outside.

A small boy, carrying a white stick, came out of one of the houses opposite, looking for playmates. It was Frank. Cornelia used to play with him. The stick signalled that he was living with someone who was stricken. I wondered if any other child would come to join him. No one did.

Rembrandt had experienced it all before in the thirties and told me that things would get better when the weather cooled. I fetched a bucket and cloth, rubbing away at the soot. It was satisfying to see it come off, as if I was removing impurities from the world. I longed to taste some fresh air. As the cart had gone, I considered it safe to open the window. Instantly I was caressed by a warm breeze, although it did carry the fetid whiff from the canal. I leaned out over the windowsill, looking down at the water lapping at the foot of the building. The wet cloth was still in my hand and a big droplet of water slipped from it and sped towards the canal. It would hit the surface in an instant and be subsumed, gone but not gone. I smiled, and as I smiled I felt as if someone was watching me but the face behind the window opposite was gone. There was a slight pain in my head. I probably needed a rest as I'd been up since five. No doubt as soon as I drifted off to sleep Cornelia would come and wake me. I closed the window, went to the adjoining room and lay down on the bed. How sleepy I felt.

But pain barred my sleep. My thoughts started wandering. It was strange to think that we'd been in the Jordaan for five years already. Cornelia had not even been two when we were forced to leave the old house as a result of the bankruptcy. The Jordaan was a poor quarter, crowded and noisy, and the four of us were cramped into only four rooms, with the studio doubling as living quarters. And yet he painted, if anything, more prodigiously than before. If nothing else, our financial affairs had been simplified by losing everything. Although I wished Rembrandt would not waste so much time trying to find a way of getting some of Titus's inheritance back. Sometimes I thought that he and Geertje had more in common than they liked to think. But Geertje had fought her battles with virtually no means. She made up for it in determination. After her release, even though she was seriously ill, she'd managed to have her name added to the list of his creditors. And it may well have been her comparatively modest claim that had caused his fragile edifice of loans and credit notes to collapse like one of Cornelia's badly constructed towers. Or perhaps he just could not stand the thought of this particular creditor holding him to account and so he decided to give the tower a good kick by filing for voluntary bankruptcy. That way he'd eluded his responsibilities – at least that's how his creditors saw it. Poor Geertje died before she could receive a stuiver from the auctions of his possessions.

The pain was getting worse and thoughts about the troubled past were not helping. I'd direct my thoughts to something pleasing: him painting. A few days after moving here he'd gone out and bought a mirror and a large canvas from money we'd hidden. And soon we'd settled into a daily routine. I spent many hours each afternoon with him in the studio, doing the accounts at the desk. He started a new portrait bigger than any I'd seen him do before. It was almost eleven foot by three. The mirror was propped up a few feet away from him so he could use himself as a model. He began by applying the grey-coloured ground. His arm and hand flowed from canvas to palette and back like the water brought in and out of the harbour by the tides. Over the next few weeks a formidable presence emerged: a man in golden robes, with a staff like a sceptre and the bearing of a king. However, on his head he wore no crown but a simple brown beret. His face and stature were Rembrandt's and yet his golden attire made him look so unlike the grey-haired man in painter's garb that served as a model.

For a few weeks I watched the enormous portrait come into being from a distance. Then one afternoon I got up and looked over Rembrandt's shoulder to see what he saw in the mirror. There was his dear familiar face in deep concentration. It was then that I noticed – I think for the first time – that he had the face of an old man.

I looked at the canvas. He'd used his face most honestly; there was the slack skin around his eyes and cheek, and the pallid flesh tones were rendered with cruel accuracy. And yet the impression conveyed by the king was one of absolute triumph. Yes, the body was growing old, but the paint told a different story, as if the entire figure was imbued with the vigour of each brushstroke; the clothes were not merely ostentatious but almost alive, the large hands chiselled, sharp. As if to say, there's more that animates a man than the youth of his flesh. The paint had been placed with supreme self-belief. As if he'd felt the need to put his brush against the Reaper's scythe and won.

I watched his hand at work; and it seemed to me, as it dragged lead white across the sleeve of the robe, that not only was it investing the canvas with a life of its own but making it into something more than a portrait of himself: a mirror to each and every soul who cared to look at it.

We'll be fine, I thought, there'll always be buyers for this.

*

The pain in the end forced me to abandon these memories. Titus and Rembrandt were both still out. Cornelia was downstairs but I did not want to call her in case this was the sickness. It could be something else of course. I'd had headaches before, but not like this. If only he'd come back soon. I'd ask him if headaches were a symptom of the distemper. He'd know.

I adjusted my position, but the slightest movement caused a stabbing pain in my head. I wanted a drink but could barely move. I decided to cool my forehead with the cloth from the bucket. I kept low, crawling on all fours, dragging the bucket and cloth back to the bed, and then put the filthy wet cloth on my forehead. It helped a little.

Finally I heard the front door open and called for him. His step paused and then quickened up the stairs.

'What is it?' he asked, his voice wavering.

'My head's in agony. I don't know why.' The sound of my voice was splitting my head.

'Have you exhausted yourself?'

I tried to speak quietly and with few words. 'I don't know. Nothing unusual. The pain's getting unbearable. Call a physician, please.'

'It's risky,' he said.

'Why?'

'Physicians visit plague victims, they often carry the infection and also . . .'

He did not continue.

'What?'

'Well, they might report you – wrongly report you – as being infected. If our house gets marked we won't be able to sell a thing.'

'What if I am?' I thought of the unspeakable screams we heard every day from houses nearby. One man had been in such agony that he'd roared almost incessantly all night. I'd lain awake pressing my hands to my ears. At last he'd fallen quiet and in the morning I'd seen his body thrown on the cart. I imagined my own body lying on the corpses, wearing nothing but a shift.

I wanted to take Rembrandt's hand but then I paused for fear of passing the sickness to him.

The ache in my head pinned me down as if someone had driven a giant nail right through my skull and into the bed frame. Then it was as if something icy cold flowed in my veins. I wanted to see his face but I could no longer open my eyes. I felt an urge to scream and flee the house. It was said that sometimes the fear killed people before the disease. Those were the lucky ones.

He must have noticed my quiet distress, for I heard him coming closer to the bed.

'No,' I said, holding my arm outstretched, my eyes still closed.

But he took my hand and I felt the warmth of his. 'Don't be silly, Rika.'

Silly was good. A word from a world of minor worries.

Then he added quietly, 'It can't be.'

'Why can't it be?' I managed to half-open my eyes.

'It will be fine. You did not leave the house,' he said.

Then I remembered the all-important question. 'Headache, is that a symptom?'

He looked at me and then away.

'Is it?' I cried.

'It's also the symptom of the common headache and a dozen other illnesses.'

'Fever, do I have a fever?'

He put his hand on my forehead. 'Yes, I think you do. Are you thirsty? Of course you are.' He saw the dirty cloth. 'I'll get you water and a fresh cloth.'

He patted my hand. 'Don't worry, people still get ill with all the usual ailments and recover. It could be from the food. Maybe something is spoiled. You cannot trust the merchants – they try to flog anything, for folk are desperate.'

He got up to leave.

'Did Titus come back with you?'

'Yes.'

'I don't want Cornelia or Titus in here until we know.'

He nodded.

After he'd gone I thought of Saskia. I didn't want him to have to see me like this. My body was boiling. I had not asked him about other symptoms. I knew that swellings were a sure sign and then there were 'tokens'. I'd heard about them when I was a child. People had whispered that so-and-so had tokens and I knew they would die. The word was both intriguing and terrifying. Tokens of what? Something too grizzly to imagine.

He returned and held out a mug of diluted beer.

'Please put it on the table. Don't come near,' I said. 'We must be careful, for Cornelia's sake. She'll need you.'

'And she'll have you too,' he said, and sat down on the edge of the bed, ignoring my request to stay away. Then he helped me drink.

'Many a nurse does not fall ill despite touching the sick.'

'And many a nurse does,' I said.

'It's not the plague, Rika.'

Plague, did he have to use that word? His denials were reassuring but the throbbing in my skull was not. For Titus and Cornelia's sakes we could not afford to delude ourselves; perhaps he could still flee with them.

'Tell me the symptoms,' I said.

He stared into space as if struggling to remember. 'A high fever or shuddering cold, along with vomiting, headaches and dizziness.'

'Tell me how it progresses.'

'Usually visible marks start to appear – buboes, blisters or spots.'

'And after that?'

'Rika, please, what good is this? You're only frightening yourself.'

'I want to know how it ends!' I said, raising my voice again.

He sighed. 'Some die quickly, within a few hours of the first symptom, others last about a week, a great many survive. There's often a faintness at the end, a kind of swooning.'

'What about tokens?'

'Oh, they are an old-wives' tale.'

He clearly was not telling me everything. I felt with my hand for swellings under my arms and in my groin. Nothing.

'Bring me the mirror,' I demanded.

He did not move.

'It's either the mirror or a physician,' I said.

He went to get the mirror and held it up for me. 'See! No red spots or anything.'

I didn't know what *he* was seeing but my face looked like a ghost's, drained of colour, black circles around my eyes. Again the peculiar sensation of ice water trickling through my veins. I felt quite unwilling to draw another breath, as if by pausing the heave for air the inevitable march towards my fate could be halted.

I thought of Cornelia. I must not leave her while she needed me. And he must not lose another wife. Then I felt hope again; some survived, maybe I would – even if it was the distemper.

He was sitting there, looking out of the window, his face vacant.

'Get me a nurse,' I said.

He took the mirror from my hand and leaned it with the shiny side against the wall.

'Why? I can look after you and you'll be up and about again in a few days.'

'No,' I said, 'I'll be in agony before long. She might know how to ease it and help me recover.'

'You're right. I'll get you a nurse. I'll find a good one. Now try to sleep – you'll be better when you wake again. I'll go right away.'

'How long?' I said.

He stroked my hair.

'Don't touch me,' I pleaded, with little conviction.

'I can't help it,' he said, shrugging his shoulders and smiling. 'I'll be as quick as I can. Not more than two hours in any case.'

As he left, I shouted after him, 'Look in on Titus and Cornelia and forbid them to come up.'

He shouted back his agreement from halfway down the stairs.

I tried to sleep but I could not – it was as if my skull was being wrenched apart. I hoped it would take him less than two hours.

I tried to console myself with thoughts that it would be a relief to have a nurse, someone who'd know what to do. As I lay, I began to wonder if God had decided the time had come for me to pay for my sin of living with Rembrandt outside the bounds of marriage. But I'd not even thought of it as a sin for a long time. Everyone treated us like man and wife. Could the Almighty be more begrudging than man? Were we not married in his eyes too?

He could only think of one person who could get him a competent nurse at this time: Jan Six. He broke into a run. But soon he was out of breath and had to slow down again; besides, he needed time to work out what to say to his friend – if he was still his friend.

How striking the sky looked tonight, streaks of pastel pink, green and blue. What an unfitting backdrop to what was unfolding beneath. The few people who were out walked close to the edge of the canals, avoiding the houses because of the smell wafting from many a door and for fear of infection.

When the distemper had first started he'd found it heart-wrenching to listen to the screams, but as things got worse he'd grown used to it, even used to seeing the bodies. Sometimes they were slumped in a doorway or had simply collapsed dead in the middle of the street. The only reason he even noticed the corpse floating in the canal was that the unusual beauty of the sky had seduced him to use his eyes again and now he wished he hadn't.

What to say to Six? He might not want to help him, and besides he might have gone to his country estate. The last time he'd seen Six, many years ago, was to warn him of his imminent bankruptcy so that he could sell the credit note while it still had value. On that occasion he'd also asked Six for a loan, as he could have bailed him out, but Six had flatly refused and not seemed too pleased that he had even asked.

He'd arrived at the old gates. There was no footman in sight so he pushed them open and walked up to the house. The hedges looked unkempt and the path was littered with dry leaves and twigs. He banged the giant lion head door-knocker as loudly as he could. An old manservant opened a window above.

'How may I be of assistance?' The man's demeanour belonged to another time.

'Is your master at home?'

'He is receiving no one.'

'Tell him it's Rembrandt. I need to speak to him, it's urgent. If he can come to the window.'

'Please wait a moment, Mijnheer, I will enquire.'

After a few minutes Six's head appeared in a first-floor window. He looked pale from being indoors.

'Rembrandt, what brings you here at a time like this?'

'Hendrickje is ill.'

'With the plague?'

'No, no, it's only a fever but she needs a nurse and they are rather hard to come by at the moment.'

Six gave a tired smile. 'Yes, somewhat, I dare say.'

'I know we did not part on the best of terms, but I was hoping you might ask Dr Tulp to make a recommendation.'

'I happen to know a good nurse myself. She helped us greatly with our children last year. If I write a note, she might be persuaded if she is free. She's good.'

With that he disappeared inside and after a time threw down a weighted piece of paper and said, 'I'm so sorry, my friend.'

'No, Jan, it's nothing, just a common fever, but she's got a terrible ache in her head.'

There was a change in Six's expression that frightened Rembrandt. 'Tulp is retired but there is no one who knows more about migraines . . . and the plague. He issued guidelines during the last epidemic on which medicines to take, in order to put a stop to all those concoctions created by quacks. I will write you a letter to give to him, asking him to advise you which physician to call – should things get worse.'

Six disappeared again for several minutes. Then he came back and threw down another paper, folded up and weighted like the first.

Rembrandt put it in his pocket. 'Are you all right? Why have you not left?'

'I'm needed here. The Church is making sure the poor are fed enough to keep them alive if the plague does not get them.'

It was hard to believe, but Six was risking his life for the common good. And how wrong he'd been, thinking his old friend might not help him.

'I'm sorry, too,' said Rembrandt, craning his neck to look at Six above.

'Whatever for, my man?'

'For asking you for money just before I went bankrupt. For being less than warm when you did not give it to me.'

'Don't think of it for another minute; you were in desperate straits – of course you tried. You thought you were heading down the drain and that I could prevent it.'

Rembrandt nodded. Six probably could have prevented it but then he'd only have struggled on for longer and possibly still failed to pay it all back.

'Have you done much these last few years?' asked Six.

'I have indeed. I have had much more time.'

'Good, good, I was hoping you'd be working prodigiously.'

'But I'm selling less than I used to. Of course, if I adapted my style a little . . .'

Six interrupted, 'You've never bothered with that – why start now? You can't go backwards.'

'No, quite right,' he said, grinning at his friend.

Six continued, 'You know the portrait we did, I mean you did – I look at it every day. It's a masterpiece.'

Rembrandt smiled. 'I know.'

Six laughed, 'That's better.'

'You must come by when things are back to normal,' said Rembrandt.

'I will,' said Six. 'And keep on painting, especially now. It'll keep you out of trouble.'

'What a complete bore you have become,' said Rembrandt.

'Take a look at yourself,' Six laughed. 'Paunch, children and devoted to your lovely wife.'

Rembrandt had to press his lips together to stop despair getting the upper hand.

'Send word if you need anything else,' Six said. 'No need to come in person. You'll be needed at home.'

'Thank you, thank you so much. May God love you as much as I.'

Six laughed heartily. 'There's a man of true faith, asking God to try to measure up to Rembrandt. Only you could see it that way.'

*

As he hastened through the dark streets towards the nurse's house he kept feeling that he'd missed something obvious, something in plain sight – like the corpse in the canal. It was one thing to be blind to the ravages of the plague but to go for months without looking at the sky . . . He looked at it now. An inky black. And yet he could still discern the remains of the fading light. Or was it the afterglow of something luminous he'd seen in another life? It seemed a very long time since he'd last set eyes on something truly bright.

I must have drifted off into some kind of stupor for the next thing I knew he came through the door with a little woman who wore a perfectly starched white cap that was fringed by the fairest wisps of hair. It was possessed of so little weight that it refused to clump into strands and instead hovered around her face.

'I'm Anna. I'm going to look after you,' was all she said for introduction.

Her voice was like the notes of a small flute. There was something child-like about her. This alarmed me at first; how could a slight thing like her stand with me against the sickness? I needn't have worried for she immediately set to work.

'Looks like you're running a fever, my dove.'

She'd brought a large basket with her and from it she produced herbs, tinctures and cloths from which she quickly assembled poultices and applied them to my legs.

'To draw out the heat,' she said.

And indeed for the first time I felt a lessening of the pain in my head, at last allowing tiredness to win out.

'There, there,' she said, 'let sleep take care of you.' Through half-closed lids, I watched her white lace cap and the near-white hair, a blurry halo about her face.

Rembrandt visited every few hours but stayed away from the bed, as I had wished. In the evening Cornelia came to speak to me from the doorway. As much as I longed to see her, the thought that I might never hold her again made me feel wretched and hopeless.

The next time I woke, the pain had subsided a little. It was dark night and yet Anna was there in her chair. I was able to speak so I asked her about how others fared that had been stricken. She told me that in many cases they turned to the Almighty. And that the closer death came, the more the heart was moved to repent. She'd heard the most desperate confessions and pleas of forgiveness from the sick on their deathbed. Many had advised her not to leave things as late as they had. Perhaps when death draws near the urge to cleanse oneself is inescapable. I too started to feel troubled. Not by the recollection of my sins but by my failure to think of any. It must be my pride obscuring them, I thought. And I had been excluded from partaking in the Eucharist for over ten years now. My sins must have stacked up all this time and brought the plague upon me.

My limbs grew hot again with fever and my mind was taken by it too. I thought I was in the dark, cavernous chamber of the Church

Council, summoned there for the one sin I did remember. The first thing I noticed were not the twelve men that sat behind a long rectangular table but the table itself. It was very beautiful, with gold trimmings and carvings, possibly a leftover from the old Church. How strange that it had not been replaced with something much less wonderful.

I could not bring myself to look up but had a vague impression of a row of gloomy figures lined up behind the table. My hands were shaking uncontrollably, whether from present fever or past fears I did not know – they were as one.

The heat was so overwhelming that I looked for its source and saw two great stoves, one on each side of the chamber. A servant stood by to keep them well fed with coals. Old men are often cold.

'It says here you've been living in whoredom with Rembrandt the painter,' a voice declared.

I looked at my feet.

'Do you admit to having fornicated with the painter Rembrandt van Rijn?' asked another.

'It's too hot,' I said to the man with the coals and felt Anna dab my forehead with a damp cloth.

'You must understand that someone like you cannot partake of the Lord's Supper? He who eats and drinks unworthily, eats and drinks judgement to himself. You must see this?'

My shoes were full of mud.

'Look at us!' one of them shouted.

But I could not face them.

Another whispered, 'She won't look at her sins either.'

'That's not surprising.' They laughed.

'Shhhh,' said Anna, 'there's always hope.'

'No hope for her,' several council members muttered at once. 'She's a whore – once a whore, always a whore. And all whores go to hell.'

I made an effort to look at them but all I could see were shadowy bodies wrapped in thick shawls. And when I tried to see their faces, my vision blurred.

The servant was throwing coal into the fires by the bucketful. It was boiling hot and my body was shaking violently.

'It's the evil in her,' one of them whispered.

'Marriage is honourable amongst all; but fornicators and adulterers God will judge.'

'Repent your sins.'

'Ha, look at her, she can't. It's too late.'

Their shadow heads were nodding.

It was not too late. I'd ask forgiveness. But I could not prise my lips apart, as if they'd become sealed with hardened varnish.

'See, the devil's got her.'

'But we still have a duty to her soul. Who eats and drinks unworthily, eats and drinks judgement to himself.'

'She must not partake for her own good.'

'Hendrickje Stoffels, you are hereby excluded from partaking of the Lord's Supper.'

*

I felt Anna rubbing my hand and I could see the walls of my room again. I told her I wanted to repent and she said it did not matter *when or where* – I could repent in my own heart and save my soul and she would listen. But again, the words would not come. How could I possibly turn to a God that infected mothers? I thought of the poor women who'd given birth, even as they were falling ill with the plague. They had to choose between suckling their child and thereby infecting the baby or watching it starve to death. Wet-nurses were not to be had. I forgot all about repentance and probed Anna for more and more descriptions of the horrors that took place and she obliged, telling me that scores of women died in childbirth because there were no midwives. Nobody could be moved to help a neighbour for fear of even breathing the same air. But still the bonds of blood were strong, she said; many families stayed together. But it meant – more often than not – that they died together.

When I was tormented by my pains that night, instead of seeking forgiveness, I thought of the hundreds who were suffering like me and worse. I kept the mothers in my mind and heart. And only then did I find a measure of peace.

The next time I saw him it was light. Anna as usual got up and left and he took her seat by the window. He remained silent for a long time.

Eventually he asked, 'How are you feeling?'

'Much the same,' I replied and asked if he was working.

'Yes,' he said.

'Good,' I said. I felt an urgency to speak to him of more important things, but I could not fathom them or lift them into the realm of words.

'Titus has gone out to get some materials,' he said.

'I'd better try to sleep,' I said, even though I wanted him to stay.

'Good, my love,' he said, 'I'll be back later.'

For the first second of awakening I knew absolutely nothing of my condition, not until a moment or two later when the awful pain and nausea once more wormed its way into my spirit and with it the thought that I might be dying. Anna put a cup of beer to my lips. 'You slept very peacefully and for a good time.'

'How long since I got ill?'

'I came here yesterday, the day you fell ill, I believe. You've been sleeping since noon. It's late afternoon now.'

I could not believe how much time had passed. 'Where is he?'

'In the studio, I think.'

In addition to the pain in my head, my calves were now contracted in a constant muscle spasm. I'd assumed that I'd feel better after sleeping and as a result of her medicines.

'I'm feeling worse,' I said. 'I'm getting worse all the time, aren't I, Anna?'

'Yes, poor child, no good denying it.'

'Why aren't you doing what any sensible person would do, leave me and protect you and yours?'

'Oh, I could not do that.'

'Why not?' I asked. 'What's there to be gained? The money won't do you any good when you're dead.'

She simply shrugged her shoulders. 'There's always hope,' she said.

Hope, that word again that stood in for *nothing*. She should try wiping her arse with *hope*, then she'd see how much use it is. She sat by my bedside, smiling beatifically. 'I know, dear, you're terribly worried.'

I pushed my hands into the bed, trying to sit up. 'I've had enough of being slowly tortured to death.'

Immediately I was overwhelmed by dizziness and nausea, but still I tried to roll myself off the bed.

'Hendrickje, please . . .' she said and pushed me back onto the pillow.

I started sobbing. 'That ill-begotten cunt of an illness. I'll die from it, I know I will. I'll die from the plague . . .'

'Shh . . . I know.'

'No, you don't . . .'

She tried to stroke my forehead and I batted her hand away. 'There's only one thing that would help: put an end to me right now.'

I lay there, so completely spent that I could not wipe away the tears that spilled from my eyes.

'My love,' she said, 'nobody knows who will live and who will die; besides, it would not be right, you know that.'

'Who cares about what's right? Is this right?' I protested. 'I have a child. I can't die, but if I must die, I might as well die now and relieve everyone.'

'No one would be relieved by that but you.'

'That's good enough.'

'Only be glad it's you and not your child.'

I considered this. If I kept railing against my fate, maybe God might wreak revenge on Cornelia.

'You need him to help you more,' she said calmly.

'Who?'

'You know that it is the sickness but your husband doesn't want to see it. Normally it's the other way round, with those stricken by it claiming it's naught but a sore throat, or a little fever.'

'I need to rest,' I told her. 'He's been here, he's got eyes, hasn't he? Better eyes than most!'

'But he's keeping them shut. You're quite alone in the knowledge of it. No wonder you're in despair.'

As if the plague was not reason enough to despair! I closed my eyes.

'You don't want him to have to suffer,' she said.

I kept my eyes shut, feeling an impulse to stick my fingers in my ears.

'You wish to protect him but it's not helping him. Whether you live or die, it is better for him if he goes through it with you. He will be hurt less that way even if you die.'

I could not help but consider her words, even through the curtain of pain.

'What is it, child?' she said.

I shook my head. I could not say that I was afraid he'd leave me the way he'd left Saskia in her final hours. Never mind, I told myself, what difference did it make? In the end everyone dies alone.

Woman Bathing in a Stream

It was getting dark. Something bothered him, but he could not name it. He went back to her room. She was asleep like last time.

Anna told him, 'She's been very troubled, talking in fever about the Lord's Supper and not being absolved. If there's anything you can do to relieve her, you must try. I don't know what she thinks she's done and why she can't or won't ask for forgiveness.'

She left before he could reply. He sat down. He remembered all too well how dismayed she'd been the day the Church Council had excluded her from the Lord's Supper. Perhaps old fears were preying on her, but what was he supposed to do about it? He'd found a way then, but it had always been easier to allay her fear while she was sound in mind and body. There'd been a lesson for him in it too. Perhaps one he ought to remember.

How strange that the painting in question was within arm's reach even as he thought of this. Then again, not so strange. It was no ordinary picture, even by his standards. And it was never to be sold.

He picked it up from where he'd leant it against a wall months ago with the intention of hanging it up. He put his feet up on the window ledge and propped the two-foot picture on his legs. How beautiful she was. Normally what mattered most when he worked was to achieve his intention but this one had been all about her. He'd wanted to serve her, to help her, with everything he had at his disposal as a man and as an artist. He'd wanted to work a miracle. And he had to admit – it was. Letting the canvas lie flat on his legs, he regarded the sky. There were some hazy clouds, illuminated by the rising moon.

That evening almost ten years ago the sky had been beautiful too. He even remembered the taste of the pickled herring he was chewing when she'd wordlessly slid the writ towards his plate. Her hand had stayed motionless in the middle of the table. As if it had forgotten the way home. Her eyes were unable to rest on anything, least of all on him, it seemed. He'd wanted to take the lost-looking hand, kiss it and put it back in her lap, where she normally liked to keep it. The very life that normally animated her had been absent.

He emerged from these memories and looked at her sleeping form. Still the same Hendrickje, but not the same.

He'd picked up the thing. He remembered how thick it was, inexpertly fashioned, the paper probably locally produced, certainly not from China or Japan. It was a decree issued by the esteemed gentlemen of the Church Council. Until that moment he had not even known that she'd been summoned, let alone that she'd gone without telling him.

It did not surprise him that the bigots had finally got down to it. The pregnancy had been showing for months. It said she was *excluded from the Lord's Supper for living in whoredom with the painter Rembrandt van Rijn.* To him it amounted to nothing more than black ink on poorly milled fibre. To her, it was a whole world of grizzly goblins. Her arms and elbows were heavy on the table, propping up the rest of her.

His words would make no difference. As for actions . . . Marry her? No. He would not do it, even if he had the money to pay off Saskia's clan. He had to show her something that was worth a million times him marrying her. Something so beautiful and true that all the bigots in the world could never make a dent in it.

'Look at me,' he said.

She lifted her head, her eyes unable or unwilling to meet his. The roundness of her middle had increased and he imagined the baby inside, curled up and safe.

He pointed at the paper. 'This is just what's in their heads. A woman shamed for being pregnant without a piece of paper to say it's officially sanctioned, sanctified, stupefied or whatever you want to call it. If you carry this turd of a notion around with you then they've got you on a leash and every time they pull, you'll feel the tug. Besides, you'll be stuck with a stink for the rest of your life.'

She pulled her tunic about her, covering her belly.

'It's not the truth,' he bellowed. This was not helping.

He looked at her face. The answer would be written there, it always was. She sat hunched forward, her right hand tightly pressed against her eyes as if trying to keep tears from spilling out. Occasionally there was the hollow sound of footsteps passing by the house.

'Let's go out into the back yard,' he said. 'It's a warm night.'

She did not move but when he put his arm under her elbow she came with him. They sat down on the old bench. It was a cloudless sky with millions of stars scattered across it like glowing grains of sand, some big, some small. There she was: Ursa Major, the bear, high up in the sky.

Rika kept her head bent, unaware of the splendour above, but at least she seemed more comfortable out here in the darkness.

'I'm thinking of doing a Callisto,' he said. 'She was Diana's hunting companion along with a gaggle of other nymphs, until she was seduced by Zeus and fell pregnant. It must be hard to resist a god.'

Nothing, not even the beginnings of a smile.

'When Diana discovered this, she responded much like the elderly gentlemen of the Church Council. She lectured Callisto on how terrible it all was and expelled her from her band of nymphs. As if that was not enough, she also turned her into a bear. Callisto wandered the wilderness, where she soon found that being a bear in a forest was a bit like being the Pope in Rome. Food was plentiful and life was easy. But it got even better. Zeus, out of love or guilt, who knows, gave her a dream of a gift. Immortality. Look.'

He pointed up at the stars. Her eyes followed his finger.

'She's right there. See the very bright star – that's the North Star, and right next to it that's the constellation of Callisto. She has an eternal place of honour in the skies, so close to Polaris that she'll never drown in the waves. She's always above the horizon.'

Rika said nothing but when he put his arm around her, she leant against him.

'Will you come to the forest with me tomorrow and let me paint you as Callisto?'

'As a bear?'

'No, my pumpkin-bellied-tulip. I want to paint you just as you are.'

She shrugged her shoulders.

'As long as we keep the picture and don't put it where people can see it.'

'We'll do with it as you wish.'

Early the next morning he had Jacobus prepare a canvas and pigments. They set off in a carriage with cheese, bread, easel and materials. He almost never painted outside but this was different. He took the lead and she followed him past the bordering shrubs. He had a sullen companion. Even when the growth canopied into a spacious forest, she would not walk by his side.

'Do you remember where any of the pools are?' he asked.

She pointed with her hand but remained silent. They continued in single file and soon reached a pond. She sat on the first rock she saw. Her hair was not arranged in a bun or under a cap as it normally was but loosely tied behind her head with a string. She wore a brown bodice, white shift and a black skirt that spilled over the rock. One of the sleeve buttons had not been done up. She sat without purpose, as if she was made of soft wax, slowly flowing apart.

He unpacked pigments, oil and tools. The light was good from this side. He could not wait to see it on her.

'Rika, can you go over to the other side?'

She used her arms to push herself up from the rock. She must be feeling heavy by now. What must it be like to carry something alive? She walked around the pool and stood waiting on the other side with one arm propped against an oak tree. The oval of water was only about eight feet wide and fed by a mere trickle of a stream. Several fat oaks stood guard around it. A cloud must have moved, for a shaft pierced the canopy, making the brackish water glow amber.

'Can you take off your shoes and wade in a little?'

She did as he asked. 'Brrrr,' she said, holding up her skirts.

'Wait, that's a good spot.'

There were soft highlights on her right cheek and forehead. And the rest of her body was illuminated by a shimmering light which carried with it the green and brown of leaves, water and earth. This is what I call light, he thought.

She giggled. 'There are plants growing in here!'

She was moving her legs a little, playing with the green, stringy plants. Little wavelets glistened where the water met her shins.

'What are the plants doing there?' he said.

'Wondering what's trampling on them.'

He smiled. Now she was standing still, looking into the water with the faintest of smiles on her lips. She was happy. Something inside him slipped off an edge and took a fall.

'Will you take off your cap and . . .' he hesitated, wondering if she'd take offence '. . . I'd like to paint you in your shift.'

She smiled, waded back to the bank and undressed. He set up the easel and organized the paints. Jacobus had done well; the ground he'd painted on as a foundation was the right shade of ochre. She was in her shift now, on the bank, looking up into the trees. The white linen hung loosely about her body, coming down to her knees. He longed to see the shape of her belly but it was entirely disguised by the folds. You could not have everything in life, they said. Around her neck the shift had a large opening which went right down between her breasts, allowing a glimpse of their gentle shape. 'Are you warm enough?' he asked.

'Yes, I love to feel the air,' she said, touching her half-bare shoulder. Did she know the power she had over him?

'Can you wade in again to where you were before?'

The light seemed brighter now on her face. He had never known skin to glow like this. He could look at her as long as he wished. What treasure.

Her legs, so strong; her hands full of bunched-up fabric by her hips. And the drape of fabric between her hands was just hiding where her legs met, casting a shadow full of promise. She was smiling, looking at the water. She must be seeing the reflected canopy with flecks of blue sky beyond. She'd forgotten about herself.

Now he too had to forget so he could paint her. He started with little brushes but soon put them aside and reached for bigger and bigger ones. Finally, he used the widest brush he'd brought. He dipped it into lead white mixed with various earth shades and a little cobalt and swept it across the canvas, creating a swag of fabric at the very top of her thighs. His fingers knew where to place the paint. He worked in a rhythm allowing chance to play her part. Palette, canvas. Load and stroke. Load and stroke. He stepped back – the accidental grooves, made by the impasto paint, seemed to add to the illusion; by virtue of being three-dimensional, they fooled the eyes into believing they were seeing a thing that could be touched.

He'd never worked this roughly before. He wanted to swear out loud in joy. Why would anyone want to spend all day applying paint like flea droppings?

Thankfully he had brought enough paint, for he was using it as thick as plaster.

He stopped and looked and then looked some more. She stood without that tension in the body that told you that she was aware of being looked at. She was as she was, more real than anything he'd ever seen or anything he'd ever paint. That thing inside him was still falling. And it would go on falling until his dying day.

He looked at her as she was now, hot from the fever, asleep, and put the picture down. He could just sit a while with her.

I woke and did not know where I was but sensed that he was near. I wanted him to know I was awake. I tried to open my eyes and rouse myself to speak, but my tongue was like lead and the fever impenetrable. Then I thought myself to be by a stream watching water gush over a stone and plunge into a vortex. Had I not found him once in such a whirlpool? I searched for him but there was only foam, no up or down.

Now I was a child, lying in bed for my afternoon nap but watching patterns of light and shadow on the whitewashed wall. The light was dancing. The wind was buffeting the tree outside my window. God's breath.

There were the shadows of two leaves. With each little gust they moved closer together and at the nearest points their shadows formed tongues, then leaped into a bridge; touching for the blink of an eye. How strange, I thought – it's as if being so close, they need to be conjoined. I too wanted to leap – to him.

I was by a pool. Looking up, I was blinded by the blazing light, which slipped through the swaying branches. I closed my eyes, feeling the sun on my face and his eye, his hand, his brush and his attention all about me like a warm nest. He was painting me. I wished I could wear nothing at all, to better feel his gaze. Water lapped at my calves and soft wind blew over my arms and legs, making me giggle.

He was standing with his easel by the pool, stepping from one foot to the other, painting with his whole body in broad movements, singing his song about me. I was no different from the sparkling water, the oaks and the tall firs. He was so concentrated; both his face and his hands. What miracle his brush had performed – dissolving my solid body, making me the air.

And then I was awake and I could speak.

'My love,' I said.

'I'm here,' he answered.

And then he came and knelt by my bed to be closer and I felt him as if someone had lit a light inside my heart.

The Shell

He'd sat with her for a long time. They didn't speak much but he kept looking at her eyes, which were there for him, so steady, despite the illness, feeling unaccountably happy. Then he watched her eyelids grow heavy as she drifted off again.

He continued to watch her sleeping face and wondered how long it would be until she was well again. Then he felt the need to do something. He stood up and walked the few steps across to the studio. The easel was there, waiting, but work was not what he wanted. He wanted to feel something in his hands, that's what it was. There on the shelf was a shell, a *conus marmoreus*. He took it. It had a beautifully marbled surface of white dots on black, perfectly placed to make a satisfying pattern and yet no two white dots were shaped the same. He'd stood holding it just like this many years ago on the day they'd been forced to start selling his collection to ward off bankruptcy. He'd walked into the *kunstkammer* and stood gazing at the shelves, unable to choose what to put into the crates for auction. He needed the costumes for his work. His collection of etchings would potentially fetch a high price but only if he sold them at the right time and he needed them for reference. As for the shell in his hand, there really had been no good reason to keep it.

How could nature sculpt something so perfect? The creature who dwelled in it wasn't capable of appreciating the splendour of its house. And the only interest any other beast might have in it was to devour its occupant. Eventually the shell would be tossed about by the waves, first losing its sheen, then its edges. In the end nothing would remain but grains of sand. Only because a man had stumbled across it had it been transformed into an *objet d'art*.

Back then he'd concluded that it was of no real value, and placed it in the crate. He'd added feathers, nuts and precious stones and works of art, including Lucas van Leyden's prints for which he'd paid an astronomical amount just to make a point to the market about the true value of art.

Rika had walked in, holding a vest she'd knitted for the baby, letting him feel how soft the wool was. Then, understanding his struggle to part with things, she'd said, 'The babe will come into this world with nothing at all and it won't care as long as it's fed, warm and loved.'

She put her arms around him for a moment before she left. The idea of the unencumbered babe made him smile, a special freedom shared by babies, birds and fish. What would it be like to walk out of this house, with light shoulders and nothing in his hands? After all, one day he'd have no choice in the matter. That was not only how we entered the world but also how we left it. All these objects, the shelves thick with them, they were merely borrowed. And when he made his exit they'd pass into the hands of another borrower, another fool who thought they were his for ever.

He'd riffled through the crate until he'd retrieved his shell and rescued it. With the *conus* still in his hand, he went back to her room.

She was still sleeping of course. He tried and failed to get comfortable on the rickety chair and his fingers felt sweaty clutching the shell. He placed it on the chest of drawers by the window. It was dusk, the sun low in the sky, throwing the shadow of the window's central partition on the top of the chest; a crisp beam of black. He placed his thumb into the light, his nail lining up with the edge of the shadow. How fast the shadow moved. It had but kissed the crest of his thumbnail and was already advancing to the middle of his nail. Nothing could stop the shadow's progress, nothing. He lined his thumb up again and again, retreating until the sun had finally set. Nightfall a matter of minutes. It sickened him. He looked at her – she was breathing, steadily. How many breaths until she woke?

I woke up to a knock at the door. Rembrandt was sitting by my bed. Titus came in and told us that Anna had left because her own daughter had been taken ill and that we must assume her gone for good.

Rembrandt looked at me and all I could think was that I did not want him to rush out to find another nurse. 'Draw me, please,' I said.

He looked surprised but got up and returned with paper. Then he lit some candles because it had grown dark by now. By some miracle the weight of the distemper had lifted a little. I gave up worrying about him touching me. He'd tend to me now that Anna was gone. I asked him to help me sit up.

He put his arms around my back and pulled me into a sitting position. I must smell awful, I thought. He held me for a long time. I was surprised that even a body as ill as mine could feel longing: desperate, urgent, headless desire. And then fright that we might never meet again in flesh and soul at once. I calmed myself; perhaps we could still meet in each and every part – by passing through the gate to the visible.

He let go of me and started drawing. I closed my eyes, listening to the familiar sound of his pencil, feeling his eyes on me, thinking of how his pen had made me once and was now unmaking me. He drew the ridge of my nose, and it became transparent like glass. Having been recorded, it consigned itself to oblivion. Then my cheeks went; my sunken eyes were no more, my ears, my hair, my mouth – all gone to nothing. Where my head had been there was an empty space, a window through which I looked, seeing his face, the lines of concentration on his forehead, his hand and eye in closest kinship; drawing as one.

Her brow so soft. Her eyes bright. Impossible to render. Her face; so much more than the lines and shadings his pencil can produce. The eyes again. Looking at him so constantly – even from the shadows. Abjure that thought. But it's there; the hollowness of the cheeks, the shape of the 'skull' beneath the all-too-thin flesh. He can see it all and more. She's soft like cherry blossom borne skywards by a breeze.

Her pupil, an opening that lets the light in. His pencil follows it, round and round until the paper too becomes a hole, a black dot, threatening to suck in everything: the wisps of hair that have escaped the cap, the shadows under her eyes, the sweat that glistens on the tip of the nose. So bright. The skin, green, grey, but in a few places still with a hue of pink. The bones of the cheek, protruding, requiring the sharp end of the coal. He must return to the aperture, the black emptiness that demands something more to do it justice, more black, more coal and round and round it goes, abrading its cremated wood and still the black reflects the light, not dark enough – press, press – the charcoal pencil snaps.

He looks at what he's drawn. More death-mask than face. Then he looks at her living face, dismayed by the accuracy of his record. She looks like a corpse, so much so that it's surprising to see her chest rise with another breath. He must not think like this, but can anyone look that ill and live? Her eyes are still her eyes, though. She's reading him. She has known this was the way to get him to see. He has at last arrived in time with her. Now and here. Her breath is putrid as if something is eating her body from the inside. He turns away. It's getting late. He should go out and find another nurse.

He's been sitting on this chair for too long – his legs need movement, his lungs air. There is a world outside this room. But he stays. Stays.

He picks up the empty glass from the table by her bed. Searches the rim until he finds the ghostly print of her lips from the last time she took a sip. How long ago was that? His finger traces life's echo, the glass cold in his hand. He searches his own heart for marks she might have left there – indelible ones. They will have to last him for ever.

It is now perfectly dark outside. She starts to sing – a lullaby from long ago, when his world was still tolerable. Her voice soars above his silent world, clear and untouchable:

I pray you may sleep until you are home.
I pray you not suffer the tiniest storm.
When we're together we'll sail once again
The waves gently rocking, our two hearts to one,
As vast as the ocean, till all else is gone.

Even against his will he feels comfort seeping through him. He closes his lids. Her fingers stroke his hand, their very gentleness uncorking his emotion. His body doubles over, somehow producing sobs despite his efforts to prevent them. Suffering – how inadequate a word for his apocalypse.

He tries to roll in on himself, as if that could prevent anything. His hand is pressed against his heart. It's empty. A violent kind of empty. He hears a sound, a knock, knock, knock, then realizes he is banging his own head against the wooden bed post. But it's the only thing to do. Knock, knock, knock, knock, knock.

'Oh love,' she says from far away.

He slips off the chair, down on his knees, his arms and head lying on the bed and on her. Her hand on his shoulder. He is mouthing her name. Soundlessly, over and over again. She cannot help him. No one can. For soon he will be all alone.

I don't know how to comfort him. He is silent now but his body is trembling under my hand. I find his hand and hold on to it.

'I can't, Rika,' he says.

'Can't what?'

'Watch you die.'

He feels her fingers in his hair, her touch burning right through him. She tells him, 'One hour at a time. A minute even.'

He squeezes her hand, agreeing, straightening himself. One minute at a time. He wants to look at her but fears what he will see; still he focuses his vision, sees her wan face yet glowing eyes and feels an unexpected warmth in his chest. He is lucky in a way. But he doesn't know it. He leans towards her so he can whisper in her ear, 'I love you.'

She smiles, her soft fingers touching his cheek. 'I love you too.'

'Yes,' he says. 'Now what is next?'

'Finding another nurse?'

'I'm the nurse,' he says, pointing at himself, grinning to further lift the mood. 'But we could use an expert physician.'

He shows her the bundled-up note. 'See, Jan gave this to me. An introduction to the great Dr Tulp no less.'

She looks relieved. As he unfolds the note, he sees Six has used a valuable silver coin as weight.

The Anatomy Lesson of Dr Nicolaes Tulp

He'd first met Dr Tulp over thirty years ago when he painted his anatomy lesson, but he remembered it clearly. The doctor had been in his late thirties and he in his mid twenties. After months of waiting Tulp had sent word that an executed murderer's body had finally become available. As he made his way to his home, he thought back to the occasion, and it had been an occasion! He'd never been inside the Waag before. It was a bulwark of a building as befitted a former city gate built two centuries ago. He had to make his way all around to find the entrance because each of the four guild rooms was accessed through one of the round towers. When he finally got to the surgeons' room on the first floor, he was pleased that it had large windows which cast an even light. There were about two dozen men, mostly dressed in black, milling around the pallid body on the table. The small room was replete with noisy chatter. They pointed at and even poked the corpse – curious as boys.

Tulp clapped his hands and his students and colleagues arranged themselves off to one side to allow him to commence his lesson. The doctor picked up his scalpel and without hesitation cut into the skin along the length of the forearm. Rembrandt half expected the dead man to cry out in pain. He also expected blood to spurt out, but of course it didn't. His heart was for ever idle now. Tulp started to peel back the skin with his fingers and the scalpel, revealing a layer of fatty tissue and Rembrandt had to look away as a sick feeling rapidly gathered in his stomach. So he studied the men, none of whom seemed to be affected by the butchering. But it was not butchering, for when he looked again, he could appreciate that Tulp had shaved away layers of tissue with the most delicate and precise motions of his scalpel, like a sculptor working on human flesh. After a while he had laid bare the mechanism that animates the hand, the flexing tendons and ligaments. They had been picked perfectly clean, yellow strands against the red meat of the hand. Tulp used his pincers to grab at tendons on the back of the hand and pull at them as if they were the strings of a marionette. Rembrandt was not sure what came first – the dead man's fingers straightening or the collective gasp of the audience.

This was the moment to depict. He sketched the dissected arm as fast as he could. This sitter would not return for another session.

The painting had made his reputation and Tulp had been extremely pleased with the work. But that was a long time ago, and the doctor must now be near seventy and he would know of Rembrandt's dishonourable bankruptcy. He did not rate his chances of wringing much help out of him.

The manservant showed him straight into Tulp's study, a surprise given how cautious everyone had become. The room was dominated by a huge oak desk that looked seaworthy enough to sail to the Americas. The walls were hung with detailed anatomical drawings. One of them showed a valve that operated at the junction of the small and large intestines. He remembered hearing about it. Tulp's valve it was called, for he had discovered it.

'Rembrandt, it is good to see you,' said Tulp, walking in with the stride of a busy and important man. 'Are you well? What is your business?'

He'd often seen Tulp from a distance at public gatherings with his snow-white hair but now that he was shaking his hand, he felt the full force of the man; sprightly and as sturdy as his desk.

'My wife is taken ill and I am in desperate need of a good physician. Jan Six sent me here and kindly wrote this letter.'

Tulp perused it. 'A letter of introduction was not necessary – we know each other, don't we? Of course I'll try to help. Do you suspect it is the plague?'

'She's got a fever, dizziness and sometimes vomiting and headaches.'

Tulp nodded. 'It is very difficult to summon a good doctor at this time – most are in the country tending to the wealthy.'

'How come you haven't fled?'

'At my age you either fret all the time or not at all. I've chosen the latter.'

Rembrandt had a feeling he was about to find out if this was really true.

Tulp walked to the window, looked out and then turned back to him. 'You know it's strange, but I think your painting did a great deal for my rise in the profession. People started treating me as if I was important.'

Rembrandt laughed. 'If that's how you were regarded, then you earned it.'

Tulp smiled. 'Perhaps, but regard and reputation depend on people's memories and memory is a fickle entity. Your picture did the trick of making me and my work unforgettable.'

Tulp felt indebted to him, good.

The physician stood scratching his chin. 'But I am sorry, Rembrandt, I cannot think of anyone.'

Rembrandt held his eyes. Tulp must have something.

'Well, there's me,' said Tulp. 'I'm a doctor, of course.'

'You are most kind,' said Rembrandt.

Tulp waved his hand to silence him. 'I'm fed up with being holed up in here anyway. Let's go.'

Back at the house, Tulp's demeanour changed. Gone was the commanding voice. He was more like a grandfather seeing his favourite grandchild. He pulled a footstool right next to the bed and said softly, 'How are you feeling, my dear?'

'The worst is the pain in my head and legs,' she answered.

He nodded understanding. 'Shall we have a look at you?

Rembrandt, can you lend a hand?'

Rembrandt only gently pulled up the shift but even that slight movement caused her to cry out in pain. There were red splotches all over her body.

Tulp said, 'I'm sorry, I'm going to have to prod around a bit.'

He felt in her armpits and groin. 'I cannot feel any swelling. Here, Rembrandt, you have a try so you know how to check over the coming days.'

Rembrandt put his hand where Tulp's was and then Tulp put his fingers on Rembrandt's. 'You press down a little to see if you can feel anything hard.'

After she was covered up again she said, 'Is it the distemper, Dr Tulp?'

He looked at her as if to get her measure. 'When I'm asked a direct question I must give a direct answer.'

She nodded.

'Sometimes it helps to know your enemy so you can focus your resolve. I fear it is the distemper. All the signs point to it: the vomiting, headache and most of all the rubescent areas. There are many rumours about the plague, making it seem more terrible than it is. It is a serious disease but it is also a disease that a great many survive. You are not too old or too young – you can get through it.'

Rembrandt saw him to the door and tried to pay him with Six's silver coin but Tulp refused. 'You'll have more need of it than I.'

He gave him a long list of instructions, herbal brews and poultices.

'But none of this is a cure; it only makes the symptoms more bearable. I'm afraid it is very much a matter of chance and good care who survives. You should look out for further signs which will alert you if the end is coming. Those who have soft and puffy white swellings, rather than red ones, especially if they appear suddenly, very rarely live. Some never get any swellings at all, the disease overtakes them so quickly. Also if tokens appear, little hard spots like flea bites, this is a sign that death is near.'

Rembrandt nodded, wondering what the point was of telling him all this. Perhaps if the time were to come, it would be better not to know.

'You must now mark your house.'

Tulp made to leave but Rembrandt held him back by the arm.

Again their eyes met. 'What do you think?' said Rembrandt.

'She may well live.'

'How long, if she doesn't?'

'Between three and five days,' said Tulp. 'If she's still here after seven it's a good sign.

'Thank you.'

Tulp was standing by the door. He dipped into his bag and produced a small bottle with a yellow-brown liquid.

'Have you heard of laudanum?' he said.

'Yes.'

He handed it to him. 'The pain can be very bad, so bad that some are killed because their heart gives out or they are driven to lunacy. But you must not tell her this as it will only frighten her. If the pain is unbearable, put three drops of this on to her tongue, but use it sparingly for too much of it will cause a delirium and difficulty breathing. No more than twelve drops per day, with at least a three-hour gap between doses. It's an opium tincture but not all laudanum is the same. Most of it is little more than a cough suppressant. But this works. I've tried it. It's a powerful analgesic. I had it shipped from England, before the quarantine, for my own use.'

Rembrandt thanked him as profusely as he could.

After Tulp had gone he held the bottle tightly, the most valuable possession he'd ever owned.

He went up to the studio, and poured chalk, some lead white and linseed oil on to the mixing block. He used a spatula to fold it all together and then scraped the thick paint on to an old palette. He picked out one of his students' brushes, then he went back downstairs and out of the front door. He could not help looking up and down the street, like a furtive criminal. There wasn't a soul in sight. Not that it made any difference whether he was observed or not. The letter he was about to paint would bring a whole string of consequences on their heads: no more callers to the house, no business, no money and eventually no food. He loaded the brush with paint. It took only a few seconds. He stood back. His 'P' gleamed whiter than all the others. Of course, they had not gone to the trouble of using proper pigment. He shrugged his shoulders.

From the adjacent bedroom she could probably hear him cleaning the palette, brush and mixing block; he'd have to go back before too long. Surely she would live. Unlike him, she was still in the midst of life and strong. The notion of her dying within three to five days was absurd. When he reached the door, he put his hand on the latch – maybe not quite yet. He sat back down on a chair in the studio, to collect himself. He thought of the many who had fled the plague; children had left parents behind, husbands their wives, and gone as far as England. It was all down to him now. Why hadn't he asked Tulp for another nurse?

It was time to get up and go back in, but something kept him in the chair. He commanded his legs to walk through the door. He couldn't fail her, as he'd failed Saskia.

She lay curled up, clutching her middle.

'What took you so long?' she said.

'Just thanking Tulp,' he lied. 'He's been very kind.'

'Now we know for sure it is the plague,' she said between gasps, 'you must take me to the plague house. It's for the best.'

'Don't be stupid, Rika.'

She tried to say something but was prevented by a cramp. She pointed at the bucket. He fetched it and held her as she vomited. He could feel every convulsion, draining her of strength. The retching did not stop for a long time, in the end bringing up nothing but bile.

When it was finally over he gave her a drink to rinse her mouth. She spat all of it back out.

She sank back on to the pillow, catching her breath. He wiped her face and saw that around her eyes a network of purple lines had sprung up; burst capillaries from the retching.

'Don't you want to drink?' he asked.

'No, I'll just be sick again.'

Her lips and skin were dry. She needed to drink. 'Are you not thirsty?' he tried.

'I told you. It's not worth the effort.'

Nothing more was said. He was grateful when she drifted off, whether into sleep or a swoon he could not tell.

He went down to the kitchen and there were Titus and Cornelia sitting at the table. Cornelia jumped up. 'Pappie!'

She came running towards him. He put out his hand as if to stop her but thankfully Titus had already caught her around the waist and now was holding on to her because she continued to struggle.

'I'm so sorry, my sweet,' said Rembrandt. 'Pappie would love to hold and kiss you but we have to be careful not to make you ill.'

She started crying, still pushing with her arms against Titus's chest. Rembrandt felt himself on the point of breaking, so he stepped into the corridor, closing the door, but still he had to listen to Titus trying to calm Cornelia as she sobbed angrily. He stood with his back against the wall and then slid down to sit on the floor and buried his face in his hands. He made sure not to produce any sounds as despair overtook him.

After a while Cornelia fell silent. Titus opened the door and Rembrandt looked up at him, realizing as if for the first time that his son was a grown man.

'She's gone to sleep,' said Titus.

Rembrandt nodded.

Titus held out his hand to help him up but then remembered and withdrew his arm. Rembrandt pushed himself up, holding on to the wall. His legs had gone to sleep; he felt like an old man wobbling back into the kitchen. On the bed by the fire lay Cornelia, sleeping. He walked over. Her face was still wet with tears. He sat down at the table. Titus put beer in front of him.

'Some bread and cheese?'

Rembrandt nodded.

For a while he ate in silence.

'If there's anything that needs fetching just write it down for me. Or anything else I can do.'

Rembrandt nodded.

'How is she?' said Titus.

'In pain, cramps, vomiting,' said Rembrandt, looking again at his grown-up son. The fact of which, for some reason, made him feel even more helpless.

When he'd finished eating he wanted nothing more than to sit with Titus, to talk about the relative merits of nut over linseed oil or where the best herring could be bought, but he took himself off to the makeshift bed in the corridor. He must sleep now so he could be of use to her.

*

Titus must have roused him not long after. Hendrickje was screaming, his son said. Rembrandt found her doubled over. He felt panic. He was so ill-equipped, so lacking in experience. How much pain was considered bearable? When should he give the laudanum? Tulp had said to hold off for as long as possible as there was a limited amount and whether she lived or died, it had to last a few days. But how was he supposed to know how many? He resolved to wait.

She was still suffering bouts of agonizing cramps and vomiting, with only very brief periods of respite in between. Like labour, he thought, but without anything to show for it in the end. He'd watched the midwife when Cornelia was being born, calm and efficient. Perhaps that's what he had to become: a midwife helping his wife into the next world. He applied poultices of saffron, pigeon droppings and mustard as instructed by Tulp. They were meant to take the heat out of her body but how inadequate these measures were.

Some time in the morning she cried out, 'The bed's on fire, I'm burning. Help me.'

'It's the fever, my love.'

'No, quick, Rembrandt, put it out. Help me.'

She screamed so violently that he had no doubt that she suffered the sensation of burning. He pulled the bedclothes off her and lifted her out of the bed on to the floor but she was still writhing as if being burned alive. He touched her back; the skin was very hot.

Using a jug he sprinkled some water over her hair and chemise. It helped. Her panic subsided.

'There is no fire, is there?' she said. 'My body is burning itself up. I wish it was over. How long do you think until I can be dead? My body, it's too strong. It will go on for many a day yet.'

Her body was strong. It was a good thing.

'Don't give up, Rika, you'll come through this.'

But the words had left behind a great hole where his faith used to be.

She looked at him, as if wanting to believe him. But what good was there in giving her false hope? Perhaps the kindest thing would be to encourage her to forgo drink, to hasten things along as was her wish. He even considered for a moment offering her all of the laudanum. She would die instantly and without pain – but this he could not do. Only God knew if there was still hope.

But given her intense pain and his despair, it seemed time to start administering the laudanum. 'Tulp gave me this,' he said. 'It will help with the pain.'

'What is it?' she asked and already opened her mouth to receive the drops.

'It's made from opium.'

'Why did you not tell me about it before? I was in agony,' she said.

'We have a limited amount of it and I did not want us to run out too early, with the pain getting worse all the time.'

'What if one takes more than the allotted dose?'

Was her mind bent the same way as his or was she merely wondering about the dosage? 'Tulp said it would cause delirium and great difficulty in breathing,' he told her.

'I just hope each dose lasts for a good while. To know it's there and not be able to take it would only be another kind of torture.'

How bitter she sounded, but she was speaking more easily; perhaps the laudanum was already effective. Her chemise was soaked so he helped her take it off, and that's when he saw the swelling in her armpit. The monstrous thing was sticking out half an inch. It looked as if a bone was poking out, stretching the skin and making it appear white and hard. Was it one of the deadly swellings Tulp had described? It was hard to remember his words. He dared not touch it and anyway it was better not to tell her while she was in such despair. She was shivering so he heaped on the blankets.

'Lie with me,' she said.

'By Jove,' he replied, 'the lady is feeling better.'

She smiled. 'Consorting with a plague victim will easily make you the talk of the town once again; whether you'd get much custom afterwards is another question.'

He laughed, wondering what to do. He was exposed to the disease anyway, so why not lie with her? He'd continue to be strict about keeping a good distance between himself and Titus and Cornelia. He slipped under the blankets. It had been three days now and she was still alive, and what a miracle the few drops of laudanum had worked. He'd discovered a swelling and yet he was feeling hopeful. He had to remember that the laudanum was no cure. It was only masking the pain.

He closed his eyes, lying on his side. She lay facing away from him so he stroked her back and down her arms. He could feel all her ribs, so much of her flesh was gone. Then he held her frail little body against his. He wanted to protect her but all he could do was to look on.

He woke to the sound of chattering teeth. 'Please, more medicine,' she begged.

'I'm sorry, Rika, but three hours have not passed since the last dose, not even two.'

She said nothing.

'We'll have to wait until the clock strikes five. We'll manage till then.'

'That's easy for you to say.'

'I'll tell you something to keep your mind off things.'

'That will have to be some tale,' she said between spasms of chattering. 'Tell it to someone on the rack – more chance it'll distract them.'

'Just listen,' he said. 'We're in the forest, you know, the one you like.'

She groaned, sounding angry, but he continued. 'It smells of summer grasses and flowers. We are by the pool where I painted you. Remember the big oaks, sheltering us from wind and rain?'

'Shut up and give me the laudanum.' Her body was shaking ever more violently. But he carried on. Maybe he only kept talking to stop himself from fleeing the room. He focused on the tone of his voice, making it deeper, to try and penetrate through her pain, to let her know that there was still this world for her to return to. His voice resonated in his chest. The sensation made him feel less panic-stricken.

'The surface of the lake is smooth, a mirror, not a breath of wind. A few leaves are floating there on the water. The sky, trees and shrubs reflected in it.'

She cried out in pain, unmasking the futility of his efforts. Maybe he could ask Titus to sit with her for a little while. No, he could not expose Titus.

Her eyes were closed, face muscles stretched taut. He closed his eyes to see better, to beat a path to her somehow.

'Rika, can you hear me?'

There was no answer. Then he thought of something he'd heard the midwife do. 'When the next cramp comes I'll count so you'll know when it will be over.'

She screamed and he counted, 'Ten, nine, eight, seven, six, five, four.' She relaxed. He stopped counting. 'There, now it's over. You can rest a while.'

When he noticed her body tensing again after a few minutes he counted again, this time from seven, so that the end of the count-down would coincide with the ending of the cramp. It did. She breathed out. They went on like this for the best part of an hour. They were ruled by the rhythm of the cramps; he had to keep pace with her pain, hoping she could use his voice as an anchor to keep her from insanity.

Finally the cramps lessened of their own accord, which was probably just another stage of the illness. She lay still and he relaxed, relieved that things had eased for the moment.

Then she whispered, 'Open this. Undo the buttons, please!'

But she was not wearing anything. Had her mind gone? He pulled away the cover to make her feel that she was unconstrained.

To his surprise, she pushed herself up a little to a half-sitting position and then pointed at her stomach and legs. 'This, look at this.'

He could not comprehend her meaning. She continued in a very reasonable tone. 'That body there – can you not see – it's dying. We need to get rid of it. See? It stinks. Do something!'

She looked at him, expectant and so sanguine. Then, with a speed he would not have thought possible, she grabbed the knife he'd left on the side table for chopping herbs for poultices. It was sharp. She held it to her stomach, the point digging into her.

'I'm sewn into this thing; we need to cut it open so I can get out.'

'No, my love, it's your body. You can't get out.'

'What do you mean I can't? You cannot expect me to stay in this cadaver.'

He grabbed her wrist with one hand and wrested the knife from her. She screamed and struggled.

He did not know what to do or say so he locked his arm around her until she tired. Then the clock struck five in the afternoon and he gave her more laudanum. As her body grew heavier and looser beside him he whispered, 'I'm walking with you to the gate and if it opens we'll go through it, together.'

'Yes, my love,' she replied, 'to the invisible.'

He played with the idea of drinking all the morphine as soon as she'd died, then perhaps they really could go together. It was such a comforting thought that he held on to it. The sensation of the glass vial against his lips, the liquid going down his throat, a soft nothing embracing him. And then he sang to her to help her into sleep.

I pray you may sleep until you are home.
I pray you not suffer the tiniest storm.
When we're together we'll sail once again
The waves gently rocking, our two hearts to one,
As vast as the ocean, till all else is gone.

I'd never heard him sing before. And once I'd drifted off – not into the dullness of sleep but into a clear and present wakefulness – I was deep inside the forest, deeper than I had ever ventured before. The birds were singing, as if right by my ear, and the air was like balm. I let my wrap drop from my shoulders, not caring where it fell, skipping like a young girl ever further into the wood. After a while, I slowed to an ambling pace. My skirt seemed an encumbrance, so I undid it and left it behind, along with my cap and chemise. I could feel each blade of the soft grass brushing against my calves. When I reached a small clearing I stopped to contemplate the realm of green; the canopy above, the light-speckled grass, the network of branches and leaves that formed the undergrowth and grassy ground that led across the clearing to the other side. There was no path, only the glittering light which beckoned between the leaves, making me wish to reach it. I crossed the clearing and soon arrived at the shimmering waters of a round lake, as vividly blue as Rembrandt's azurite. He always said to use it sparingly, for it likes to draw attention to itself.

The air, thick with honeysuckle, roused me to walk on, along the bank through the tall grasses. Occasionally I climbed over a fallen tree or branches. There was no trace of anyone having set foot here – a virgin place. A heron stood on stalky legs poised to dart for fish.

I looked at the water, smooth and alive. The entire lake a mirror, containing heron, shore, sky and overhanging trees. On a whim, I turned my back to the lake and looked at it through my legs. Everything was upside down, throwing what had previously seemed solid into question and making the fluid world seem tangible. As I righted myself I did my best to hang on to the illusion that the lake was the substantial world. I would dive into the impenetrable bank and find myself a pigment suspended in a fluid universe of countless things. Of course as soon as my foot touched the water a flurry of ripples passed through the syrupy green.

I waded in further. The water was pleasantly cool. I wanted to be fully immersed. It scaled my stomach, breast and neck, sending before me spreading circles.

I swam a few strokes to get warm, underwater plants brushing against my legs, but soon they were left behind as the water ran deep. A breeze rustled through the trees and then whipped up wavelets all around me, spraying my cheek. I looked up at the vast sky above. A heron crossed the blue, taking no notice of me.

I held my breath, floating still, buoyed up by the water. What an expanse of swaying azurite. Then, with my eyes only just above the surface, I noticed tiny pondskaters, their feet making indentations on the water. Little waves lapped against the back of my head and then my body was gone as if I'd bled into the blue. I did not have to move at all and yet I did not sink.

I breathed out a long breath. No care for ever breathing in again, breathing out was all. Empty – full, as the mirror-lake, waves, sun sparkle, a drop of dew. Water in water.

He woke up, still in bed with her. It was night now. She was so quiet, no laboured breathing. Was she still breathing? He put his ear to her mouth and yes, he felt her breath. Relief, but would it not be better if it was over? No, he decided, not yet, it was too soon, too soon for him.

Just then she opened her eyes, smiling at him. Her lips moved but he heard no sound so he put his ear by her mouth. 'I love you,' she said.

'I love you too,' he whispered.

‘Love Cornelia for the two of us,’ she said.

‘Yes.’

‘I’m sorry.’

He wanted to tell her it was all right but only managed to nod.

Then he said what he knew he must say. ‘You can, you know. If it’s time, if you can.’

He couldn’t say the word *go*.

He was not sure if she had heard him, for she closed her eyes again; her breathing so very faint. He cradled her hand in his and lay down next to her again. He knew that she could feel him. When would they be lost to one another? The next minute, the next hour? Would the sun ever rise again for her? The church tower struck two. He remembered someone telling him once that most people die in the early hours because the body is at a low ebb. He tried to stay awake, having convinced himself that she would go soon and wanting to keep his promise, but he fell asleep again.

The next time he woke up he was surprised to see her standing in the corner of the room. It was very dark but he could just about see her. She had put the shift on again. He felt hope. She had somehow found the strength. He looked where she had lain and saw her body there on the bed, eyes open, lifeless and next to her he saw himself asleep.

The girl in the corner was smiling as she told him, ‘I have died.’

She was holding her hand out to him. He went and took it. It did not occur to him to question what he saw, so relieved was he to see her happy. Something had changed about the room as if it had grown larger and the walls seemed less solid. Even though he could not see it with his eyes, he felt a sensation similar to that of sunlight on his skin. As if an invisible light was shining down on them, embracing them. She felt it too, for she was looking towards it.

He wanted to get closer to this warmth that seemed like the very distillate of love. Holding hands, they moved towards it, or it towards them, and he found himself thinking that he would not have expected that pure love felt thick and warm as treacle. Not only on the outside of him but inside too. It filled him so entirely that he could not imagine ever feeling fear again, or even remembering what the sensation of fear felt like.

He'd always believed his life to be the mill and grist of existence; but now his life seemed so insubstantial compared to this. He also knew with perfect certainty that this was where she belonged.

He watched her happy face, and all the time they were going further into the heart of the invisible light. He was only too happy to come along but then she looked at him. There was a pause and even though she was not telling him, he knew to go no further. She kissed him. And he still felt the warmth of her lips on his mouth when he awoke.

The light of dawn blinked in the shutters and he knew without needing to look that she had died. Her body was lying as he had seen it in his sleep. He got out of the bed, opened the windows and shutters wide, letting the orange sunrise flood the room. He stood surveying the city – how the light sparkled on the rooftops and on the little ripples in the canal. He felt as if he'd not seen light until today, or only a narrow part of it. He'd pay proper attention to it from now on.

He went into the yard to wash and dress before Titus and Cornelia were awake and then he'd have to tell them and comfort them.

PART IV

Four years later

Self-Portrait with Two Circles

Rozengracht, Jordaan, Amsterdam, 1667

The sun is dim and hazy in the sky, kissing the IJ before disappearing. The North Star is there as the gracht falls perfectly silent. The ropes hang slack. No carts or goods, the doors are shut for sleeping – until the morrow. But there are footsteps. Prince Cosimo stands at a familiar door, in puffed-up robes, a dozen courtiers fringing him. He takes it upon himself to knock. An old man opens the door and the prince with a little bow explains, 'I could not have left Amsterdam without seeing Rembrandt.'

The painter looks unimpressed. He'll likely tell him – prince or not – that he has closed up for the day, but he thinks better of it and invites him in. It's probably because he hopes to relieve him of a fair few guilders. He always liked on-the-spot sales best.

After they have gone, the sweat and sickly perfume of the prince's party still hangs in the air, so Rembrandt opens the windows wide and returns to the three-quarter-length portrait of himself that is sitting on the easel: an imposing figure on a mottled grey background, one hand on the hip, the other holding a palette, brushes and maulstick. The clothes in the picture are simple, a long brown tabard and white cap. He frowns – the composition has all the vitality of a cowpat drying in the sun. He sits down in an armchair, closes his eyes and considers finishing for the day. Then he gets up again, goes to the window for some fresh air. There's the Ursa Major constellation – Callisto. She's not the brightest constellation in the sky but he likes her best. To avoid melancholy creeping up on him, he goes back to the canvas, loads his brush with brown and starts the motion of a circle in the air like the stars around Polaris. When the brush reaches the canvas, it deposits paint on it. He's drawn a perfect half circle. He does the same on the other side. But the traces of his brush are faint so he retraces them with small brushstrokes. The cowpat of the mantled figure is now wedged between two arcs. That's all it's taken to bring the picture to life. He no longer feels tired or sad.

For a moment the figure he has painted looks like a mirror-image of himself; solid, weight on both feet, arm on hip, palette poised. The two globes will be interpreted as two separate worlds, as there's a tradition of depicting the initial unity of Creation ruptured in two: heaven and earth, invisible and visible realms.

He wonders which of the two circles represents the invisible and if he should make one circle look different from the other. But is heaven really another place from earth? He leaves the two circles the same. Let whoever is looking at them make up their own mind about which is which, or if they are one and the same.

There is yet another knock on the door. He tries to ignore the thumping, but whoever it is has the persistence of a courting pigeon. So in the end he goes downstairs and opens the door to tell them to come back another time. It's a couple, a man and a woman. They stand at a demure distance, a few steps down from the front door, their faces a mixture of surprise and embarrassment.

Both are dressed in immaculate black from head to toe. The only aspect that can be construed as ornamental is the man's curly hair. It hangs rather listlessly about his head. She has fair skin and a full mouth but the lips are drawn in, as if she is wishing herself to be elsewhere and yet her honey-coloured eyes look up at him. The young man finds his voice. 'May we speak with you?'

'About what?' says Rembrandt. He's still only interested in finding a reason to get rid of them.

'A commission,' says the young man.

The woman has her arm hooked through the man's and both exude such unabashed hopefulness that he cannot bring himself to say no. Not yet anyway.

'Please come in,' he says and leads the way to the studio. Once they get there, the couple look around; there is nowhere for them to sit. He always hated the place to be crowded with chairs. Seats only encourage students to take breaks. The couple appear to be waiting for an invitation to speak.

'What can I do for you?' he says.

'We have just become betrothed.'

They look at each other and there's a long pause as if they've fallen into a reverie. At last the man says, still unable to take his eyes off her, 'We would be honoured if you were to paint our portrait.'

Rembrandt says nothing. He does not want to paint them.

The young man clasps his hands together like a petitioner, tries hard to think of something heartfelt to say, but the only word that comes is, 'Please.'

'Both of us,' she adds and blushes. 'I mean, both of us together in one picture.'

She has the kind of face that displays her sentiments whether she wants it to or not. The kind of face he likes to paint. Oh, look at them! How close they stand together, their elbows always touching. He really ought to paint them.

He says he'll do it. They look surprised and he is too.

Isaac and Rebecca

A few days later they arrive for their first sitting. He asks them to stand where the light is good. They are both a little beyond the customary age for marriage. He is much taller but he stoops so as not to tower over her. She has rosy cheeks and her face is a picture of half a dozen conflicting emotions. The young man, perhaps aware of her discomfort, stands somewhat awkwardly by her side as if trying to wrap himself around her, like a safe harbour. Dear Lord, thinks Rembrandt, what have I got myself into? At least they are not the types to interfere.

'Come a little this way,' he tells them, trying to turn them more into the light but without losing that intertwinedness. But now they stand like choirboys, arms by their sides, and the humble black they are wearing won't do at all.

'I'll make a quick sketch now,' he tells them, 'and then you'll be back for more sittings.'

Eager nodding from the couple.

'I have my own way of working. It will take several months.'

Not quite so eager nodding.

He sits down in his chair, paper on his lap, and watches them. She's anxiously fingering her dress and the man's arm creeps further around her back.

Rembrandt is getting impatient with their unease. He jumps up and tells them, 'I'll paint you as the biblical couple Isaac and Rebecca – you know, a sacred marriage.'

They look pleased.

He continues. 'Remember, they had to flee and live in exile. Isaac feared, with Rebecca being so beautiful, that other men desiring her for themselves would want to do away with him. So they pretended to be brother and sister.'

Now they look confused.

'A hazardous situation,' says Rembrandt, 'but remember they were chosen for one another by God. I'd like to paint them – you – when meeting in secret, in an arbour. You must imagine yourselves in this kind of place. You have not been alone with one another for many a week, you are man and wife . . .'

The woman is trying to catch the man's eyes. He even considers telling them that Isaac and Rebecca were caught sporting with one another by King Abimelech. But if he does they will certainly leave.

He takes a bench over to them and motions for them to sit down, to calm them. He says, 'Just pretend I am not here.'

They are sitting as if in the stocks. The story he's told them has made everything worse. But it matters that he gets to paint this picture.

'Lovely,' he says, 'I must fetch my chalks. Please excuse me. I have to go to the furthest corner of the attic to retrieve them. I'll be ten minutes at least.'

He leaves and closes the door. As soon as he's gone they start exchanging glances. She still looks very uncomfortable. It's a wonder she does not insist they leave. They must badly want their picture. Time passes.

The young man puts his arm around her. His hand is resting lightly on her shoulder. There's a stillness in the room. He has his head inclined as if he is listening to her every breath. She finally settles into his embrace.

Rembrandt must see this – where is he gone? He is outside the studio, staring at the white wall. Then he crouches down to a little hole in that wall but he stops short of putting his eye to it. He's lined them up with that hole – a peep-hole into bare humanity. What a clever ploy, but now he can't bring himself to look through it. If only he would look. He must look.

But he won't because he's afraid. And now the noise of rain against the window is drawing his attention. He watches the droplets flowing down the glass, merging and then away. He too wants to be washed away.

He thinks of the two circles he's drawn – would they be joined one day or is he, standing in the middle, the bridge between the spheres?

He makes his choice, goes back and looks. The woman gathers up the fabric of her dress, bunching it tight within her hand, as if it is the next best thing to gathering him, her love. She takes the ball of cloth and presses it against her womb. Rembrandt steps away again, unable to bear the longing in his heart. But all the same, he has decided that he will paint the dress in red.

He stands looking at the white wall, notices a spider making a web between the wall and window. It is excreting a near invisible thread, making the radial spokes. Rembrandt probes his cheek with his fingers, feels the slack place where his teeth used to be. Perhaps another year or two, he thinks. The spider has begun a loose spiral from the centre of the web. Next he'll do a second tighter spiral. Methodical. He shrugs his shoulders and puts his eye back at the hole.

The woman's gaze, like the man's, is inward. They have forgotten where they are. The man's right hand rests on her breast – her heart – his fingers soft, receptive as if it were possible to listen with his hand. Rembrandt knows it is. It is.

The woman's hand comes up to welcome his. She places her fingertips on the back of the man's hand, as if to seal their union. And so they stay.

Rembrandt tells himself that he is a gout-ridden fool for not having brought any paper. He rushes to the door, opens it a crack and whispers to them, 'Stay as you are, I beg you.'

Then he walks in quietly as if trespassing on a holy scene. He sketches them quickly, then dismisses them and starts painting from memory as soon as they have left.

Over the next few weeks, while the spider sits in its web waiting, Isaac comes to wear gold, not the usual tired brocade but a highly textured fabric that glistens with a light of its own. Rembrandt takes the palette knife and plasters paint onto the canvas, layer upon layer. He is the maker of mountain ridges and valleys. More sculpture than painting. The sleeve of the man is becoming the brightest part of the picture and the more he models it into being the more he feels a great ease of movement in his limbs. It takes no effort at all. On this at least age has no claim. The oil paint flies on to the canvas as if each lump knows where it belongs. So solid a thing and yet as ethereal as song.

Finally the vast golden sleeve is done and he turns to her carmine dress. He weaves strands of orange, brown, gold and his own soul into the red until it dissolves into a rubied sea of all compassion. He drizzles the same red over her shoulder and works it into the background too. Nothing is excluded.

Finally, when he reaches the outer edges of the canvas, he does not want the painting to stop there. And so he wills the golden light and the sea of carmine to go on, beyond the edge.

He feels the thing he could not name before. Feels it so clearly now. A glow within; it is the same light he is painting. The light he has seen in the night of her death and now he knows – it is for this world too. The visible and invisible. Not two separate spheres but one.

Rembrandt continues to work on the limitless dress. A dress to dress all things. And as he does, all the world is clad in the immeasurable.

Would you believe it, and I honestly mean what I say, I should be happy to give ten years of my life if I could go on sitting here in front of this picture for a fortnight with only a crust of dry bread for food?

Vincent Van Gogh in a letter to his brother Theo in 1884 about Rembrandt's *Isaac and Rebecca*

Author's Note

I remember standing in front of Rembrandt's *Self-Portrait at the Age of 63*, in 1999, for a very long time. I looked at the artist's ageing face, depicted with such unflinching honesty and found myself moved. Since that day, I've been intrigued by the power of Rembrandt's art to engage our emotions.

Perhaps it's because his works touch on what it means to be human, to live, to love and to die. These big questions are like sparkling jewels at the bottom of a dark pool. And it's that sparkle, more than the potential answers, that have kept me looking at his paintings, etchings and drawings.

His art and the events of Rembrandt's life are rich and deeply interesting and some of them are stranger than I could have imagined. I have studied the historical documents and theories of Rembrandt's life and work and they are woven into the fabric of this novel, but they are not why I wrote it. I read and write for the experience, to journey to a place either familiar or unknown. *Rembrandt's Mirror* therefore, is not intended as a proclamation of facts or beliefs but as a means of transport.

Rembrandt van Rijn (1606–69)

We know a great deal about Rembrandt's life. This is largely thanks to hundreds of historical documents that have been discovered in archives. Many are related to Rembrandt's numerous legal proceedings. They include an inventory that was drawn up of his possessions when he filed for *Cessio Bonorum*. Other sources of information are writings by contemporaries, such as Samuel van Hoogstraten, or the works themselves.

Some art historians believe that the change in style and drop in Rembrandt's output after Saskia's death was the result of some kind of breakdown but Ernst van de Wetering, the chair of the Rembrandt Research Project, argues that Rembrandt's work changed as a result of his artistic process – he had pushed his style of dramatic light and dark to such an extreme that it meant he had to sacrifice too much pictorial detail and texture in order to achieve extreme spotlight effects. Consequently he had to find a new approach. It is impossible to know with certainty what motivated his artistic choices.

What we do know is that towards the end of his life, with the onset of old age and the experience of severe personal losses, his art lost nothing of its potency. If anything, he seems to have delved even deeper into what it means to be human and his late works are considered to be amongst the most moving and timeless works of art ever created.

Hendrickje Stoffels (*c*.1626–63)

Hendrickje entered Rembrandt's household in 1647/8. Her date of birth is usually given as about 1626 (genealogy directory of Bredevoort); however in a document from 1661 she declared she was thirty-eight, which would make her year of birth 1623. Either way she would have been in her early twenties when she entered Rembrandt's workshop. Hendrickje was the youngest of four children. She had two brothers and one sister. Her father died in July 1646, possibly the victim of an explosion of the gunpowder tower in Bredevoort. In January 1647, after half a year of mourning, her mother, Mechteld Lamberts, married a neighbour, Jacob van Dorsten, a widower with three young children. As a consequence of her mother's marriage, Hendrickje seems to have left home for Amsterdam.

Rembrandt never married Hendrickje; however, almost two years before her death, on 20 October 1661, Hendrickje and two neighbours made a deposition as witnesses about an intoxicated surgeon who 'showed great insolence and wantonness while holding a glass of wine in his hand, by accosting every male person who passed him and forcing him to drink or fight with him' (*Rembrandt Documents*, 61/12). On this legal document she is named as 'Hendrickje Stoffels, wife of Rembrandt van Rijn the fine art painter aged 38'. The document provides evidence that Hendrickje's status as Rembrandt's wife, without having been formally married, was accepted by her neighbours and the notary.

Hendrickje Stoffels was buried in a grave in the Westerkerk on 24

July 1663. It is not known with certainty that she died of the plague, but her sudden death, while the epidemic raged in Amsterdam, suggests that it was the cause.

Saskia, née *van Uylenburgh* (1612–42)

Saskia married Rembrandt in 1634. She was twenty-two and he twenty-eight years old. She died seven years later, probably of tuberculosis, after the birth of their fourth child, Titus. In the preceding years she suffered several bouts of illness, confining her to bed for many months. Their three children born prior to Titus all died within weeks of being born.

Samuel van Hoogstraten (1627–78)

Samuel studied with Rembrandt between 1642/3–1646/7 (according to Thijs Weststeijn, although other sources suggest he may have been with Rembrandt as early as 1640). We know he had returned to his native Dordrecht by January 1648. Having spent between five and seven years in Rembrandt's workshop, he was one of the longest-staying pupils. His writings are a source of information about Rembrandt's views on art and painting. Samuel wrote a book entitled *Introduction to the Academy of Painting, or the Visible World* (original title: *Inleyding tot de hooge schoole der schilderkonst: anders de zichtbaere werelt*). And it seems likely that some of the content is based on the methods and theories Rembrandt taught in his workshop.

Geertje Dircx (*c.*1610–*c.*56)

Geertje grew up in a modest family in Edam. It is unclear when exactly she entered Rembrandt's household. It is likely that she was hired in 1641, the year before Saskia's death, to help look after baby Titus. It has been suggested that she is the model of *Woman in a Bed* (Scottish National Gallery) but there is no evidence that she was the model for any of Rembrandt's works.

Titus van Rijn (1641–68)

Titus was named after Saskia's sister Titia. On 28 February 1668 he married Magdalena van Loo but died soon after on 4 September 1668 and was buried in the Westerkerk in Amsterdam. His wife and Rembrandt both died a year later. Magdalena gave birth to their daughter, Titia, six months after Titus's death. Titia had no children and died in 1715. She was the last of Rembrandt's descendants.

Cornelia van Rijn (1654–84)

In 1670, at the age of sixteen Cornelia married Cornelis Suythof and together they emigrated to Batavia, Indonesia. She gave birth to a boy in 1673, called Rembrandt Suythof. She had another boy in 1678, Hendric Suythof. Neither of them had children of their own.

Jan Six (1618–1700)

Jan Six was the wealthy son of a merchant family and a patron of the arts who had a long association with Rembrandt. In 1655, through his marriage to Margaretha Tulp, he became the son-in-law of

Nicolaes Tulp – the surgeon and then mayor of Amsterdam. Six himself became mayor of Amsterdam in 1691 at the age of seventy-three.

Pupils

Rembrandt had a great many pupils throughout his working life. Most of them had already completed an apprenticeship with another painter before joining Rembrandt's workshop, finishing their education by learning his style of painting, which was very popular for many years. When fashions changed many adopted the popular style of detailed brushwork. However, Rembrandt never pandered to contemporary tastes.

Notes by Chapter

I have relied on research and theories by a number of scholars, some of which I have adapted for fictional purposes.

For links to all of the images below, please visit: http://kimdevereux.co.uk/Rembrandts_Mirror/Pictures.html

PART I

The Night Watch

The Night Watch (1642), Rijksmuseum, Amsterdam. Originally titled *The Company of Frans Banning Cocq.*

I have taken inspiration from Ernst van de Wetering's description of the painting in *A Corpus of Rembrandt Paintings, vol. 3*

St Jerome in a Dark Chamber

St Jerome in a Dark Chamber (1642), Metropolitan Museum of Art, New York.

This chapter is based on the theory of Joseph J. Schildkraut in *Saint Jerome in a Dark Chamber: Rembrandt's Metaphoric Portrayal of the Depressed Mind*

PART II

The Supper at Emmaus

The Supper at Emmaus (1648), Louvre, Paris, signed and dated.

Acting and emotions

In this chapter Rembrandt asks the pupils to act out the *Supper at Emmaus*. Some of its content is informed by Thijs Westerstein's *The Visible World*. According to Samuel van Hoogstraten's writings it was important to depict emotions in such a way as to evoke a strong response in the viewer.

Rembrandt himself appears to have practised different facial expressions in front of a mirror as a series of early etchings shows him surprised, laughing and scowling.

Rembrandt's speech about drawing

The ideas contained in this speech are based on Fredrick Franck's *The Zen of Seeing: Seeing/Drawing as Meditation*. Franck's writings also inspired the scene of Hendrickje drawing Rembrandt, in particular the idea that when drawing a face, mask after mask falls away.

Self-portrait at the age of 34 (1640), National Gallery, London.
In this self-portrait Rembrandt depicts himself as well groomed, with a self-assured pose and elaborate sixteenth-century costume. It seems that Rembrandt deliberately alludes to Titian's *Portrait of Gerolamo*

Barbarigo, thus declaring himself to belong to the same canon as the famous Old Masters.

Prostitution and attitudes to women

Many of Petronella's attitudes towards sex are based on Lotte van de Pol's *The Burgher and the Whore: Prostitution in Early Modern Amsterdam*, which draws on seventeenth-century writing such as descriptions by travellers, as well as witness statements which were taken in the process of prosecuting women for prostitution. Extracts are used by kind permission of Oxford University Press.

Van de Pol paints a vivid picture of attitudes at the time:

Intercourse while undressed was considered abnormal.

The sexual appetite of women was feared and considered greater than that of men.

The dialogue 'Doggy, where are you going? Come, go with me to my house, we'll share a jug of beer' is a quotation from a statement by a constable who lingered at the head of the Kalverstraat, pretending to be drunk.

A chamber cat was a female prostitute who plied her trade at home often with only one or a few regular clients.

Silent whores were prostitutes who hid the fact and outwardly led respectable lives.

Woman on a Gibbet

Woman on a Gibbet (1664), Robert Lehman Collection, New York.

Elsje Christiaens was the first woman to be executed in twenty-one years. Rembrandt was not the only artist to draw her body. She is also visible on the far right in Anthonie van Borssom's 1664 ink-and-watercolour painting of the execution site.

This is one instance where I have deviated from the chronological order of Rembrandt's works. The drawing appears in the novel in the year 1647 but Rembrandt made it towards the end of his life in 1664. It is a good example of his lifelong practice of making studies from life (and death). These included many extraordinary subjects, amongst them a lion, an elephant, a defecating dog and corpses being dissected.

Sermon of Jodocus van Lodenstein

Most of van Lodenstein's words are quoted from the sermons reproduced in *In Quest of Pentecost: Jodocus van Lodenstein and the Dutch Second Reformation*, by kind permission of University Press of America.

The French Bed

The French Bed (1646), Teylers Museum, Haarlem. Also known as *The Ledikant*.

Due to a revision made by Rembrandt, the woman has three arms!

A Woman Sleeping

Woman Sleeping (*c.*1654), The British Museum, London.

Saskia Lying in Bed

Saskia Lying in Bed, a Woman Sitting at her Feet (*c*.1635–8), Staatliche Graphische Sammlung, Munich.

The Mill

The Mill (1645–8), National Gallery Washington, Widener Collection (oil painting).

This chapter is loosely based on the painting *The Mill* for which Rembandt may have made preparatory drawings. See also the etching: *The Windmill* (1641), Harleem.

Self-Portrait by a Window

Self-Portrait by a Window (1648), Rijksmuseum.

The idea of the inherent freedom of 'looking' is inspired by Douglas Harding's writings.

Self-Portrait Wearing a White Feathered Bonnet (1635), Buckland Abbey, National Trust Collections.

This painting was reattributed to Rembrandt in 2014, based on stylistic criteria, the quality of the paintwork and the fact that X-rays revealed exploratory paint work related to the conception of the painting which is proof that it is not a copy. As a result, the value of the painting is now about £30 million.

Jan Six with a Dog, Standing by an Open Window

Jan Six with a Dog, Standing by an Open Window (*c.*1646), Six Collection, Amsterdam. See also the etching *Jan Six* (1647), Teylers Collection, Haarlem.

Rembrandt and Geertje appear before the Commission of Marital Affairs

Many documents associated with Rembrandt's and Geertje's negotiations (if one can call them that) have survived. Most of what is read out by the notary and the exchange in front of the tribunal are quotes from the original documents, such as Rembrandt's response to Geertje's claim, 'I do not have to admit that I have slept with Mistress Dircx. It is for her to prove it.'

Rembrandt's wrangles with Geertje and his financial decline stretched over several years. In the novel the events have been grouped closer together for the sake of narrative flow.

The Return of the Prodigal Son

The Return of the Prodigal Son (*c.*1650–55), Fondation Custodia, Collection Frits Lugt, Paris.

Sometimes referred to as *The Departure of Tobias*.

'Miracle of our age'

'The miracle of our age' was how the South German art-lover Bucelinus (1599–1681) commented on the fifty-eight-year-old Rembrandt in his list compiled in 1664 of 'The Names of the Most Distinguished

European Painters'. Rembrandt's was the only name out of 166 to attract such a tribute.

Samuel's drawing of balance scales

The idea of this drawing is based on Thijs Westerstein's discussion of 'Noch hallt het over', an emblem depicting a woman holding a balance by Jan Lyken, *Voncken der liefde Jesu*, Amsterdam, 1687.

Daniel in the Lions' Den

Daniel in the Lions' Den (*c*.1649), Rijksprentenkabinet, Rijksmuseum, Amsterdam.

Portrait of Jan Six

Portrait of Jan Six (1654), Six Collection.

Rembrandt's portrait of Jan Six is still owned by a direct descendant of Jan Six, Jan Six van Hillegom.

PART III

Self-Portrait

Self-portrait (1658), The Frick Collection, New York.

Rembrandt painted himself at least forty times and etched himself thirty-one times. The question of the raison d'être of so many self-portraits is touched on in the novel a number of times and inspired by the conflicting views of Perry Chapman, who suggests that Rembrandt strove to define himself as an artist and ultimately as an individual, and Ernst van de Wetering, who argues that the fact that they sold well was the primary motivating factor in their creation.

In 1999 a *Self-Portrait at the Age of 28* (1634), was discovered by Ernst van de Wetering and Martin Bijl and then restored to its former glory. It had been overpainted by Rembrandt himself and turned into a tronie, *Man with a Russian Hat*. The fact that Rembrandt himself overpainted his self-portrait suggests that he did so because it had not sold, perhaps because it depicted him at a much younger age and therefore no longer resembled him. He may have hoped to increase his chances of selling it by turning it into a tronie.

My own view is that, whatever other motivation Rembrandt had for depicting himself, he must also have been deeply interested in the process and the pictorial opportunities it represented. The convenience of using oneself as a model may also have played a part.

Woman Bathing in a Stream

Woman Bathing in a Stream (1654), also known as *Callisto in the Wilderness*, National Gallery, London.

This chapter is based on Ernst van de Wetering's suggestion that Hendrickje is portrayed as Callisto. It was Jan Leija who first suggested that the woman's shift could be interpreted as a reference to the story.

Rembrandt rarely painted outside, so this painting may well not have been executed in the open air. We do not know with absolute certainty that any of Rembrandt's paintings do in fact show Hendrickje, but I believe that this one does, as well as the *Portrait of Hendrickje Stoffels* in the National Gallery, London.

The Shell

The Shell (1650), The British Museum, London.

The Anatomy Lesson of Dr Nicolaes Tulp

The Anatomy Lesson of Dr Nicolaes Tulp (1632), Mauritshuis, The Hague.

PART IV

Self-Portrait with Two Circles

Self-Portrait with Two Circles (1665–9), also known as the Kenwood Self-Portrait, Kenwood House, London.
The idea of the two circles as two worlds is based on Thijs Westerstein's *The Invisible World*.

The myth of Rembrandt's decline into obscurity is contradicted by the fact that he was still famous enough for Prince Cosimo III de' Medici, Grand Duke of Tuscany, to make a point of visiting him in the Rozengracht in 1667, two years before he died.

Isaac and Rebecca

Isaac and Rebecca (*c.*1665–9), Rijksmuseum, Amsterdam. Also known as *The Jewish Bride*.

The name change occured after the painting became related to a drawing by Rembrandt that depicts Isaac and Rebecca caught in amorous engagement by King Abimelech. This was the result of interconnected observations by Wilhelm Valentiner, Cornelius Müeller-Hofstede and Hans Kaufmann.

This link was further strengthened by X-ray examinations by Ernst van der Wetering and the discovery of a detail previously hidden by the frame. The detail shows a window's edge which is assumed to be the window from which King Abimelech was spying on the sporting couple.

Acknowledgements

I am greatly indebted to the many scholars who have contributed so much to our understanding of Rembrandt's life and art. Foremost I'd like to thank Ernst van de Wetering, who kindly met me in 2004. This novel draws extensively on his work and that of the Rembrandt Research Project. Thank you also to Simon Schama for our brief exchange many years ago and the inspiration of his writings. I'd also like to acknowledge Thijs Weststeijn's book *The Visible World*, which brings to life the intellectual, philosophical and artistic climate of the time and Paul Crenshaw's *Rembrandt's Bankruptcy*. One statement in particular by Crenshaw lodged itself in my mind because it rang so true: 'The events surrounding Rembrandt, and the choices made by him, demonstrate that Rembrandt handled his money and marketing in the same manner that he led his life and made his art: he was unconventional in every respect.'

I'd also like to thank my mother for her unwavering support, and Alex for his belief in my writing and his help, on many fronts, in brining this novel into being. Thank you also to my writing group friends Gill and Sam and to Ian for everything. I'm deeply grateful to

Samantha Harvey and Gerard Woodward for teasing out the writer in me. And I'd like to thank Richard Francis for his wisdom.

Heartfelt thanks to my agent at Curtis Brown, Karolina Sutton – a writer's fantasy made manifest – and my brilliant and inspiring publisher and editor, Margaret Stead at Atlantic Books.

Select Bibliography

Jonathan Bikker, Gregor J.M. Weber, Erik Hinterding, Marjorie E. Wieseman, Marijn Schapelhouman, Anna Krekeler, *Rembrandt: The Late Works*, National Gallery, London, 2014.

A. Blankert, *Rembrandt: A Genius and His Impact*, National Gallery of Victoria, 1997.

David Bomford, *Rembrandt (Art in the Making)*, Yale University Press, 1994.

J. Bruyn, B. Haak, S.H. Levie, P.J.J. van Thiel, *A Corpus of Rembrandt Paintings I: 1625–1631 (Rembrandt Research Project Foundation)*, 1st edn, Springer, 1982.

J. Bruyn, B. Haak, S.H. Levie, *A Corpus of Rembrandt Paintings II: 1631–1634 (Rembrandt Research Project Foundation)*, 1st edn, Springer, 1986.

J. Bruyn, B. Haak, S.H. Levie, P.J.J. van Thiel, E. van de Wetering, *A Corpus of Rembrandt Paintings III: 1635–1642 (Rembrandt Research Project Foundation)*, Springer, 2010.

Christopher Leslie Brown, Jan Kelch, Pieter van Thiel (eds), *Rembrandt: Paintings: The Master and His Workshop*, National Gallery, London, 1991.

H. Perry Chapman, *Rembrandt's self-portraits: a study of Seventeenth-Century Identity*, Princeton University, 1990.

Paul Crenshaw, *Rembrandt's Bankruptcy: The Artist, his Patrons, and the Art World in Seventeenth-Century Netherlands*, Cambridge University Press, 2006.

Frederick Franck, *The Zen of Seeing: Seeing/Drawing as Meditation*, Vintage, 1973.

Amy Golahny, *Rembrandt's Reading: The Artist's Bookshelf of Ancient Poetry and History*, Amsterdam University Press, 2014.

E. H. Gombrich, *Art and Illusion: A Study in the Psychology of Pictorial Representation*, Phaidon Press, 2002.

Douglas Harding, *On Having No Head: Zen and the Rediscovery of the Obvious*, Inner Directions, 2002.

Julia Lloyd-Williams (ed.), *Rembrandt's Women*, Prestel, 2001.

Shelley Perlove and Larry Silver, *Rembrandt's Faith, Church and Temple in the Dutch Golden Age*, Penn State University Press, 2009.

Lotte van de Pol, *The Burgher and the Whore: Prostitution in Early Modern Amsterdam*, Oxford University Press, 2011.

Rembrandt van Rijn, *Drawings of Rembrandt; With a Selection of Drawings by His Pupils and Followers*, vol. 1, Dover Publications, 1965.

Rembrandt van Rijn, *Drawings of Rembrandt*, vol. 2, Dover Publications, 1965.

Simon Schama, *Rembrandt's Eyes*, Penguin Books, London, 1999.

Carl J. Schroeder, *In Quest of Pentecost: Jodocus Van Lodenstein and the Dutch Second Reformation*, University Press of America, 2001.

Walter L. Strauss, Marjo van der Meulen, *The Rembrandt documents*, Abaris Books, 1979.

Thijs Weststeijn, *The Visible World: Samuel van Hoogstraten's Art Theory and the Legitimation of Painting in the Dutch Golden Age (Amsterdam Studies in the Dutch Golden Age*), Amsterdam University Press, 2009.

Ernst van de Wetering (ed.), *A Corpus of Rembrandt Paintings IV: Self Portraits (Rembrandt Research Project Foundation)*, 1st edn, Springer, 2005.

Ernst van de Wetering, *Rembrandt: Quest of a Genius*, Waanders Publishers, 2007.

Ernst van de Wetering, *Rembrandt: The Painter at Work*, University of California Press, 2009.

Ernst van de Wetering (ed.), *A Corpus of Rembrandt Paintings V: The Small-Scale History Paintings: Small Figured History Pieces (Rembrandt Research Project Foundation)*, Springer, 2011.

Ernst van de Wetering, Volker Manuth, Marieke de Winkel, *Rembrandt by himself*, National Gallery, London, 1999.

Marike de Winkel, *Fashion and Fancy, Dress and Meaning in Rembrandt's Paintings*, Amsterdam University Press, 2014.

Paul Zumthor, *Daily Life in Rembrandt's Holland*, Stanford University Press, 1994.